SILENCE FOR THE DEAD

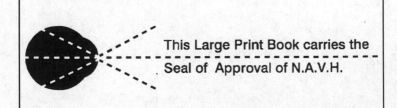

This Large Print Book carries the
Seal of Approval of N.A.V.H.

SILENCE FOR THE DEAD

SIMONE ST. JAMES

THORNDIKE PRESS
A part of Gale, Cengage Learning

GALE
CENGAGE Learning·

Farmington Hills, Mich • San Francisco • New York • Waterville, Maine
Meriden, Conn • Mason, Ohio • Chicago

GALE
CENGAGE Learning

Copyright © 2014 by Simone Seguin.
Thorndike Press, a part of Gale, Cengage Learning.

LIBRARY OF CONGRESS CATALOGING-IN-PUBLICATION DATA

St. James, Simone.
    Silence for the dead / by Simone St. James. — Large print edition.
        pages ; cm. — (Thorndike Press large print romance)
    ISBN 978-1-4104-7344-8 (hardcover) — ISBN 1-4104-7344-9 (hardcover)
    1. World War, 1914-1918—Veterans—Fiction. 2. World War, 1914-1918—Medical care—Fiction. 3. Nurses—Fiction. 4. Large type books.
    I. Title.
    PR9199.4.S726S56 2014b
    813'.6—dc23   2014026490

Published in 2014 by arrangement with NAL Signet, a member of Penguin Group (USA) LLC, a Penguin Random House Company

Printed in the United States of America
1 2 3 4 5 6 7 18 17 16 15 14

For Adam, again and always

■ ■ ■ ■

PART ONE:
ANGEL OF MERCY

■ ■ ■ ■

Selfishness is pre-eminently a defect which disqualifies a woman from the nursing profession.

— Eva Luckes,
Matron of London Hospital,
1880–1919

CHAPTER ONE

England, 1919

Portis House emerged from the fog as we approached, showing itself slowly as a long, low shadow. I leaned my temple against the window of the motorcar and tried to make it out in the fading light.

The driver watched me crane my neck. "That's it, for certain," he said. "No chance of confusion. There's nothing else around here."

I continued to stare. I could barely see cornices now, the slender flutes of Grecian columns just visible in the gloom. A wide, cool portico, and behind it ivy climbing walls of pale Georgian stone. The edges faded in the mist, as if an artist's thumb had blurred them.

"A good spot, it is," the driver went on. My silence seemed to make him uncomfortable, had done so for miles. "That is, for what they use it for. I wouldn't live here myself." He adjusted the cap on his salt-and-pepper head, then stroked a thorny finger through his beard. "Table's low here, so it gets wet. These fogs come off the water. It all ices over terrible in winter."

I pulled away from the window and tilted my head back against the seat, watching through the front windscreen as the house came closer. We jolted over the long, muddy drive. "Then why," I asked, "is it a good spot?"

He paused in surprise. I tried to remember when I'd spoken last since I'd hired him at the train station, and couldn't. "Well, for those fellows, of course," he said after a moment. "The mad ones. Keeps 'em away from everyone, doesn't it? And the bridge from the mainland means they've nowhere to go."

It was true. The bridge was long and narrow, exposed to the wind that had buffeted us mercilessly as we navigated its length. Any man who attempted to reach the mainland on foot would be risking his neck. I wondered whether anyone had tried and fallen to his death in the churning ocean below. I opened my mouth to ask, then shut it again.

The driver seemed not to notice. "It wasn't built as a hospital, you see. That's what I mean. It was built as a home, and not too long ago, either. Twenty years, give or take. Family named Gersbach, with children, too. God knows how they did it out here. Four hours on the train from Newcastle on Tyne to town, and then over that bridge. No place for a child, I say. No one saw them much, and no wonder — it was all they could do to get supplies from the mainland, and they never could keep servants for long. I guess there's no explaining the rich. They left during the war. I hear they were standoffish folk. Typical for Germans."

We were drawing up to the house now, and he steered the motorcar around the drive, headed for the front portico. We circled a stone fountain in the center of the lawn, unused, sitting dry and stained in an empty garden bed. Patches of mist moved across it, sliding soundlessly over the sad-eyed carved Mary as she opened her blessing arms over the empty basin, blank-faced cherubs flanking her on either side.

"You mustn't worry." The driver stopped the motor before the front steps. "It's remote — that's certain — but I've never heard of anyone being mistreated at the hospital. Your fellow is probably just fine. It'll be too late for me to come back tonight,

11

but they've nice guest rooms here, for family. I'll just come by tomorrow morning, then, shall I?"

I looked at him for a moment before I realized he thought I was a visitor. "I'm staying," I said.

For a second his eyebrows flew upward, as if I'd said I was checking myself in. Then they lowered in consternation. "A nurse? I thought —" His gaze flicked to the rear compartment, where my valise lay. It was small enough to be an overnight bag. When he looked back at me, I met his eyes and watched him understand that the valise contained everything I owned.

"Well," he said. The silence sat between us for a moment. "I'll just get your bag for you, then."

He got out of the car, and I opened my door before he could come round, pulling myself from the painfully hard seat. He flapped his hands in frustration and retrieved my small bag. "Be careful," he said as he handed it to me, his friendly tone gone. "These are madmen, you know. Brutes, some of them. You're just a tiny thing. Young, too. I had no idea you were coming to nurse, or I would have said. Most of them don't last. It's too lonely."

I handed him payment, the last money I

12

owned. "Lonely is what I want."

"I get called out here to pick the girls up sometimes when they leave. They're quiet as ghosts, and we never see the nurses in town. Maybe they're not allowed. I'm not even certain they get leave."

"I don't need leave."

"What kind of nurse doesn't need leave?"

Now he sounded almost annoyed. I turned away and started up the steps.

"It's just you don't seem the type," he called after me.

I turned back. "You needn't worry about me." I thought for a moment. "It isn't a German name, Gersbach," I said to his upturned face. "It's Swiss." I glanced past his shoulder to the fountain again, at Mary's slender, draped shoulders, her elegant arms. Then I climbed the steps toward the front doors of Portis House.

"Katharine Weekes." The woman glanced through the papers in her hand, shuffling them deftly through her long fingers, the corners of her mouth turned down in concentration.

"Kitty," I said.

She glanced sharply up at me. We were in a makeshift office where perhaps the butler or the housekeeper had once sat, tucked in the back of the building, the room furnished with only a scabbed old desk and a mismatched wooden filing cabinet. Out the window, the fog drifted by.

She was a tall woman, with square shoulders, her hair cut in a blunt fringe that was almost mannish. She wore a thick cardigan over her uniform, and a pair of half-glasses that she didn't bother to use dangled on a chain around her neck. The white cap she wore seemed out of place and almost ridiculous on her head. Her eyes narrowed as she looked at me. "You will not be called Kitty," she said. "You will be Nurse Weekes. I am the Matron here, Mrs. Hilder. You will call me Matron."

I filed this piece of information away. It was stupid, but I would need it. "Yes, Matron."

Her eyes narrowed again. Even when I tried, I had never had an easy time sounding obedient, and something must have slipped through my tone. Matron would be one of those women who never missed a hint of insolence. "It says here," she continued a moment later, "that you come from Belling Wood Hospital in London, where you worked for a year."

"Yes, Matron."

"It's a difficult hospital, Belling Wood. A

lot of casualties came through there. A great many challenging cases."

I nodded mutely. How did she know? How could she know?

"We usually prefer more experienced nurses, but as you were at Belling Wood, it's to be assumed your skills are higher than would strictly be required here at Portis."

"I'm sure it will be fine," I murmured. I had carefully placed my hands on the lap of my thick skirt, and I kept my eyes trained on them. I wore my only pair of gloves. I hated gloves, but I hated the sight of my hands even more. At least the gloves hid the scar that traveled from the soft web between my thumb and fingers down to the base of my wrist.

"Are you?" Mrs. Hilder — Matron — asked. Something about the careful neutrality of her tone set a pulse of panic pumping in the back of my throat.

I risked a glimpse up at her. She was regarding me steadily from behind a gaze that gave nothing away. I would have to say something. I quickly searched my memory.

"Belling Wood was exhausting," I said. "I was hardly ever home. I began to think I couldn't really make a difference." Yes, this I remembered hearing. "I was tired of casualty cases, and I had heard of Portis

15

House by reputation."

A bit thick, perhaps, but I felt it had been called for. Matron's expression didn't change. "Portis has no reputation," she said without inflection. "We opened only last year."

"I hear that the patients are very well treated," I said. Also true, even if I had heard it only from the taxi driver twenty minutes earlier.

"They're treated as well as they can be," she replied. "You also have a letter of reference here from Gertrude Morris, Belling Wood's head nurse."

I watched her extract the page and read it carefully. Her eyes traveled down the handwritten paper, then up again. Sweat beaded on my forehead.

It was a lie, all of it. I'd never set foot in Belling Wood. My London flatmate, Alison, had worked there, and in her few hours home between shifts, she'd told exhaustive stories of what it was like. It sounded like hard work, but hard work didn't bother me, and I wanted a job. Washing bandages and emptying a few bedpans didn't seem like much compared to the factory work I'd been doing, and when I was let go, I found myself with no way to pay my half of the rent.

16

Ally'd had two nursing friends over one night, and as I sat in my tiny bedroom, I listened through the thin walls to their talk. One had a pamphlet from Portis House advertising for nurses and was thinking of applying. She was sick of London and the work sounded easy — just a few shell-shocked men, if you please, far from the blood and the vomit and the influenza in the city. But the others said the place was so far away she'd likely go mad. Besides, rumor had it Portis House couldn't keep staff past a few weeks, though no one could say why, and it was desperate for girls. Who wanted to give up a good London job and go all that way to a place that couldn't keep nurses? Best, all the girls agreed, to stay in London and hope for a promotion — or, even better, a husband.

I'd sat on my thin bed listening, hugging my knees, my heart pounding in excitement as they'd tossed the idea away, and after they left, I'd fished the pamphlet from the trash bin. It was the perfect solution. A far-distant place, desperate for girls, and all I'd have to do was wait on a handful of soldiers. I'd sent off an application claiming Ally's experience as mine, complete with a letter of reference from the head nurse. Ally had talked about her often enough; it was simple

17

to change my handwriting and use the woman's name. Who would check too closely in these days of chaos, with the war just over?

I'd received a reply within a few days — an acceptance sight unseen, accompanied by travel instructions. I'd told Ally a made-up story about getting another factory job and packed my bag, leaving her none the wiser. If it doesn't harm anyone, I'd always thought, it's fair game.

Matron folded the paper again and put it on the desk. The pulse of fear in my throat slowed.

"This all seems in order," she said.

I swallowed and nodded.

"Conditions here can be challenging," she went on, "and our location is isolated. It isn't easy work. We have a hard time getting girls to stay."

"I'll stay."

"Yes," she said. "You likely will." She tilted her head and regarded me. "Because Gertrude Morris happens to be my second cousin, and that isn't her handwriting at all."

My heart dropped to my stomach. No. *No.* "I —"

"Be quiet." Her voice was kept even, and her eyelids drooped over her eyes for a brief moment in what almost seemed an expression of triumph. "I should not only turn you away. I should report you to Mr. Deighton, the owner. A word from him to your next employer and you'd be out on the streets."

"But you brought me all the way here." I tried to speak calmly, not to sound shrill, but it came out a croak. "You can't just turn me away. Why did you bring me here?"

"I didn't. Mr. Deighton did. I was away for several days, and your application fell to him. Believe me, if he'd waited to seek my counsel, none of this would be happening." She sounded a little disgusted, as if the slight was a frequent one. "But now it's done."

What did that mean? I waited.

Matron leaned back in her chair and examined me. "How old are you?" she asked.

"Twenty."

"Have you had measles?"

"Yes."

"Chicken pox?"

"Yes."

"Do you have varicose veins?"

"No."

"Susceptible to infection?"

"I've never been sick a day in my life."

"Are you capable of holding down a man who is thrashing and calling you names?"

Steady. She was trying to throw me, but I wouldn't let her. "I don't know about the thrashing, but I've been called every name in the book and then some."

She sighed. "You seem awfully confident. You shouldn't be. You're a pert one, too, and don't think I can't tell. I don't care for your attitude." She glanced down at the papers before her again, then back at me, and now her jaw was set. "I don't know what you're up to, Miss Weekes, and I don't care to know. As it happens, I'm in dire need of a nurse. I haven't been able to keep a girl past three weeks, and it's put the work far behind. Frankly, I'm about to lose my position over it."

I blinked. I hadn't expected candor. "I'll stay," I said again.

"I'll thank you to remember that, and not come crying to me."

"I don't come crying to anyone."

"You say that now. Another thing — I keep rules here at Portis House. Show respect to myself, to the doctors, and to Mr. Deighton when he comes for inspection. Cleanliness and neatness at all times. Always wear your uniform. Shifts are of sixteen hours' duration, with two hours of leisure

20

time in the early afternoon, and one week's night shift per month. You get a half day off every four weeks only, and no other leave will be given. Curfew is strictly enforced, and no fraternizing with the men. Breaking the rules is grounds for immediate dismissal. Do I make myself clear? And for the last time, you're to call me Matron."

I couldn't believe that this was happening, that I would be staying. That my wild plan had worked. *This place is perfect — so perfect. I'll never be found.* "Yes, Matron."

"I will not discuss your background, or lack of it, with anyone for now. But you are expected to perform all the duties of a nurse, to the level of your fellow nurses. How you do that is your problem. Is this fully understood?"

"Yes, Matron."

"Fine, then. I'll have Nurse Fellows show you around the place." She stood.

I stood as well, but I didn't follow her to the door.

"Well?" she said irritably when she opened the door and turned back to see me standing there. "What is it?"

"Why?" I said. "Why did you accept me, really? You don't like me at all. Why didn't you turn me away?"

I could see her deciding whether to answer, but her distaste for me won out and she went ahead. "Very well. Because I think the only girls who will stay here will be the ones who have nowhere else to go," she said bluntly. "Normal girls haven't worked, but someone desperate might do." She shrugged. "And now I've found you." She turned to the open doorway. "Nurse Fellows, please show Nurse Weekes to her quarters."

CHAPTER TWO

"Linens in the second cupboard," said Nurse Fellows. "Matron keeps the key and I keep a copy. One pillow, one sheet, and one blanket for each man — no extras allowed. In winter we add a second sheet and a second blanket, but it's only June, so they're to have summer blankets only. The third cupboard under here is for disinfectant — refilled once per week; take note, you'll need it. Sponges on the shelf here. For larger spills call Paulus and he will bring the other orderlies. This button here rings Paulus's office. Orderlies are to be called only for emergencies, not for everyday problems, or Matron will hear about it. Are you following me?"

"Yes." I hefted my valise in my hand. They'd offered to have an orderly come take it for me, but I'd refused. I didn't like the idea of a strange man pawing through my things.

Nurse Fellows was spare and thin hipped, perhaps twenty-four, though the pockmarks on her face and the thin line of her lips made her look older. She wore the shawl-collared blouse, long pale blue skirt, and full apron that was the Portis House uniform, the apron tied at her boyish waist. Under the starched cap her tightly pinned hair was of a bright yellow hue I'd never seen in nature.

"Breakfast is at seven sharp, followed by morning exercise. Luncheon is at noon, afternoon tea at three o'clock, and supper at six thirty. Curfew for the men is nine thirty, no shirking, and ten o'clock for the nurses. Any disturbances past ten o'clock will be reported directly to Matron."

We left the back corridors, lined with supplies and storage closets, and started up a servants' staircase. The house was much larger even than it had appeared when I approached; I hadn't yet seen anything but the servants' quarters, and those were finer than anyplace I'd ever lived. The floors were worn, but the wood was fine; the banister of the winding servants' stairs was smooth and heavy beneath my hand. I wondered exactly how rich the Gersbachs had been.

Nurse Fellows kept talking, seeming to need no reply from me. "The doctors come every second Wednesday to see the patients. They do inspections, so be sure the patients are quiet and everything is clean and ready for presentation."

"The doctors don't live here?"

She gave me a look. "I'm not sure what hospital you're from, but no. Doctors don't usually live on the premises."

Cold sweat on my neck again. "Well — no, of course not. I just thought —"

"Perhaps you're used to casualty cases. Injured men requiring round-the-clock care?"

"Yes — I am."

"Right. You'll have to adjust. We aren't dealing with sick men here, Nurse Weekes. Not truly sick, anyway. They are treated with rest, quiet surroundings, and routine. The doctors just come to mark their progress."

"I can handle that."

"Don't be so certain. Without discipline, the men can be unruly, and some of them are sly. I wouldn't trust one of them past the end of my nose. Meals are served in the dining room here."

We were in the main house now, walking a wide corridor lined with dark wainscoting. There was the scent of wood polish, but underneath it was a damp smell, as if the

25

fog were creeping through the windows. We turned a corner and she opened a set of double doors, revealing the room beyond. "Oh," I said.

Whatever the original furniture had been, it was gone now, replaced with two long tables and rows of chairs running the length of the room. Molded plaster in the shape of leaves crowned the high walls where they met the ceiling, itself decorated with vines crawling between its thick beams. Two windows adorned one wall, heavy brocade curtains framing an indistinguishable view of fog. Blank squares mapped where the family artwork had hung, and the uncarpeted floor rang with the empty echo of our footsteps. The room looked stripped, as if it had come down in the world, but the elegance was still there, like an aristocratic woman in a simple set of clothes.

The sheer size of it amazed me. "This was a dining room for one family?"

"Well, yes. This was a private home. Didn't they tell you?"

It sat twenty people easily along the tables, and where I'd come from, a room like this could have housed two families. "Did they move because they had no money?" I asked.

The look she turned on me was incredulous. "How in the world should I know? It's nothing to me, and it's nothing to you, either. Why would you even ask such a question?"

I looked at her and realized that under the brusque manner that she probably used on everyone, she genuinely disliked me. Well, well. "I'm just curious about the rich, that's all. Aren't you?"

"I am not. If you want my advice, you should keep a quiet tongue in your head if you want to get by here. The doings of people who own grand houses are none of our business."

"Fine," I said, but I narrowed my eyes at her behind her back as she turned away.

"We have nineteen patients here," she continued as we left the dining room again, I still carrying my valise. "Each man has his own room, which he should certainly be grateful for. There's the nurses' room, separate quarters for Matron and myself, four temporary rooms used for the doctors, families of patients, and Mr. Deighton. Quarters downstairs for orderlies, kitchen staff, and the gardener. Even with all that, there's a section of the west wing closed off. That's how big the house is."

"Where are the patients now?"

"In their rooms. It's part of the schedule for late-afternoon rest. Supper is in an hour, and after that, they're allotted ninety minutes of leisure time in the common room." She swung open another door at the end of the hall. "That would be this one."

This room was larger than the dining room; even stripped of its artwork and furniture, it was grand. It was opulently paneled, with a lower section connected to an upper section by three wide steps. At the far end of the upper level a bank of French doors — three pairs, I counted — looked out on a verandah and a set of manicured gardens beyond. The doors were latched closed now against the fog, the verandah damp and empty, the gardens only shadows of trimmed hedges hunched in the mist.

Like the dining room, this room had been emptied and the furniture replaced with hard, functional pieces. Thin-cushioned chairs were positioned on cheap rugs in clusters meant to be social. Two sagging sofas had been placed next to a scarred bookshelf piled with ratty magazines and books with dark, puffed pages. A single table featured a chess set and two facing chairs. I looked up and saw the same plaster vines that had decorated the dining room, looking down on this meager sight from their majestic place on the ceiling.

"There is no smoking," Nurse Fellows

said as I craned my neck. "Cards are forbidden. We get newspapers, but they cannot be current and they must be vetted by Matron first. All letters coming in and going out are read and censored if needed. Dice and gambling of any kind are not allowed. We have tentatively encouraged amateur theatrics, but so far none of the men has shown an interest."

"Blimey," I said. "What do they do in here, then?"

A look of unmistakable disgust crossed her face, and she answered as if swallowing something sour. "There are books on the shelf. Some use the time to converse, or simply to sit and think. Many are not capable of much else — you'll see. The vicar comes from time to time."

"Coo," I said, just to irritate her. *You're not so high and mighty yourself, miss. Your vowels give you away.* "Impressive. We had nothing like this at Belling Wood."

Nurse Fellows rolled her eyes. "Well, of course you didn't. Belling Wood is entirely different from what we have here." She pulled a watch from her apron pocket, checked it. "Late-afternoon rest is almost finished. I'll take you up to the nurses' quarters to wash and change. You'll need to be ready for supper duty."

29

"Very well," I said as I followed her narrow back out of the room and along the corridor toward the servants' stairs. "I'd like a smoke first, if you don't mind. It was a long trip from the train station."

She started briskly up the stairs. "Weren't you listening? There's no smoking here."

I stopped. "What do you mean, there's no smoking?"

"I just said it."

"I thought that was for the patients."

She stopped at the first turn of the stairs and looked down at me, her yellow hair nearly glowing in the dim light. "Nurse Weekes, there is no smoking anywhere at Portis House. The smoking of cigarettes is not healthful."

"Not healthful?" I tried to keep my voice from rising as I pictured life without cigarettes. "What kind of mad rule is that?"

"The nurses are to set a proper example for the patients — an example that is healthful, helpful, and moral." She gave slight emphasis to the last word as she pronounced this little speech, which was quite obviously memorized. "A nurse's duty is to give comfort with quiet obedience, which is the highest calling there is. Surely they didn't let the nurses smoke in London?"

I had no idea about the hospital, but Ally

30

had smoked steadily when not on duty. "What about in my free hours?"

"It isn't allowed."

"That's ridiculous." I put down my valise. Even at the factory, the shift supervisors had looked the other way when we slipped out the back door for a smoke. "The last I checked, I'm not mad, and I'm not a patient here. How can you make rules about my free hours?"

"Because we can," she said simply. "You are an employee here, and you are being given room and board. As such, you are setting an example twenty-four hours a day. Aside from the fact that the mad are lacking in moral judgment, it is simply the rule. And if Matron makes the rule, you follow it. Now, will there be a problem, Nurse Weekes? If so, I can inform Matron."

I gritted my teeth. I'd only just got the job, and I couldn't lose it. "No," I made myself say. "There will be no problem."

"Good. Then I'll show you to your quarters."

We looked at each other for a long moment, and I saw how it would be. When I picked up my valise again, the corner of her mouth quirked in triumph. Then she turned away, and I followed her up the stairs.

The nurses' quarters were on the second floor, in a long, narrow room that overlooked the front gardens and the drive. Five cots, each neatly made, were set up along the windows. Makeshift curtains, now tied back with strips of cloth, were strung up between the beds; the effect was a little like a hospital ward, though it was offset by the mullioned windows, the rich wood flooring covered with only the thinnest of rugs, and the dark wainscoting that matched the rooms below. Again I had the impression of a room that had once been opulent.

Atop one bed sat a girl with dark blond hair, wearing full uniform and cap, leaning against the headboard with a magazine propped against her knees. A pair of heavy shoes was discarded on the floor, and she rubbed her stockinged feet together as she read, moving the sole of one foot over the top of the other. She looked up as we entered, and I saw her face was heart shaped, her eyes wide and gray.

"Oh — hullo!" she said to me.

"Nurse Beachcombe," said Nurse Fellows before I could reply. "Supper is in fifteen minutes. Have you washed and prepared?"

The girl blinked. "No — that is, Nina is
—"

"And where is Nurse Shouldice? She
should be preparing as well."

"I'm here." A woman's low tenor voice
came from the doorway behind us, and I
moved aside. A second girl came into the
room, this one tall, her shoulders wide, her
hair mousy brown, her face doughy and
slack. She regarded Nurse Fellows with
naked hostility from behind a pair of wire-
rimmed glasses. "Who's this, then?"

Nurse Fellows's lips pursed even thinner.
"This is Nurse Weekes, who starts today."

"Is it?" The big girl swung a look at me.
"Will she last longer than the last one,
then?"

"That was unfortunate," said Nurse Fellows. "Matron has taken it under advisement."

Now the look swung back to Nurse Fellows. "Will she take it under advisement
that Martha and I have been doing double
duty for four days?"

"Nina," said the girl on the bed weakly.

Nurse Fellows's returning stare was icy.
"Matron is well aware of the staffing levels
here, I assure you. That is why we have a
replacement. The two of you will have to
train her, as I am far too busy. I expect you

33

to teach her properly." She turned to me. "I'll get you one of the uniforms from the cupboard. I'll remind you that you are expected to wear your uniform at all times." She darted a glare at Nurse Beachcombe, who was still sitting shoeless on the bed. "Even during breaks. I'll see the three of you in fifteen minutes."

"Where does she get off?" grumbled Nurse Shouldice after Nurse Fellows had gone.

"It was only my shoes," Nurse Beach-combe said uncertainly as she scooted off her bed. "I'd no idea it was against regulations."

"Of course not," the bigger girl replied. "*Too busy?* Too busy doing what, I'd like to know."

I stared at the heaping pile of cloth Nurse Fellows had deposited on the bed. The outfit looked ridiculously complicated. "I'll never get into all this," I said.

Nurse Beachcombe slid her shoes on and stood next to me. "It isn't so hard. I'll help." She assisted me out of my blouse and skirt and gave me a shy smile. "I'm Martha," she said to me, "and this is Nina. Where are you from?"

"London," I said. "And I'm Kitty."

"I like that name," said Martha. "I've only

been to London once myself, and wasn't it wonderful! You see, this is rather simple — underskirt, skirt, then blouse and collar. The apron goes on last."

"So you're the new girl," said Nina. She was watching me with a wariness I couldn't quite fathom, as if she thought I'd steal her valuables, whatever they might be. "You've already met Boney, I see."

"Boney?" I frowned as Martha helped me with the skirt, trying to place the reference. "You mean Napoléon?"

"Oh, you're an educated one, then." This was said with disdain. "Yes, our little dictator. That's what we call her, though not to her face, of course. Matron's pet, she is, don't you think?"

"I've no idea." Without knowing the lay of the land, I wasn't about to insult another girl behind her back — even if she *was* obviously Matron's pet. "I'm not educated," I said. "I just read books."

"Well, there won't be any time for that here." Nina's glasses glinted in the waning light from the windows. "You'll be worked off your feet. Six o'clock we're up, and on duty at seven. You're on duty until nine thirty, lights out at ten. Then it starts all over again."

"Nina's engaged," said Martha. "To a man

35

named Roland. He's coming to collect her next month. Isn't that romantic?"

"Martha, hush," said Nina, though she couldn't quite keep the superiority from her voice. "We've only just met her."

"Well, she's one of us now, and shouldn't she know? I think it's so exciting. I had a boy back in Glenley Crewe, but I had to come here for work, and he married someone else. Do you have a fellow, Kitty?"

In every group of girls I'd ever encountered — girls working together on a factory shift, girls living together in boardinghouses — the girl who was engaged had the highest status. It was probably the reason Boney, so fond of her superiority, disliked Nina so much. I would have to tread carefully. "No, I don't."

"Oh, that's too bad. You shouldn't have trouble with the men here — they're not a bother in that way. Some of them don't much know what's going on, really, so they don't get any ideas."

"Ideas?" I tried to button the detachable collar with fingers that were suddenly cold and clumsy. "What do you mean?"

"For goodness' sake, Martha," Nina chided. "They're patients. And madmen."

Martha shrugged. "It doesn't mean they can't get ideas, does it? That's all I was saying. There, now you fit right in."

I stared down at myself. My long, slim serge skirt and serviceable blouse were gone, replaced by layers under a full apron that nearly brushed the floor. There had been grumblings that hems six inches from the ground were too short to be proper on a girl, part of the immorality we girls had learned during the war, though the grumblings never discouraged us from wearing the shortest hems we could find. Now I'd gone back in time, like a woman in an old photograph, one of those stiff biddies with sour expressions. The blouse's shawl collar sat heavy on my shoulders, and the long, puffed sleeves ended past my wrists and halfway up my hands. How was I supposed to work in this?

"Your shoes," said Martha. "Are those your only ones?"

I looked at my only pair of oxfords where I'd discarded them on the floor, their leather starting to separate from the soles. "Yes."

"Oh, that won't do. The floors are *cold* here, and you'll be on your feet all day."

"Didn't you need thicker shoes in a London hospital?" This was Nina, regarding me closely from behind her glasses, with the suspicious look again.

"No," I fumbled. "That is — there was no

regulation. For shoes."

"No matter." Martha bent next to my narrow bed and rummaged on the floor. "The last girl left her boots; they'll fit just fine, I think. She was the same size as you. There, do you see? How lucky!"

I took them from her. They were ankle boots of thick leather, well made and low heeled, like something a girl would wear on a farm. I pulled them on — they did fit surprisingly well — and stared at my feet in dismay. I had no desire for elegant clothes, and no money for them if I had, but I barely recognized myself. What had I gotten myself into? And what kind of girl, I wondered, left her boots behind when she left a job?

"We'll just add the cap," Martha was saying. "It has to be worn straight, see? If you put it on an angle, Matron will notice." She took a closer look at my head. "Your hair is just perfect for it. Did you do these braids yourself?"

I ran my fingers along the pattern of hair where I'd wound long braids around the back of my head. "Yes."

"It's so pretty. Don't you think, Nina?"

"I think we're going to be late."

Martha reached up to place my cap, and I saw her forearms were bare, her sleeves shorter than mine. It took me only a minute

38

to puzzle it out — I noticed small fabric loops along her cuff as she adjusted my cap. *So that's how one works in this dress. Detachable sleeves. Clever.*

I slid my fingers along my own sleeves, finding the buttons and undoing them one by one. I kept my expression calm, almost bored, as if I had known all along.

"I hope I won't need these," I said, dropping the sleeves on the bed when she finished.

Nina stared at me uneasily, then headed for the door. "You'll need them for inspections, so keep them ready."

"I won't lose them," I said.

"See that you don't. Come now, or we'll be late for supper."

CHAPTER THREE

Twenty minutes later, after hastily eating a bite of bread and cheese and taking a gulp of lukewarm tea, I was standing again in the doorway of the grand dining room. I was finally getting my first look at the patients, the madmen of Portis House.

They filed past me into the room, quiet and orderly. They were of all kinds — tall and short, skinny and fat, light and dark. Each man wore a uniform of oatmeal-colored heavy linen: a simple pair of trousers and a long-sleeved buttoned shirt with the words PORTIS HOUSE HOSPITAL stenciled across the front and the back. I realized I had been picturing them all in military uniforms and puttees, as if the war were still on; to see them dressed in hospital dress was disconcerting and somehow diminishing.

They didn't look at me. They spoke to one another in murmurs, if they spoke at all, as they took their seats. They seemed almost docile, and my first, incongruous thought was: *They don't seem mad.*

Nina sidled up beside me. "No belts or suspenders," she said. "If you see either, you're to confiscate it. Straight razors, too."

She watched for my reaction from behind her lenses. I kept my face straight, but I noticed she was right: Not a single man in the room wore a belt or suspenders on his trousers. The trousers seemed to have just a drawstring. String being, perhaps, deemed too difficult for a man to hang himself with.

I cleared my throat, spoke as softly as I could. "How do — how do they shave?"

"Safety razors only. Most of them are used to it from the war. There are one or two complainers, but we're not to take chances. No matter what a man says to you, there are no exceptions to the rule."

I nodded, trying not to picture what would make a man want to leave this place so badly that he could not be trusted with a straight razor — trying not to think that the rule must have grown out of experience.

Nurse Fellows — I'd already started thinking of her as Boney — joined us, Martha at her shoulder. "We're ready," she said. "The kitchen is loading the food now. Nurse Shouldice, take a tray to Mr. West — his

41

legs are particularly bad today, and he is in bed. Mr. Childress will also need his broth in the infirmary."

"I'll do them both," said Nina. "Mr. Childress usually eats something when I coax him a bit."

"Very well. Nurse Beachcombe, you're to take a tray to Patient Sixteen. I haven't heard from him, but I assume he'll want something."

Martha brightened. "Yes, Nurse Fellows."

"Who is Patient Sixteen?" I asked.

Nina and Martha exchanged a look, but Boney ignored the question. "You're to supervise the dining room," she told me. "I'll help you serve, but then I must see Matron and supervise in the kitchen. They seem in a decent mood tonight. Can you handle it?"

I glanced out at the men sitting at two tables under the extravagant vines plastered into the opulent ceiling. I hoped my bravado was convincing. "Of course."

"Good. Get moving, or Matron will hear of it. Let's go."

The orderlies — four men in white linens, one of whom was massively tall and large — had wheeled carts into the dining room. The tall one unlocked the panel to a dumbwaiter and opened it. With a loud creak of pulleys, a platform containing plates of food appeared, presumably from the kitchen. The orderly emptied the plates onto his cart, shouted *"Hup"* down the shaft of the dumb-waiter, and the platform lowered again. I watched, mesmerized, as this was repeated many times over. I'd seen dumbwaiters in restaurants, but never in a house before.

Boney turned to me as the other two nurses loaded trays and vanished toward the stairs. "We used to say a prayer at meals, but some of them couldn't sit still for it and it had a disrupting effect on the others, so we stopped. I'll pour the water. Each man gets a plate. And set them down *gently.* For God's sake, no loud noises. Do you under-stand?"

"No loud noises?"

She pursed her lips. "They can't handle it. I've yet to work with a nurse who takes the proper care. No bangs, claps, or sounds of that sort — half the men will hit the floor, thinking they're in a trench. Portis House is supposed to be a restful place of healing, and lack of stressful sound is part of the treatment. Doctors' orders."

I glanced into the room again. *Half of them will hit the floor.* "I understand."

I picked up plates from one of the carts as she took a large pitcher of water and poured

43

for each man. With three patients — Mr. West of the bad legs, Mr. Childress in the infirmary, and the mysterious Patient Sixteen — out of the room, we had only sixteen men in the dining room, eight to each table. Each plate contained a square of beef, a lump of potatoes, and a spoonful of watery peas. I set down one plate, then another, taking care to set them gently. I had been hungry, even after the bread and cheese, but as I looked at the plates of food, my appetite drained away.

The men ate without complaint. Boney finished with the water and gave me a nod before leaving the room. A hush fell, heavy and pregnant, as soon as she was gone.

"A new nurse," came one man's voice. It was impossible to tell which, as no man raised his head.

"A pretty one, too," said another.

I quietly set down another plate.

"Where's the freckled one?" This came from a blond man with a short beard who was in my line of sight. "We haven't seen her in days, and she's not on night duty, either."

None of the nurses had freckles; this must have been the last girl, whose boots I was wearing. "Yes, where is she?" said a man with big shoulders and bright red hair who

44

was sitting farther down the line I was serving. The look he gave me was jeering. "Do tell us poor fellows, won't you, sister?"

"I'm not your sister," I shot back at him.

To my surprise, he laughed, as did the man next to him, though no one else joined in. I set a plate in front of a tall, gangly man who had spectacles placed atop his large Roman nose. He looked up at me kindly. "I believe Creeton means a nursing sister," he said, his accent proclaiming Oxford or Cambridge. "A member of your order."

"Order?" I couldn't disguise my horror as I stared at him. "You mean like a nun?"

"A nun!" The red-haired man laughed again. "Thank God she ain't one of those!"

"A nursing order," said Roman Nose. He lowered his voice confidentially and looked down as he cut into his square of beef. "It is a term, I believe, for a nurse of some seniority."

I reddened. Ten minutes into my first supper and one of the men was already covering for me. I was usually more adept than this. I'd worked for more than six months at the factory without anyone discovering I wasn't the school friend of the owner's daughter; before that, the owner of a perfume shop in Mile End still thought the shopgirl who had worked for him for nearly a year was named Theresa Baker. *For God's sake, get it together or they'll pitch you out of here.* "I'm not a nursing sister," I said to the room at large, moving down the table. "I'm only a nurse. My name is Nurse Weekes."

"Jolly good!" came a voice from somewhere behind me. "You're the prettiest sister we've had."

"I say," agreed the red-haired man. "You can tuck Captain Mabry there into bed, then, can you? I'm sure he'd appreciate it."

There was laughter, and from the way Roman Nose reddened, I guessed he was Captain Mabry. I glanced at the door, but there was no sign of Boney or anyone else. Where had the orderlies gone? "I'm not tucking anyone into bed," I said.

I had reached the last place setting, which happened to be that of Creeton — the big-shouldered redhead. He looked up at me with a wide smile. "Ah, come now, sister. It's just a bit of fun." And as I lowered his plate, a big, beefy hand landed on my behind and squeezed me painfully through my skirts.

I jumped. The plate banged on the table, rattling silverware and ringing against the water glass. Silence fell, deafening, the air stretched with expectant strain; then a high-pitched sound came from one of the other men, a keening almost like laughter.

"I'm sorry," I said, moving away from Creeton and down the table. "I'm sorry. I —"

The man making the sound had dropped his fork, and peas spilled over the edge of his plate and onto the table. He raised his hands to his face, as if embarrassed at the sound that was coming from him, and I realized the sound actually *was* laughter — hysterical, uncontrolled. He rocked forward and back again, his face reddening, the sound coming from deep inside him in loops and whorls.

"I'm sorry," I said again.

"Look what you've done!" said Captain Mabry, but he was directing this at Creeton. "You've set him off now." His tone held almost a note of fear.

"Somersham!" said Creeton to the laughing man, who continued to keen. "Crazy as a loon, are you? *Somersham!*" He lifted his plate and banged it on the table again, sending droplets of gravy flying. And again. "There! What do you think that is? Where do you think you are, then? The bloody Somme?"

The man laughed harder. The air seemed to have gone from the room, and I could

47

barely breathe. "Stop it!" I shouted. "Stop!"

"Somersham, for God's sake," Captain Mabry's voice was almost pleading. "You have to stop."

Somersham pressed his hands to his cheeks. "I'm not a coward," he said, to no one. "I'm not."

I felt a gentle touch on my arm and looked down to find a pudgy man looking up at me, his face unlined and calm. "You mustn't be too hard on these men," he said. He leaned closer, lowered his voice. "I think they've been in a war."

I took a step back, and then another. And then I was out of the room, alone in the corridor, with the empty carts and the deep, growing gloom. I made my way to the end of the corridor, where there was a window, my steps echoing strangely off the walls, and looked hopelessly out at the dark drifts of fog.

I couldn't do it. I couldn't. I'd been so certain, but I'd miscalculated. That hand on me — I could still feel it, and it made me sick. I'd thought I'd be caring for madmen, simpletons, drooling idiots. I hadn't thought they'd be *men.*

And now I was locked up with them in this place, miles from anything.

I put my palm on the glass, felt its cool

dampness, the slick chill of it. Watched the fog go past my fingers. The paint was chipping along the sill and coming off the top of the window in strips. Strange, to see paint peeling already in a house apparently so new.

I closed my eyes. From the dining room, the laughter had stopped, and there was an ominous silence. Calm came over me, almost cold, along the back of my neck and shoulders. It robbed me of my fear and made me feel strong again. Did the door to the nurses' bedroom have a lock on it? Was there anything in Portis House I could keep as a weapon, just in case?

The silence was broken by a hoarse shout from the dining room, the smash of dishes, the clatter of overturning chairs. From down the corridor came the heavy sounds of orderlies running up the stairs from the kitchen, a shout of surprise. But I was closest, and it took me only seconds. And so I was first into the dining room, and the first to see the blood spilled on the floor.

CHAPTER FOUR

I didn't think; I only sank to my knees, fighting with my skirts, beside the man prone on the ground. He was wedged between the two tables, curled in on himself, his hands up. When I leaned over him I saw that it was Captain Mabry, his glasses tumbled off to the floor, his face streaked with blood.

Creeton. It must have been. Or perhaps Creeton with the help of another. Or someone else altogether? I didn't know any of the men well enough to be sure. I pulled the captain onto his back as the room erupted into chaos behind me, chairs scraping as men pushed them back, excited voices. "He's done it again!" said someone.

"All right, then." A man's voice boomed over the others. I looked up to see the orderlies had come into the room, and the biggest one, a huge man with pale hair cropped close to his scalp, was giving orders. "We're going off to the common room. All of us. In order. Single file. Nice and quiet."

His vowels flattened over one another, the consonants crisp and brittle. British, and yet somehow alien. I had just placed it as South African when Matron appeared behind the huge orderly and peered past him, her expression livid.

"What is the meaning of this?" she barked to the room.

I looked back down at Captain Mabry. He was lying in my lap, as docile as a trained dog, looking up at me. His nose was bleeding profusely, a great gush of blood down the front of his face, over his lips and chin, onto his shirtfront and the floor. It was a nosebleed in full flush, more gobbets of fresh black blood moving sluggishly out of his nostrils.

Nina appeared over my shoulder. She took in the situation briefly, said, "I'll get the Winsoll's," and was gone before I could ask what that meant.

I swallowed. "Right, then." I rolled him farther up over my knees. The nose didn't appear broken; it seemed, unbelievably, like a simple nosebleed. I lifted his torso and tilted his head back — he cooperated with perfect obedience, as if I knew what I was doing — and crooked my elbow under the back of his neck. "Lean back. Lean on me as far back as you can and look up."

A bloody nose, of all things. The one thing — the only thing — I knew how to treat, at least temporarily. The only thing I had experience of.

Captain Mabry tilted his head back. With practiced precision I pinched his nostrils shut, high up, just under the hard section of bone. He gurgled a bit. The men were leaving the room, muttering, as the big orderly watched them go. I could smell the captain's shaving soap, could feel the texture of his linen shirt against my supporting arm. There was a spot of dried soap at his temple. I looked away.

Behind me, someone shuffled and walked away, but I couldn't see who. The captain went very still.

A pair of masculine feet, clad in worn leather shoes, came into my line of vision. Creeton crouched next to me, his wrists draped over his knees, and looked the two of us over. "Well, well," he said, his voice pitched low, dangerous, and strangely pleased. "Hello, sister."

I glared at him and said nothing. This man had put his hand on me. My skin crawled.

He leaned closer until his breath, hot and

damp, fanned the wisps of hair behind my ear. "Having a good time, are we, on our first day with the madmen?"

"Be careful," I said back, just as low. "I bite."

He recoiled. He must have seen something steely in my eyes, because uncertainty flickered across his face, but he covered it quickly with a leering smile. "Perhaps I'd like that."

"Where I bite, I promise you wouldn't."

Surprise again, but he had no chance to answer before Matron stood over him. "That is quite enough, Mr. Creeton."

Creeton pushed himself to his feet slowly, obeying with an air of open defiance. He turned and followed the others from the room without another word.

Matron stepped forward and looked down at us. "Mr. Mabry," she said, disappointment in her voice.

Mabry blinked up at her, his expression impossible to read beyond my hand and the trail of blood.

"Another nosebleed," said Matron. "I thought we were past this. You haven't had one in several weeks, and it seemed you had conquered this particular problem. But now I see I was wrong. You realize I'm going to have to report this to the doctors, don't you?"

"I'm terribly sorry," said Mabry.

"I realize you may be. But it doesn't change the fact that I must put this in my report to the doctors. If you had refrained, things would be different."

"I'm terribly sorry," he said, his voice fainter this time.

"Nurse Weekes," she said without acknowledging him further, "please see that he is cleaned and sent to his room for rest. The sight of him will upset the other patients."

"Yes, Matron."

"And report to the kitchen in twenty minutes. I presume you know where it is."

The kitchen was downstairs, a huge, utilitarian room full of ranges and instruments I couldn't put a name to. A male cook and several kitchen boys were cleaning up after supper with the help of two orderlies, and in one corner a small table had been set with simple bowls and spoons. Matron, Martha, and Boney were all seated at it when I arrived. Nina came behind me; she had helped me clean up Captain Mabry with the aid of Winsoll's, which had turned out to be a kind of disinfectant. I could still smell it in the back of my nose and behind my eyes. We'd also changed my bloodstained apron.

A kitchen boy put a pot of stew on the table, and at its savory scent my appetite returned. It seemed this was the nurses' evening meal.

When we had all taken a bowl, Matron spoke. First she bowed her head and recited a prayer; we all bowed our heads in silence. Then she straightened and gave us her eagle stare again.

"Nurse Fellows," she said. "Please begin."

Boney lifted her chin, as if reciting in front of the class. "I ordered the linens you requested, Matron, and they should come with the next delivery. I also completed the inventory of the storage room in the west hallway."

"Very well. I expect a written report on my desk by morning."

"Yes, Matron."

The stew was delicious. The shaken, horrified feeling I'd had in the dining room began to recede. This seemed to be a sort of nurses' meeting. I ate and listened with half an ear, thinking about nosebleeds.

"Nurse Beachcombe?" said Matron.

"Patient Sixteen ate his supper," said Martha. "Or I think he did, as the orderlies

55

brought down an empty tray. He didn't want me to stay in the room."

"And how did he seem?"

I wondered whether that was a blush on Martha's cheeks, or whether she was just overheated. "He was no worse than usual, Matron. He was sitting on that window seat he likes. He barely spoke to me."

"But did he appear improved at all? Sociable?"

"No, Matron."

For a moment Matron looked almost uncertain. "I had so hoped for improvement. Though of course I realize he's —" She broke off. Martha and Nina exchanged a glance.

I put down my spoon. "He's what?"

Matron regarded me for a moment. "Patient Sixteen is the least of your worries, Nurse Weekes," she said. "Carry on, Nurse Beachcombe."

"Yes, Matron. The coal was low in the fires today, so I spoke to one of the orderlies about it. He said there's water leaking somewhere in the cellar, and none of them want to go down there to the scuttle, and they're having to draw straws."

"What do you mean, they don't want to go down there?"

"Well." Martha's eyes went even wider in

her heart-shaped face. "They say the water leaks constantly, they can't make it stop, and the scuttle is placed far in the back. You have to cross the cellar to get to it. And sometimes, at the back, they hear sounds in the water behind them closer to the stairs, like — like splashing footsteps. And so they won't go down."

We all fell silent. Finally Matron spoke. "Are you telling me," she said, her mannish voice slow with disbelief, "that the orderlies — grown *men* — are afraid of a few mice in the cellar?"

"Unacceptable," said Boney.

Martha bit her lip. "But they say it's true."

"It sounds like poppycock to me," said Nina, as she shoveled in another mouthful of stew. "Send me down there. I'll go."

"There will be no need, Nurse Shouldice," said Matron. "I will speak to Paulus myself."

Paulus, I gathered, was the huge orderly, the man with the South African accent. Nina shrugged. Martha worried her lip, her supper forgotten.

Matron turned to me. "And you, Nurse Weekes? What nonsense have you brought me? Or are you a girl with even a minimum of intelligence?"

There was a glint in her eye; she was waiting for something from me, something she

57

expected. I lifted my chin. "What happened in the dining room today," I said. "The nosebleed. I'd like an explanation."

"Would you?" said Matron.

"From the way you spoke to him, there's obviously a history. If I'm to care for him, I'd like to know what it is I'm to expect."

She frowned. If there'd been a test, I wondered whether I had passed it. "Mr. Mabry has a particular psychoneurosis," she said. "He often seems calm, but he is prone to fits. They can be violent, so you must take care if you're in his presence when he's struck with one. He has broken several items during his time at Portis House."

I digested that. "And the nosebleed?"

"Is one of his recurring fits. The doctors believe it is of particular concern. They have been focusing their treatment on it, and before today he hadn't had one in nearly three weeks."

"Treatment?" I looked around the table. "Do you mean he somehow *makes* himself have nosebleeds?"

"You saw it yourself," said Boney. "How else did he get it?"

I decided not to mention that I hadn't been in the dining room at the time. "It's just — I didn't know a nosebleed could be caused by force of will."

"He doesn't will 'em," said Martha. "He gets afraid. He thinks he sees something."

"That's bunk and you know it." Boney turned on her, her lips tight, spots of red high on her cheeks. "He does no such thing!"

"Nurse Fellows is correct," Matron broke in. "Mr. Mabry suffers from delusions, as do many of the men here. Mind over matter, Nurse Weekes. Mind over matter. It is what many of the men here still have to learn." She pushed back her chair and stood. "And now, I expect you all to return to your posts for the evening. We have work to do."

CHAPTER FIVE

"It was a test, wasn't it?" I said much later in the nurses' quarters as I sat on my narrow bed and pulled off my shoes. "Supper, I mean. Putting me in there alone."

Martha, standing before the washbasin and pouring water over her hand from the pitcher, glanced sympathetically at me. "I wouldn't worry about it. Boney does it to all the new nurses."

"She leaves them alone with the men to test them? Does Matron know about this?"

"It's Matron's *orders,*" said Nina, landing heavily on the edge of her own bed. "Boney would never think up anything on her own."

I rubbed my feet. The bed was hard and the mattress thin, yet my body nearly groaned aloud in relief. We had spent the evening cleaning the dining room, mopping the floor in the front hall, polishing the banisters, carrying baskets of clean linens up the stairs from the laundry, checking the lavatories, closing the windows in the bedrooms, and making sure the men behaved in the common room. The only real nursing we'd done was for Mr. West, the soldier with the bad legs — it turned out he'd had both legs blown off below the knee, and sometimes needed medication for the pain. The sight of those two shortened legs, the empty expanse of trouser pinned carefully over them, had made me almost wish for my twelve-hour shifts at the factory.

"It's really for the best, you know," said Martha, drying her hands. "Not everyone can handle it here. It's best to know right away."

"We've seen enough of them come and go, God knows," said Nina. "You won't be here long yourself, Martha, if you keep repeating the orderlies' scary stories to Matron."

"He wasn't lying," Martha protested. "He was *scared.*"

"It's this place," said Nina. "Anyone who stays here long enough goes just as mad as the patients, with the exception of you and me. And sometimes I wonder about the two of us, working here as long as we have."

"That's not fair. This is a good job."

I listened to them and remembered Matron's words. *I think that someone desperate might do.* I wondered what made Martha and Nina — and Boney — so desperate that they were the only girls to stay.

Money, perhaps. Or perhaps, like me, they were girls with nowhere else to go.

"This was the nursery," Martha said to me, gesturing around the room, her eyes shining just a little. "This room here. Isn't that nice? It's so pretty." She looked up and down the long room, taking in the grandness of it despite the shabbiness of the current furniture. "I like to imagine what it was like to grow up here. The children, tucked in their beds. There were only two, you know, and they had this room all to themselves. Wouldn't it be lovely, to grow up in a room like this?"

She was smiling, and her eyes were sweet and kind, but her skin was sallow, her bones sticking through the shoulders of her dress like broomsticks. She'd grown up, like me, where children didn't live in grand houses, and now she worked a job with madmen — a job in which I'd seen her carry linen baskets twice her weight up two flights of stairs — and she called it "good." She dried her thin, chapped hands, and I knew that deep down she was hard, but she wasn't hard enough. No one ever was.

"The children sound like spoiled brats to

me," I said.

"Now there's a bit of sense," said Nina from her bed. She was untying her apron, her head bent down, her stringy hair coming loose from its bun and dangling. "Besides, who wants to grow up in a damp old house in the middle of nowhere, no matter how rich you are?"

"You're just not picturing it," Martha persisted, her eyes half closed and looking somewhere far away. "I like to imagine Christmas. The whole room decorated and lit with candles. Gifts of oranges and wooden toys. The children on Christmas morning. It must have been wonderful."

"Christmas!" Nina snorted. "You're out of your mind. It's only June. And why aren't you undressing, anyway?"

Martha shrugged. "I'm working night shift."

"What?"

"Matron's orders. She told me after supper. She said that since we've had no one on night shift since Maisey left, I will have to do it."

"That's ridiculous," I interjected. "You've been working since six o'clock this morning!"

Martha bit the edge of her thumbnail. "I'll be tired, for certain, but I can make it through."

"What do they need one of us on night shift for, anyway?" Perhaps I was exhausted, but for some reason, this injustice — Martha having to work twenty-four hours straight — made me angry. "Don't they just lock the men in their rooms and be done with it?"

Nina gave me the *you're stupid, aren't you?* look that I was beginning to recognize. "Of course we don't lock them in. We're not allowed."

"They're madmen. This is a madhouse. Why in the world not?"

"Obviously you haven't seen what a man can do to himself in a locked room, have you?"

I thought of the rule against belts, against straight razors, and said nothing.

"The bathrooms, too," Nina said. "The inside bolts are taken off, and we aren't given keys. So that means someone has to work the night shift and check in on them. We get nightmares, sleepwalking, insomniacs. Some of them want to harm each other over some petty argument, or get deluded into thinking they can walk out the front door and go home."

"It isn't so bad," Martha said gently. "There's an orderly on duty all night,

64

though he sleeps in his chair most of the time. Matron has us count linens. It's usually quiet, except when someone starts screaming."

"Oh, God." I rubbed a hand over my forehead. "I need a cigarette."

"Look what you've done," Martha accused Nina. "You don't have to be so harsh. Now she'll run off and leave us, just like the last girl."

Nina turned to me darkly. "If you do, and I have to do double work again, I'll find you and skin you myself. Do you hear me? Besides," she added, "you shouldn't smoke. I hear it isn't healthful."

It was hours before I slept that night. I lay endlessly on the lumpy, narrow bed, shivering in my thin nightgown under the single regulation blanket, staring at the far-off beams of the ceiling. The coal fire we'd laid in the nursery fireplace burned low and hissed in the damp, and feverish wisps of clammy air passed over me in drafts. The house made distant noises as it settled and groaned in the gloom. Nina snored, oblivious.

I listened for screams, but heard none. I wondered where Martha was, whether she was counting linens. I wondered whether

65

Ally would ever find out about the deception I'd used to get here, and what she would think of me if she did.

Perhaps she'd be angry, or perhaps just disappointed in me. Most people were, sooner or later.

I tried rolling onto my side, but it was no warmer that way. It was the beginning of summer, but the nights were still chilled, especially this far north out on the marshes by the sea.

Who were the Gersbachs and why had they built a house here? I wondered where they'd gone. I saw my brother Syd's bedroom, the bed so neatly made up, the coverlet folded down precisely, the way it had looked on the morning he left for war without saying good-bye. *Shut up, Kitty, and go to sleep.*

I pressed my eyes shut. My nerves were waiting for the screaming, waiting, waiting. *He gets afraid,* Martha had said of Captain Mabry. *He thinks he sees something.*

Cold sweat trickled down my body. Creeton's hand on me, the blunt intrusion of his fingers through the fabric of my skirts. Captain Mabry's blood, his stillness on my lap. Someone moving behind me, though I never saw who. I dozed, part of me still waiting for something to come — the hard

66

grip of fingers, or the screams. Or the shuffle of feet behind my back. Dawn was years away.

And Syd's cold bedroom, dark and abandoned. Someone moving behind me that day, too, as I stood in the doorway.

No matter how bad it gets, I said to myself just as I did every day, *I'm never going home.*

CHAPTER SIX

Over the next two days of grueling work, I came to know more about Portis House. I learned to coax water from the reluctant taps in the laundry, where we filled our buckets for daily washing. I learned how to rub polishing wax onto a floor so it wouldn't look opaque. How to buff the convoluted knobs of a brass bedstead without missing a spot. How to carry a bowl of hot soup up a flight of winding stairs without spilling any on the tray. How to fold a bedsheet properly at the corner of a bed, though I was slower and clumsier than Nina, and had to watch her more than once from the corner of my eye, admiring the fast, sure way she hefted the mattress with her beefy hands.

I also learned how to spend just five extra minutes in the lavatory, rubbing my aching feet; and, for a wonderful, beautiful quarter hour, I found a deserted spot outside the kitchen door, out of sight of the windows, where I smoked a cigarette, my eyes closed in a rapturous daze, the breeze blowing last autumn's leaves over the cobbles in front of me and out over the low, rolling grounds beyond.

West, the soldier with the missing legs, had lost them to a grenade lobbed into his trench by advancing German infantry; his fiancée had abandoned him after he came home in a wheelchair, and his family had sent him to Portis House after he'd embarrassed them by weeping at his coming-home party. Other men were here because of anger fits, drunkenness, the inability to get out of bed, and — the worst cases — delusions and even catatonia. The last catatonic patient, however, had been removed some three weeks earlier, it having been decided that Portis House was too remote and far too understaffed to care for such a case.

All of this I learned from Archie Childress, the soldier Nina had taken broth to on my first day. On the second day he was assigned to me. "He can't eat. You'll have to coax him," was all Nina said. "You'll see for yourself."

The infirmary was on the same floor as the men's bedrooms, though down a corridor and near the entrance to the west wing of the house, which was completely closed off. It was large enough to accommodate three beds, a working sink, a cupboard with linens and basins, two wooden chairs, and a small table, which I assumed was for dressings or doctors' instruments. It had a single window, and the patient lay here alone, unattended and looking at nothing. It took me a moment to realize that the room was so large because it had once been the master bedroom.

That first day I entered, carrying a bowl of hot soup and a cup of tea on a tray, I found a man sitting on one of the beds, fully clothed but for shoes, leaning on the headboard with his legs stretched out, his hands folded politely in his lap. The curtains on the window were closed and his face was half lit, though I could see he was too thin for the patient's uniform he wore.

I set the tray on the table and straightened. The quiet fell like a blanket. The man on the bed made no move.

Perhaps I should say something, I thought. No one had told me what ailed this man, so I had no idea what to expect. "I've come with your supper," I said, my voice loud in the silence. He took a deep breath and shifted a little, and in the intimacy of that sound I realized this was the first time I'd been alone — completely alone — with a patient. We even had this section of the house to ourselves; the rest of the men, with the exception of mysterious Patient Sixteen, were downstairs. My throat closed a little.

What was I supposed to do? He didn't look feverish, or bleeding. What was wrong with him that he couldn't eat supper with the others? My back hurt; my hands stung from the disinfectant we'd used to wash the main-floor lavatory. My arms were shaking with exhaustion, but I readied myself anyway, wondering whether I could defend myself. He looked well enough to come off the bed and at me.

He breathed again — it sounded like a sigh this time. He leaned forward and unfolded his hands.

"My name is Nurse Weekes," I said in my nervousness. "I can help you. That is — do you understand?" I bit my lip. "Can you speak?"

He leaned farther forward. His hands now rested on his narrow thighs, on their backs, cupped loosely as if waiting to catch something. The daylight filtering through the window made everything as sharp as a pencil drawing, and I saw that his hands shook, both of them, shuddering against the fabric of his trousers, an uncontrolled tremor that moved with its own rhythmic

71

purpose. He curled forward over them a little, as if they were injured, looking down at them. He had sandy brown hair, a gaunt face, a narrow, well-shaped nose, lips set in a determined line. Stubble lined his jaw and cheeks.

I blew out a breath. The shaking hands must be why he had trouble eating. My mind turned the problem over. "Perhaps we could —"

"I sss—" The sound came from him in a resentful growl, and I stood in silent surprise, watching him wrestle with himself. "I speak," he said finally to his hands. "It's just that I am tongue — that I am tongue-tied when I am around ladies."

Well. No one had ever mistaken me for a lady, but I let it go. "You should eat something."

"No, I'm quite well, thank you. Are you the new nurse? Nurse R— Are you Nurse Ravell's replacement?"

It was a curious stutter he had, in which he sometimes backed up and ran over his words again as if in a motorcar. "Yes, I suppose I am. Was she the one with the freckles?"

"Yes. A curious girl. Very — very quiet." He glanced up at me, something embarrassed in his expression. "Do you know if she's all right?"

"I don't know, I'm afraid. I think she quit suddenly. You really should eat."

"No, thank you. You sound — you sound like a London girl."

"Yes."

"That's nice."

"Look, Mr. Childress —"

"Archie. Call me Archie."

"Archie, then. You really —"

"How long have you worked here?"

Now I realized he was parrying me. "You should eat your supper."

"No, I'm — I'm quite well, thank you."

"But I just think you —"

"Do I *look* like I can eat my supper?"

His face flushed red. He was still but for his shaking hands, glaring at me.

I took a breath. I would not back up. I would not run. "You look like a man who can try."

"Do you think I haven't tried? Do you?" Anger made his stutter disappear. "I have tried. My hands have been shaking for sixteen months. It takes an hour to cut and eat a simple piece of meat. I have to be — I have to be fed like a *child*."

Suddenly I was near tears, wanting to scream. "Very well." I turned for the door. "It's nothing to me. Good night."

"What are you — ?"

"I'm leaving," I said, the words pouring out of me. "For God's sake. I'm tired, my feet are throbbing, my own supper is waiting, I'm bloody starving, and I have hours of work to do before bed. I've no time to coddle you while you feel sorry for yourself."

"Wait."

I paused, blinking hard, my face turned away from him.

"I'll t—" His stutter was back, and I winced. "I'll try. You're — you're right. And I — I am hungry."

I heard the bed creak, and turned to see he had moved to the table and was sitting down before the bowl of soup. He took the spoon in one shaking hand, dipped it in the broth. I stood frozen by the door, watching in helpless fascination. The spoon lifted slowly, so slowly, from the bowl of soup. He levered the spoon up, with painful deliberation, the tremors shaking the liquid from side to side, jettisoning broth over the edges. By the time the spoon reached his mouth, only a tiny amount of liquid was cradled in the bottom; much of this was lost down his chin as he tried to empty the single swallow down his throat. The entire maneuver was executed in perfect silence.

Sixteen months like this, I thought. All I could say was, "Archie."

He dabbed the napkin to his chin with a shaking hand and looked me in the eye, speaking with perfect clarity. "You're not much of a nurse, are you?"

I shook my head. "No. Actually, I'm the worst nurse you've ever seen."

Suddenly we were both laughing. And that's how I made friends with my first patient at Portis House.

"You should be eating your meals downstairs," I said to Archie the next night as we managed his soup. I'd dumped out his tea and transferred the soup into the cup. It wasn't perfect, but it had a better success rate than the spoon.

"Do you think this" — he gestured to the setup, he and I at the little table, trying to get food into him — "would go over well with the others?"

It wouldn't, of course. "I only meant that the infirmary is horrible, and you've nothing to do. You should at least be getting exercise with the other men."

"I'm mas-master of the house here." He gestured around the former master bedroom. "The finest — finest suite. And I have something to do now," he said, taking a

75

shaky sip of soup. "I can gossip about the others with you."

"Is it so bad?" I said.

He shrugged. "Matron — Matron gives me extra time to eat my — meals in the dining room. I do — I do the best I can. The others like to have a go at me, especially Creeton, but I can — I can handle it." He looked at me. "You're wondering why I'm in the infirmary, aren't you?"

"It crossed my mind."

He scratched his forehead slowly, his hand juddering. "A few days ago I had a par— I had a par—" He took a breath. "I had a particularly difficult episode."

That seemed to be all. I frowned at him. "What happened?"

Now he looked distressed. "I had a particularly difficult episode."

"I'm sorry."

He closed his eyes. "Is it Monday?"

"Yes."

"The doctors will — will be here in two days, then. Wednesday is when they come. Matron said I'm to — to stay here until the doctors say I can leave. It's safer here."

What did "safer" mean? I looked at his gaunt arms, his sunken cheeks. "You said you could handle it."

"You don't — you don't like it here, do

you?" he said.

I crossed my arms. "You're parrying me. Again."

He smiled a little.

"Well," I said, "perhaps it's best if you do come down. It's extra work to bring your meals, you know. You and the mysterious Patient Sixteen."

A spark of interest crossed Archie's eyes. "He hasn't come down, then?"

"No."

"I see."

I pictured a man disfigured, his face part gone, or maybe burned away. Ally had seen men like that in London, their noses blasted off or their eyes seared shut, and she'd been quiet when she spoke of them, dragging painfully on her cigarette, her eyes looking old. "I don't even know what he looks like," I ventured, hoping for a warning. "The other nurses take him his meals. I haven't seen him."

"You won't," said Archie, the words slipping out softly as if he spoke to himself. "They won't let you see him."

I looked at him, stunned. "What do you mean, they won't let me?"

He dropped his gaze and stirred his soup, the neck of the spoon chattering gently against the lip of the cup. "Ask them," he said. "You'll see."

CHAPTER SEVEN

"Patient Sixteen," said Boney as we cleared plates from the empty dinner tables, "is a special case. A *confidential* case." She raised her chin. "The fact is, you don't yet have clearance."

"What does that mean?" I protested. I'd thought I had a handle on the politics here, but I could see that I'd been wrong. The idea panicked me a little. "How can I need clearance to give a man his supper?"

The inevitable words came from Boney's mouth: "Matron's orders. Nurses come and go here. Not all of them are trustworthy. The clearance to deal with Patient Sixteen is not given until a nurse has proven herself to Matron."

With what Matron knew about me, the likelihood of her giving me clearance was almost nil. Not that I cared about it, of course. "Listen," I said. "The doctors come on Wednesday. Nina told me that the patients have to attend the group sessions. So it mustn't be so secret then."

"Patient Sixteen is an exception." Boney stared disapprovingly at my confusion. "The doctors see him in private. His door is allowed to be closed, but not locked. He is not to mix with the other patients. He does not attend group sessions, meals, or exercise. Paulus Vries and two other orderlies have clearance, as well as Nurse Beachcombe and Nurse Shouldice, myself and Matron. And no one else."

"Why?" I asked, though I already knew it was futile to try to get Boney to spill anything. "What's wrong with him?"

"That's not for you to know. And only nurses with clearance can assist the doctors at all. You've only been here three days, and you've proven yourself sloppy and insolent. If you think you'll get clearance, you're sadly mistaken."

She said those words — "the doctors" — with such righteous awe it was obvious she had her precious clearance. I thumped a stack of plates on the cart. Of course I was sloppy — I had no idea how to nurse. And as for the insolence, well, this was my attempt to be *nice.* Boney had no idea what thoughts I clamped my jaw on daily.

"Just keep trying," said Boney with a

superior smirk as she pulled the cart into the hall. "It takes time. The last girl wasn't here long enough to get clearance before she left. Improve your attitude and perhaps Matron will consider you. Now — please go see Paulus. He's to give you some work to do."

Paulus Vries wore the orderly's uniform of shirt and trousers of white canvas, and sported a thick mat of pale, springy hair on his forearms past the short sleeves of his shirt. He wiped his large hands on a towel as he spoke to me, regarding me with indifferent eyes. "It's the lav," he said without preamble. "All that knocking in the pipes, and the toilet won't stop gurgling. Do you have the same problem in the nurses'?"

I shook my head. The nurses had their own lavatory on the third floor, near the old nursery where we slept. The patients shared a lavatory on the second floor, on the east side of the house that contained their rooms. The infirmary was the only room with a separate bathroom.

"Well, it's a problem," Paulus told me. "The fellows have been complaining about the noise, and it isn't just in their barmy minds, either. There are sounds, and a smell, too. Probably an animal in the walls chewing the pipes, or something's died in there. It's driving some of them more out of their minds than they already are."

I frowned. We were standing in the downstairs hallway, just outside the kitchen, and orderlies brushed past us back and forth. "That's all very interesting. Why is it to do with me?"

"Because two of my men did a bit of exploring in the drains with a length of rubber hose, and something in there was backed up nasty. Caused a bit of a mess." He tucked the towel into the waistband of his trousers.

I waited for him to go on, but he didn't. "I'm to clean it?" I asked. "Is that what you mean?"

He shrugged. "I'll carry the mop and pail up for you if you like."

"A nurse?" I said. "A nurse is supposed to mop the patients' lav? That's orderly work."

"Not today, it isn't. Matron's orders."

I watched him, feeling sick, as he pulled a heavy metal bucket and thick mop from the closet. *She's testing me,* I thought as I followed him up the east staircase. *Of course she is. She wants to see if I'll quit, like the others.*

The smell hit me before we even approached the lavatory door. It was a dank, horrible miasma, not a smell of bodily fluids, but of something rotting. It seemed

82

to creep from the crack under the closed door like a living thing. My stomach turned.

Paulus seemed not to notice, or perhaps he'd smelled worse. As he approached the door, a voice came from the hall behind us. "Sister!"

Creeton stood in the open doorway to his room, watching us. He put his hands in his pockets and leaned on the doorframe, taking in the bucket and mop and starting to grin. I turned away.

"What a good little nurse you are," Creeton called after me. "Cleaning up like this. We're a bunch of brutes here, I'm afraid. It looks like someone left a nice present in the lav just for you."

"Shut up," I said.

"Sweet scented and something to remember us by." He laughed. "Has any man ever given you a present quite so nice?"

"Leave off," said Paulus. "You're supposed to be downstairs in the common room."

"I forgot something. I'm glad I did now. This is much better than watching Somersham giggle or Mabry mop his bloody nose."

I found I was gripping the mop handle, my hold so tight my knuckles were white. I'd been heckled before, plenty of times, but there was something about being heck-

83

led by Creeton that made my skin crawl.

"You go," Paulus said over my head to Creeton, "or I'll carry you down there myself."

But Creeton's steps left the doorway and came toward us. "I want to watch. Will she be on her knees scrubbing, Vries? I'd like to see that."

"You go," said Paulus again, as I stared at the door and smelled the unspeakable smell, "or I get angry."

There was a long pause, as if Creeton was weighing his chances; then his steps turned away with the same slow, deliberate insolence he'd used on Matron. I brushed a forearm over my eyes.

Paulus was watching me. There was no mockery in his expression, but there was no pity, either. "You have to," he said simply. "It's her way. You either do this now, or you do something else later. Something worse."

I nodded.

He put his hand on the doorknob. "Just don't vomit. If you do, I have to tell her." He opened the door.

It was the largest, most modern bathroom I'd ever seen, and if it didn't have a vile sort of black mold sprayed over it, I'd have thought it beautiful. A claw-foot tub dominated one corner; in the other was a sink, elaborately styled, and a toilet. In an oval mirror mounted on the wall, set in a gold-painted frame, I could see a matching foot-bath on the facing side of the room. Tiles of pristine white set in a diamond pattern covered the floor, and smaller tiles hand-painted with blue flowers decorated the walls. Over it all, above the bathtub, was a high window, opaque with blue-and-white stained glass.

They had put the hose down the drain in the bathtub; most of the mess was concentrated there. Something was spattered on the walls, black and dripping over the pretty hand-painted blue. It seeped from the edge of the bathtub and pooled on the floor, running between the tiles. The stench was rotten. As I stood in the doorway, a black drop disengaged itself from the curled edge of the tub and landed on the floor with a fat *plip.*

I put a hand over my mouth. "How did they manage to do this?"

"A hose has two ends, doesn't it?" said Paulus. "What came up one end came out the other. They tried to put it in a bucket, but you can see it didn't work very well."

"But what *is* it?"

"Buggered if I know. Something dead, most like, as I said. It made a sound coming up — Well, I've put the soap in the bucket. Just do the best you can."

I couldn't even nod.

"I'll be outside the door," he added before he left. "I'm needed in the kitchen, but I can stay a few minutes. In case Creeton comes back."

Then Paulus was gone, and I was alone. I filled the bucket in the sink, turning the pretty china taps. I soaped the mop and began to clean, my eyes watering from the smell. I started on the floor, but the black stuff smeared and wouldn't come off. I scrubbed harder, dousing with more soap and water. It was definitely some kind of disgusting mold, thick and viscous, blackening the grout. Suddenly I was thirteen again, cleaning my father's vomit from the floor of our rancid old flat, my stomach heaving at the sour smell, sweat dripping from my forehead into the mess, trying not to clatter the brush against the bucket, trying not to make any sound as he slept in the next room. *Please, please, don't let him wake up. Please* —

There was a sound in the wall.

I stopped. It came again — a low groan from deep in the building, far off and down below. Somewhere, something clanged against a metal pipe with a hollow sound.

I'd been at Portis House for three days, and I'd never heard anything like it.

I stood frozen, half bent over my mop, cold sweat on my temples, staring at the wall.

It wasn't a precise, mechanical sound; the groan came and went, now closer, now seeming farther away, like breathing. The clangs came irregularly, and then came a low ticking, as of something dripping in rhythm. It sounded for a while — *tick, tap, tick* at perfect intervals — and stopped.

"Paulus?" I said.

My breath came hard in my chest. It was just the house, of course — the walls settling, water coming from somewhere in the roof. It was a big place, and there were bound to be sounds. The groan came again, and I pressed my eyes shut. For some reason, the thought I'd just had came to my mind again. *Please, please, don't let him wake up . . .*

The noise eased off and quiet fell again. I dunked the mop into the bucket and scrubbed with renewed vigor. The sooner I got out of this horrible, solitary bathroom, the better.

As I finished the floor, my arms shaking with strain, there was a single far-off clang. I jumped as if someone had touched me.

Behind me the toilet gurgled and I nearly dropped the mop handle, grasping it again at the last second and leaning on it like an old woman, my heart pounding. The sound from the toilet was thick and sucking. I kept my back to it and imagined turning around to look, seeing black mold in there instead of water. I deliberately walked away and twisted the taps on the bathtub, letting the gush of water drown out the sound.

Leave. Just get out of here.

And tell Matron I couldn't do it? No. I can't. I needed this job. *Needed* it. Matron was looking for a reason to dismiss me. *She's told you to clean the bathroom. So stop jumping at sounds and bloody well clean it.*

It took another half hour with a scrub brush to clean the bathtub, and by the time I finished, I was wet with sweat, tendrils of hair coming from my braids. My sleeves — even though I wore them at the shorter, elbow length, as always — were edged in black at the cuffs, and I had wet smears on the chest and front of my apron. My arms shook with the strain of scrubbing, and I could smell myself, the rotten smell of the mold mixed with the pungent odor of sweat.

But the lav was clean. I dropped the brush in the empty bucket and ran my forearm over my eyes. I suddenly felt like weeping.

Nothing was worth this — nothing. This humiliation, this disgusting work under a woman determined to break me. I'd sold my pride, bartered my soul for a job. But what did it matter? Who cared about the pride and the soul of one stupid girl? I didn't even have enough train fare to leave.

In the wall behind me, the groaning started again, far off and low. I gripped the bucket and raced for the door, away from that horrible sound that seemed to crawl up my spine, to grip my brain. I had to get out, get out. *Don't let him wake up, don't let him wake up, don't let him —*

Paulus Vries was not outside the door. He'd had to go back to the kitchen, leaving me alone in there, if he'd ever stayed at all. I closed the door behind me and set down the bucket, the sweat on my body and neck icy cold. My head throbbed and I looked around the dim corridor, part of me surprised to find I wasn't actually in our old flat, dizzy with exhaustion from a sleepless night. I was only in the east wing of Portis House, in a hallway lined with the men's bedroom doors, quiet now as all the patients were down in the common room, the last of the twilight fading into darkness. I could no longer hear sounds in the walls; but whether they'd stopped, or I could just no longer hear them, I had no idea.

My eyes burned with some unnameable emotion, and my legs felt weak. I was still standing there, trying to gather the strength to take a single step forward, when someone came toward me down the hall. It was a heavy, skirted silhouette — Nina, I already knew from the slouch of the shoulders.

Her doughy face looked alarmed, her eyes frazzled behind her glasses. "Kitty — for God's sake. Where have you been?"

My voice croaked. "Matron's orders."

She glanced down at the bucket and the blackened mop. "Oh. Well, she could have picked a better time, I have to say. West's legs are hurting him, one of the others needs a headache powder, and I've just realized I never collected the supper dishes from Patient Sixteen. If the kitchen tells Matron, she'll kill me."

"It's all right," I heard myself say, as if from far away. "I'm finished now. I'll get the supper dishes for you." When Nina paused, her expression uncertain, I pushed on. "Don't worry. I have clearance. Boney just told me tonight."

"Are you sure?"

"Yes, of course. You go get the headache powder. I'll collect the dishes and bring them down."

"I suppose that works. It's the fourth door to the right." She turned and hurried back the way she had come.

I approached Patient Sixteen's closed door, my bones aching and a shrill, painful sort of excitement in my spine. I walked in without knocking.

The room was dim and quiet. A single lamp burned on a table next to a narrow bed, but the bed was empty. My gaze traveled over the washbasin, the dressing table, and the single chair. These were also empty in the reflected light, tidy and uncluttered but for a set of dishes stacked on the dressing table. I blinked, my eyes becoming accustomed to the dark.

"You should have knocked," said a voice.

Unlike the other men's rooms, this one had a large window, dark now, looking out over the vista of trees and marshes behind Portis House. I could see the low humps of soft hills rolling away into blackness that must be the ocean.

The curtains were tied back from the window, framing a narrow alcove. A man sat there, visible only in silhouette, his knees drawn up, looking out the window at the darkness.

The sound of the voice jolted me from my strange, exhausted reverie. It was familiar in

91

some impossible way, the sound resonating in my brain like an itch. "I came for your dishes," I said.

"Did you?" Again, the familiarity stunned me; I tried to place the voice. He sounded as if he cared not at all. "I left them on the dressing table." He glanced at me only briefly, his face in shadow, before turning back to the window.

I took a step into the room. From the shape of him, he looked like a normal man — all legs and arms present, no fits or shakes. His wrists were draped over his drawn-up knees, his back pressed to the wall of the window seat. I saw an outline of hair, tidy and short. His body was big but lithe, curled with the thoughtless ease of an athlete, his large bare feet on the ledge. I knew I had been picturing some kind of monster — deformed, perhaps, unrecogniz-able, like the ones Ally had described. *Better off dead,* she'd said of them.

But now I knew that made no sense. No patient would require *clearance* for a set of injuries, no matter how awful. *A confidential case,* Boney had said. It was something to do, then, with the man himself.

Someone important. Someone secret. Someone no one was supposed to know was here, in a madhouse. And I knew that voice.

He was still looking out the window; he seemed to have forgotten me, lost in whatever he was contemplating. I walked to the dressing table and looked at the tray. He had arranged the emptied dishes in a tidy stack, centered for easy balance, the cup placed in the middle of the empty bowl. Considerate, then. I couldn't ask him who he was, why he was here. Once Matron found out what I'd done, how I'd lied and broken the rules, I'd never be allowed in this room again. But there was nothing to do but obey, take away the dishes like the servant I was, and leave.

I had raised my hands, nearly touched the edges of the tray, when he spoke again.

"Nice weather we're having, isn't it?"

I looked up. He had turned toward me now, squaring his shoulders in my direction. He slid one elbow over and crooked it on his knee, the better to see me. At this angle the lamplight fell more fully on his face; I saw dark eyes, high cheekbones, and a sharp, shadowed jaw. His eyes on me were kind, and as I watched, he tried a tentative smile on his lips, as if it were costing him a great effort.

I dropped my hands. He must have heard my intake of breath, for his smile slowly faded.

"My God," I said, "it's you."

The smile nearly disappeared, just the last remnants of it touching the corners of his mouth. His eyes narrowed and he looked at me more closely.

I walked toward him, staring at his face. It was all there now, every one of his features burned into my brain, familiar from the dozens of times I'd seen them everywhere — the magazines, the newspapers, the newsreels. His voice familiar from the one unforgettable time I'd heard it. The dark curling hair, the blue eyes under winged brows, the high cheekbones, the elegant jaw now covered in second-day stubble. Though I'd never seen him close up and in person, I could see now that the photographs, the films that made him look so handsome to hundreds of poor, stupid factory girls like me — none of them had lied.

"Oh, God," I said, unable to help myself, "you're Jack Yates."

CHAPTER EIGHT

When I said his name, the expression in the man's eyes dimmed a little, and a shuttered blankness came carefully down. "Do I know you?"

"You can't be here," I said. "Not you."

Jack Yates. *Brave Jack,* the papers called him, the hero of the war. Newsreels flashed in my mind, imprinted on those rare nights I'd gone to the cinema with a few other girls: Jack Yates at a navy dockside, his long coat open and flapping in the wind, his hair blowing, a smile on his face, shaking the hand of Winston Churchill. Jack Yates on the steps of a swank party, posing with Lloyd George's arm around his shoulders, and the caption *Our brave soldiers saluted by none less than the Prime Minister!* Newspaper photos of Jack standing at the Dover shore in uniform, his puttees high on his long legs, his hands clasped behind his back. *Send Me Back to the Front, Brave Jack Says.*

I stepped closer and he slid his feet from the sill and stood, facing me. He was a head taller than I, and something about him took all the air from the room. We'd all adored him, my girlfriends and I, each of us thrilling a little at the pictures of him, at the stories.

He'd been a soldier, an ordinary private — an uneducated boy from Somerset, orphaned and raised by foster parents. *Truly from nowhere,* the papers marveled, because it was impossible to imagine that someone without a title, someone who had to work for a living, could matter. Thousands of men like that died every day, our sweethearts and husbands and brothers and cousins, and none of them mattered a damn.

But not Jack. In the thick of battle, when his CO and all the officers of his dying battalion had been killed, lowly Jack had led the remaining men on a complex sortie across No Man's Land, a half-mile stretch littered with barbed wire and bodies. He'd brought them into enemy lines, holding two trenches alone until reinforcements came. When it was over, the Germans had retreated from that section of the line, and a mile of the Western Front had been reclaimed for the Allies. All because of one man, who had not lost a single soldier in the entire suicidal operation.

The newspapers had loved him. He'd been given the Victoria Cross, had been feted everywhere, was seen in every newsreel. *Brave Jack Asks the Women of England: Are You Doing All You Can?* The girls at the factory wanted to marry him, but when I told that to Ally, she only laughed, saying she'd had enough of soldiers with no money.

I looked into his face now. "You didn't go mad," I said. "You never did. Not *you.*"

He rubbed the back of his neck and was silent for a long moment. "Do I know you?" he asked again.

"Trafalgar Square," I said. "I was there."

The hand dropped. "Ah."

"I froze my arse that night, watching you. Me and my friends."

"Yes, well." He moved to brush past me, and I breathed the scent of him, an unfamiliar tang that went straight to my bloodstream. My own smell must have been much less pleasant, but he made no mention of it. His arm, where it brushed mine, was warm. "I'm sorry about your arse."

"That wasn't a madman," I said, "speaking on the platform that night. We were moved to tears."

It was true. Even I, who hadn't cried perhaps in years, had cried that night in Trafalgar Square, where we'd gone to see Jack Yates speak as the winter of 1917 settled in. It was supposed to be a recruitment speech, a war bond speech, the kind we'd heard countless times in the past three years. *England will endure. England will not be defeated. Your brave soldiers need you.* But Jack's speech had been different. He'd been over there, he'd fought, he was one of us, and he was the only one, in those four long years of propaganda, who spoke to us with honesty. Who had actually meant what he said.

"It was a written speech," he said to me.

"Of course it was. And you wrote it."

Surprise made him pause. "What makes you say that?"

"Do you think," I said, insulted, "that I don't know the difference between a speech written by a government official and a speech written by a real soldier?" Something about the entire situation made me angry: that magnificent man in Trafalgar Square, his breath puffing icy clouds as he spoke, moving us with his words — that man here, reduced to a madhouse, telling me it had been nothing. "Do you think I'm that stupid?"

"I have no idea." He rubbed his eyes, his fingers slowly pressing into the sockets. "I

98

don't even know who you are."

He didn't care. My anger stuck in my throat. "Never mind. I'll take the dishes and go."

I had turned and moved back to the tray when his hand landed on the dressing table next to me. "Wait."

I froze. He was too close, his body too near my own. Heat was coming off him as if he had a fever. His arm was solid, the sleeve of his uniform shirt rolled up past the elbow, his forearm sinewy and strong. I felt my back go rigid, my neck begin to knot. I didn't speak.

"Wait," he said again, as if I'd said something, and for the first time I realized he was speaking slowly, as if dragging words up reluctantly from his brain. "Trafalgar Square. My speech. Let me explain."

I swallowed. *Drunk,* a shrill part of my mind screamed. *Or on a narcotic. He outweighs you by three stone and could overpower you as easy as breathing. He could put those hands around your neck in an instant. Damn him anyway. None of the things you believed in mattered to him at all. Get out. Get out now.*

"There's no need," I managed, my voice stiff and strangled.

His hand touched my bare forearm, and I

jumped. "It's just —"

"Don't touch me."

He didn't let go; I didn't think he'd even heard me. His fingers were long and agile, the nails cut short, the hand an almost perfect study in the dim light, curling to touch the sensitive skin on the inside of my arm. It wasn't a tight grip, but I thought of the last time a man had touched my bare skin and I felt like screaming. The fact that my blood raced under Jack Yates's fingers made it worse.

"You're right," he said, the drag still on his words, just a slight lag that a casual observer might not notice. He was fighting it hard. "I did write the speech. I thought they'd censor me, cut me off somehow, but they didn't. I think they knew what I would say. I believed it." He took a breath, began to quote the speech itself. " 'I'm just a regular soldier . . .' "

"Let me go," I said.

" '. . . but despite this war, in this new world, I am more. I can be more. You can be more. Anyone can be more . . .' "

I turned. I thought I was fast, but — drugged or not — he was damnably faster. He caught my wrist before I had the ghost of a chance to slap his face.

"What is your name?" he said, his dark

eyes looking into mine. His pupils were dilated, but somewhere in there I saw a spark that made me want to look away.

"Kitty Weekes," I said, holding his gaze.

"Kitty Weekes," he said slowly. "I think you're in some sort of trouble."

"Nurse Weekes."

I whirled. Matron stood in the open door behind me, the massive bulk of Paulus Vries at her shoulder. Wedged in on her other side was Boney, her eyes nearly bulging out of her narrow face.

We made quite a tableau, Patient Sixteen and I: I filthy and covered in mold, my hair askew, my uniform damp, my wrist in the grip of a man wearing only a loose shirt and a pair of trousers. I wrenched my hand and he let me go.

"Nurse Weekes," said Matron again. "You do not have the proper clearance to be in this room."

"I —"

"According to Nurse Shouldice, you claimed the proper clearance. An untruth." Matron's eyes blazed with real anger, and I wondered what had so dearly set her off. "Nurse Fellows tells me the procedure has been clearly explained to you, so there can have been no misunderstanding. Have you any explanation for your actions?"

"Of course she does," Jack Yates said from behind me. "I asked her here."

Boney was nearly choking with indignant energy; this was likely the most exciting thing that had happened to her in a month. But Matron narrowed her eyes, her anger cooling under a swift look of uncertainty. "Mr. Yates. The nurses at Portis House are required to follow the rules. You needn't cover for this girl."

I made an outraged sound in my throat.

"I wanted these dishes cleared," he said smoothly, moving up beside me. I did not look at him. "When I opened the door, Nurse Weekes was passing. I asked her to come in and take them." He gave a remarkable impression, under pressure, of a sober man. "I see no reason to discipline her. She was only doing as she was told."

It was patent nonsense; if he'd hailed me as I was passing, why had I told Nina I had clearance beforehand? I expected Matron to call him on it, to put him in his place and foist me out the door. Instead she said, "Mr. Yates, you are kind, but this is not necessary."

This seemed to annoy him. "I asked," he said slowly, "her here."

Matron swallowed, as if actually swallowing his absurd fiction. "Very well. Thank you, Mr. Yates." She turned to me, her gaze unfeeling. "I've told you I expect cleanliness at all times. Please go clean your slovenly appearance and resume your duties."

I felt my jaw clench. "Yes, Matron."

"Go."

I moved for the door, but Jack Yates spoke again. "I have another question."

"Yes, Mr. Yates."

"What did you mean by 'clearance'?"

There was a surprised beat of silence. "Yours is a sensitive case, Mr. Yates," said Matron. "We have a number of nurses and other staff at Portis House, some of whom come and go, not all of whom we know as thoroughly as we would wish."

"So you give them clearance?" he said. "To come here?"

"Yes, of course. It's a requirement for your own protection. Surely you were aware of the situation?"

"No." I gripped the doorjamb as he said the word, staring down at my hand, my heart lurching at the bare confusion in his voice. "No, I wasn't aware."

I could turn. I could look at him once more, reassure him somehow. But I raised my eyes to see Boney goggling at me, Matron's narrow stare on me. I wondered whether Jack Yates was looking at me, too.

"I have no time to deal with you tonight," said Matron to me in a low voice. "There will be an incident report. We will speak tomorrow."

I nodded and brushed past her. I set my shoulders, mustered the best dignity I could in a filthy uniform, and left without looking back.

CHAPTER NINE

To my surprise, when I arrived at the old nursery, I found Martha Beachcombe standing at the washbasin, looking in the dim mirror and pinning her hair. She was already dressed in her skirts and blouse, and her apron was neatly laid on her bed.

"You're awake," I said. "It's early for night shift."

She sighed. "I just couldn't sleep anymore. I'm restless tonight." She gestured at the curtain between our beds, which she had tried closing. "It doesn't help much," she admitted. She turned to me, and her eyes lit with surprise. "My goodness! What happened to you?"

I glanced down at myself. "I had to, ah, clean the men's lav. Matron's orders."

"The lav?" She stared at me agog. "In the east wing?"

"Yes. I had to mop it."

"What was wrong with it?"

"You don't want to know."

She bit her lip, and an uneasy look crossed her face. I felt sure for a second that she'd heard the strange noises in that bathroom, that she'd seen the black mold coming up from the drains, but the expression passed and the moment was gone before I could think how to seize it.

Martha looked down at her apron on the bed. "It isn't so bad," she said. "Matron can be strict, I admit. But she's really a good person. Deep down, she's very good."

"If you say so." Just thinking about the lav, of what I'd heard in there, made me feel exposed, undefended in some raw way, as if everyone could see my secrets on my face. I moved toward my bed while she wasn't looking at me. "I don't much care what kind of person she is. I just want to get cleaned up and out of these clothes."

"Do you need help?"

"No, I'll be fine." I kept my voice steady. I'd learned the trick of getting in and out of my uniform alone. It was a bulky, complicated outfit, but I reluctantly admitted it had its usefulness; I wouldn't have wanted to clean that mold in my thin skirt. I began undressing. "I've met your Patient Sixteen, by the way."

I didn't need to be looking at her to know

her jaw dropped. "You what? I didn't think you had clearance!"

"I don't. I met him anyway." I remembered Matron's tone as she'd spoken to him, the way she'd backed down. "So we have the great Jack Yates here, then. What is his story?"

"Oh, Kitty, I don't know."

"You may as well tell me." I jerked off my filthy blouse and dropped it. "I'm going to find out anyway."

"No, I mean I really don't know. I have clearance, but I'm not privy to the doctors the way Boney is. He came here about six months ago. He was moved here in the middle of the night, and we were told not to bother him. He never leaves his room." She bit her lip. "The only thing I know is — well, it's just hearsay."

"Tell me."

She didn't take much convincing. "I overheard Boney say once — I didn't mean to hear it, really I didn't — that he came here after he tried suicide."

That made me stop. I straightened and stared at her. The room seemed to actually tilt for a long moment. "What did you say?"

"It might not be true," Martha insisted. "I don't know, not really. I don't even know how he — well, how he tried it. But he's labeled as a suicide risk, Kitty. Even more so than the others. We have to search his room regularly, those of us with clearance. Matron is very fussy about how he's treated. I think she worries about him. We've never yet had a successful suicide here."

She caught my gaze for a long moment, then looked away. So there had been unsuccessful suicides, then. I didn't ask. I couldn't. "But Matron doesn't make him leave his room," I said, "and follow the rules like the others."

Martha shook her head, biting her lip again.

"Why not?"

"Kitty, he's *Jack Yates*! You're more worldly than me, I suppose, but even I saw the newsreels."

"That's no reason." I undid my skirt and let it fall to the floor, then started on my underskirt. Jack Yates, trying to kill himself. That man who'd stood before me in his room, so vital and alive. My fingers were numb on the buttons and loops at my waist. "So no one knows who Patient Sixteen is? Not even the other patients?"

"Oh, no. He doesn't talk to the other patients. We aren't allowed to mention him by name. I don't think any of the patients know."

He uses that lav, I thought. *Even Jack Yates has to use the lav at some point.* But I'd get nowhere pushing the issue. I had finished undressing, and wore only my underwear and stockings. I pulled another uniform from the wardrobe where the spares were kept and dropped it on my bed next to the dirty one. Then I put my back to Martha and sat on the edge of the bed.

"He was on some kind of drug," I said. "I could tell by his pupils, and his speech was slurred."

"Kitty, you have so many questions! He can't have been." I could hear Martha's apron slide over her sleeves. "I told you, we search his room. Twice a week at least."

I stared down at my knees for a moment. "Martha."

"Yes?"

"Do you think he's weak?"

"Mr. Yates?" Her voice was surprised. "Whyever? Because he tried to kill himself?"

I leaned down a little, slid my hand under the mattress. My fingers slid along the slats of the bed, seeking that one thing I'd hidden. "Everyone knows that men who try to kill themselves are weak. Aren't they?"

"Oh, no," she replied in earnest. "Certainly not. He's just had a terrible time like the rest of them, that's all. The war made some of the men sick. The unlucky ones. It isn't their fault. They got sick, that's all. And so we nurse them."

Under the mattress, my fingers found the handle of the knife I'd swiped from the kitchen my first night here. It was long and its blade had gleamed silver in the lamplight of that first night as I'd tilted it to and fro. I'd looked at it closely, making sure I saw every detail. Looking at it had made it more real, so that when I hid it under the mattress within easy reach, I could still see it before my eyes as I lay down every night.

I'd taken it because I'd been afraid, because I wanted to be armed. It was that raw, exposed feeling again, as overwhelming as a drug. I couldn't get the sensation of Creeton's hand off my skin, the way he'd looked at me, and I'd known I'd never sleep unless I had some way to protect myself.

From my patients.

I'd nearly screamed at Jack Yates. I'd nearly struck him. I'd come within inches.

He's had a terrible time.

It isn't their fault.

I rubbed my hands across my eyes. Well, Martha was a better person than I was; most people were. Most people were kinder, more trusting, more forgiving than I.

I had my reasons.

I let go of the knife, but my eye caught on something square and dusty pushed up against the wall below the headboard. The corner of it was in plain view. I slid off the bed to my knees and reached for it.

Something metal tinkled, a smaller item tucked between the object and the wall. I pulled it out and looked at both things. One was a book: *Practical Nursing: An Everyday Textbook for Nurses.* The other was a circular locket on a thin chain. I popped it open and saw a photograph of a pretty blond girl, perhaps fifteen, looking soulfully at the camera from under a halo of hair. I latched it shut again. It must have been left here by the last nurse. Perhaps Nurse Ravell with the freckles. Maybe she'd dropped the locket and the book and never thought to look under the bed before she quit.

I had just opened the book and touched the edges of the pages when Nina came into the room behind me. "Kitty, Boney is asking for you. She says you're taking too long up here. Oh — hullo, Martha. Up already?"

"Oh, God," I said. "What does she want me to do now?"

"The common room. There's no one to supervise."

I dropped the book and the locket and kicked them back under the bed, taking up

111

my uniform and putting it on as fast as I could. When I looked up I found Nina looking at me, uncertainty washing the usual sullen expression from her face. "What is it?" I asked.

"The trouble with Matron. Is it very bad?"

"I don't know," I replied. "She said there will be an incident report."

"That's bad. I'm sorry. She asked. I can't lie to her. I need this job."

By lying my way into Jack Yates's room, I could have gotten her sacked. The thought bothered me, something I was far from used to. "It's my fault."

"What got into you? For God's sake, just follow the rules or we'll all be out the door. Though that bathroom was a nasty one — I'll give you that. I've never seen Matron make a girl do that before. When I started, she had me rake leaves out of the back garden. I thought it horrible at the time."

"I suppose I should be honored."

"No. You cleaned it, though, right enough; I checked. What's Matron got in for you?"

"I don't know," I lied.

Martha chimed in, "I don't think Matron does it on purpose."

"No." Nina sighed. "Of course *you* don't. Get your cap on, Kitty, and let's go."

■ ■ ■ ■

The men took daily exercise after breakfast, as long as the weather was fine. As the next day was a textbook example of June in all its beauty, a painting of sunny skies and soft breezes, the men were duly shuffled out behind the house to the grounds. I was sent with them to supervise, in the company of Paulus and one other orderly.

I was starting to understand the intricacies of the staffing at Portis House. Matron hadn't exactly been truthful with me; in fact, she had outright lied. Even with only nineteen patients, Portis House was grievously understaffed. Everyone — nurses and orderlies alike — was stretched to the breaking point. *One week per month on night shift,* Matron had told me, but that would require four nurses on rotation; we had only three. Boney was permanently assigned to "special duties" and never had to work nights, part of the reason Nina despised her.

My inexperience meant I hadn't noticed as quickly as I might have, but I was starting to see. When the last nurse had quit, days had gone by with no nurse on night shift at all. There were only six orderlies, including Paulus, covering twenty-four-hour duty; they did all the heavy work and one of them always had to be on call in case a patient became unruly. They walked around as gray faced as we did. If Matron told me now, as she'd said that first day, that I'd get "two hours of leisure time in the early afternoon," I would probably laugh in her face, for the idea was as likely as taking a trip to Monte Carlo.

And so now there were three of us — and I a woman — supervising eighteen grown madmen on the open, sun-drenched lawns of Portis House. There was no fence or wall around the grounds; only the manicured garden near the house was circled with a low garden wall and a waist-high gate that opened out to the grasses and hills beyond. Even a child could have unlatched this gate, or climbed over it, and so the men were essentially given free rein.

"But aren't they even looking for more staff?" I asked Paulus as we walked through the garden gate and onto the open grounds. Since we had only one gardener, the grasses here were indifferently manicured and they brushed midway up my skirts.

Paulus shaded his eyes and looked about. The men had scattered, some of them walking the hills, others staying close to the house. I had wheeled West in his chair to the terrace and left him there at his own request, unable to spend all of my attention on one man even if he was helpless without me. "They won't get more staff," he said. "Not now."

"Why not?" The men were given no games to play, so they simply wandered, or sat on the ground in the sun. They looked strange, dotting the landscape in their matching uniforms reading PORTIS HOUSE HOSPITAL, against the greenery and the bright blue of the sky. I realized with a chill that no one wanted to give these men a tennis racquet or, worse, a croquet mallet.

"Money, of course," said Paulus in his usual brusque way. "They have to make a profit, don't they? That's what it's all about."

"They could take more patients," I said. "Open the west wing. It isn't being used."

"Then they'd need even more staff, wouldn't they? And in order to use the west wing, they'd have to fix it."

"What do you mean?"

For the first time he glanced down at me, his big face mildly alarmed. "Has no one actually told you? Don't go into the west wing. It's dangerous in there. It's falling down."

"Falling down?"

"I mean it," he said. "I've been in there

and it's a mess. There are parts of the ceiling coming loose. The last thing we need is a nurse breaking her neck in the west wing. Then we'd be really understaffed."

I thought perhaps he was joking, but he kept his face utterly straight and I couldn't tell. "Thank you. For the warning."

"Hodgkins is wandering off again." Paulus trotted off after the short man with no memory, who was as lost as a sheep.

"He's right — he's right, you know," said a voice behind me.

I whirled. "Archie!"

He looked abashed at the greeting, waved a hand briefly at his surroundings. "Matron said — Matron said I could."

"I'm glad." He was so pale he nearly glowed in the sunlight, which showed in painful relief how very thin he was, how his uniform hung off him. He was sitting in the grass, propped on his hands behind him, his feet together and his bony knees poking upward. When he sat like that, leaning on his hands, he didn't shake; he looked like a sick man, but one who might sit in the sunlight and recover.

"The west — the west wing," he said, as I grabbed my skirts and kneeled next to him. "You forget my palatial suite — my palatial suite is closest to it. Paulus is — correct.

116

Don't go there."

"I wasn't planning on it," I said. "I've enough to do, thank you very much."

"It's the — the damp. It's very bad. Much of it — is rotting."

I looked over at the west wing, with its bare, darkened windows. It curved out over the landscape, away from us. "Why there, and not the rest of the house?"

He only shrugged and looked away.

I brushed my palms together and pointed to an especially large set of windows, winking sunlight back at us. "I wonder what those windows are. It must be a large room."

Archie still said nothing. I'd noticed that, as talking was difficult, he often just liked to listen as I kept the conversation going alone. But this was different. His previous good mood seemed to have suddenly fallen away and he seemed almost sullen.

I kept trying. "I'm going to hazard a guess," I said. "I think it's a ballroom. That sounds like something rich people would have. I can't imagine being so rich. Living grand like that." He still said nothing, but he was listening, so I continued. "That room there," I said, pointing to a set of windows at the very end of the west wing of the house, culminating in a door to the outside. "I think that room is —"

"That's the library," said Archie. His voice was curiously flat.

I turned to him, but he was still looking away. He had only tilted his head, looking at me from the corner of his eye. "All right," I said, stepping carefully around this volatile mood. "How do you know? I thought the west wing was closed off."

"Not the li — not the —" He swallowed. "Not the library."

I frowned. "So the patients go in there?"

"No."

What was he getting at? I glanced at the library again, but it sat silent. None of the patients, not even wandering Tom Hodgkins, had gone anywhere near that lonely door. I opened my mouth to speak again, but Archie swiveled toward me now. The sullen mood was gone.

"Sometimes," he said, "when I'm out here, I imagine — I imagine going that way." He lifted a hand and pointed, shaking, in the direction of the woods. "I imagine there's a pub just past those trees. And I go in and — I go in and order bangers and mash and beer." He smiled at the thought, then looked at me and tapped his temple wryly with a trembling finger.

I sat fully on the ground and pulled my knees up, hugging them. "What's over there?" I asked Archie, pointing in a different direction, toward a sloping hill.

"The thea— the theater," he said promptly. "It's a — a comedy. Very — very good." He smiled at me again. "Don't worry. I won't go. There's nowhere to go — nowhere to go, is there? Not really. It's why they don't bother with fences. We could walk away, but we have no — we have no money, and no one will help a man wearing one — wearing one of these shirts. We all know it. You'll find us — find us very well behaved today, by the way. The doctors come tomorrow and we — and we have to be well."

I thought this over and frowned at him. "Be well for the doctors? Archie, I don't understand."

He shook his head once, and for a moment his contented expression fell away again and something very bleak, very sad, replaced it. "That's because — that's because you're not a patient here."

I swallowed. For a long second, which seemed to stretch on forever, he'd left me. It took a moment before his expression turned back to normal, but in that moment I suddenly wondered what had happened to Archie in the war.

"Tell me," I said, when he had come back

to me, "about this part of the country." I gestured around us at the landscape.

He looked at me pleasantly. "What do you know?"

"Nothing." My laugh was quick and held a note of bitterness. "I know the streets of London, and that's all. I know nothing about this place."

And so he told me about how the hills and the trees gave way to marshes in one direction, and in the other direction, where the land sloped upward, were the rocky cliffs going down to the wild sea. How this entire section of land sloped like a piece of pie, with Portis House sliding down it. He told me about what birds nested here, and which ones migrated through. He told me how the wind blew off the frozen sea in winter, turning sleet into ice on the windows and the branches of the trees. How the bridge to the mainland was often flooded over in rainstorms, and they'd had to wait for the water to come down before getting another delivery of supplies.

I listened, fascinated despite myself. And even as he spoke I couldn't help letting my gaze drift upward, to the wall of the house behind us. On the second level was a distinctive window, where our final patient stayed inside, alone in his room. From here I could

see the window seat. There was no one looking out at us, but the curtain moved, and I
knew someone had disturbed it.

CHAPTER TEN

I awoke to the howl of warm, damp wind against the panes of the nursery windows. I scrubbed my face and looked out over the dark marshes under lowering clouds, the lonely clumps of trees bowing, the air as dense as cotton wool with oncoming rain.

"Hurry," said Nina from behind me. "Get dressed or we'll be late for inspection."

She was in some kind of tizzy, and she pulled off her spectacles and polished them vigorously as we hurried for the stairwell. "The doctors come today," she explained to me. "They'll do inspection promptly at eleven. Everything has to be cleaned and ready by then. And I do mean everything."

It was true. We had to wipe windows, wainscoting, the backs of chairs; we had to stack linens with mathematical precision and line up spare pillows in perfect piles. By the time the men had gone to breakfast and I'd polished each bedstead, I was already exhausted, as much by the keyed-up tension in the air as by the work.

The men were almost eerily quiet. They had shaved with their safety razors, buttoned their shirts, tied their shoes, straightened their beltless trousers the best they could. They ate breakfast in silence, then sat at windows or on chairs in the common room, their jaws tight and their eyes drawn. Two men played a halfhearted game of checkers. Others looked blankly at nothing. We cleared the dishes with soft clicks in the dining room, loading the dumbwaiters.

What is it? I wanted to scream. *What is it?* But I kept my questions to myself, watching Nina polish her glasses again, hearing Boney snap at the orderlies, her lips pressed into a line so thin they nearly disappeared.

"It's a good day, isn't it?" This was Tom Hodgkins, the patient who had no recollection of the war — or of much else, for that matter. He was thirty-five-ish and pudgy, with a spreading middle and thick, doughy thighs. He sat in the common room and smiled at me as I wiped an end table yet one more time. "The doctors are so kind."

"Are they?" I asked.

"Oh, yes. We get the best care here at Portis House. Regular checkups. Concern about our well-being. We're positively

123

spoiled."

I looked at him sitting in a stripped-down room far from home, reading a newspaper three weeks old with a square very clearly blacked out from the front page — probably an article about the war — and wondered, as I sometimes did, where he thought he was. "That's nice."

"Some of these men, you know —" He looked about and lowered his voice confidentially. "Some of them seem rather ill. I've heard that injections of a vitaminic compound can be helpful."

"I see."

"I'd ask the doctors about it, if I were you. Nurses should learn these things. One should try to excel at one's profession, even if you are only a woman and a nurse."

I snapped the dust rag rather harder than necessary, shaking out the dirt. "I'll try."

The doctors arrived midway through the morning and were closeted directly with Matron; we had to go back upstairs and tidy up, buttoning on our long sleeves as if we hadn't been working for some four hours already. I was surprised to find Martha, after catching a quick nap, getting dressed and buttoning her sleeves as well. "Inspection," she explained to me. "All the nurses must attend."

124

We lined up in the corridor outside the kitchen, all of us nurses and most of the orderlies; two orderlies had been excused to oversee the patients' exercise. The orderlies had put on fresh canvas whites, and we all stood awkwardly, trying not to cough or shuffle our feet as Matron brought the doctors by.

There was a taller, older doctor and a shorter, younger one; the taller one was called Dr. Thornton and the shorter one was called Dr. Oliver. They wore somber wool suits. Thornton was fortyish and distinguished, with gray at his temples; Oliver was the acolyte, with a tall forehead and sweat dripping discreetly down his neck. They walked slowly down the line as Matron looked on, peering at us. I'd never seen a doctor of mental patients before, and I wondered what they were like. Dr. Thornton smelled of stale menthol and Dr. Oliver smelled of damp starch. My back hurt and I needed to go to the lav.

"The staff seems in order," Dr. Thornton said at last. "Mrs. Hilder, you are pleased with their performance?"

I glanced warily at Matron, but she wasn't looking at me. She had never spoken to me about the incident with Jack Yates, and I was waiting for discipline to fall like a guillotine.

"Yes, Doctor," said Matron.

"Jolly good." He turned to her. "Dr. Oliver and I would like to try something different today. We normally luncheon privately with you, but today we'd like to join the rest of the nurses."

From the corner of my eye I saw Boney jerk with surprise.

"Of course, Doctor," said Matron. "Let us set the table for extra places and we'll be ready."

"Thank you."

We nurses were so run off our feet we almost never took luncheon; we merely grabbed a few bites of food between tasks. But this day we had to set the kitchen table with two extra plates.

"We're here really as observers," said Dr. Thornton as he pulled up his chair. "A suggestion of Mr. Deighton's. You mustn't pay us any mind."

"We're happy to have you, if I may say so, Doctor," said Boney with shining eyes.

"Thank you, Nurse."

We sat, awkwardly rubbing elbows, and served our meal. I tried to take Dr. Thornton's measure, as I always took the measure of men who had the authority to sack me. A

126

tyrant, a bully, a lecher? Did a doctor of minds, instead of bodies, have some kind of all-knowing ability to read thoughts? Perhaps he did, in order to heal patients. All I could see was that he was younger than our oldest patient, Mr. MacInnes — who had been an orderly in a casualty clearing station and had come home from Vimy with shell shock — and that he ate ravenously.

I slowly came out of my woolgathering to discover that they were discussing Patient Sixteen. Dr. Thornton was frowning.

"I don't like this," he said. "Can he not be dissuaded?"

"I don't believe so, Doctor," Matron replied. "I spoke to him this morning, and he was quite insistent that he wanted to join this afternoon's sessions."

"But he's never done so before." Dr. Oliver was amazed. "He's always seen us privately. Why join the group sessions? Why now?"

"I can't say," said Matron. "He told me only he thought he was ready."

"I don't like this," Dr. Thornton said again. "It will disrupt the other patients. And he'll be seen by orderlies and other staff without clearance. This is expressly against Mr. Deighton's orders. The situation with Patient Sixteen is supposed to be contained."

He glared at Matron as he said this, as if this were her doing. I glanced at the other nurses. They were sitting silently, as if taking in a tennis match. Nina, of course, was eating her lunch.

"That isn't all, I'm afraid," Matron said. "He's also asking permission to exercise out of doors."

"With the others?" Dr. Thornton was horrified.

"No," Matron replied. "He says he would like to go running alone at dawn every day. He says he's beginning to feel the lack of activity in his room. He says he thinks the exercise may be beneficial to him."

What are you playing at, Jack Yates? It was the first thought through my mind, and immediately I silenced it. Perhaps the request was a sincere one. Why did I doubt it?

Dr. Thornton's eyes narrowed. "Patients taking excursions alone is expressly discouraged by Mr. Deighton."

"He should be refused," Dr. Oliver agreed. "On both requests."

"I don't believe he means to be disruptive," Matron said. "His isolation, up until now, has been a voluntary one."

Dr. Oliver nodded. "That's true. But if his changing his mind is going to disrupt the others, I wonder if enforced isolation may be of benefit. I believe we're equipped for it. What do you think, Dr. Thornton?"

Enforced isolation? What did that mean? Locking up Jack Yates? I tried to keep my alarm from showing on my face.

"Wait, now. Wait." Dr. Thornton held up a hand. "Dr. Oliver, in the case of any other patient, you would be correct. But this is —" He glanced around the table at us, and suddenly I was certain he had no idea which of us had clearance. "This is Patient Sixteen. His are special circumstances."

Dr. Oliver looked helpless.

"Patient Sixteen's voluntary isolation has worked well for us," Dr. Thornton said. "But enforced isolation may not work as well with his particular neurosis. He is, as we know, a special risk." He paused, thinking. "I do wish Mr. Deighton were here to advise. As he is not, we may have to rethink. Matron, how sane would you say the other patients are?"

She blinked at him slowly. "They are all quite ill, Doctor."

He nodded. "Yes, yes. That may work. Their letters are censored before they leave the building, are they not?"

"Yes, Doctor."

"Quite so. Really, the risk comes if one of

129

these patients was to recover. And even if he did, he would have to tell of what he saw in a believable way. I don't think such a scenario is likely." He nodded again, satisfied that he had solved the puzzle. "Patient Sixteen will be seen with the first group, and only orderlies with clearance can attend. I do think we can manage it."

I glanced around the table again. Was he actually counting on the others being mad enough not to be believed? On none of the patients ever getting well? Had their entire policy been based on the hope that Jack Yates would never be well enough to leave his room, even for a minute?

Everyone had lowered their eyes to their lunch plates, even Matron. But Dr. Oliver saw the look on my face, and his expression sharpened.

"Matron," he said, "you seem to have a new nurse on staff?"

Dr. Thornton looked up from his chop in surprise.

"Yes, Doctor." Matron seemed as wary of this subject as the last. "This is Nurse Weekes."

"How long have you been here, Nurse Weekes?" Dr. Thornton asked me.

It took me a moment to calculate. "This is my fifth day, sir."

"Your fifth day!" He turned to Dr. Oliver, almost peevish now that another problem had come up. "Did you notice this change on the staffing roster?"

"It isn't there, sir," Dr. Oliver replied, mashing some peas onto his fork. "A Nurse Ravell is listed on the staffing roster."

"Nurse Ravell left quite suddenly," Matron said.

"But her replacement has been here for five days!" Dr. Thornton seemed distressed. "The staffing roster must be kept current, Matron. You know it is an important part of your duties."

Matron said nothing, but Boney was going red. She was as easy to read as a book. The staffing roster must obviously have been one of the jobs Matron had assigned her.

"Now all the paperwork is suspect," Dr. Thornton complained. "Matron, please tell me that at least the *patient* roster is up-to-date?"

Matron sat straight in her chair, her shoulders squared, her glasses dangling on her chest, her blunt face unhappy to be receiving a dressing-down in front of her staff. *Tell them to stuff it,* I urged her, but she said only, "It is, Doctor. I do beg pardon. It will not happen again."

131

"See that it doesn't. Nurse Weekes, what are your qualifications?"

I swallowed my food, which was suddenly as dry as sand. "I worked at Belling Wood Hospital, sir."

"Jolly good," he said, taking another helping. "Perhaps you can share with us some of their latest methods."

I wasn't a practiced liar for nothing. "I could, sir, but none of those skills are needed here."

"True, true," said Dr. Oliver.

"Yes," Dr. Thornton agreed. "These men aren't actually sick. This must be very different for you. Still, I would like to know —"

"Nurse Weekes is eminently qualified," Matron broke in. I silently thanked her at the same time I admired her moxie. "Mr. Deighton hired her himself, while I was away for a few days on personal business."

Dr. Thornton's fork actually clicked down on his plate. "Did he!"

"Bravo," said Dr. Oliver.

"You must tell me" — Dr. Thornton leaned forward across the crowded table toward me, his menthol scent wafting in my direction — "what you *think* of Portis House."

Was it a trick question? Was he assessing

my mental state? I hated trick questions. I put on a very serious face. "I wasn't hired to give opinions, sir. I was hired to work."

"Ah, that is very admirable. But you must have some opinion, Nurse Weekes. The food, for instance." He gestured to the table between us. "The diet here has been scientifically designed to maximize the physical health of a fully grown man. What do you think of it?"

I should have been afraid of him, of both of them; everyone else was, even the men. Part of me knew I should be afraid. But when, at sixteen years old, you've been held down on the dirty linoleum by a man twice your size, the blade of a kitchen knife put in your mouth as he tells you to be quiet or he'll cut out your tongue, something inside you shifts. It wasn't courage — far from it. Being afraid like that made you understand, as you moved through the world of men, just how very afraid you should be. But I found in that moment that my fear had an edge to it. It came, perhaps, from a thin slice of anger.

"I don't know anything about it," I told him. "If someone offers me a meal, sir, I just eat it. I'm no fool."

Dr. Oliver laughed, but Dr. Thornton leaned back in his chair, a thoughtful smile on his face. Perhaps I had pleased him. Although I'd been cursing the work of polishing bedsteads an hour earlier, I wished I were doing it now.

"My goodness," said Dr. Oliver, an interminable time later. "Dr. Thornton, I must remind you of the hour. It's time for the afternoon sessions."

"Yes, of course." Thornton dabbed his napkin over his lip. "Matron, please have the men assembled as we discussed. We'll go upstairs and begin."

We all pushed back our chairs and stood. Boney moved to lead the doctors from the room; Matron rose to assemble the men; the rest of us prepared to clear the dishes and go about our afternoon work.

"Nurse Weekes," said Dr. Thornton.

I put down my dishes and turned.

He smiled at me. "I would like you to accompany today's sessions. I believe it will be instructive for an experienced nurse such as yourself. She does have clearance, of course, Matron?"

There was a beat of strained silence.

"Yes," said Matron from the doorway, her sharp eyes staring at me like chips of stone. "Of course."

"Very good," said Dr. Thornton. And he and Dr. Oliver left the kitchen, Matron hurrying behind.

I glanced around at the others. Nina was amazed; Martha shooed me toward the door with one hand. But it was Boney who drew me. She stood aside from the door and stared down at her feet, her gaze furiously fixed, her bright yellow hair garish under its cap. Her lips had lost their prim, important line. Dark red spots flushed high on her cheekbones, as angry as a fever. Hurt crossed her face, but she fought it off. She was so damned easy to read.

Then she blinked hard, and her expression shuttered over again.

I dropped my napkin on the table. It was more important to her than to me; it was everything to her, and it was nothing to me. She had experience and I had none. I didn't even like these men. And yet, when the doctors told me to go, I went. Because when someone offers me a meal, I eat it.

And I tell myself I am no fool.

CHAPTER ELEVEN

So that the doctors could come and go in an afternoon, the patients were seen in small groups. "We really must be away by supper," Dr. Oliver explained to me as we climbed the stairs.

"And what do I do?" I said.

"Be ready," he replied. "Sometimes the patients get upset, and sometimes they need assistance. We don't allow orderlies in the room — what is said is far too confidential. But there should be one posted outside the door. If things go smoothly, you simply sit. And observe."

His tone told me I was lucky to have the opportunity. I said nothing.

We used the common room, where the chairs had been set in a rough circle. I was directed to an extra chair off to the side by the wall, where I would not intrude on the conversation. I sat, crossed my ankles under my chair, and smoothed my long skirts over my legs.

Jack Yates arrived with the first group.

There was silence as the men filed in: Archie, Creeton, Captain Mabry, and Mr. MacInnes. Jack had shaved, combed his hair, and put on shoes. He looked at me as he entered, his dark-lashed blue eyes registering quiet surprise, and then he turned to the others and sat in the chair with his back to me.

Dr. Thornton cleared his throat. "Ah. We do have someone new with us today. I hope no one will find this too disruptive."

The men shuffled their feet and glanced at one another. They said nothing.

"This is, ah, Mr. Yates," Thornton tried again.

They knew. All of them. I looked at their faces and understood that the doctor wasn't telling them anything they hadn't already known, probably from the first. It was Archie, after all, who had warned me about the clearance to see Patient Sixteen. I'd been right; there was no hope of privacy in the close conditions these men lived in, not after being here six months. The happy little fiction that no one knew Jack Yates was here was just that: a fiction.

But the men said nothing, and Dr. Thornton and Dr. Oliver continued to look pained at this supposed breach in the rules.

The tension stretched unbearably. Creeton opened his mouth, a smirk on his face; then his gaze traveled over the other faces and he closed his mouth again. Finally Mr. MacInnes nodded. "How d'ye do," he said.

"Yes, hello," said Archie.

Thornton looked relieved. "Let's begin." He pulled a leather-bound notebook and pen from his briefcase, crossed his legs, and prepared to write. "Dr. Oliver, which patient is first?"

Oliver consulted his own list. "Mabry, sir."

"Mabry." Dr. Thornton made an obvious note of the name. "Please proceed, Mr. Mabry."

Captain Mabry — Matron and the doctors called him "Mister," but the rest of us couldn't help but call him "Captain," he was so obviously a captain — swallowed and nervously pushed his spectacles up on his nose. "I've been doing much better," he said.

"Is that so?" Dr. Thornton regarded him. "I seem to recall, Mr. Mabry, that you were having hallucinations, though we had seen improvement in recent weeks."

"Yes, sir."

"I see. And what are you requesting?"

"I would like to see my children." Mabry

138

sat stiff and brittle, as if a single tap would shatter him.

"I'm sorry?" said Dr. Thornton. "Would you repeat that, please?"

"My children," said the captain, a little louder. "I would like to see them — please, sir."

"Your children." Dr. Thornton wrote in his notebook. "Yes, you've made this request before." He turned in his chair. "Dr. Oliver?"

As Dr. Oliver riffled through his papers for something, I watched Captain Mabry's face, so plainly stamped with contained emotion, and I understood what Archie had told me the day before. *We have to be well for the doctors.*

Dr. Oliver handed Dr. Thornton a piece of paper, and Dr. Thornton looked it over. "I have here," he said, "an incident report written by Matron. It states that you had one of your delusional attacks only a few days ago."

That day at supper, Mabry lying in my lap with a nosebleed. The room was painfully quiet.

"Sir," said Mabry.

"Well? Was it an attack? Or is Matron lying?"

"I had a nosebleed, sir. That was all."

139

"A nosebleed."

Captain Mabry's gaze flicked to me for the merest second; then it flicked in front of me, to Jack Yates. Jack leaned forward in his chair, his elbows on his knees, looking down at the floor as if tuning out the scene around him. He raised his head, looked at Mabry long enough to catch his eye for a second, and dropped his gaze again.

"I have a request here," said Dr. Thornton, "from your wife, Mr. Mabry. She has applied to visit you, along with your children. If you are still having attacks, you must understand that for the safety and well-being of your family, as well as of yourself, I would not be able to allow this visit. Do you understand?"

Mabry did, with agonized clarity. "Yes, sir."

"Do you still maintain you had a nose-bleed and not a delusional attack?"

I was shocked. Thornton had no superior powers, no higher insight. This wasn't medical treatment; it bore no *resemblance* to medical treatment. It was bartering, pure and simple. I wanted to scream.

"Yes, sir," said Mabry.

"Nurse Weekes." Thornton turned in his chair and suddenly all eyes were on me. "The incident report lists you as witness.

140

What is your assessment?"

My face grew numb, and for a second my voice wouldn't work. "I'm not familiar with Captain Mabry's attacks, sir."

Thornton closed his eyes briefly, as if greatly tired. "First of all, he is not a captain here. We have no ranks at Portis House."

Except for you, I thought. But I said, "Yes, sir."

"Please explain, in your capacity as a medical professional, what Mr. Mabry experienced."

"Cap— Mr. Mabry experienced a nosebleed, sir."

"It seemed to spontaneously bleed?"

"Yes."

"And when it spontaneously bled, did Mr. Mabry ask you for assistance?"

"No."

"And why was that?"

I could feel something closing in on me, like the drawstrings of a bag tightening over my head. "He wasn't speaking."

"He chose not to speak? Or he could not speak?"

I said nothing.

"Answer the question, Nurse Weekes."

I looked around the room. Mabry was staring straight ahead, at nothing; the others gazed down at their laps. Even Creeton

141

was subdued. They all had their own requests to make, their own cases to plead. Jack Yates still leaned forward on his elbows, his body somehow coiled and tense in his casual pose. He was, I thought, the only man who could have helped — if he had been in the dining room to witness it, and not shut in his room.

I'd be dismissed if I lied, and everyone knew it. I choked out the words. "He couldn't speak."

Thornton's gaze drilled into me. "Because he was lying on the floor barely conscious — is that correct? Precision is the most important part of diagnosis, Nurse Weekes. Please be precise."

I gritted my teeth. I could not look at Mabry again. "He was lying on the floor, unable to speak."

Thornton turned back around in his chair and wrote in his notebook. "This request is denied, Mr. Mabry. And next time, don't try to lie to me."

It was hard to understand, the feeling that settled downward on my shoulders and my chest, the feeling that I could be sick if only I had the ambition to move. I'd done as I'd been asked; I'd told the truth. I'd avoided getting sacked, my only goal in this job. I risked a glance at Captain Mabry, who had not moved, had not spoken, and yet his entire demeanor had sunk into despair. Thornton had taught me a lesson, intentional or not: *You are not their friend. You are not ever their friend. Not ever.*

It had to be public, of course. We'd had a supervisor in the wool factory who always chastised girls in public, in the middle of the work floor. He'd fired girls in front of us, sending them out the door in tears as we watched. It was the same with these sessions; nothing — no humiliation or lesson — could be private. I'd never cared about being fired from the wool factory — which, of course, I was. But I cared about keeping my job at Portis House. I cared.

"We'll move on to you, Mr. Creeton," said Dr. Thornton now.

Creeton shrugged. "There's nothing to say about me, gov."

"Your parents have filed an application to visit you."

For a second, sheer surprise crossed Creeton's face; then he lit up with a gleeful smile. "Wouldn't you know!" He turned to Captain Mabry. "Sorry about that, old chap. Looks like you can't see your family, but I can see mine."

"Leave him be," said Mr. MacInnes. He was whip thin, with graying hair and a close-trimmed mottled beard. "Just leave him be."

Creeton turned on him. "You changed bedpans in the war, you drunken old sot. They won't let you see your family, either."

"I did change bedpans," MacInnes shot back as if grateful the tension had finally broken, "and I wiped the bums of men better than you."

Archie laughed; Creeton turned on him next. "Shut it, you idiot. I shouldn't even be in here with the likes of you."

"Gentlemen," said Dr. Oliver.

"Tell them," said Archie. "Tell them about — about the nightmares and see if they say you're not crazy. Do it — do it."

"You think I won't beat you stupid just because you were in the infirmary?" Creeton's beefy hands curled over the arms of his cheap wooden chair. "Do you?" I started wondering whether Paulus Vries was outside the door as promised.

No one moved.

"Creeton," said Jack Yates into the silence. "Enough."

Jack's elbows were still on his thighs. He raised his head, his hands still dangling between his knees, and the pose immediately went from casual to that of a man ready to spring. He and Creeton exchanged a long look I could not read.

"I don't have nightmares," said Creeton at last.

"We all have nightmares," said Jack. "It doesn't matter."

The other men exchanged alarmed looks. "Not me," said MacInnes.

"No," said Archie. "No."

Jack looked at all of them and sighed.

Dr. Thornton finally broke in. "Right, then, Mr. Yates. Do we have the session under control now?"

Jack leaned back in his chair, crossed his arms over his chest. "Go ahead."

"Thank you," said Thornton, his voice cool. He turned back to the room. "Gentlemen. Let's continue, shall we?"

CHAPTER TWELVE

By five o'clock the day felt endless, as if it had begun far back in a tunnel I could no longer see the entrance to. My head throbbed and a sinister pulse of pain had started behind my eyes, growing with bloody force with each successive heartbeat. I blinked my sandpaper eyes and tried to keep focus.

We had finished all the groups; every patient at Portis House had been evaluated, or at least checked off a list. Dr. Thornton spoke the name of the man; the man mumbled something about how he was feeling much better; Dr. Thornton told him what request had been made by family, if any, and publicly told him whether it was granted or denied.

Jack Yates simply said he had not been sleeping. No one had requested to see him.

Thornton had made notes in his small book all afternoon, his pen scratching busily, but Dr. Oliver had had to remind him of the names of each of the men. I'd sat quietly in my corner as instructed, rousing myself only when voices were raised.

There had been a single nightmarish moment when Somersham had spoken about his dead sister — he became hysterical and had to be sedated. Thornton had turned to me with a simple barked command: "The syringes in my case, Nurse Weekes." I'd grabbed the small black bag and unlatched it with damp fingers, but when I hesitated, Dr. Oliver reached in, removed a syringe, and quickly injected the patient as I stared in panicked nausea. It had taken me half an hour afterward, sitting in a corner with my hands pressed into my skirts, to stop shaking.

It was a long afternoon of misery. Patients were a means to an end, part of my job — not my friends, as Dr. Thornton had demonstrated. Lunatics. And yet as I heard a man plead to see his mother or his sweetheart, or burn with shame as he admitted to uncontrolled vomiting or the inability to sleep with a simple blanket touching his arms, I felt the stirrings of a burning, angry dissatisfaction. I started trying to understand.

I'd spent the war in London, going from

shared flat to factory shifts or shopgirl work. The war had loomed large and encompassing, yet in the background. It was the topic among the girls at the lunch counter or the pubs, sweethearts shipping out, sweethearts home on leave. It was felt in the rationing, in the black-blazoned headlines that shouted at me from newspapers left in discarded trash bins or on park benches in early dawn on my way to work — stark, angry words like Mons and Passchendaele and Ypres, incalculable numbers of dead, ships sunk, blurry photographs of battles.

My brother, Sydney, had enlisted in the first weeks of war and had never sent home a single postcard. The first few months after he'd gone were the worst of my life; then I'd left home myself, and the war had sunk into a miserable background din, and I was certain he was dead. I had enough problems of my own to worry about what happened in France anymore.

Or so I had told myself.

But these men had been there. They had experienced something so otherworldly, so catastrophically horrible, that I would never know what they saw when they closed their eyes at night. Or what they heard when a plate banged on a table. They'd washed off the mud and the blood and been sent home, unlike Syd, and it had been so bad they couldn't cope with it. They'd ended up here. Something sounded in me, deep down like a bell being struck in the depths of the ocean, something that saddened and frightened me and made me exhausted in the same way one is exhausted after vigorously, repeatedly vomiting up one's supper.

Mabry hadn't seen his children because of me. *You are not their friend.*

"I hope that was instructive," Dr. Thornton said to me as the last few men filed from the room. "Have you any questions, Nurse?"

"No, Doctor."

"Come now," Dr. Oliver chimed in. "There must be something?"

I turned to them. "It just seems . . . it just seems that it isn't actually treatment the men get. Medical treatment, I mean. They're just . . . motivated to behave." *Like in a prison.*

Dr. Thornton nodded. "You've come from casualty cases, so the confusion is understandable. Mental cases are very different, Nurse Weekes, especially cases of shell shock. Did you think we could give them a bandage, perhaps, or a pill, and cure them?"

"These men," said Dr. Oliver, "need to *learn.*"

I looked from one man to the other.

"What about Jack Yates? Does he need to learn?"

"Ah," Thornton said. "That went better than expected, did it not? Perhaps I should explain. Patient Sixteen came to us with instructions from the highest level of government — the highest, I repeat — that his stay here was to remain confidential. I don't think anyone will trust a madman's account, but it's good to be certain. You've been given great trust today. I hope you can keep it."

"But why?" I asked. "Why the secrecy?"

Thornton leaned in so he could not possibly be overheard by anyone except Dr. Oliver. "Mr. Yates was a great hero to this country. To know that he has fallen to this . . ." He gestured around the room. "To know that he has fallen to such a low level would, I think, be detrimental to morale."

My head throbbed with pain. "But the war is over."

"Our great country is involved in many operations the world over," he replied, "and will continue to be. The will of the people behind government is important. If it were to be known that Jack Yates had become a coward . . ."

I choked, any anger I'd ever felt at Jack evaporating. "Jack Yates is not a coward."

Dr. Oliver patted my hand. "You're a loyal lady, and we admire you for it. But you must understand that there is nothing lower for a man than this, than to come here. To be one of . . . these."

"Nothing lower," Dr. Thornton agreed.

I followed them to the corridor, the two of them conferring quietly together. I waited for them to finish their conversation, for them to dismiss me at last. There was a single crack in the wall, hairline thin, making its way down from the ceiling. Outside, the sun struggled to break through a thick cotton layer of cloud. I had the sudden desire to walk out the door and keep walking, walking, breathing the warm, damp air.

Why had none of the men admitted to having nightmares?

"Doctors." Matron approached us, only slightly reddened from her climb up the stairs from the lower reaches of the house. "You are finished, I see."

"Yes," Dr. Oliver replied. "We are ready for the weekly debriefing."

"Certainly." She looked at me in a signal of clear dismissal, for which I could have kissed her feet. "Thank you, Nurse Weekes."

"Actually," Dr. Thornton said, "I'd like Nurse Weekes to accompany us to the debriefing. I believe it could be beneficial to her training."

Matron was already flushed, so I couldn't tell whether her color deepened. "That won't be possible."

"I do believe I have Mr. Deighton's authority, Matron, in matters of protocol."

"You do, of course. What I meant is that Nurse Weekes can't be spared just now. She goes on night shift as of tonight and is scheduled to take some rest before her shift begins."

That stunned me out of my exhausted reverie, but before I could open my mouth, Matron had turned her gimlet stare on me. "Come with me, Nurse Weekes."

We stood at the foot of the servants' stairs before she spoke again. "I'll send Nurse Beachcombe to you when I can. She'll tell you what's required on night shift. You're to report at eleven, after the others have gone off duty."

"This is it, isn't it?" I said, childish in my outrage. "This is my punishment. The incident report wasn't good enough for you. Why don't you just sack me and have done with it? Or is it because you're so understaffed?"

Matron sighed. "Please go now and prepare for night shift."

"What was it?" I said to her. "What made

152

you hate me so? Was it the fact that I was requested by the doctors without your *clearance*? Or was it that I actually cleaned that disgusting lav?"

She looked at me for a long moment. I knew nothing of Matron; I didn't know where she came from, or whether she had a family or friends, or even what her first name was. I realized as I looked into her hard, square face with its blunt fringe of hair that this opaqueness was utterly deliberate on her part. If she had her way, I would learn no more about her than I could learn from the statue of Mary on the front lawn. For a second she seemed about to say something; then she changed her mind, her eyes glittering as she looked at me.

"You have a great deal to learn, Nurse Weekes," she said.

I turned to stomp up the stairs, but she gripped my arm. "Dr. Thornton left his notebook in the common room. Please fetch it; then, for God's sake, go."

I fetched the notebook, the fine leather smooth and heavy in my hand. I was in such a storm of emotion that I had nearly left the empty common room again before I realized what I was holding.

I remembered Dr. Thornton scribbling diligently all afternoon, his pen scratching. I felt queasy, not with unease at what I was about to do, but with a horrible, creeping suspicion. I opened the notebook.

There was a page of names, the names of our patients. Beside each was a thick black check mark.

And the rest of the pages — four in all — were covered in inky doodles, of clumsy giraffes and splotchy elephants, a dog sitting on his hind legs begging, a cat with long whiskers. A hillside dotted with trees and houses.

I snapped the book shut, and I did not notice that my hands were shaking.

There was no point in undressing, as I'd only have a few hours to sleep, so I dropped onto my narrow bed in the nursery, untying my boots and letting them fall to the floor. I lay on top of the thin quilt fully clothed and rubbed my eyes.

Exhaustion took my body, but my mind was alive with all I'd seen. Something in me was shifting, changing. I felt as if I'd been touched with an electric wire. I'd never sleep. I rolled over and reached down, finding the book and the locket under the bed.

I pulled both of them onto the bed next to me and propped myself up on an elbow, opening the book. *Practical Nursing: An*

Everyday Textbook for Nurses. I ran my finger down the table of contents.

Nina had told me there would be no time to read at Portis House, and she'd been right. I owned no books myself, but I had perused the shelf of books in the common room — *Ethan Frome, The Thirty-Nine Steps* — and silently selected the ones I wanted. Books were a means to an end, even novels; for the more a person knew, the less she could be taken in.

Treatment of infectious disease. Bandaging practices. The lancing of boils. On disinfection. Correct suturing. I'd been caught unawares earlier when Dr. Thornton had expected me to inject a patient and I'd hesitated. I'd been lucky neither man had noticed. I turned to the chapter titled "Intravenous injections" and began to read.

Footsteps approached from the hall and I flipped the book shut, shoving it under my pillow just as Martha came to the door. "Matron sent me," she said. "Do you want the curtains shut?"

"No," I said. "I won't sleep."

"It doesn't help much anyway," she agreed. "Matron says I'm to bring you supper if you like."

I'd been sent away before supper. Matron wanted to get rid of me that badly. I had no wish to put yet more work on Martha, who had handled night shift already. "I'm not hungry."

Martha sat on the edge of the bed and groaned as the weight came off her feet. "I'm sorry about night shift, but I can't say I'm sorry for my own sake. I'm so tired. I'll appreciate a good sleep tonight — that's for certain."

I was still lying on my side, propped on an elbow, and from my position I could see the thin bones of her shoulder blades through the back of her blouse. How someone as small and thin as Martha accomplished the monumental workload at Portis House was rather surprising. "What do I do on night shift, then?" I asked.

"Oh, yes." Martha rubbed her ankles, not willing to go quite so far as to remove her shoes. "Well, there's a desk next to the stairwell door in the men's hallway — you've likely seen it."

"Yes. In the nook built into the wall."

"That's the one. That's the night nurse's desk. You sit there, though you make rounds once per hour, checking on the men. Their doors should be open, or at least ajar, except for Patient Sixteen. Those are the rules. You go as quietly as you can and you check to see they're sleeping."

"It sounds dull."

Martha rubbed her eyes. "Perhaps. It's easy, unless any of the men has a bad night. Then it gets more exciting than you'd like."

I thought of the sessions I'd listened to earlier that day. "They have nightmares?"

"If it happens, you get the orderly — I think Roger is on duty tonight. Though you likely won't have to fetch him, because he'll hear and come on his own. You shouldn't approach the patient without an orderly, because when they're in that state, they tend to thrash. You probably know all of this from London."

"Just tell me."

"Well, all right. Most of them calm down nicely once they're awake. If a man wakes and he doesn't calm down, there are hypodermics in the nurse's desk, locked in the drawer, for emergencies."

I lay back, feeling the hard edge of the book under my pillow. I'd have to study before I went on duty tonight, and pray that things were calm. "And what do I do the rest of the time? When the men aren't having nightmares?"

"You count linens," said Martha. "The inventory lists are in the top drawer of the nurse's desk, as well as a pen and ink. Both the upstairs and the downstairs closets.

Make sure to count the linens on each man's bed, or the count will be off."

I stared at her. "We count the linens every night?"

Martha yawned. "Yes, and the inventory goes to Matron in the morning. She always checks, so you can't cut corners. Write a nightly report and leave it in the desk drawer; Boney takes it to her every day. Oh, goodness — I have to get up or I'll fall asleep where I'm sitting." She moved to rise, but when she put her hand down on the mattress, she stopped. "What's this?" She picked up the locket and peered at it.

"I found it," I said, trying not to sound defensive. "It was under the bed. It isn't mine."

"This was Maisey's." Martha turned it over in her hands. "She must have left it."

"Is that Nurse Ravell? The one who was here before me?"

Martha nodded. "Her initials are engraved on the back, just here."

I looked closely as she showed me. "Martha, don't you think it strange that she left her boots and her locket behind?"

Martha frowned, uneasy. "Perhaps. She was an odd girl."

"What did she say when she left?"

Now Martha looked away. "Nothing. She

didn't speak to us, that is. We didn't see her when she left."

"What does that mean?"

"She went on night shift one night, and in the morning she was gone."

I could do nothing but stare.

Martha glanced at me, caught the look on my face. "I'm sure there was nothing strange about it. She kept to herself, that's all. Perhaps she'd just had enough."

"Martha, for God's sake. She left in the middle of the night?"

"Not necessarily." She bit her lip. "She could have gone at dawn."

Something uneasy turned in my stomach. Portis House was far from anything, deliberately so. How would a girl get out of here alone, in the dark or in the first reaches of light? Had she walked all the way across the bridge? What made her want to leave so badly that she would walk out during a shift, leaving her boots, her locket, and her book behind?

After Martha had gone, I pulled the book from under my pillow again. A page at the front featured a drawing of Florence Nightingale treating the wounded in the Boer War, etched in ink. She was a female silhouette in long sleeves and Victorian skirts carrying a lantern across a battlefield, its light shining from the folds of her cloak. On the ground before her a wounded man reached up, begging for help, his gaze on her benevolent face. *The Lady with the Lantern,* the caption read. And beneath it: *The angel of the battlefield, which every nurse should aspire to be.*

I looked at Florence for a long time. She was as perfect, as impassive, as the statue of Mary outside, but there was something about the way she stood, the confident sway of her cloak, that I found myself liking. They drew her as pretty, but I imagined her as tough as old leather. I scoffed at myself and turned back to the chapter on hypodermics.

The first time I read the chapter, I stumbled over words I didn't know, so I read it again. I stared at the diagrams, memorizing them, and then I read the chapter yet again, sentence by sentence. I'd never had much education, but education, in my experience, was no match for doggedness. If I wanted to learn something, I was capable of studying it in a book until I understood it, no matter how long it took. In the end it was a matter of winning over the words that refused to obey, of comprehending them through sheer determination.

No one had ever accused me of a lack of determination.

I hadn't thought I'd sleep, but as the faint sun vanished into darkness, as I heard the creaks and groans of the house around me, and somewhere below me the men sat to supper, my eyes drifted closed. I put the book under my pillow again, the image of Dr. Oliver's soft hands behind my eyelids, replaying the way those hands had handled the hypodermic, pushed the needle under the skin. The words from the pages pricking my brain like pins, I drifted to sleep.

Night shift was coming, after all, and I had to be ready for the dreams.

■ ■ ■ ■

PART TWO:
NIGHT SHIFT

■ ■ ■ ■

We don't want to lose you but we think you
    ought to go,
For your King and your country both need
    you so.
We shall want you and miss you,
But with all our might and main,
We shall cheer you, thank you, kiss
you, When you come back again.
— "Your King and Country Want You," 1914

CHAPTER THIRTEEN

Nina woke me at ten o'clock, and as I was still dressed I had only to wash my face, tidy my braids, and don my boots. As the other girls went to bed, I descended the darkened spiral servants' stairs to the lower floors.

My first stop was the kitchen. The few hours I'd slept had strangely refreshed me, and I was ravenous. The entire house was dark; I had to feel my way down the corridor on the servants' level, but I found the kitchen lit with two paraffin lamps, one perched on a high counter and the other in the center of the wooden worktable in the middle of the room, around which sat four figures in the postures of people just recently off their feet.

"Hullo," I said, recognizing Paulus Vries's large frame and the wide pot-bellied figure of the head cook, who I thought was called Nathan. "Is there any food?"

Nathan moved his toothpick from one corner of his mouth to the other and regarded me flatly. "You night shift?"

"Yes."

"Might be something for you. Bammy, check the stew pot."

The smallest figure rose from the table, and I saw it was a kitchen boy, no older than sixteen. He wore a greasy cap of fabric tied behind his head like Nathan's and a set of stained and well-worn cook's whites. He lumbered to the darkened stovetop without a word. None of the other figures moved; they sat with their hands resting on their thighs or on the tabletop, their fingers curled, their shoulders a little slouched. It was the timeless pose of a person first sitting down after an endlessly long shift on his feet, wanting nothing but to sit and not think and not be ordered somewhere for a few blessed minutes, and I recognized it well.

I pulled up a chair for myself. Bammy thumped a bowl of stew and a slice of bread down before me, even remembering a spoon. I thanked him and he responded only by dropping into his chair again, sprawling as if he'd just done an expedition to Kilimanjaro.

"So you're on night shift." Paulus's accent

166

sounded exotic in the humdrum English kitchen. "Did you sleep?"

"A little," I said between bites. "Did you?"

"I'm finished," he replied. "I'm off now. You have Roger tonight." He nodded to the fourth. figure at the table, a second orderly much smaller than himself. Roger was tidy, with brown hair slicked neatly back from his forehead. He looked at me with a flinty stare and nodded.

"All right," I said. "Why are the lights out? Why the lamps?"

"Electricity goes off at night," said Paulus. "We're not on the main lines all the way out here — far from it. The electricity runs off generators, and we turn 'em off at night."

I stopped tearing my piece of bread. "There's no electricity all night?"

"No." This was still Paulus. "We kept the generators on at first, but they kept malfunctioning at night — something kept getting into 'em, though we don't know what. We don't have the manpower or the supplies to repair them every day, so we decided to turn them off at night. No need to light this whole place anyway."

"Well, that's wonderful," I said, "except for the part in which no one can see."

"We've lamps. We light 'em along the men's corridors — most of them don't like the dark. Roger gets one and so do you, to carry."

The Lady with the Lantern, I thought wryly. I had almost been in a good mood — something to do with the rest I'd had, and the fact that the doctors were gone. I was unsupervised for the first time since I'd arrived, and it felt a little like being a child left home when its parents are away. But at the thought of walking Portis House in the dark, my good mood drained away.

Nathan was still watching me. His expression looked like a cross between disinterest and reluctant amusement. "Your first night shift, I see."

I tried to take another bite of stew. "Yes."

"This house scare you?"

I wanted to sound bold, but thought of the black mold in the lav, the sounds in the walls, and said nothing.

"I hope you're not the susceptible type," Nathan said. "Those don't last long in this place. Especially after night shift. It isn't just the nightmares. Most of the men say that something walks the halls, especially at night."

"Nathan," said Paulus in a warning voice.

"Oh, shut it. You know it's true. Every nurse goes running. We didn't even see the last one's tail." He turned back to me.

168

"Some say it's the ghosts that make the patients try to top themselves."

"What?" I managed.

"A few have tried it," Nathan said. "That spot outside the library, you know. That seems to be the spot they go to. The last one had stolen a blade."

There was a long silence. I thought of that lonely door I'd seen while I sat on the lawn with Archie, how none of the men had gone near it. Bammy the kitchen boy looked at his shoes.

"They're just madmen," Roger put in. He was perhaps over fifty years old, something I hadn't noticed when I'd first seen his dark hair. "I've done night shift plenty of times here. I never see anything walk but the sleepwalkers. These patients sleep tidy if you make 'em. We'll have a quiet night tonight."

"You say that," said Nathan, "but even you won't go near that library."

"That's a bald lie," said Roger.

"Why the library?" I broke in. I wouldn't think about suicides. I wouldn't. "Why isn't it closed with the rest of the west wing?"

"It's the isolation room," Roger said. "They took the books out, of course. It's big, and it's secure. Keeps the patients in solitary confinement far away from the others."

"Works like a top," said Nathan. "Not a single man of 'em wants to go to the isolation room. Not for love or money. And not overnight."

Dear God. "Is anyone in there now?"

"No. It's empty." Nathan put his toothpick back between his lips. "Except for the ghosts."

"There are no ghosts," said Roger.

"So you say. The men know. It's getting worse, too. Did you hear the last one screaming? Said he could see something from the window."

"He screamed because he was mad. They're all mad here, or didn't you notice?" Roger shrugged. "It's nothing to me. If they act up, day or night, they know me. They know me very well."

"All right." This was Paulus, who sat in his chair tilted with its front legs off the ground, rocking back and forth on his huge long legs. "Well-done, lads. You've tried your best to frighten the new night nurse. That's enough."

"She didn't need any scaring." Nathan grinned at me.

"Go on to bed," said Paulus. "Bammy, you're dead on your feet. You're back on shift at six. Roger, just do your job tonight and don't tell tales. Got it?"

Paulus tilted the front of his chair back to the floor and rose. I could get no proper read on him; he'd defended me more than once, yet seemed indifferent to my existence. It didn't matter. He was large, and I wished he were on night shift instead of beady-eyed Roger.

I took the lamp Roger handed me and followed him down the corridor and back up the south stairs, thinking about the old library used as an isolation room. I could see now why Archie hadn't wanted to talk about it. I wondered why a man would try that spot in the grass, in front of the library door, to try suicide. Why more than one man would try it there.

Roger walked me to the nurse's desk. "I'll be around about," he said. "I have duties to attend to. You may not see me, but I rarely go out of hearing distance. If one of the men gives trouble, just yell."

He was small and slight, not much larger than me, but when I looked closer, I saw he was wiry, with nothing but gristle under his canvas shirt, and his knuckles were pitted and scarred. Another drifter from God only knew what walk of life who had found his way here. "All right."

He smiled briefly at me with his narrow mouth, a smile that didn't reach his eyes.

"If one of them has his dreams, don't go near him alone. But they'll be no trouble, I warrant. They know me." He flexed his hands a little so the scarred muscles moved. "They know me very well."

After he'd gone, I sat briefly at the desk, which was set in a nook in the wall and was long and thin as a toothpick. I slid open the first rickety drawer, pulling out the linens list and staring at its crabbed, inked columns. Already the words and numbers blurred. I put the list down again and pulled on the other drawers. One was empty, and the other was locked. Martha had given me a ring of keys and I pulled them from the loop at my waist, perusing them. The linen closets, Martha had explained, and the medical supply closets, and the food and tea stores. One small key fit the desk drawer, which opened to reveal a set of hypodermic needles.

They gleamed dully at me in the lamplight: four of them, set in wooden holders, detached from their syringes, the needles impossibly long. They were of wicked metal, lined up with precision, carefully waiting. Set in the compartment next to the needle heads were glass syringes, their silver plungers fully compressed, and four vials of brown liquid, unlabeled. I remembered the chapter I'd read before sleeping. A nurse would attach the needle head, draw the liquid into the syringe, and inject the patient. I shut the drawer and locked it again.

Portis House consisted of a large central section with a smaller wing tilting off on either side — the west wing, which was closed off, and the east wing, which housed all the staff rooms except the nurses'. The fenced garden was set between the curves of the two smaller wings, as if enclosed in a pair of hands. It was the central wing, easily triple the size of either of the smaller ones, that contained the men's bedrooms, with the nurses' old nursery on the floor above, the common and dining rooms on the floor below, and the kitchen and laundry in the basement.

I walked the long corridor of the main section softly in the quiet. Mullioned windows lined one wall, looking out over the front portico and the statue of Mary. The other wall had doorways to the men's bedrooms, and turns to secondary corridors lined with even more doors. I had been in this place a dozen times, but never in the dark and silence of night shift, and never alone. Pale light from the silver quarter moon gave only the faintest shimmer to the windows, the light giving up even before it hit the sills. From paraffin lamps in holders along the walls between the windows rose curls of pungent smoke.

Each man's door was, as per the rules, unlocked and open. Most had pushed their door almost closed, trying for as much privacy as possible. Perhaps, with a new night nurse on duty, they were testing how strict I'd be. I didn't much care. I wasn't of a mind to pick arguments over whether I could see into their rooms or not.

I approached the first door and read its wooden placard:

Thomas C. Hodgkins

D.O.B. 7 January 1890

Admitted 21 December 1918

Tom, the man with no memory of the war. He'd been in this place six months. I pushed the door open and looked in, noting the tidy room with its faint smell of used socks, and the heaped and snoring figure on the bed. I pulled the door to again and moved on.

It went like this, room by room. Each man was asleep, or at least pretending to be so. I moved as quietly as I could. I had just begun to hope my first "round" might be a success when from the room I was approaching came a moan and a thundering crash.

Oh, God, I thought. *A nightmare already.* I pushed into the room to find Somersham, who'd been sedated during the afternoon session, on his knees on the floor, his bedclothes tangled around him. It looked as if he'd been trying to get up for some desperate reason.

"Somersham," I whispered, but he didn't hear me. I raised my lamp and saw the glassy, sick look on his face and knew he was not having a nightmare. I swung around, looking in the dark for a basin. There was none, but I grabbed the pitcher on the washstand and, putting down the lamp, barely got it under his chin before he started vomiting.

He did so for a long time, though he had been asleep through supper and there was nothing in his stomach. The sound of it went on, torturous, until I was wincing. It paused only long enough for him to briefly take a breath, look up at me, and say, "I think it's stopping," before he was bent over helplessly again.

"Somersham," I said to him in a low voice when he stopped again. "What in the world is the matter? Is there anything I can do?"

He straightened. His hair was on end, his face slick with oily sweat. He was only twenty-one or so, and the stubble on his cheeks was sparse. His eyes rolled back, the lids closing. He threw up — or his body made the motions — one more time, and then he slouched back against the bed frame, his legs still tangled in his blankets, his fingers dropping the jug into my waiting hands.

He closed his eyes again. I stared at him, crouched and ready, imagining every kind of incurable fever. "Somersham? Are you ill?"

He moaned a little, raised one hand in a weak effort, and let it fall. I leaned forward, took his shoulders gently. "Let's get you back into bed."

It took some doing, as even though he was young and small, he still weighed much more than I did. He tried to help, but his eyes kept rolling back in his head in that alarming way, the lids fluttering open and closed. I touched his forehead, the only thing I knew how to do. It was the sedative, I figured, wearing off and tearing him apart as it did so.

My hands were cold as I pulled the bed-clothes up from the floor and tried to tuck them around him. Was this what sedatives did? Was this normal? I knew nothing — nothing. Was there something I should be doing? What if he died on me? For the first time, alone on a dark floor with a semiconscious patient, I was struck by what I had done, what monstrous thing I was pretending. He could die in an instant and I could only look on, helpless.

What had been in that injection?

He seemed to settle, the drug sucking him back into sleep again. "He's coming," he said to me with the voice of exhaustion, unable even to open his eyes. "He's coming. I can hear him."

"Somersham?"

His eyelids fluttered, the eyes beneath them moving. One chilled hand brushed my arm like a leaf falling in autumn. "Help me," he whispered, so low I almost thought I'd imagined it. "I'm so afraid."

My mouth had gone dry. *He's mad, that's all,* I thought, and yet almost without willing it I leaned forward, closer to his face as it slowly went still. "What?" I whispered back to him. "What is it?"

Nothing.

I leaned back again. Silence descended around me, broken only by the rasp of Somersham's breathing. The lamp I'd set down cast a yellow circle of light on the floor.

I took the fouled water jug and the lamp and stepped into the hall. The commotion hadn't roused anyone, or if it had, they lay in their beds trying not to listen. Roger, for all his talk of being in earshot, was nowhere to be seen. The moonlight hadn't moved in the windows. I turned and walked, alone, toward the lav, my footsteps sounding softly on the floor.

In the lav, I turned the tap on the sink. It was still clean in here, and smelled of disinfectant, yet I nearly fumbled as I rinsed the jug as fast as I could.

This house scare you?

"Shut up," I said aloud to no one. "Shut up." I scrubbed harder, the jug slippery in my hands.

He's coming. I can hear him.

Clang. A single sound, low in the walls. Then the groan again, faint at first, and a second time closer. As if something had just realized I was here.

He's coming. Help me. I'm so afraid.

"Shut up," I said again, twisting the taps. In the dark the bathroom was an echoing chamber, the floor radiating cold, the moon-light colored blue in the high window. I stood in my bubble of lamplight, trying not to smell the stench of vomit, the hair on the

178

back of my neck alight, trying not to think, trying not to remember —

"He isn't coming," I heard myself say. "I left. He isn't." I didn't think who I was talking to, who I meant. That it wasn't who Somersham might have meant. "He isn't."

The groan came again, and I hurriedly closed the taps, nearly dropping the clean and dripping jug in my haste. I picked up the lamp again. *Run, Kitty.* But no. He'd always hated it when I ran. It had always made it worse. I walked slowly instead, setting down each foot with silent care, holding my breath to bursting. *He must not hear,* I thought wildly.

I let out a harsh gasp of breath when I reached the corridor. I backed against the wall, put down the jug and the light by my feet, and raised my horrified hands to my face. I was nearly sobbing. Nothing made any sense; my thoughts were a jumble, disconnected, insane. *You are falling apart, Kitty.* This wasn't me. I was the girl in control, the one who always had her eye two steps beyond everyone else, the one with schemes and plans. I was the girl who could get through anything, think on her feet, lie, endure whatever life tried to throw at her. I was not the girl who was reduced to a sobbing wreck, incoherent with terror over a vision from her past, from her imagination.

This house scare you?

My feet moved away and I left the jug and the lamp on the floor. In the lamplight of the corridor I counted the doors. I knew which door I was heading for.

It was shut. Special rules. But it was not locked. I turned the handle and opened it wide enough for me to slip through the opening and stand in the dark, my eyes trying to adjust, listening for breathing, for any sound.

All was silent for a long, black moment. Long enough for me to consider retreating from the room as quietly as I had come. He was probably asleep, oblivious to the sounds outside, oblivious to me.

"Nurse Weekes."

That voice. So soft now, in the depths of night. Intimate. Coming from the direction of the window, where I'd found him before. Not sleeping, then.

"Patient Sixteen," I replied.

I couldn't see him against the darkened glass. Still, I fancied I heard a breath, heard his body shift just a little. "Have you come to check on me, then?"

"You're not asleep."

A low laugh that tapped down my spine

like fingertips. "No. I'm not. How is Somersham?"

"Asleep." I wondered how many men suffered insomnia, sitting or lying in their
rooms night after night. I could do nothing
for them. I could do nothing for any of
them, not even for myself.

I tried to say something else. Something
important that burned my throat and at the
backs of my eyes. But nothing came, and I
could only stand helpless with hot tears
moving down my face, grateful that he
couldn't see me in the dark.

He moved again, came off the windowsill
— I could tell as clearly as if I could see
him, so attuned to him was I — and came
closer. I heard his bare feet on the floor.
"Nurse Weekes," he said gently, as if sens-
ing my tears. "Are you all right?"

I took a breath, and to my horror it
hitched on a sob, half of which I desperately
tried to swallow. "My name is Kitty," I said,
my voice cracking. "I'm not a nurse. I'm
not anything. I don't know what I'm doing.
And I don't — I don't think I can do this."

A long pause followed. I supposed it
wasn't often nurses came into his room at
night, teary eyed and confessional. "Sit
down," he offered at last.

"I can't." Another stupid utterance that

made no sense. I leaned back against the wall and sank to the floor in a slow glide. I took another sobbing, hitching breath and pulled my knees to my chest, thinking I'd die of humiliation.

"Wait," he said, and he padded from the room, returning with my lamp. He set it on the bedside table and sat down on the floor himself, close enough to the lamp to be illuminated in its globe of light. He didn't look bleary now, his pupils not dilated. Dark stubble had started on his chin, but he didn't even look puffy with sleep or exhaustion; he fixed me with a gaze of intelligence and concern. It didn't escape my notice that he'd placed the lamp in just such a way that I could see him but he could not see me. The consideration of it only made me cry harder.

"Tell me," he said simply.

I did. I told him about overhearing my flatmate, about taking the pamphlet from the trash, forging the letter from Belling Wood, getting on the train sight unseen. I told him how Matron had seen through my ruse and hired me anyway, of how it had been only blind luck I'd known what to do with Captain Mabry's nosebleed, how the doctors had chosen me for the afternoon session and I hadn't known how to inject

Somersham with a sedative, and how I'd been helpless when Somersham had woken up tonight. I told him how I'd found a book under my bed but had no time to read it properly in time and wouldn't know how to save a life. The hot rush of words, once started, had to run its course before at long last I wound down into silence.

He seemed to think for a moment. I waited for judgment, but it didn't come. "I didn't guess," he said finally. "From what I've seen, we all think you're competent and reliable."

I rubbed my drying cheeks. "I'm neither."

"Then you fit in well here." He gave a wry smile. "Thornton was fooled."

I shook my head. "What were you doing, asking to come to the sessions today? Asking to go running alone? You put everyone in a tizzy."

"Did I? That wasn't my intent. I just . . ." He rubbed his jaw, searching for words. "I've barely left my room for six months. It suddenly bothered me. I don't know why."

"Well," I said, glad to change the subject, "there was a great debate over what to do, since no one is supposed to know you're here. Thornton eventually decided the other patients wouldn't be believed if they ever went to the newspapers with it. That is, assuming any of them ever get well."

"Bloody hell," said Jack softly. "I don't want to affect anyone's recommendations for release. I'll put the word out that the men are to be quiet about it."

I stared at him. "They all already know you're here, don't they? Every one of them."

"Kitty, try living in these close quarters for six months and see if you have any privacy," he said. "Most of them have seen me at some point or another, and Mabry and I have talked more than once. If Thornton had ever spent a day in here, he would never have believed he could make such a stupid rule. I had no idea he'd tried."

"But Matron lives here. She should know." I thought back, went over everything again in my mind. Now that I recalled it, Matron had not seemed particularly panicked about the other patients seeing Jack. She had been more concerned about the nurses and the orderlies, since they were the ones who could leave Portis House and tell tales. "She may have pointed out the flaws and been overruled. Thornton doesn't value her opinion much," I said. "Even if Matron thought a rule was nonsense, she would keep her thoughts to herself and follow it anyway. She'd lose her job otherwise. Keeping quiet and following the rules seems to

184

be the policy here."

"And you have trouble following rules."

"I can follow rules," I countered, stung. "I cleaned the lav, didn't I? That wasn't a picnic, either."

Jack frowned. "Wait. They made you clean the lav?"

I smoothed my palms over my braids. "It's clean, isn't it? Who do you think mopped up all of that horrible black mold? Why do you think I looked such a wreck when I met you?"

Even in the gloom I could see his gaze sharpen, the skin around his eyes tighten, as he became alarmed. "I didn't notice what you looked like. And I assumed an orderly. Are you saying Matron had you do it alone?"

"She does it to all the girls." Since I had stopped weeping, my head felt heavy and light at the same time. My eyes burned. "It's a sort of test. But I'm getting the worst tests she can think of, because of what she knows about me."

"For God's sake. Alone." He rubbed his hands over his eyes, agitated. "Kitty — this is going to sound strange, but I'll say it anyway. You should get out of here. You have to go. Find another job."

I barked a laugh. "Right."

"Go to Newcastle on Tyne," he said. "Or farther, if you can afford the ticket. Apply wherever you can. Find something."

I stared at him. "Are you serious?"

"Kitty, it's dangerous here. You shouldn't stay. Frankly, you should run."

"Run? Because of a bathroom?"

"It isn't just a bathroom. It's this *place*. Don't you feel it?"

We stared at each other for a long moment. My head spun. *He is insane,* I thought. *This place . . .* But perhaps he was just trying to get rid of me. Perhaps he wanted me gone.

The thought drew me up like a splash of cold water. I'd thought I couldn't do this, but the idea of turning around and leaving, of Jack asking me to leave, panicked me. "I can't leave this place," I said.

"You can," said Jack.

"No," I said. "And I don't mean that I won't. I mean that I can't." He frowned, and I stumbled on. "Weren't you listening when I told of how I got here? How I lied? I'm desperate. I don't have enough money for a ticket to Newcastle on Tyne or anywhere else. I own three blouses, two skirts, a pair of shoes, three pairs of cotton stockings, one hat, one pair of gloves, one wool coat, and four pairs of underwear. My last

186

employer sacked me owing three weeks' pay. I spent my last coins on my ticket here and the hired car, and I had to steal a stale bun from a baker's stall because I couldn't afford to eat at the same time. I've been running for four years, and I can't go any farther."

"My God, Kitty," he said. "Running from what?"

I shook my head. "That's my own business. If I leave here, I am on the streets. Perhaps a man will pay me a few shillings for a quick one. Is that what you'd rather I do?"

"I never said that," he said, angry now. He leaned forward and reached into the dark, his hand finding my wrist. I watched his bare arm flex in the lamplight, the tendons on the inside of his forearm tense, my mouth gone dry and my pulse beating in the base of my throat. "Bloody hell, Kitty."

His grip was strong, his skin hot on mine. The feel of it put me in a state near panic, and everything else burned away. "Why are you here?" I said desperately. "You're Jack Yates. Who sent you here?"

"No one," he said, not letting me go. "I checked myself in."

"No. I don't believe it. You're not —"

"Yes, I am." The shadows from the lamp

played over the beautiful planes of his face, and I thought of what Martha had said, of how he'd tried to kill himself. "I'm as mad as the rest of them, Kitty. Never doubt it. For the last part of my life, I've wanted nothing more than to die. I don't sleep. I don't speak. I have nightmares . . . things I barely even remember, and I wake up wanting more than ever to be dead. I see visions, ghosts at night. I hear footsteps. Does that sound mad to you?"

"You're not mad," I said again.

His eyes left me, flickered to something over my shoulder through the door, and their expression changed so entirely I nearly gasped.

"He's coming," he said.

And from somewhere down the hall, the screaming began.

CHAPTER FOURTEEN

It was Archie. He was half off his bed by the time I got to him, his head and body twisted back, arched as tight as an archer's bow. His hands were up, the fingers flexing, grasping air. From his throat came a jagged scream unlike anything I'd ever heard from a grown man.

"Archie!" I reached past his hands and grasped his shoulders, tried to shake him. "Archie!" Too late, I remembered I wasn't supposed to approach a man in the grip of a nightmare alone — but by then he was thrashing beneath me and his wrist clouted the side of my head. I switched my grip to his arms and tried to pin him down. "Archie!"

Footsteps came behind me; it was Roger, at last. "I'll take him," he said, but I was already tangled with Archie, his bony arms entwined with mine. Archie's eyes opened and he looked past me unseeing, staring at something that wasn't there. His arms spasmed again and I dodged them. Then he shut his eyes tight and pressed his face to the pillow; his hands flew up to his ears as if he heard something intolerable; he drew his knees up in a posture of defense. "I won't go!" he screamed. "I won't go!"

A wiry hand, scarred and unspeakably strong, gripped my arm. "Move." Archie had huddled down as if trying to burrow, his hands still clapped over his ears. I stepped back and Roger stepped in.

My knees were weak. I watched Roger shake the writhing Archie and tried to gather my jumbled thoughts. Water? The hypodermics? Surely the other men must have woken. Where had Jack gone?

I stumbled out into the dim hallway. There was no sound, no movement from any of the doorways. Surely this could not be commonplace, those screams a usual occurrence. Jack's door was shut; I had no time to think of it as I swung my gaze the other way and saw a shirtless man pass the nurse's desk and disappear into the stairwell.

Jack? I couldn't tell. Why had he removed his shirt? Or was it another patient, choosing just this moment to try an escape? What if he was sleepwalking? Behind me, Archie screamed again, his voice going hoarse.

You are losing control of the situation, Nurse Weekes. I dashed back into the room and grabbed my lamp, which I'd taken with me from Jack's room. Leaving Roger to wrestle with Archie, I hurried down the hall as quickly as I could. If it was a sleepwalker, he could hurt himself or get into trouble. And if he woke from his nightmare in another part of the house . . .

I swung past the nurse's desk and plunged into the stairwell, pausing at the top landing. "Hey!" I whispered loudly into the dark, hoping that whoever it was had woken up. "Who are you? Where are you?"

There was no answer, so I held the lamp before me and lit my way carefully down the first steps of the spiral, the wood creaking beneath my feet. I went slowly, feeling my way, peering into the darkness ahead of me in case he'd stopped in his tracks, not wanting to crash into the back of a sleeping man. "Wake up!" I hissed into the darkness. "Wake up!"

Still no answer. I descended one round of the spiral, then another, the faint light of the men's corridor receding behind me. I was plunged completely into the blackness; the stairwell was usually lit by daylight coming from its high windows, now blank and starless. I had only the globe of my paraffin

191

lamp to light my way from step to step.

Where could he have gone? One floor down, the door led to a corridor behind the dining and common rooms, but it was heavy and fastened with an old iron latch; if the sleepwalker had pushed it open, I would have heard it. That meant he either was still on the stairs or had descended past the main floor, continuing down to the lower floor where the kitchens and the servants' rooms were.

Still, I came to the first door and took a moment to run my hands over it. The latch was fastened, the door unmoved, the metal of the latch icy cold. I pulled my fingertips away and rubbed them together to warm them. "Come back!" I tried whispering into the dark again. "Come back!"

Perhaps I shouldn't try to wake him. Wasn't that the wrong thing to do with a sleepwalker? I didn't know. If I found him, I'd try to get him back to his room, and —

There was a faint sound at the bottom of the stairwell, as of a shuffle of feet. *Sssh.* So he was at the bottom door, then. I did not hear that door open, either. He seemed to be just standing there, still.

I lifted my lamp and plunged downward again, trying to peer ahead, my hand sliding along the banister, my legs disappearing into the gloom. And suddenly I noticed the cold: icy, thickening cold, climbing my ankles and legs as I descended, as if I were walking down a set of steps into icy water. The skin on my legs and thighs rose in goose bumps even under my layers of skirts, and my feet in their boots ached with numbness.

I slowed, bit my lip. There was still no sound from below.

I took another step — the cold rising almost to my waist now — and stopped. I leaned over the banister and swung my lamp in the dark, trying in vain to see something, anything, and failing. The only thing I saw in the dim glow of light was my own breath, puffing in the cold air as if I were outdoors on a winter's night instead of indoors on a stairwell in June.

I stood still for a long moment, the lamp raised, watching as one breath and then another plumed out into the dark air. There was only the sound of my breathing echoing in the stairwell now, the inhales a high whistle, the exhales gasping with fear. There was silence from the bottom of the stairs, a waiting silence, of something patiently watching me come closer, something with all the time in the world.

Every instinct told me to turn and run; and yet, if I did so, I would turn my back on it to climb the stairs again. And if it followed me . . .

I pushed myself backward and up one step, my boot scuffling on the stair, my hand sliding on the banister and pulling with the slick grip of my palm. My breath rasped. And from below I heard it move in response, heard a footstep and the soft creak of the sole of a foot on the bottom step.

"Nurse Weekes!" Roger's voice boomed down the stairwell. I glanced up to see him silhouetted in the upper doorway, a place that seemed miles away. "Come quick! Mabry's nose is bleeding again."

In a second, purely by instinct, I launched myself up the stairwell toward him, pounding up the spiral as quickly as I could. He gave me a queer look as I reached him, breathless and undoubtedly ghastly. "What were you doing down there?"

I shook my head, unable to form words for an answer, and brushed past him. No sound had followed me up the stairs; the cold was gone. I headed down the hall on legs that wobbled, Roger's footsteps the only ones behind me.

"It's nothing," said Captain Mabry. "I'm quite all right."

He stood at his washstand wearing the

flannel top and trousers that were standard-issue pajamas at Portis House. It was an ensemble that, truthfully, did not look much different from the outfits issued to wear during the day. I thought of the shirtless man I'd seen and gripped the back of the room's only chair to keep myself upright.

"I can get you something," I managed. Archie had quieted and I had sent Roger to make sure every patient was accounted for, so we were alone. "Aspirin. Disinfectant."

"It won't be necessary." He was wiping his nose with a flannel, catching the last trickle of blood. This nosebleed was tidier than the last one, as he'd made it to the washstand as soon as it started. Now he glanced at me in the mirror, his tone neutral and not exactly welcoming. "You should sit down."

I did. There was silence for a long moment. I couldn't blame him for his demeanor, considering what had happened with the doctors. I took a breath and tried to focus. "I'm sorry," I said. "I truly am. About earlier. I'm sorry."

He paused in surprise, the flannel holding steady in midair, but he did not look at me again. Instead he rinsed the flannel in the basin of water, the only sound the gentle splash. Even from where I sat, I could see the dark blood swirling as he rinsed. "It's all right," he said at last. "You would have been sacked."

"For what it's worth, I think you should be able to see your children."

His eyes still on the bloody water, he shrugged, the small gesture tight with pain. "They're right. I'm not fit."

"That's rubbish," I said. "You have a few nosebleeds, that's all. Your children would survive it."

"Is that all you think it is?" He dabbed his nose again, then rinsed the flannel, swirling it for longer than necessary. "After the war," he said slowly, never raising his eyes to me, "I wasn't myself. I began drinking. It got . . . very bad." He pulled the flannel from the water, wrung it out slowly. "Antonia — that's my wife — was frightened. She told her father she didn't want me around the children anymore. And her father told me that I would come here and recover, or he would move them all back to the family home and I would never see any of them again."

I sat very still.

"So," he continued, "I came here. I thought I'd dry out — you know, a few days of the shakes, stiff upper lip, carry on and that sort of thing — and go home and take up my life. And then . . ." He looked up at the blank wall where a mirror would be, though no man was given a mirror in his room at Portis House. He stared at the wall as if he could see himself. As impersonal as a doctor, he pulled downward on the skin of one exhausted, bloodshot eye, and then the other. "The first time it happened," he said, "I pissed myself. And they told my father-in-law. They told him."

That bell sounded inside me again, somewhere deep down. Oh, I understood that kind of fear. I understood it well.

Mr. Mabry, said Matron's voice in my mind, *has a particular psychoneurosis.* And then, Martha: *He gets afraid. He thinks he sees something.*

He's coming.

I leaned forward in my chair, unable to keep quiet any longer. "What is it?" I asked him, unable to keep the pleading from my voice. "What *is* it? What do you see?"

"You'd like me to tell you, wouldn't you?" His gaze cut to me. "You'd like to know what we all see. And when the doctors make you tell them, I'll never see my family again."

"No," I said. "No."

"That's how it works," he said. "That's how it is for all of us."

197

I was silent.

"I'm quite all right, Nurse," Mabry said after a moment. He looked away. "I'd like to get some rest, if you don't mind."

"He all right?" Roger asked when I came out into the corridor. He leaned against the wall, his arms crossed over his chest.

"Yes," I managed. "He just wants rest, that's all."

Roger's eyes watched me keenly in the gloom. "All patients present and accounted for," he said. "Tucked into their beds like children on Christmas Eve."

"All right." I had known it, of course — known that whatever I had followed down the stairs had not been a man. "And Mr. Childress?"

"Sleeping like a little baby."

There was something nasty in his tone. I wanted to get away from him, the sooner the better. "Very well. I suppose —"

"What should I do with Patient Sixteen?"

A low bell of alarm sounded in my gut. "Beg pardon?"

"He probably wants out by now, but I think we should leave him in. At least for a while."

"What are you talking about?"

Roger's eyes gleamed as if he'd been waiting for me to ask. "I locked him in."

"You what?" I launched myself down the hall, fumbling for my keys. "You can't do that. What's the matter with you?"

"He wanted to come out when the shaky one started screaming," said Roger, following me. "He was getting agitated. I needed him to stay put."

How long ago had that been? Half an hour? I reached the door and knocked on it. "Jack? Mr. Yates?" I clumsily tried my keys, one after the other, in the lock. There was no answer.

"You don't have the key. I do."

I looked up at Roger. He was half smiling. He'd heard me use Jack's first name. My heart was in my throat, my head pounding. I was nearly sick with panic. Half an hour. It was long enough. He'd tried to kill himself once before. *For the last part of my life, I've wanted nothing more than to die.*

"Give me your keys," I said.

"He wouldn't stay in his room. It teaches them a lesson."

"Give me your keys."

He sighed and handed them over as if put upon. I called Jack's name again and pushed each key into the lock, my fingers sweating, until one of them turned.

The door swung open into darkness. I

took a gasping swallow of panic. If anything had happened, if he was dead, it would be my fault alone. I'd seen the door shut half an hour ago. *Stupid, stupid. If he's dead, you've killed him.*

"Jack?" I whispered into the dark.

A long moment of silence, and then something moved. I swallowed another breath.

"Jack," I said again.

He got up from the window seat and walked toward me. He propped a forearm on the doorjamb and leaned on it, looking down at me. "Hullo," he said.

I looked into his face, taking it in for a long moment. "Are you all right?"

"I'm fine. And you?"

Something was wrong. I reached up and tilted his face farther into the light from the corridor, studying him more closely. My hand was icy with the aftereffects of terror, but he didn't complain. His skin was rough with stubble. I stared into his eyes and found the pupils dilated.

"What did you take?" I asked him.

"Nurse Weekes," he drawled, and I realized how close our faces were. He smiled and tweaked the edge of my pinned cap.

I squeezed my fingers harder along his flawless jawline, pulling him back to attention. I could have shaken him. "You took this before. What was it?"

"The doctors gave it to me."

"Liquid?" I said. "Shots? Pills?"

The large pupils focused on me again. "Pills."

"How many?"

"Two." He blinked slowly. "Three."

Three pills had done this to him? And how many had the doctors given him? A bottle? If he swallowed the whole thing, no unlocked door, no rule about belts or braces, would save him. "Give me the bottle," I said.

He leaned a little farther forward, his gaze soft on me. "You're damned beautiful."

Something jarred inside me like a shard of glass. No one had ever called me beautiful before. Oh, I knew I wasn't ugly, but "pretty" was always the word applied to girls like me. As in, *Come over here, pretty girl,* or *Do you like a drink, pretty girl,* or *Are you going home, pretty girl?* I squeezed my legs as my knees went weak. He was drugged; that was all. Too drugged to notice the shock on my face as the word "beautiful" rolled from Jack Yates's tongue. I kept my voice careful. "Give me the bottle," I said, and let him go.

Obedient as a child, he went back to his room, fetched the bottle of pills, and gave it to me. I turned away from him and saw Roger still standing behind me, watching.

His eyes followed my hand as I dropped the bottle into the pocket of my apron.

"Everything is under control here," I said to him. "Go back to your duties. I'm going to count linens."

He left, giving me what he must have thought was a knowing look. I stood in the hall for a moment, gathering my strength. I walked away without looking back to see whether Jack Yates was watching me, but when I'd sat down at the nurse's desk, the list of linens in front of me, the gaping doorway to the darkened stairwell behind me, I pulled the bottle from my pocket and looked at it.

A full bottle of pills. A locked door. A man who had attempted suicide before.

It was as if, I thought, someone thought Jack Yates better off dead.

CHAPTER FIFTEEN

Hours later, when the soft light of dawn had finally appeared, I sat on the edge of the bathtub in the nurses' lavatory, slowly unbraiding my hair. I was nearly shaking with fatigue, and the only thing I wanted more than my bed was a long, hot bath.

Nina and Martha had gone on duty, and I was alone. I opened the taps on the tub as full as they would go. I felt filthy, rank with dried sweat, and a decade older than my twenty years.

I let my hair fall and undid the braided knots one by one, tugging gently, working my fingers through the strands. The motion of it, the slow repetitiveness, started to soothe my wild brain. Too much had happened, even though for the quiet remainder of the night I'd counted linens as the wind moaned on the darkened marshes outside the window.

Now dawn had come again. I thought it

would be a warm, pretty summer day. I turned the taps off and listened to the last drops of water. The nurses' bathroom wasn't half as luxurious as the men's. The tiles were plain white and there was only a simple sink, toilet, and bathtub good enough for the use of children, overlooked by a narrow window now glowing pink with early light.

My nerves were still ragged, and they had not forgotten the terror of that other bathroom. But this room was quiet. There were no sounds in the walls. The air was not sharp with fear in here. This was just a bathroom, the house just a house. An English home at the start of an early-summer day.

I stood and dropped my nightdress, then stepped naked into the tub. I tried to remember the last time I'd had a long, hot soak in a bath all to myself and couldn't. Well, then, there was one small advantage to living in the leftover riches of the Gersbachs.

I pulled my knees up, sank my shoulders under the water. I was too thin. My body was already narrow, boyish, but I could see the lines of my ribs. My hips were only a little rounded, my legs longish and thin with muscle, my breasts small. None of it mattered to me. I never looked at myself, not really.

I plunged my head under the water and scrubbed at my scalp. The memories came worse with my eyes squeezed shut; I saw that pale, shirtless figure walking to the stairs, and Archie's face as his hands flew up, and even poor Somersham as he vomited into his water jug. I saw my breath cloud in that stairwell, heard my voice echo off the walls. I heard Archie say, *I won't go.*

I pushed back up with a gasp. I dashed water from my eyes and stared at the ceiling. This was not just a house. It was quiet now because it chose to be, because it dozed. It left this bathroom alone because this room did not interest it. It let me sleep for now because it chose to.

Never turn your back on danger, Kitty.

Something was going on, something outside of normal rationality. Something mad. And I couldn't leave, which made things simple. I'd have to stay and face whatever it was. I pressed my hands to my eyes. This thing had not bested me yet, but it had come close. I was tired, so tired of doing everything alone.

Jack Yates's jaw had been rough and hot when I'd touched it. I could still feel the scrape of his stubble against the pads of my fingers. He'd listened so calmly as I'd cried, letting me stay in the dark. My skin prickled at just the thought of him, curious and aware, as if my body was imagining what his hands would feel like.

You didn't tell him everything, I reminded myself, and pulled the plug, letting the water spiral down the drain.

I was six years old when my father first hit me. I was pulling myself up the arm of the sofa, pretending to be a mountaineer, when I'd looked up to see his hand swinging toward me, as large as the moon. As I'd lain on the floor, my face stinging and a jolt ringing up my tailbone, as I bit back a cry — for even then I'd known better than to make a noise — what registered first was not pain but surprise. It had been so fast, so random. *Did that happen?* I'd thought stupidly. *Did it really?*

Over the years, long past when it should have vanished, that surprise had been constant every time. My mother was most often the target of my father's anger; she had it worse than either me or Syd. We were nuisances, slapped casually out of the way with a muscled arm, but something about my mother infuriated my father, no matter what she did. She simply made him angry.

And when she finally left, when I was thirteen — ran away with a man from the local soap factory, like a bad theater melodrama that no one would ever want to see — my father turned that anger on me.

He hit me while Syd was out. He called me names, disgusting and crude, when Syd couldn't overhear. He twisted my arm behind my back, his fingers digging into my skin, silently when Syd was in the next room, and told me if I screamed, he'd kill my brother. If Syd noticed my black eyes, he never spoke of it. I didn't blame him, and I didn't ask for help. It was I who made my father angry: the way I looked like my mother, the way I was growing into her body, the way my lower lip curved like hers. I infuriated him. There was nothing anyone could have done.

The morning after Syd went to war, I stood in the kitchen frying two eggs on the stove. My father came in behind me on silent feet. He took the back of my neck in a viselike grip, bent me forward, cracked my forehead on the edge of the counter hard enough to bleed, and threw me to the floor. My arm hit the handle of the pan and the hot eggs and grease went flying, splattering the wall.

"That's for leaving my socks on the

dresser," he said, and left the room.

I lay on the linoleum, thinking that the eggs were ruined, wondering whether he'd be angry because they'd been wasted. I absently wiped the blood from my forehead. And then I realized: The surprise was gone. I lay on the floor and felt nothing. And something heavy coiled in my stomach, something that was almost fear and almost anger. *You are going to die this way,* it said. *Perhaps not today and perhaps not tomorrow, but this is how you will die.*

The year that followed was the worst of my life. Syd had gone to France and vanished; we had no idea whether he was alive or dead. My father drank. He put a knife in my mouth and threatened to cut out my tongue; he held my hand under hot water until it scalded; he pulled me screaming from under the bed one night, not knowing or caring when my hand caught on a bent nail and the skin ripped from the base of my thumb almost to my wrist. He told me that if I ran, he'd find me, no matter where I went; he'd find me and kill me, dump my body. I believed him. I had no other family, no money, no friends, and nowhere to go.

I could have married, I supposed. I was fifteen, and the local boys liked to catcall as I walked down the street in my ill-fitting dress. But by then I knew men were as dangerous as snakes. If I married one of them and he was the same, then what? Then what?

One night he came drunk into my bedroom. He crawled on top of me, a big, painfully heavy man, pressed his knees onto my thighs beneath the covers, and pinned my hands over my head. He savored the way I froze, my breath in my throat. Then he laughed, his breath hot and painful on my cheek, his body shaking. He got up and stumbled from the room.

I lay awake for hours after that, trembling. Tears leaked down my temples and into my pillow. The heavy coil came back into my stomach. *I am going to die this way. I am going to die.*

Nothing had changed. I still had no money, no friends, no family, and nowhere to go. I had just turned sixteen. I was utterly alone and helpless.

It didn't matter. Three days later, I ran.

CHAPTER SIXTEEN

I woke to Nina's face as she shook me in bed. The sun was high in the windows, glaring through the thin curtains.

"Matron wants to see you," Nina said.

I blinked at her. "What time is it?"

"Three o'clock."

"What?" I sat up. "I'm not on duty yet."

Nina frowned. "Matron's off duty at night. She wants to see you now."

I dressed and braided my hair, anger rising within me. Of course I would be expected to attend to Matron's convenience; how else would it be? That I had been dragged out of bed after working a twenty-four-hour shift, given only a few hours' rest, would be nothing to her.

The men were being served tea in the common room. A few of them passed me in the corridor and nodded. Somersham stopped me and apologized for the night before.

"It's all right," I said to him. "Are you feeling better?"

He moved his gaze from his feet to the window behind my shoulder. "Yes, ma'am. I'm well, thank you. I didn't mean to bother you last night."

In the afternoon light he looked haggard, as if he hadn't slept the sleep of the drugged for some twelve hours. Somersham and I were about the same age, but like most of the men here, he looked much older. I didn't have the heart to keep him there, asking him questions. Instead I said, "Are you certain? I can fetch you an aspirin."

"It's kind of you, ma'am, but if it's all the same to you, my stomach won't quite handle it."

"Of course. Go have tea. I'm on night shift again tonight. I'll see you later."

Boney appeared at my shoulder as he left. "There you are," she said. "Matron has been waiting."

Boney's face had its usual expression, but there was a distinct smugness about it. And so I wasn't surprised when Matron turned thunderously on me when I entered her office.

"Nurse Weekes," she said curtly. "Sit down."

I sat in the hard chair opposite her desk,

the same chair I'd used for our first interview.

Matron thrust a paper at me. "What is the
meaning, exactly, of this?"

I took the paper and looked at it. "It's my
report from last night's shift. I was told I
was supposed to write one."

"Read it, if you would."

I cleared my throat. " 'Patient Twelve,
Somersham, vomited twelve thirty a.m.
Patient Six, Childress, nightmare two a.m.
Both now resting quietly. Nothing else to
report.' "

I raised my eyes. Matron was glaring at
me.

"Well?" she said.

"Did I do it wrong?" I asked.

"Do it wrong?" There was high outrage in
her tone, and I realized she was truly angry.
"Nurse Weekes, I have been told on good
authority that this is far from a complete
report. I have been told that you spent a
good deal of time alone with Patient Sixteen
in his room, which is against regulations
about fraternizing with the men. I've also
been told that Mr. Mabry had another
nosebleed, a fact you were apprised of, and
yet you utterly failed to note it here." She
took the paper from my hand and raised it.
"This is an *incomplete report.*"

I blinked. Perhaps exhaustion was coloring my perception, but it seemed a vigorous overreaction to me. "I didn't think it was important," I said.

"You may want to rethink that answer," said Matron. "You may want to rethink it very carefully."

I pushed my mind into gear. I'd been tattled on by Roger — that much was clear; he'd told her everything. He'd done it because he'd known I would catch hell for it, though why he wanted me to, I couldn't yet figure. I honestly hadn't meant to lie to Matron; I'd written the report in a haze and I barely remembered thinking anything at all as I wrote, except that I wanted Captain Mabry to see his children.

But I'd miscalculated. Matron was furious. The list of things that could put Matron into such a tizzy was easy enough to guess, and I figured I knew the item at the top.

"The doctors," I said.

"The doctors," Matron shot back at me, "are responsible for the medical care of these men. Completely responsible. They report directly to Mr. Deighton. If an incorrect diagnosis is made and a man is sent home when he shouldn't because the night nurse didn't think a man's symptoms were important, what do you think the consequences would be?"

"I didn't —"

"If a man goes home," Matron continued, "and harms his family or himself, the inquiry will lead directly here. Directly to you and to me."

At our first meeting she'd told me that she was about to lose her position because she couldn't keep a girl past three weeks. She was as worried about her own job, then, as I was about mine. The thought surprised me. I had never imagined Matron worried about anything.

I bit my lip, thinking. "All right. It's just that I spoke to Captain Mabry and I don't think he's a danger to himself or others, not really. He has fits of nosebleeds, that's all. I'm not even certain he's mad." *Except that he sees things. But then, so do I.*

Matron gave me a withering glare. "*Mister* Mabry, like every other patient in this institution, will say anything he can think of to win your sympathy, and therefore gain himself a better chance of escaping Portis House."

That utterly stopped me. I stared at her, openmouthed. "Escape?"

"Of course, escape. This is an institution, Nurse Weekes."

"But the doors aren't locked. There are

no fences. The men can leave whenever they wish."

"And where would they go? Off over the marshes into the ocean? Or over the bridge to the mainland? We confiscate all of their personal belongings when they come here, including identification papers, money, and clothes. They wear clothing identifying them as patients." Matron pulled a handkerchief from a pocket in her apron and began vigorously polishing the spectacles dangling on her chest. "There has never yet been an escape from Portis House, but if there were, no man could effect it alone. He would need help."

I couldn't calculate it. "You're saying the patients would use me?"

She shook her head and continued to polish. "Just because a man has lost his sanity does not mean he is incapable of subterfuge. In fact, the insane are quite capable of it. And when they have brooded on something long enough, they have no moral qualms at all." She dropped the glasses and let them dangle again. "So, yes, Nurse Weekes, I am saying that every man here will lie to you if he can. He will tell you what he thinks you want to hear in order to gain your sympathies. He will tell you he is a victim, that he is unjustly accused, that he is unfairly

215

imprisoned. He will not tell you about the people close to him who are so badly frightened that they wanted him locked away for safety." She looked me in the eye. "Trust me, Nurse Weekes, there are people right now who are terrified these men will come home."

She had a way of looking at you that made you think she knew everything. But she couldn't have known how those words made me shiver. I understood terror of a man coming home in a way I had never spoken of to anyone.

"You hadn't thought of that, had you?" said Matron.

I shook my head.

"I didn't think so. You need to *think*, Nurse Weekes, if you're going to succeed here. Do you know why Mr. Somersham was vomiting?"

"The drugs," I said numbly. "They were wearing off."

"That is, in fact, incorrect. Persistent nausea is part of Mr. Somersham's particular neurasthenia. For the first three weeks he was here, we had difficulty getting him to take food at all. It usually recurs when he's had some excitement, such as I understand he had yesterday."

I sat silent. I had been so sure.

"Mr. Mabry," said Matron, "is subject not only to nosebleeds and delusions, but to violent fits as well. It took us nearly two weeks, I might add, to dry him out. And Mr. Childress assaulted one of the nurses a few days before you started here."

"What?" Archie?

"He assaulted Nurse Ravell, your predecessor, during a night shift. She was so frightened she left right away without notice."

That was why she had departed so quickly that she hadn't taken all of her belongings. I rubbed a tired hand over my forehead. Everything in the dark of night, when I was alone — everything had seemed so different. In the light of day, I questioned what I had seen, what I had thought. *I had a particularly bad episode,* Archie had told me.

Matron wasn't finished. "As for Patient Sixteen, can you explain why you entered his room?"

I shook my head.

"Did he request your assistance? The truth this time, Nurse Weekes."

"No," I croaked.

She sighed. "I know you believe the rules don't apply to you, but believe me, they apply to you more than to any other nurse I've ever had. A condition of Patient Sixteen's care here is confidentiality. And that is the second time you have entered his room without any authority. He came here to be privately treated for the breakdown of his mental faculties, not to be followed and fawned over by foolish girls who won't leave him alone. To disregard the rules of his treatment is to set it back."

And there I'd been, barging in uninvited, demanding comfort for my own problems. He'd listened so patiently while I'd poured out my stupid mistakes and contravened the conditions of his own recovery. "I'm sorry. I am. It won't happen again."

"That isn't good enough, Nurse Weekes. I have already written another incident report. I had no choice. Your behavior has compromised the effectiveness of this institution."

"The patients all know who he is," I blurted, my cheeks stinging. "They all know. You can't truly think there was a way to avoid it."

For a second, her gaze flickered. She knew. "A rule is a rule, Nurse Weekes."

"But —"

"I've just explained it," she snapped. "Your job as a nurse is not to question the rules, but to follow them. Failure to follow the rules results in an incident report."

I swallowed. "And the incident report is read by . . ."

"Dr. Thornton, Dr. Oliver, and Mr. Deighton, yes. They all receive it."

So I was ruined, then. I had no one to blame but myself, as usual. I blinked back tears, and a flare of anger burned over my shame. "Did he tell you he locked the door on Patient Sixteen?" I asked her. "When he tattled on me? Did he tell you that much?"

Matron didn't bother pretending she didn't know who I meant. "Yes, he did. Orderlies are given keys and can make special judgments if they feel safety is being compromised."

"Whose safety? Patient Sixteen is *on suicide watch,* for God's sake. What if he had killed himself while locked in? What would your Dr. Thornton or your Mr. Deighton have said then?"

Creases bracketed her mouth, forming deep grooves. "That has been taken into consideration. In the end, no harm was done. The incident will not be repeated."

"Will there be an incident report about him? About Roger?"

"Incident reports are none of your concern, Nurse Weekes."

"They are when I'm about to get sacked."

"That is enough, Nurse Weekes."

I looked away. It was scathingly unfair. It had taken five days — no, six. This was my sixth day at Portis House and I had already ruined it, ruined everything. I thought about the bottle of pills I'd taken, hidden now under the mattress on my bed. I could tell her — what? That I thought the doctors and orderlies were conspiring to have Jack Yates die by his own hand? What if the admission just doomed me further? What if Jack had stolen the pills and the doctors hadn't given them to him at all? I'd never asked him. If I revealed the pills now, I could cause him more trouble than I had already.

Well, she was right about one thing. I'd taken the bottle. The incident would not happen again.

I was actually sitting there thinking of strategies to keep Jack Yates from trying to kill himself again. It hit me in a wave of awful disbelief. I didn't realize I'd spoken until I heard the words, tired and quiet from my own lips. "Six months ago he was a hero."

Matron sighed. "I am not concerned with heroes," she said, though her own voice had softened a little. "I am concerned with patients."

"Then you should let Jack Yates come out of his room if he wants to," I said.

For a second she actually looked surprised, as if I'd said aloud something she'd been thinking. Then she shuttered her expression again. "Let me tell you something, Nurse Weekes. Nursing is a job, and not a glamorous one. You do not get to choose the patients you treat. No one will ever thank you or even tell you you've done well. Our only task, which we must perform from waking to sleeping, is to do our duty. That is the profession we've chosen." She put an emphasis on the word "chosen."

"*Nurse* Weekes."

I tried to glare, but it probably came across as sullen. I was too tumbled up to do it properly. "How long do I have?"

"If you are asking if you will be dismissed, that isn't up to me. Mr. Deighton receives the incident reports every few weeks, and it usually takes him several days to get to them. Three weeks, perhaps."

"May I go now?"

"Yes. You are on duty tonight, though since you're dressed now, it's likely the other nurses can use your help with supper."

I pushed my chair back. "I'm going for a walk first. I've barely been out of doors since I arrived."

She thought about it, likely concluding that if I had the benefit of fresh air, she could get more work out of me. "Very well.

One hour. Don't go far."

"May I ask one question?"

"What is it?"

"Where did she go?"

Matron looked surprised. "Who?"

"The nurse before me. Maisey Ravell. Where did she go when she left here?"

She frowned. "To the village, I assume, unless she got another position."

"The village?"

"Yes. Bascombe. The village on the mainland, at the other end of the bridge. You would have passed through it on your way here." Her gaze narrowed. "Why do you ask that?"

"Because she left some belongings behind. A locket and a few other things. I thought perhaps she might want them. I'd like to write and ask her, if that's allowed."

Again Matron considered. "Very well. I'll have Nurse Fellows give you the address we have in the records. The post goes in the morning."

It wasn't much, but it was something. And before she could speak again, I was off, my steps taking me down the corridor and away from Portis House as fast as I could go.

CHAPTER SEVENTEEN

July had almost arrived, and true high summer was beginning. To me, the season was usually marked by humid, smoggy London days, clothes that stuck to my skin as I worked, sheets I had to dampen with water so I could sleep in my airless room at night, the smells of smoke and dirt and motorcar fumes like lingering gas attacks. I had never spent summer out of the city.

The air was fresh here, blowing over the marshes in a warm exhale tinged with earth and salt. I unpinned my cap, untied my apron, and dropped them on one of the chairs in the garden as I went through the garden gate.

Past the back of the house and the gentle rise of the hills were hunched clumps of low trees, bordering the marshes themselves. I pushed on, farther than I had ever gone while supervising the men at exercise. Long grass, each blade as wide as my thumb, brushed at my skirts with a silvery shushing sound matched by the persistent whistle of the wind in my ears and punctuated by the calls of birds. I leaned my body into the climb up the slope, feeling my legs stretch in their cotton stockings, the pull of the muscles on the backs of my calves. My feet in Maisey Ravell's practical leather boots sank into the soft earth. Sweat trickled between my shoulder blades, not the slick sweat of fear but the honest sweat of effort, dried quickly by the summer wind.

I had to lift my skirts as I climbed. I should have been cursing my uniform, with its fussy blouse and petticoat, but I was growing used to it. I had never worn a corset — it seemed a pointless extravagance to me, and I had no desire to look like an old biddy — and the uniform, mercifully, did not require one. After several days of hard work in it, I had to admit that it was easy to move in, easy to bend and stretch in, sturdily sewn with minimum fuss. What had seemed prudish a few days earlier I now realized covered everything no matter what difficult position I found myself in. It was nice to know you could help a man vomit into a pitcher on the floor without showing him your calves or giving him a look down your blouse.

So I pushed myself along now, skirts rustling in the grass, beginning to enjoy the blood pumping in my body despite how tired I was. By the time I reached the top of the rise, my cheeks were hot and I felt damp sweat under my pinned-up braids.

From here I could see the thicket of trees, clustered like a crowd of commuters on a busy train platform, that were solid land's last gasp before the marshes began their march to the sea. The grass grew thicker there, tangled with brush and undergrowth, uncut by any visible path. Beyond the trees, the marshes stretched like patchwork, mossy and silvery, their colors strange even in the workaday summer sunlight. They faded into an impenetrable horizon that must be the sea, though I saw no sign of any boat or mast in the long moments I searched for them.

I turned back to the house. It looked different from here; it was so large I'd only ever seen pieces of it, like the portico on that first day in the fog. There was something both magnificent and ominous about it from here. It stood alone, showing its wealth and outright splendor, spreading its wings against the tremendous expanse of the marsh and the horizon, as if flung down by a giant hand. It was a massive, wide square of pure stone, dwarfing its ornamental gardens in shadow, its windows staring indifferently at the sky and the sea.

I walked along the rise, unwilling to descend just yet. My hour was likely up soon, but the sun was shining, and this far from the house I could almost feel the ghosts and the devils falling away. The house was just a house from here, after all. I should have been amazed at the quiet and the loneliness, or even horrified, being a London girl; the emptiness here was entirely new to me. But I'd always craved solitude, even on a crowded factory floor. Solitude was safe.

There was movement in one of the upper windows of the house. Someone was watching me.

For a second my eyes wanted to see a shirtless man, but no. It was a dark-haired man in the pale shirt of Portis House, sitting on a familiar window seat in an unmistakable pose. Even from here, I knew Jack Yates.

I had no idea how long he'd been watching as I'd stood staring out to sea without cap or apron, oblivious, my skirt blowing against my legs. He lifted one hand now in salute, palm out, a silent greeting. I raised my own hand in return, held it there. We were locked together for a long moment, and I imagined my hand pressed to the glass of his window. Matron had been right. I should never have burdened him with my problems or sought comfort he was in no position to give. My first priority should have been his care. I'd been selfish, as always.

I lowered my hand, made myself look away. I turned my gaze to the deserted west wing, its dark windows, and then I froze.

A woman stood on the grass before the door to the isolation room. She wore a blouse and skirt, the hem lost in the long weeds, her hair tied back, hatless. In the shadow of the looming walls, I couldn't see her features clearly. But I could see that she stood with her hands at her sides, unmoving. And she was staring steadily at me.

My heart thumped in my chest. For a long moment I just stood there, my breath short, wondering what I was looking at. A woman? A ghost? I thought of the shirtless man I'd followed into the stairwell and I had the wild instinct to run. But my feet did nothing, rooted to the ground like clay.

Then she moved.

She turned with a slow, eerie calm and walked away, back toward the isolation room door and past it. Her skirt shifted as she passed, though in the tall grass I couldn't see her feet. She *moved* like a real woman. But then, the shirtless figure I'd seen had moved like a real man.

She turned the corner and disappeared around the side of Portis House. I stayed frozen for another long moment, but she didn't reappear. I should go back into the house, I knew. Even though it was improbable, likely impossible, that a woman had come so far alone with no transportation, I should report what I had just seen. Instead, I followed her.

The breeze died as I descended the rise toward the west wing, giving way to still, oppressive air before I reached the house. I stepped into the curve formed by the cup of the west wing's walls and my vision was dappled with shadow. Jack Yates's window had vanished from sight, and no one could see me here. The weeds smelled rank and without the breeze there was no sound, no soft shushing of grass, only the sound of my boots on the choked, soft earth.

I looked around me and realized where I was standing.

That spot outside the library, you know. That seems to be the spot they go to. The last one had stolen a blade.

I glanced down at my feet, as if expecting

to see blood still beaded on the grass. For a second I could imagine it clearly: a patient in his Portis House whites standing here with a stolen knife. Shouts, orderlies running. The man raising the blade. When I had first heard it, it had seemed strange that men would supposedly be drawn to this place for such an impulse. Yet as I stood there myself, the loneliness was unmistakable, with the air of a place that was more toxic and sick than any other place in this vast madhouse.

The windows of the isolation room had been fitted with iron bars, and a heavy lock hung on the door, its keyhole staring vacantly at me. I tried to imagine being locked in there alone, far from the rest of the house, looking out at these hideous weeds. Would they tie a man up? Put him in a straitjacket?

I had to cup my hands to the glass of the window, between the bars, before I could see inside, and it took a moment for my eyes to adjust to the gloom. I saw a cot, a basin on a nightstand, a single wooden chair. The walls were stained; water had come in during a rainfall, perhaps. Dust littered the floor. This was the room's only window. A man would sit here and stare at nothing, see no one, count the stains on the wall, on the ceiling . . .

The men know. It's getting worse, too. Did you hear the last one screaming? Said he could see something from the window . . .

I pushed away. My skirt caught on something, and I looked down to see a weed growing along the wall, my skirt hooked on its sticky tendrils. I pulled myself free as other weeds scratched my legs. I was in the grip of something strange. I felt as if someone had slipped me a drug, something that made me see more than I wanted, as if I could peel up the edge of the visible world and glimpse what lay underneath. The woman watching me. This horrible, strangely awful room that made the hair on the back of my neck stand on end. I took a step back. I saw my reflection in the window, and behind me something moved.

It was a figure. Tall, indistinct. A gleam of sunlight on metal, and then it was gone. Not my father. And yet —

He found you, a voice said in my head — the same crazy, panicked voice I'd heard in the men's lav. *You broke the rules and he found you and you know what happens when he gets angry.*

I whirled around. Nothing there. Only the hot, dead air and the sour smell of the weeds. And then another voice came, this one deeper, indescribable. *You coward.* I took a step and something hit me hard in the stomach.

I bent double, moaning low and terrified, and the impulse to scream was so overpowering I pressed my hands over my mouth as another mad sound escaped me. I breathed out in a hot rush of air. As impossible, as insane as the situation was, my brain still recognized what was happening. I was about to get a beating. I had to run.

I forced my legs to move, one step, and then another, pushing through wave after wave of panic. *Just move, move.* I staggered through the fetid grass and out of the shadows into the sunlight again, and then I dropped my hands and kept running.

I had little memory of the hours after that. I know I put on my cap and apron and helped with supper. I was a shell, functioning like an automaton on the outside, my brain rattling with wild terror on the inside. It was a familiar feeling, a reaction I could not control. It was a survival instinct born of many beatings, of the need to appear normal, not to let on. My mind was very good at this, at moving my hands and feet and working while the rest of me shut down. My life, for a short time, was happening to someone else, and so I got through one moment, and then another, and then another.

You coward.

My feelings were gone, gone.

It was only much later that I hid in the nurses' lav and got up the courage to take off my apron and unbutton my blouse. I stood before the dim mirror and ran my hand over my smooth, white stomach, looking for a bruise. I knew what they looked like, the bruises that came from a blow like that. My father had given me dozens of them.

There was nothing.

I had not known I was crying.

I wiped my tears and stared at my unblemished skin in the mirror for a long, long time.

CHAPTER EIGHTEEN

"There were four Gersbachs," said Nathan the cook. "Two parents, a boy, and a girl. Kept to themselves, I hear."

"How old were they?" I asked, spooning my stew. It was night again and I was back at the table in the kitchen, eating before my proper shift began. I sounded almost normal. I tried not to let the spoon clatter against the bowl. "The children?"

"Bammy's age." Nathan jerked a nod at the kitchen boy, who was about sixteen. "Or so Bammy himself says. He's from the village."

I looked at Bammy. "Did you know them?"

" 'Course not." He looked at his shoes. "They was rich."

"Why are you asking?" Nathan said to me.

I turned and found him looking at me closely. Before my shift I had rebraided my hair, sponged myself off, tried to rest. It didn't matter that I was cracking up inside; I couldn't show weakness, not to these men. "What's it to you?" I said to Nathan, and was rewarded with an approving grin.

I turned back to the others. "But they were outsiders," I said. "The Gersbachs."

"Germans," said Nathan.

"No," I said. "Swiss."

"Never."

"They were Swiss," Paulus Vries cut in. "She's right. Not everyone's a Hun, you simpleton."

"And what the hell are you?" Nathan shot back at him.

"I'm South African. Did you think I was a Hun, too?"

"I don't know what the hell you are." Nathan looked stubborn. He hadn't liked being wrong. "Maybe you're a spy."

"I fought in German South-West Africa in 'fifteen," Paulus said tightly. "I killed as many Huns as any man here. We buried them in the heat and left them there. The Germans ought to have no love for me."

"All right," I said. "Back to the Gersbachs. They came here and built this place. Then what? Where did they go?"

"They moved away," said Paulus.

"They didn't," Bammy broke in.

We all stared at him. "What's that supposed to mean?" said Nathan.

Bammy shrugged. He was gawky and painfully shy, but he was warming a little with newfound authority. "There was talk in the village, that's all. They built the house — we saw the trucks haul everything over the bridge for months. But no one saw them move out or drive away. There's only one way off here, and that's over the bridge. No one saw it."

I thought of the figure I'd seen in the reflection in the window. I put my bowl down.

"Someone must have seen something." This was Roger, who had been listening quietly until now. He looked uneasy. "What about the servants working here?"

"He fired them all," Bammy said. "Mr. Gersbach. Said they were moving away, taking none of the staff along."

"There you go, then," Roger said. "They moved."

Or he knew, I thought. *He knew that, for whatever reason, they wouldn't need servants anymore.* "Perhaps they left in the middle of the night," I said. "Maybe they had debts and had to get away."

"You haven't lived in the village," Bammy replied. "No one would miss an event like the Gersbachs' moving out, even at three in

235

the morning."

"Well, they must have done it," said Paulus. "The place is empty. Their things are gone. They did it quiet, that's all."

Bammy shrugged and dropped his gaze back to his shoes.

There was a moment of silence. I bit my lip, my courage deserting me. I was going onto another night shift, alone. *I saw a ghost today,* I wanted to say. *I saw another one last night. Please tell me I'm not the only one.* I felt fragile, and I didn't like it. I opened my mouth and took a breath, but it was Bammy who spoke first.

"They never left," he said softly.

We all looked at him again. He lifted his gaze, defiant.

"They never left," he repeated. "That's what you're thinking, isn't it? The sounds in the basement, in the lav. Everyone knows it, but no one wants to say. No one saw them because they never did move away. They're all buried here somewhere and their ghosts are haunting the place."

I exhaled.

Nathan chewed his toothpick, uncomfortable. Roger had gone red in the face. It was Paulus who spoke. "Lad," he said, "you've been listening to too many stories. It's just an old house that's falling apart."

"But that's it," Bammy protested. "It's not old at all. Why are there cracks in the walls? Why is the west wing falling down? Why is there mold in the men's lav? Why is it getting worse? No one has an answer to that, do they?"

"The air isn't good here," Nathan said. "There's something about it. That I know. What do you think, Nurse?"

He was looking at me again. "It's strange," I managed. "I suppose."

Roger scraped his chair back and stood. "Well, you ladies can sit here and gossip about ghosts all you like, but I've a shift to start." He glared at me from gimlet eyes. "So do you, Nurse."

Of course. My watcher. There would be no love lost between Roger and me tonight. I gave him a hard look in return and stood.

It was a warm night, not a breath of wind to rattle the windows or sigh in the eaves. Through the panes of glass in the upstairs corridor I saw the garden unmoving, the clusters of trees still as soldiers. In a cloudless sky the stars had appeared, speckling the deep black canopy with small diamonds of light. I wondered whether the air smelled sweet, whether it was a perfect summer night for strolling and looking at the sky. The perfect night to do things I'd never have the time to do, with people I'd never be able to do them with.

The conversation in the kitchen dogged me as I sat at the narrow nurse's desk and pulled the linen lists from the drawer. The Gersbachs dogged me. Only one family had lived in this house. Only four people. And now I lived in their house, slept in their nursery, looked from the same windows they had looked from, ran my hands along the same stairway rails they had smoothed with their own palms. They were not just the absent owners of giant dining rooms and paintings gone from the walls. One heard about people disappearing, perhaps, but never entire families. Never entire families, just vanishing into the air.

And I had followed something into the stairwell the night before, felt it waiting for me in the dark at the bottom of the stairs. I had seen something in the library window, something that had hit me.

The need to talk to Jack Yates was like an itch. I wanted to confide to him what had happened to me, and — I admitted it — I just wanted to see him. But I was being watched, and tonight I would behave. Jack had to get well. That had to come first.

I slid aside the linen lists and drew out *Practical Nursing,* which I had slipped into the desk drawer earlier in the evening. I opened the book and looked at Florence Nightingale again. Florence would never have gone into a patient's room and started crying about her problems. She would never have seen things and started to crack up. I pulled my lamp closer to me on the desktop, turned to the chapter on sutures, and began to read.

Two hours later, it seemed as if the night would be a quiet one. The men slept without nightmares; Roger had disappeared to his other duties; and when I did my rounds, if Jack Yates was awake he made no sound. No moans came from the walls of the lav, and the drains sat undisturbed.

I studied until my eyes blurred. There was nothing for it; I would have to count linens soon. This was how Martha and Nina did night shift, then: a numbing repetition of making rounds and counting, with no company in the silence, nothing but the slurring thoughts in your head. Listening to one's own quiet, creaking footsteps in the corridor, shivering a little as the night wore on, looking out the darkened windows, trying not to think of sleep.

I caught my reflection in a window's darkened glass. My face had filled out just a little, the effect of a week of regular meals.

It was a narrow face, heart shaped, the nose longish, the eyes dark and long lashed, perhaps, but overall unremarkable. The only feature that set my face apart was the lower lip, my mother's lower lip, which was soft and full, yet curled in almost a sensual sort of disdain. I had no control over the look of that lip, but men seemed to find in it an invitation, and it had enraged my father. I had paid, I thought, a very high price for such a small thing.

I slid my own face out of focus and looked past it to the garden, wondering what it would feel like to be out there, feeling the warm night air breathe gently across me.

I was cold. My shoulders rose instinctively, flexing upward. I put a hand to the back of my neck and rubbed it. The body grew cold at night on its own, but this was different. A distinct icy chill, on my neck and back, between my shoulder blades. A draft. Or —

"No," I said softly to myself.

The word came out on a breath of frosted air.

Reflected in the glass, something moved behind me.

From one of the rooms came a scream. I recognized the voice: Archie again. My hands were icy, my feet made of clay; I did not want to turn around, but at the second scream I was already moving.

There was nothing in the icy corridor behind me. I ran to Archie's door, never fast enough, pressing as if moving underwater. The air was cold and strangely heavy. Somewhere deep in the walls a pipe groaned, punctuated with a familiar *clang.* I gripped the jamb of Archie's door and propelled myself into the room, grabbed the brass foot of the bedstead, and pulled myself toward him.

He was arched again, just like the night before, his head thrown back and his mouth frozen in a rictus of terror. I took his shoulders and tried to shake him. "Archie!" He thrashed, his sinews twisting like leather under my hands. *This is last night,* I thought. *I am living it again.*

He quieted for a moment, panting on the bed, staring at me in stark fear. "Archie," I said as gently as I could, leaning over him. "Wake up. It's all right. Wake up."

There was a second in which Archie — the real Archie — was in those eyes. And then something changed. His face contorted; his teeth gritted together. Then he launched himself upward, reached his hands around my neck, and squeezed.

I was too shocked to think. The pain was tremendous. "Archie," I tried to say, but the word would not leave my throat.

He squeezed harder, pulled me toward him. "You coward," he said to me.

I tried to shake my head, but could only gasp.

"You are a coward," he said again, his stutter gone, his voice deep and eerie. Wherever Archie had gone, it was far away from the man who was gripping my throat now. I began to struggle, my fingernails biting into the backs of his hands.

Spots danced in front of my eyes, but two incredibly strong hands, their backs lined with black tufts of hair, wrenched Archie's grip from me. Roger pressed Archie's arms down into the mattress and twisted to look back at me, where I had staggered away from the bed.

"Get the needles," he said. *"Now."*

I wasted only a few seconds standing there, gasping for air, my hands on my neck, watching the small, wiry Roger pin down his patient. Archie was larger, longer limbed, and possessed of inhuman emotion that gave him strength; yet Roger bent over him and held, his forearms shaking, his face grim with deadly seriousness. It was only that Archie was weakened and underweight that kept him down, and still he thrashed and screamed, the nightmare still on him. I turned and ran from the room.

I thought the locked drawer wouldn't open; I nearly dropped the keys in my haste. Only when I pulled one of the hypodermics from its slot and felt its unfamiliar weight in my hand did I remember that I had never given an injection before. I fumbled with the needle, with the vial of liquid, and ran back to Archie's bedside.

Archie had stopped screaming, but he still struggled under Roger's grip. Sweat beaded on his reddened face and he stared at Roger with deadly hate. I approached the bed, readying the needle as I'd seen in *Practical Nursing,* trying to grip it properly between the fingers and the pad of the thumb. I jerked up the sleeve of Archie's pajama top, revealing his upper arm.

"Go ahead," Roger grunted at me. "Quickly."

I pressed the needle against Archie's skin. I swallowed. My throat was as raw as sandpaper, pain blooming at the base of my jaw and at the back of my neck. I pictured the book again, the ink diagrams, the words that ran through my head.

Quickly.

Somersham's vomiting. It had nothing to do with the drugs. *Part of his particular neurasthenia.*

Quickly.

Captain Mabry's humiliation, Dr. Thornton's eloquent little lesson. *These men are not your friends.*

Nurse Ravell, so frightened she'd run in the night. This had happened to her, too.

Quickly.

"For God's sake!" Roger nearly shouted. "I can't hold him."

I jabbed the needle under Archie's skin and pushed the plunger home.

It was messy; Archie gave a yelp of pain. I wasn't fast enough, wasn't expert enough. In a matter of seconds, it made no difference. His body collapsed on itself, a dead weight. Roger let him go and stood, wiping the sweat from his forehead.

"Bloody hell," he said. He looked at me. "You all right?"

I nodded. I was kneeling on the floor next to the bed, the emptied needle in my hand. I slumped down, my bottom landing hard on the backs of my calves, my arms dropping to my sides. I couldn't speak. I watched Archie's body on the bed, his head tilting senselessly to one side, his face slack.

"I'd strap him in," Roger went on, "but he won't need it now. One of those doses and they sleep like babies. We won't hear another peep from him tonight." He looked at me again. "You'll want some aspirin, then. Are you sure you're all right?"

"Yes," I rasped. I owed my life to this petty, bitter little man.

"A bit of a shake-up, I suppose, but you'll get over it."

"Yes."

He seemed to want to talk, now that the danger was past, or perhaps he was waiting for a rush of gratitude. "He's always been quiet, that one, until recently. I don't know what's gotten into him, but it's getting worse. Nearly did for that nurse last time, though I wasn't on duty at the time. He was on grave duty, you know."

I looked up. "What?"

"Grave duty. On the front line. Had to pick pieces of men out of the mud, try and match them up, identify them for burial. I heard they left him on it for four weeks before he cracked completely. They'll never get him well, this one. Not after that."

I stared at him, my brain turning over slowly, unable to take in anything so horrible. Roger looked at my expression and shrugged.

"All right," I said. "You may go now. Thank you."

But he was suspicious. "There'll be an

incident report, you know. I'll make certain of it."

"I'm sure you will."

When he finally left, I closed my eyes, my head spinning. I listened to the slow rasp of Archie's breathing.

I wasn't mad, not the way these men were. I hadn't been to war. I didn't have their memories, their terrible experiences, their close knowledge of death, their fears.

But after today, perhaps, I thought I was beginning to see what they saw in their nightmares.

CHAPTER NINETEEN

Three days after the incident with my father in the bed, I'd ducked into a coffeehouse in London. It was cold and damp out, and my usual routine was to stand in a crowded coffeehouse, pretending to look over the menu on the wall until it was almost my turn to order; then I'd turn suddenly, as if I'd forgotten something, and leave. It was a good way to warm one's feet and hands if one was in the middle of a long walk home.

Two women behind me had been having a conversation. The niece of one of the women had been given a chance at a position at a glove factory in Clerkenwell, but had decided to brush it off and marry her sweetheart instead. "She isn't even giving them notice," the woman complained. "She just isn't going to go. I think she's mad. What if he doesn't marry her after all? Good jobs are hard to come by. 'You're mad, Rachel Innes,' I said to her. 'It'll come to no good.' But she's determined, of course."

I'd listened a little longer, the back of my neck hot as lit coals. I waited so long it was almost my turn before I left the shop, possessed by a mad idea I had no control over, my hands and feet tingling, my legs moving on their own. I'd found our flat empty, my father not home, and where he was that day I would never know. I'd stuffed as many belongings as I could into a tiny valise and left, my nervous feet clattering loudly on the stairs.

I'd thought I'd get caught. I *knew* I would. He would come home seconds after I'd left and pursue me; he had been hiding in the closet while I'd been there, waiting in silence for me to make a move; the landlady, hearing my footsteps on the stairs, would somehow know I'd run and get a message to him. Everyone on the street was my father, or sent by him; every pair of eyes reported back to him. Even when I got to Clerkenwell and asked in a local shop where the glove factory was, I thought I'd be questioned. I thought the police would come. And when I knocked at the personnel office at the factory itself and presented myself as Rachel Innes, reporting for work, I thought they would know I was lying.

But they hadn't. They'd just put me to

work, indifferent. It seemed I'd gotten away with it. They never knew that I slept in a church vestibule all the nights until I received my first pay, that I bathed and washed my clothes in the women's lav, that I worked the line faint with hunger and fear. They never knew I was a girl who didn't belong there, who didn't deserve it, who deserved nothing but death under her father's thumb. And I began to see that if I could be smart, if I could keep moving and not get caught, they would never know.

I did not go out with men when they asked me. Not ever.

I ran my hands along the bruises on my neck, pressing them with unsteady fingers.

Archie had throttled me. My body had felt a sickening recognition of the feeling; I'd been throttled before. But this had been different. I hadn't felt the bewildered surprise of my childhood, or the deadened stillness of the day with the frying pan. I'd only felt the numbness of shock, and now rage and empty, hopeless despair. I had promised myself, *Never again.* And yet here I was, treating bruises on my neck. It was as if, even to myself, I had never believed my promise.

"Kitty."

I was still sitting on my knees in Archie's

room. I wondered whether I was going to be sick.

"Kitty."

I opened my eyes. Jack Yates was in the room with me, squatting on his haunches, his wrists dangling casually over his knees, looking at me. He was barefoot, the strong sinews of his feet balancing him without effort.

"I'll be all right," I said.

"You don't look it," he replied.

"You're not supposed to leave your room."

"No," he agreed. He reached out and put a hand on my forearm, the fingers curling over me with gentle force. "Come with me."

I stared at his hand on me. This was the third time Jack had touched me. I'd counted, remembered each occasion with perfect clarity. I stared down at his bare fingers on my skin, their darkness against my pale arm. The sight of it, the feel of it, did something to me. It made my brain feverish; it made my skin feel too small, as if I could crack it open and fly away. I had never asked him to touch me, but he kept doing it anyway. And I never stopped him. I could not take my eyes from his hand.

He pulled me up, gently, and the next I knew, I was sitting in the only chair in his room, and he'd found my lamp from somewhere. He set it on the small side table and went to the washbasin. In the warm circle of light I could see his back, the muscles flexing under his shirt.

"I'm not supposed to bother you," I said.

"You're not bothering me."

"No. I mean I'm not supposed to be here at all, talking to you. Roger is likely spying. He'll tell Matron. I'll lose my job."

Jack said nothing, only turned from the basin, handed me the flannel, and sat on the edge of his bed. He wasn't drugged this time, and his gaze was clear and intelligent as he watched me sponge my neck.

"You look rather shaken," he said.

"I saw him," I replied. "Last night, and again tonight." It had been the shirtless man I'd seen in the window's reflection tonight, his figure unmistakable. "And earlier today I saw someone else in the grass by the isolation room. A man. He called me a coward."

"What?" Jack's voice was icy with shock. "Kitty, what did you say?"

"I said I saw him." The words were a relief, but I thought of the darker shadow I'd seen in the library window and I shuddered. "Two of them, though not at the same time."

"You couldn't have, Kitty. You couldn't."

"He hit me," I said, tears stinging my eyes.

251

"What?" Jack said again. I seemed to have amazed him into repeating himself. "When I saw you from the window today?"

"Yes."

He ran a hand through his hair. "Perhaps you should start from the beginning."

I did. I told him everything, though I left out that the assault had reminded me of my father's beatings. By the time I'd finished, Jack had stood and was pacing the room. He stopped with his back to me, thinking.

"It's ghosts, isn't it?" I said. I had been through so much fear that the temptation to babble was strong. "I've never thought of ghosts before. I've never even considered they existed. I never knew. But now . . ."

Jack bowed his head, his back still to me, as if what I said affected him.

"This place is haunted." I had to say it aloud, make it real. "Ghosts." I rubbed my hand over my eyes. "For God's sake."

"I've always thought," Jack said slowly, "that it was in my mind."

"How could you?" I said.

"Easily," he replied with bitterness. "I see ghosts all the time. We all do." He turned only part of the way back toward me, so I saw his face in three-quarter profile. As if he wanted to look at me but couldn't quite manage it. "You see them when you close your eyes. Sometimes they beg you for help, and sometimes they just die again. Then you start seeing them when your eyes are open. They're just there. They're trying to stanch the blood from an artery with a piece of cloth, or they're laughing at a stupid joke right before the shell hits, or they're running next to you in a sortie before they're hit so hard you never even find the body. There are days the ghosts are quiet and there are days the ghosts never stop." He paused, the breath coming out of him with a soft sound that was not quite a sigh. "It was one more ghost — that was all. I wasn't even surprised. What was one more ghost?"

"I'm sorry, Jack," I said. "I'm sorry. But the other men are seeing them, too."

He hadn't left his room in months; he couldn't know what the others saw. But he would have heard what the men screamed in their nightmares. I tried to imagine lying in bed, listening to that at night. Wondering whether your madness was yours alone. Wondering whether what you heard was a figment of your unhinged mind.

"Part of me knew it," Jack said. "But, Kitty, I don't trust my own judgment anymore."

"Is it true that men try to kill themselves in that spot by the isolation room?"

"Yes." Jack still did not turn. "Always there. One with a razor he found God knows where. The other with a knife he stole from the kitchen."

I looked at the line of his half-turned profile, thinking about the knife under my mattress. "Why there?" I asked. "Why in that place? What is driving them? It isn't just madness."

He sighed, and finally he turned his body and looked at me. "Kitty, you're talking about something I thought I was hallucinating. It's a little hard to fathom."

I touched the cool flannel to the inflamed skin on my neck. "Are they the Gersbachs?" I asked quietly. "The ghosts?"

"I don't know."

"You've never thought about it?"

"No, Kitty. I haven't."

"No one thinks about it," I said. "No one talks about it. Let's just be quiet and it will all go away — is that it?"

"That isn't fair," he retorted. "You know why we don't talk about it. You've seen for yourself."

I held the flannel to the back of my neck, looked down into my lap. He was right. I'd attended the sessions with the doctors, watched privileges being taken away, visits denied. There was nothing to be gained by babbling to the doctors about ghosts, nothing but a careless note in a file and a longer sentence in this prison. *We have to be well for the doctors.* And as Captain Mabry had expressed so clearly, my connection to the doctors meant that none of the men would ever talk to me.

"And we don't think about it," Jack went on, "because we can't *leave.*"

I couldn't exactly criticize that, could I? I, who had never cried to a neighbor or run to a policeman for help in the middle of London when my father was hitting me? I'd never admitted what was happening, even to myself, because that would have made it real. Who was I to be brave?

I raised my chin and looked at him again. "All right. But the nurses. The orderlies. Captain Mabry's nosebleeds, the nightmares. They must have some idea."

"And what would they do?" said Jack. "People see what they want to see. They're just nurses doing their jobs."

And I wasn't. I wasn't really a nurse, and I wasn't doing my job. Martha was supporting her family back in Glenley Crewe; Nina was earning money for her wedding and marriage. What would happen if either of them had started talking about ghosts, the way Martha had talked about the orderlies being afraid of the basement? Any nurse, any orderly who hadn't left already was in desperate need of the work. And the consequences of seeing ghosts were as dire for them as they were for the patients.

"What about the woman?" I said. "Have you ever seen her?" When I'd told him the story, I'd described the woman I'd seen.

"No," said Jack.

"I don't know what she was," I said. "I didn't get the same feeling from her that I did from — from the others. But I never got very close." My mind was turning it over. I couldn't stop it. It was better than cowering in fear. "If she wasn't one of the Gersbachs, who was she?"

He watched my face for a moment. "You're not going to solve this, Kitty. You can't."

"You're right." My neck hurt, but I straightened in my chair. "But there's one thing different now."

"What's that?"

"You're talking to me. You and I are talking about ghosts for the first time. Right now."

He opened his mouth, closed it again. "You're the one asking questions."

"And you're answering them. I want to know, Jack." As I spoke the words, I felt how

256

true they were. "I want to know who they were. What they want." I felt light-headed, as if I could float to the ceiling, and the sensation, surprisingly, was not unpleasant. "I'm going to find out."

"Kitty, think," he said. "You just said you could lose your job just for being in this room. Think about what you're saying."

"If they died here," I said, "if there was a sickness, or something — where are they buried? When were the funerals? Where are the graves? Who sold this place to Mr. Deighton, the house and all the land? Four people are gone, Jack. Gone. How did that happen?"

"Kitty. You can lose everything. Why do you want to do this?"

In that moment, he looked weary. He wouldn't help me; I could see that. He couldn't. And I thought briefly, dispassionately about my mother. I wondered where she was, whether she ever thought of us. I wondered whether it mattered to her that Syd was dead, that I'd been left to fend for myself alone. I hated her with a hatred that was casual and often forgotten, but I also understood her. She'd known, just as I had, that it was life or death to leave. And when you run, you must not look back, must not check over your shoulder, must not think too much, must not wonder. For I would only drag her down and drown her.

Sometimes putting yourself first was the only thing you could do.

But it would have been nice to have someone to rely on, just once in my life. It would have hurt a little less.

"It's wrong," I said. "Captain Mabry should see his children. Archie shouldn't spend his nights screaming like that. And I'm not supposed to fix it — I'm not supposed to see the patients as my friends, as anything but a job. That's fine. But I'm about to get sacked, and I need a weapon."

"What do you mean?"

I laughed, an ugly rasp from my throat. "Jack, I'm not even a nurse. There's already been at least one incident report, and there are going to be more after tonight. I have three weeks, if Matron doesn't dismiss me herself when she hears I've been in your room again. I need something to fight back with. There's a secret here that someone's keeping; I can smell it. And if I can find it, I can use it."

"You're talking blackmail," he said softly.

"No. I've never blackmailed anyone in my life, and I don't intend to start. I'm talking about knowledge, Jack. In order to win, you just have to know more than your opponent does. I've told enough lies to know. I've been at a disadvantage since the day I came here. I need to get ahead. Digging up secrets may not be the means for my leaving. It may be the key for me to stay."

There was a silence between us. I couldn't read Jack's face in the gloom, but he looked at me for a long moment, and when he spoke, his tone was almost admiring. "I can't tell if that's brave," he said, "or just coldhearted."

It stung, but I put on my best bravado. "Coldhearted or dead, Jack," I said. "Everyone has to choose sometime."

CHAPTER TWENTY

Even among the mad, life at Portis House had a routine. Meals were served at exact times; morning awakening and evening curfew were strictly observed. The time between was a simple rhythm of rest, exercise, walks in the garden, reading, napping, or just staring out the window. Many of the men seemed barely to notice one another. Very few appeared to be friends. Perhaps that was strange, but I understood it, as did the other nurses. A man fighting for his sanity had the energy only for the simple tasks of his daily life. Friendship was a luxury.

I had thought the routines pointless at first, but it didn't take me long to see they were not only valuable; they were very nearly the stuff of life. That a man's soup was ten minutes late could upset him; that it rained during the time of his usual walk could send him into a black despondence. As the patients traveled through their weary,

260

sometimes painful days, we nurses and orderlies worked day and night in the background, our own routines never stopping. One man couldn't abide a single hair in his basin; another pulled his blankets to the floor every night and slept in the corner as if he were still in a trench, leaving us with bundled linens soaked in sweat.

Florence Nightingale had dealt with fevers, poultices, broken limbs, festering wounds. I wondered what she would have thought of the nurses on her ward tending to a man whose only illness was that he'd completely forgotten he'd been in a war at all.

I rotated back onto the day shift. There were no more nightmares on my watch; I counted linens. Jack Yates stayed in his room and I stayed out of it. I wrote a terse account of the assault by Archie and submitted it in my nightly report to Matron. I heard nothing about it, nor about discipline for breaking the rules about fraternizing with patients yet again.

After that first night, Archie was not in his room. When I was back on the day shift, Boney told me he was in the infirmary again.

"You may as well take his supper to him," she said, handing me a tray and staring at the bruises on my neck in a way I'm sure she thought was discreet. "You'll have to see him sometime."

"Is he in there because of me?"

She shrugged. "Matron's order. It's either that or the isolation room. He's been quiet, so he's in the infirmary."

"Fine," I said, and took the tray down the corridor toward the stairs. I didn't want her looking at my neck anymore.

Archie was curled on his side in bed, his thin body barely making an impression under the covers. His eyes were closed, though I knew he wasn't asleep; they stayed closed as I brought in the tray and set it on the bedside table.

"They've put your soup in a bowl again," I said. "I've told them to put it in a mug, but they don't listen."

There was a sound from the bed, and I turned to find him looking at me.

"Expected someone else, did you?" I said.

He stared at the marks on my neck, his expression one of stark horror. "Kit-Kitty —"

"Don't," I said. I dumped his tea into the sink, rinsed the cup, and began to carefully transfer the soup. "Don't say it. Don't apologize. There's nothing to apologize for."

I kept my eyes on the soup. I couldn't look

at him. I could hear his breathing, heavy and harsh.

"I'm s-s—," he tried.

I gritted my teeth, focused on not spilling the soup. "Archie, stop."

"I'm so s-s—"

I turned my back and took the empty soup bowl to the sink. I would rinse it before I took it back to the kitchen. I may as well.

"Kitty," he said again behind me. My vision blurred. I put the soup bowl down and put a hand to my mouth. I stood there for a long time, struggling to take one breath, and another. I recalled it again, the needle I'd jabbed into his arm, the scream he'd made.

It had happened to Maisey Ravell, too, and she'd run from him before he could say he was sorry. As if he were a dangerous monster. And, to all appearances, he was. Or he was just a man who had been through hell and was still there, a man who had spent weeks digging the rotting bodies of his comrades from the mud and still saw visions of it daily.

"Kitty. Pl-please —"

I turned around. His cheeks were wet, though he did not sob. I took a deep breath, took in a gulp of air that smelled of ammonia, musty old sweat, and the faint tang of vomit, the air that was the smell of this place. And then, the tray of supper forgotten, I walked over to the bed and got on it next to him, sitting up with my back against the brass bedstead. He rolled over and put one arm around my hips, his head in my lap. His shaking hand trembled in the folds of my apron.

"It wasn't you," I said to him.

He said nothing.

"I know it wasn't," I went on. "I knew it at the time, even as it was happening. It was never you. And still I gave you that needle."

The arm on my hips hugged me a little tighter.

"Who is he?" I ventured. "Do you know?"

He flinched in my lap. I heard him take a breath, but he didn't answer for a long moment. When he did, his voice was almost a whisper, but his stutter was gone.

"He comes in my dreams," Archie said. "He tells me I'd be better off dead."

I stayed silent in shock.

"I tell him no," the man in my lap went on, a quiet confession. "Always no. But it's wor— it's worse and last — last night, I don't know — it was —"

"Hush," I said softly. "I understand. I do."

"I'm sorry," he managed a long moment later.

"No." I put my hand on his back, between his narrow shoulder blades, a back that looked as diminished as a boy's beneath his infirmary shirt. My cheeks were wet, too, now, but I did not sob. "It's me that's sorry," I said through the thickness in my throat. "It's me that's bloody well sorry."

We sat there for a long time, I on top of the covers, my boots on the bed. I, who had stayed away from men for four years. I sat there in bed with a strange man, his arm around me, his head in my lap. It was against every regulation in the world. I couldn't seem to stop breaking rules, even when I tried.

Finally, he fell asleep. The soup was cold by then, but I didn't have the heart to take it away. He'd need to eat something when he woke, even something cold. He was too thin as it was.

I slid out of bed and left him, closing the door behind me.

It was time for the men's leisure hour after supper, and they had assembled in the common room, but as I approached I saw they had all stopped what they were doing. The chess players had turned away from their game; the readers had put the books and magazines down in their laps. Even the men

265

who only stared absently out the window had turned, their gazes alert.

Matron stood in the center of the room. In the soft light of a summer evening she looked the same, her face set in its familiar hard lines under her mannish hair. The electricity was still on — it would not switch off until after curfew — and the lights cast pools of yellow that were slowly losing out to the dusky blue-gray of the long summer twilight out the tall windows and the terrace doors.

I stood in the doorway and registered, with the sudden clarity that sometimes floods the brain, the scene before me as a still tableau: Matron, the men turned to face her, their expressions expectant, the dwindling of a soft, decadent day in the windows. I took in the long shadows of the men playing across the high, bare walls, the cheap sparseness of the furniture arranged on the expensive floors, the smell of polish and men's sweat and the faint smell of vinegar we used for cleaning. Every detail was as clear to me as a photograph.

Matron held up a sheaf of letters. "The mail has arrived."

A murmur of excitement went up. We'd had a delivery that morning, hours before. But, of course, there had to be time for every letter to be opened, read, and vetted.

"Mr. Creeton," Matron called. "Mr. Mabry." One at a time, each man went forward to retrieve his letter. Those who weren't called turned back to the window or picked up their book again, their faces carefully blank. I caught a glimpse of movement in the doorway behind me and saw the large bulk of Paulus Vries leaning in the corridor, his arms crossed and his gaze watchful. I wondered what scenes had taken place during previous distributions of mail.

"Nurse Weekes."

Matron held out a letter to me, a thick, creamy, clean envelope. I stepped forward and took it from her. I turned it over, apprehension pinching my spine. It did not look official, and my father could not write.

The letter was from Maisey Ravell, a reply to the letter I'd written about her belongings. She wrote in a perfect, looping hand that matched her beautiful stationery, the ink utterly free of blots. It could have been a young lady's polite letter to a friend, inquiring as to the health of her mother and asking her to tea.

Dear Kitty:
Meet me on Sunday just past the stand of trees by the west wing. There's a

267

clearing. You'll see it when you enter the trees past the rise. I need to speak to you, and not just about my locket, though I will take it back if you have it. I will be there at two o'clock. Tell Matron you require an hour's walk. The men will be at tea. She's supposed to give you a half day off, but she never does, so make her grant this instead.

Perhaps you won't come. You don't even know me. But I've had time to think now, and you can help me. You must come. Don't tell anyone. You must come.

Maisey Ravell
P.S. Thank you kindly for your letter.

Quickly, casually, I folded the letter and stuffed it deep in the pocket of my apron. The envelope had still been sealed; apparently the nurses were not subject to Matron's review of their correspondence, something Maisey must have known.

What did it mean, that I could help her? I was in no position to help anyone, but maybe she could help me. I'd have to find out.

There had been a wave of murmured excitement when the letters were distributed, which quieted down. And then, as I was thinking about making an escape, utter silence circled the room in a ripple. Every man fell still, looking at the door behind my shoulder, and I felt the heat of awareness on the back of my neck.

I turned and saw Jack Yates in the doorway. He wore the sleeves of his hospital-issue shirt rolled up to his elbows. He paused, and the merest flicker of uncertainty crossed his features; then he continued into the room, walking into the light with the easy saunter that was his natural gait, crossing the open space in front of Matron — who stared at him, her eyebrows nearly shot up to her hairline — as if he had not been in seclusion for six months.

Even the men poring over their much anticipated letters had looked up, and every eye followed him across the room.

So much for Dr. Thornton's rules, I thought.

I looked back at Matron warily, wondering when the thunder would descend, but she had schooled her face back to its usual inscrutable expression. For the merest second I thought I saw a twinkle of pleasure in her eye. Was it possible Matron was amused — even happy — that Jack had done away with an entire set of rules, just by walking through a door? It was progress, wasn't it? It meant he wanted to get well.

But the twinkle disappeared, if it had ever existed. She simply said in her usual voice, "Mr. Yates. It's kind of you to join us."

He nodded to her. "Evening, Matron. Is there a newspaper about?"

"There is," she said, "but I believe Mr. Somersham currently has it in his possession."

Somersham, sitting at the end of a sofa, held out his blacked-out checkerboard newspaper. "Oh, no, I'm quite finished. You can have it."

"Are you certain?" asked Jack.

"Yes, sir."

Jack accepted the paper from him and nodded. And just like that, the fiction that none of these men knew the identity of their fellow patient went up in vapor.

Jack had not looked at me. I took the opportunity to stare at him, since everyone else was already at it. I had seen him so often in the dark, in the gloom of lamplit shadows. I had nearly forgotten the effect of Jack Yates in the light, head to toe. He was hard to look away from.

He read the masthead of the newspaper. "This is from April," he said.

"You are aware of the hospital's policy about newspapers," said Matron.

"All right," said Jack, "I admit I don't

quite know what day it is, but April seems some time ago."

"Current events —"

"Are harmful," he said. He looked her in the eye. "Right. A man just wants the racing news. That's all I'm saying."

"I'd bloody love the racing news!" came a voice from the corner.

"Me, too," said another.

"Don't worry, old man." This was Creeton, sitting in one of the chairs, one leg crossed over the other knee and grinning a grin that didn't reach his angry eyes. "If there's anything about you in there, we'll cut it out and save it in a little scrapbook."

"Shut it, Creeton," said MacInnes. "The man's right as far as I'm concerned. I'd like to hear about the latest plays myself."

Jack folded the ancient newspaper and tossed it easily on a nearby table. "A newspaper would be good," he said, ignoring Creeton, "but a gramophone would be better."

There was a murmur of excited agreement at that. Even Tom perked up. "We could play symphonies!" he exclaimed.

In the doorway behind my shoulder, Paulus straightened, as slow as a cat. Matron's posture had gone poker stiff. "You will not," she said loudly, "be getting a gramophone."

271

"I want a gramophone!" someone said.

"So do I," said Jack. He pivoted, looked around the room, his gaze passing over me unseeing. My heart pounded in my chest. The energy he produced, just by standing there, was dangerous, so dangerous, like playing with a lit fuse. And it was only a few madmen in the middle of nowhere. But this was *it,* just the faint breath of it, just the edge of a shadow of Brave Jack. The men had all turned to him. And I knew Brave Jack was *in there,* just as I'd always suspected.

His gaze stopped on Captain Mabry. "What do you think, Captain?"

Mabry had folded his tall frame onto a sofa, half in shadow, light glinting softly from his glasses. He had not spoken, only looked on in silence. As we watched, his hand moved unconsciously over the letter that rested on his thigh.

He looked at Jack for a long moment, and something passed between the two men. Then Captain Mabry shook his head. "It's against the rules."

"Of course it's against the rules!" Matron blustered. And somehow the moment deflated, punctured like a balloon. Jack shrugged; the men subsided, murmuring. Some of them shook their heads, went back to their books, still discontented. Mabry made no move. Neither did Creeton, in his corner; I could see him sitting stiffly, his face red, his eyes on Jack, swiftly calculating. He had not expected this, and he did not like it. He caught me looking at him, and I turned away.

Jack stepped closer to Matron, lowered his voice. "May I have leave to take a walk?"

She looked bewildered. "Walk?"

"Yes."

"It's evening. The time for outdoor exercise is earlier in the day."

"I seem to have missed it," he said casually. "I'd like some exercise. Just out to the garden and back. Do you think that would be possible?"

Matron was in a spin. A walk now was against the rules, but to get Jack out of the room, away from the others, would be worth something. "You would have to be supervised."

"Of course, that's fine with me."

Matron looked around, and her gaze fell on me. Her eyes narrowed, but I shook my head and shrugged in an *I'm innocent* gesture. I watched her reluctantly conclude that I could only be an innocent bystander. "Very well. Nurse Weekes, please supervise Mr. Yates in the garden. Exercise is not to exceed fifteen minutes."

"Yes, Matron."

"You will be timed."

"Yes, Matron."

"You are not to go out of sight of the windows. Mr. Vries will be watching. And, Mr. Yates, this case is an exception. In future, if you wish to exercise, please take it at the appointed time of day."

He thanked her and I followed him toward the French doors to the terrace. Everyone watched us go, and I realized that Matron had unwittingly just approved a display — a very public display — of yet more rules being broken. I watched Jack saunter out through the doors and wondered whether he knew exactly what he was doing. In the space of a few mere spoken sentences and fifteen minutes, he had turned everything on its head, even just for a moment. He was either oblivious, a genius, or utterly psychotic. And I did not think the first option applied.

"What was that?" I hissed at him as we moved away from the doors. "What are you doing?"

He walked across the terrace and leaned on the railing. Chairs were sometimes brought out here for the men on pleasant days, but the area was empty now. "Did you like it?" he said.

"*Like* it?" I said.

"I did it for you."

There was no other word for it: I gaped at him.

He shrugged. "In a manner of speaking," he said. He turned away from me and tapped his fingers lightly on the railing. "The thing is, Kitty, you've got me thinking."

"Thinking?"

"Yes. I don't much like it, but there it is. You're brave, and you keep asking questions, and you don't quit. And the next thing I know, I'm thinking."

"About what?"

"Well." He turned to descend the steps from the terrace, and I followed him. I did not walk beside him; I was only supposed to be supervising, not strolling and chatting. But I kept close behind his shoulder as he talked. "At first," he said, "I thought about what Matron said about clearance to come to my room. That my presence at Portis House is a secret."

"Something they hadn't told you," I said.

"No. It bothered me, as I said, so I joined in the therapy sessions. And I asked for permission to go running alone. Which I'm told has been granted, by the way."

275

Thornton must have written Mr. Deighton about it, or perhaps Matron had. Even the owner of Portis House, it seemed, did not want to say no to Jack Yates.

"But still," Jack continued, "I started thinking about *why* I'm a secret. And I think the answer must be that England doesn't want it getting out that Jack Yates lost his marbles, because that would be an embarrassment. Am I correct?"

I said nothing.

"Right," he said. He turned down one of the paths through the ornamental garden, I at his shoulder. His voice grew rough. "I never told you what happened before I came here, Kitty. But perhaps you already know."

I bit my lip. "I heard something."

"I can't talk about it," he said tightly. "I can't explain it. Not yet. Not even to you."

"No," I said, looking at the line of his back and thinking about the things I couldn't talk about, either. "I understand that."

"Let's just say," he said without looking at me, "that I took some sleeping pills, and a neighbor who dropped by unexpectedly found me. That's all. I woke up and the first thing I felt was disappointment. The second was uneasiness at the thought that maybe something was wrong with me. Very wrong. So I came here."

There was nothing to say, so I was silent again.

"And I asked," Jack said, "to be left alone. Completely alone, just for a little while. I hadn't been alone all through the war, and I hadn't been alone all the time after. What I'd been through was nobody's goddamned business. I wanted privacy, but I didn't ask to be treated like a shameful state secret. And when I think about it, it bothers me."

"So you left your room and came downstairs tonight," I said. That was what that display had been, that show of defiance.

"That was part of it, yes. And I *would* like a gramophone." We had reached the edge of the garden, and he turned, leaned on the rail of the low iron fence, and faced me. His expression, through the twilight, was tired and a little wry. I glanced back at the terrace windows, which were just visible. I couldn't see Paulus watching, but I had no idea how much time we had.

"That was just the first thing," said Jack. "I've been thinking about other things, too. Do you see the effect you've had?"

"What else?" I said.

"I've been thinking about ghosts." His gaze drifted to Portis House, taking in its dark bulk. "When I came here, I thought the nightmares I was having were my own madness. I saw things . . . I thought it was my own sick mind. But now I've been thinking about the Gersbachs, and that you could be right about the others. I've been thinking about this place, and the war. And I've been thinking about you. What you've told me about your life." His gaze turned back to me, and I felt myself grow hot. "I think you're running from someone who frightens you."

The words came automatically, as if I were a windup toy. "That's none of your business."

"Ah, that's the problem with thinking, isn't it? You think about things you shouldn't." But his smile was gentle, and I knew he wasn't going to push me. "For a long time I wanted to do anything except think. Thinking made me want to die again. And that's the reason I paid Thornton for those pills."

I shouldn't have been shocked, but I was. I thought of Thornton, his self-importance, the doodles in his notebook, and it felt as if someone had punched me in the stomach with a pitchfork. Following on the heels of that was a surprising white-hot anger.

"You're not getting them back," I said after a moment. "I destroyed them." This was a lie, as the bottle was still wedged under a corner of my mattress. I'd been partly afraid that I'd be in trouble for taking them and would have to produce them again.

For a second he searched my face, as if looking for the truth. "That's inconvenient," he said.

"What are they? Morphine? Something else? A mixture?"

"I have no idea. They make me sleep, give me strange and disjointed dreams. And when I take one, the world seems far away, as if I'm watching it from outside one of those glass balls you get at Christmas. I got them by telling Thornton something about migraines."

"He gave you a whole bottle."

"Yes. He did." He rubbed a hand slowly up over his face, his forehead. "It seems strange to you — I can see that. That I'd want to kill myself. Have I told you the story of what happened after the advance at La Bassée?"

He was referring to the famous battle, of course. And of course he hadn't told me. "I read about it in the papers."

He nodded. His expression had gone still now, and he looked absently off into the garden. "I was an orphan," he said.

"I know." That had been in the papers,

too. The *Times* had featured a drawing of Jack, his plain and undecorated uniform prominently drawn, outsize like a giant, stepping on mouse-size, dark-mustached Huns. *Put me in rags, lads,* said Giant Jack, *and I'll still win the war!*

"I was adopted as a baby," he said. "I remember only my adoptive parents. They were forty-five when they took me in; I was the child they'd never been able to have. By the time I went to war . . ." He shrugged. "My mother was already sick when I enlisted. She died a few months later. My father died eight months after she did. Of grief, I think, and the pressure of running the farm alone, and of reading the casualty lists, worrying about me. They were all I had."

I bit my lip, listening.

"I thought we'd die at La Bassée," he said. "I was sure of it. I thought my plan had no chance of succeeding, none whatsoever. Everyone else was already dead. I'd been watching men die for two years, men I knew, men I liked. We kept going, and we thought we were in for it, but we didn't die. And when it was over, we were sent to the back of the line, out of the fighting."

The memory in full motion now, he dropped his hand from his forehead. I was silent, hanging on every word.

"Most of the men were sent to a casualty clearing station," he said. "We were exhausted and starving. I couldn't remember the last time I'd had water. All I wanted was to lie down, but I was separated from the others and put in the back of a truck. We drove into the countryside and a motorcar met us, and I was put in that and driven some more. The shells were lighting up the sky; we could hear them like constant thunder. Finally I was taken to a house. The family was long gone, of course, and it was a headquarters now. They took me into this pretty house in the country as the shelling continued and there sat a group of men around a dining table, loaded with food, a roast of beef and bread and cheese and bottles of wine. They were all decorated. They said their names but I didn't absorb a thing. I sat down and I didn't know what to do. I hadn't slept in thirty-six hours, and they were lighting candles at their table as if everyone wasn't dying a few miles away. I sat there, stunned.

"A man with a big, white mustache, the one with the highest rank, began talking to me. He told me he'd heard what I'd done at La Bassée, and that I'd done well. I was going to get a Victoria Cross. I was distracted by the man sitting next to him, who wore a plain coat and a civilian hat. He was the only nonenlisted man in the room, and he was writing in a notebook as the other man talked. I realized the white-mustached man was telling me I was going to be sent home, that the newspapers and newsreels would want to hear about this glorious day, and I was being sent home to tell everyone about it.

"As I said, I hadn't slept in thirty-six hours. Everything felt to me like a crazy dream. He said I was going home, and the first thing out of my mouth was, 'But, sir, I haven't had a chance to die yet.' "

The corner of Jack's mouth turned up. "My words just hung there. The man's face was like a waxwork. He'd been raising his glass to drink from it and it just stopped in midair. Then he turned to the civilian and said, 'Don't write that down.'

"I knew then. The civilian was a reporter. The entire scene — the supper, the candles, all of it — was for his benefit. The touching scene of the weary soldier being told he's done well and can go home. It was as real as a stage play. Everything wrong with my life started in that moment."

The last of the sun had gone and Jack was hard to see now, but it didn't matter. I'd never thought of it before, that he'd lived a life that had been watched, assessed, recorded. I'd never wondered what it would be like to have my own likeness drawn on the front page of the *Times*. I'd just followed along with everyone else. I, who prided myself on being difficult to fool.

"What really happened, Jack?" I said now. "What is the truth?"

"The truth," he answered, "is why I wanted to stop thinking. Why I wanted to stop everything."

The French door opened, and the moment broke. Matron's voice said, "Nurse Weekes," her tone like the rap of gunfire. From behind her two voices were rising in argument over the chessboard, and there was still work to be done before curfew. Jack stepped past me, because the patient must always proceed first, followed by the nurse, who must lock the door behind her. He paused in surprise when I grasped his wrist, still in the dark out of sight of Matron, my hand hot on his skin, and pressed Maisey Ravell's letter into his palm. But he stopped only for a second, then pulled away and walked obediently back toward the light.

I didn't know why I had done it. It was the wrong thing, the thing that would not help him get any better.

I've either started something, I thought, *or I've finished it.* Then I followed him back through the door.

CHAPTER TWENTY-ONE

That night, I had changed into my night-gown and was sitting on the edge of the bed, rubbing my sore feet while Martha brushed out her hair and Nina fastened her stockings for night shift.

"What dress will you wear?" Martha asked Nina. "For the wedding?"

Nina clasped a garter to a stocking and shrugged. "My mother's, I suppose."

"You *suppose*?"

"Well, she'll have to dig it up, won't she? It's in the attic somewhere. The moths may have eaten it to pieces."

"What color is it?"

"Lavender."

"Oh, that will look well on you." I could not imagine lavender looking well on Nina, but I rubbed my feet and said nothing. Martha went on. "What does it look like?"

Nina threw the hems of her skirts down over her substantial legs. "Like a dress, I suppose."

"Nina, you are the worst! What of the sleeves, the hem? Does it have lace?"

"There's lace at the throat, I suppose. I've only ever seen it in my mother's photograph, so what do I know about the hem? Who cares about hems, anyway?"

"I do! You know it's how I live, through picturing your wedding. I don't think I'll ever have one of my own. I'll be at Portis House forever."

She said this with such infallible good cheer, the same cheer with which she scrubbed bedsteads and mopped tiles, that I couldn't help but look at her curiously. "Doesn't it bother you?"

"Doesn't what bother me?"

"Being stuck here. So far from home. From anywhere. In this place."

She had finished brushing her hair, and she set the brush on her nightstand. In the light of the bedside lamp, the marks of tiredness and hard work faded from her face. Her dark blond hair had been carelessly tossed over one shoulder. "It isn't so bad here," she said, "especially in summer. This is a good job."

Don't you see the ghosts? I wanted to ask. *Don't you hear the nightmares?* But Jack had said the nurses and the orderlies never saw or heard things. Only the men, who were mad in the first place. To try to convince these two of what I had seen seemed pointless — an attempt to make them as frightened as I was.

"Besides," said Martha, "you said yourself that you don't have a beau."

"No. I most definitely don't."

"Well, some of us are just destined to be lifelong nurses, that's all. It isn't easy to be a married nurse, you know." She lifted her chin. "We're dedicated to our calling. Like Boney."

"Or Matron," Nina said.

"No," Martha replied. "Matron was married."

"What?" I shot back up in bed.

Martha's eyes widened as she saw our expressions. "Boney told me. She really isn't so bad, you know, if you give her a chance. Anyway, Boney said Matron used to be married, and she even had a son. But he died — Boney wouldn't say what happened, but I think it was very sad — and her husband either went away or died. I don't know which."

We all digested this for a long moment. Matron, mannish Matron, had had a son?

"Well." Nina's voice was gruff. "She's a career nurse now — that's for certain."

"Like us," said Martha.

I sighed and swung my legs up on the bed, lying down. "That's very flattering, Martha, but I'm sorry to say I'm not going to be a lifelong nurse." And I *was* sorry, now that the words came out. It was nice to have at least one person's good opinion. "I already have incident reports against me, and the chances are Mr. Deighton is going to sack me when he reads them."

Martha gasped, and even Nina stopped and stared at me. "I've never had an incident report," Martha said.

"You'll get us all in trouble," complained Nina.

"You won't have to worry about it after I'm gone." I lay back down and put my arms behind my head, pretending that raw, naked fear wasn't eating at me as I said it. "Perhaps as my last act at Portis House I'll ask Boney how she gets her hair so yellow."

Martha giggled guiltily, but Nina said, "It's natural."

"It never is!" said Martha.

"If that color's natural," I said, "I'll eat my cap."

"It's true," said Nina as Martha got into bed and turned her lamp down. "Where would she get hair dye in a place like this? Besides, her mother came to visit once and her hair was *exactly the same.*"

Martha was laughing through her nose. "Kitty, you have to eat your cap."

"Shut up," I said, throwing my hairbrush at her, though she parried it easily. "You eat yours if you're so convinced."

"Don't leave like the others," said Martha. "I like you."

"More fool you, then," I told her, blushing in the dark. "Go to sleep."

I found the clearing just past the trees, as Maisey had described. At some point, perhaps, the lady of the house had set it up as a pretty garden spot: Two wrought-iron benches were arranged at right angles to each other, looking off toward the marshes and the sea, as if guests would come out here for tea. But the lady and her guests would have had to make their sweaty way over the uneven ground, covered in clumps of grass and overgrown weeds, as no path had ever been built. The place looked disused, abandoned and left to rot.

I arrived only a few minutes past two o'clock, having successfully strong-armed Matron into giving me an hour off as Maisey had suggested. I pulled off my cap and apron as I walked, liking the feeling of shedding them even for a few moments.

A red-haired young woman sat on one of the benches, wearing a smart tweed jacket and matching skirt. Her hair was pinned up in effortless style, her gloved hands in her lap, but the ladylike impression was ruined by the wisps of red hair that escaped to frame her cheeks, the hat that sat crumpled and forgotten on the bench next to her, and the mud-splattered bicycle that had been propped carelessly against a nearby tree. She rubbed a gloved finger nervously up and down the bridge of her nose and jumped to her feet when she saw me coming.

"Oh, hullo," she said. "You must be Kitty, then."

I nodded and took her outstretched hand. She froze when I came closer. She stared at the marks on my neck. I nearly flinched, but I held myself still.

"Oh," she said. "It's happened to you."

"I'm fine." I looked around the clearing, which was overgrown with weeds. "I've never been here before," I said.

"Hideous, isn't it?" She recovered herself and smiled at me. One of her front teeth was crooked, just enough to make her face look charming and off-kilter. "It was one of Mrs. Gersbach's projects. She thought she'd have garden parties. But the wind comes in terribly off the marshes, and there's no view to speak of, so she abandoned the idea."

I blinked. "You knew the Gersbachs."

"Oh, yes. I came here scores of times. We're getting a bit ahead of things, though I do want to tell you all about it. I want to tell you everything."

She was keyed up, excited. Her fair complexion, so easily aggravated, was flushed. I looked past her shoulder again at the bicycle behind her. "Did you ride that here?"

"Oh, that?" She glanced at it as if she'd forgotten. "Yes, of course. You can ride one over the bridge if it isn't too windy, though it's jolly hard on the legs."

I stared at it. I'd never ridden one. We didn't have much use for them in London, where you walked, or took the tube when you could afford it, and anyone trying to ride a bicycle through the crowded streets would be taking his life in his hands. "Do you ride it in *skirts*?"

Maisey shrugged. She really had ridden in skirts, I realized — she must have hiked her hem up over her calves to do it. I looked her over again. She was careless but not slatternly, sporty with her sun-red nose and windblown hair. I would never have ruined such an expensive suit by bicycling across a bridge in it, but her thoughtlessness suggested she had a closet full of even nicer clothes.

We sat on the benches, and I riffled in my pockets before I could forget. "Here," I said, holding out the locket.

"Right." She took it from me, rubbed her thumb affectionately over it, and dropped it in her pocket. "Anna Gersbach gave it to me, you know. You can keep the boots."

I flushed. "I told you in my letter I'd pay you for them out of my salary. And the book is just a loan, until I'm done reading it."

She shrugged again. "It's nothing to me. Really. I can't believe they fit you so well. I never liked them much, which is probably why I left them. They're better on you."

I swallowed. The boots had been a godsend; I'd no idea how I would have coped in my flimsy shoes. But I hated to appear a charity case. "I'll pay you for them."

"All right, then." She leaned back on the bench, smiled at me again. "How are things at Portis House? You get along with Boney all right?" At my expression she laughed, an easy sound. "I can just imagine. The fireworks with an uptight girl like her."

"I don't understand," I said. "You knew the Gersbachs, but you also worked as a nurse here. I don't understand how the two are connected."

The laugh faded, and something serious flitted across her expression, something that looked quite a bit like worry. "No, I suppose you don't. I'll start at the beginning. It's what I came for." But just then her gaze rose to look at something behind me. "Oh," she said.

I turned. Jack Yates came toward us through the trees.

"Nurse Ravell, is it?" he said. "Good afternoon."

"Oh," she said again, speechless with surprise. "Mr. Yates."

Belatedly, I remembered that she'd never had clearance. She probably recognized him from the newspapers, just as I had. "Maisey, this is Mr. Jack Yates. Patient Sixteen."

Her mouth opened, closed again. The nonchalance, the easy superiority of a girl with a bit of money, had vanished. "I had heard — that is, there were rumors. But I never met —"

He was shaved and combed again, his sleeves rolled up as was his usual custom. His face was set in serious lines, and he nodded politely at Maisey. "A pleasure."

I turned to him. "What are you doing here?"

Jack didn't have what the girls I knew called movie star looks; the men I'd seen in pictures, with big, long-lashed eyes and sensual lips, looked nothing like him. His was a leaner face, as perfectly proportioned as a mathematical equation, the blue eyes striking and smart. A face that had been places, seen things, thought things, lived a life. And, I assumed, attracted a number of girls.

"You invited me," he replied. "Remember?"

"Yes, but — how did you get away without Matron seeing? Or the orderlies?"

He didn't take a seat on one of the benches but sat directly in the grass, his knees pulled up. "It's after luncheon. We're allowed to take the air. I'm supposed to exercise at the proper time of day."

An uncomfortable prickle of warning rose on the back of my neck. Taking exercise meant wandering in the gardens or the near grounds, not coming all the way out here past the trees. Didn't it? If someone saw him coming here unsupervised, wouldn't they follow and bring him back? What if they noticed he was missing? Would an alarm go up?

I remembered Matron's assurance that no man had ever escaped Portis House, as there was no means to get very far. And then I remembered Maisey's bicycle.

I tried not to glance over at it. If Jack wanted to, he could get up and take it. He was strong enough. And then he'd be gone, and whose fault would that be?

He will say anything he can to gain your sympathy, and get himself a better chance of escaping Portis House.

Maisey had gone nearly green, likely thinking the same thing. She had less to lose than I did, but being instrumental in the escape of a mental patient, especially a high-profile one like Jack Yates, wouldn't be good for her, either. As far as Maisey was concerned, she wasn't even supposed to know he was here. Still, she swallowed gamely and said, "It's nice to meet you, sir."

"I take it the bruises have healed?" he said.

She shrugged, her eyes shadowed, and glanced at my neck again. "You heard about that, I suppose."

"I did," he said, gently. "Archie didn't mean it, you know."

"Maisey," I said, "you can say anything in front of Mr. Yates. You have my word. Please start at the beginning."

She gave me one last uncertain look, then shrugged. "All right." She brushed some wisps of red hair from her face, tried hopelessly to tuck them up, and began. "Anna Gersbach — that's the Gersbach daughter

295

— and I are the same age. My papa is a magistrate in these parts and my uncle is a barrister in London — he met the prime minister at two separate suppers — so it was decided that I was an acceptable companion for Anna. The Gersbachs were so wealthy, but they were, you know, not English. It was hard to find someone equal enough."

"Go on," I said.

"It was a bit awkward at first, because Anna's English wasn't perfect, but she improved, and after a while we were friends. Wonderful friends. Like sisters, really." She pressed her fingers to her mouth for a moment, then continued. "She was a sweet girl, and lonely. They'd moved here when she was a child, so she had no one. Her father wanted to live on a big English country estate, so he picked them up and moved them here. I don't think they had anyone back home, either. They seemed . . . isolated, as if they lived in their own world. It was just Anna, her brother, Mikael, and their parents. I was Anna's only friend.

"I came here almost every week, because Mr. Gersbach didn't want Anna coming to the village. He was strange about rules — a little frightening, actually. He never came to see us when I visited, and neither did Mrs.

Gersbach. She was always ill with something or other. Mikael was older — he'd come and spend time with us sometimes. He was sweet and kind, and I liked him. But mostly it was Anna and me. We'd go walking, or ride our bicycles, or read books to each other, or on rainy days we'd just sit in her room and talk — she had the nursery to herself; Mikael had a room on the second floor, where the men stay now. At first she liked to talk because it helped with her English, but after a while her English was just fine and we talked anyway. We talked about dresses and hairstyles and getting married. Girl things, you know."

I didn't, but I nodded anyway. Jack had stretched his legs out and was leaning back in the grass, listening.

"Then the war came," said Maisey. "Anna barely noticed it. The Swiss were neutral, but the Gersbachs spoke French, and Mr. Gersbach saw himself as an English lord. He said the Germans were butchers, and that if he had been young enough, he'd go fight them himself. As for me, I waited until I was of age, and I told my parents I wanted to be a nurse."

"So you really are a nurse?" I broke in.

"Yes, of course." Maisey looked puzzled.

I felt myself going red. "It's just — the book."

"Oh, that. I knew they would only be shell-shock cases at Portis House, not casualty cases. I didn't want my skills to get rusty, that's all. Of course I'm a nurse. You can't pretend that sort of thing — that would be mad."

I said nothing, but I thought I saw Jack smile.

"I left for London in the spring of 1916," Maisey went on, "to train. Anna and I wrote each other nearly every day at first; I was horribly lonely in London, and of course she was at Portis House with no companionship at all. We told each other everything. She wrote that Mikael had joined the army and was being sent off to Belgium, that he hadn't wanted to go, but their father had told him he had no choice. He said his son would do credit to his adopted country and family name. There seemed to be some sort of awful scene over it, though Anna didn't really explain. She was even lonelier after Mikael left. She seemed depressed. She said it was awful here. I asked her if there was anything else wrong, besides her worrying over Mikael, but she said no. She wrote me less and less often, but still she wrote. And then she stopped."

298

"Stopped?" I said.

Maisey bit her lip again, her eyes worried. "Just stopped. Suddenly there was nothing. After all those letters, after years of confidences. Nothing."

"So they moved," said Jack.

"Moved?" said Maisey. "Mr. Gersbach built this place. This was his English estate, he called it. They'd lived here for only ten years. She would have told me something big like that. And she knew where to find me. Why didn't she still write me?" She shook her head. "I wrote her letter after letter, but she never answered. That's when I knew."

"Knew what?" I said.

"That something had happened to her. If Anna could have written me, if she was physically capable of it, she would have. The fact had to be that she *couldn't* write me."

Jack pushed himself back up into a sitting position, drawing up his knees again. "All right. I'll admit that's strange. What do you think happened?"

"I don't *know.*" Now Maisey's voice conveyed real anguish. "Her last letters hadn't concerned me overmuch at first, but when I reread them, they're so horribly downcast and gloomy, as if something was wrong. Papa wrote me that the Gersbachs

299

had left, but I heard that no one had seen the trucks move out." She stopped, went on. "He said they were opening a hospital here. I was working in London by then — the war was over. I took a few days' leave and came back to see for myself. There it was, clear as day: a hospital moved into Portis House. I couldn't believe it. Everyone thought it curious, but the Gersbachs had been standoffish, even snobs. They kept to themselves; they never made friends. Half the town thought they must be German. No one much cared what had happened to them. Except me. Anna was my friend, my true friend. Something had happened to her. Something horrible."

Maisey was close to tears. I remembered the face in the locket. That must have been Anna, a keepsake given to her friend. I wondered what it felt like to have a friend like that, a girl who was like a sister. It must be wonderful. And what would I do if I had such a friend and she disappeared? The answer was obvious. "So you applied for a job at Portis House," I said, "to find her."

Maisey nodded. "Matron took me on. I resigned my position in London, and Papa sent for my things. I told Papa the war was over, the men were coming home, and someone had to help the shell-shocked ones."

"He didn't want you looking into Anna's disappearance," Jack said.

"No. We fought over it. He said it was over, the Gersbachs had left somehow, Anna had forgotten about me, and that was all. She was just a girl, and girls forget. He thinks girls forget their best friends." I'd never had a friend like Anna, but even I knew that was wrong. "So I pretended I'd let it go for a while, and then I told him I wanted to work at Portis House. He never suspected. He was just happy I wanted to work somewhere close to home."

I leaned forward on the bench. "Maisey, have you heard anything about ghosts at Portis House? Anything at all?"

Her eyes widened. "Never," she said. "Not until I started working there. I had spent many nights at Portis House, you understand. It wasn't haunted. We never even joked about it. But after I came back . . ." She looked down at her lap, where she twisted her gloved hands together. "The staff talks, you know," she said. "And the house had changed. They'd closed off the west wing. Mr. Gersbach's library was an isolation cell. The gardens were overgrown. The entire house is — it's *rotting* in some weird way. It was never like that before. It was a new house. There was never as much as a scratch in the paint when I stayed there. Now the plaster is falling from the ceiling in the west wing. And the feeling is different. As if there's something wrong. I asked about the Gersbachs — I tried to be subtle — but no one knew anything. And then Matron put me on night shift . . ."

"What did you see?" I asked.

"There were sounds in the lav," Maisey answered. "There was something awful about it; I didn't even want to go in. I started thinking about Anna, wondering how she would feel if she saw her home like this, if she were here to see it being used as a madhouse, falling apart, a place of so much misery and suffering. And I started imagining that Anna really still *was* there, in the house somewhere, watching me."

She stopped and dashed at the tears that had started in her eyes, then continued. "It started to feel real, as if she was trying to tell me something. I thought if she was haunting the place, it meant something terrible had happened to her, something unthinkable, and now she couldn't rest. Then Mr. Childress had that awful nightmare, he started screaming, and —" She pressed her hand to her mouth again. "I know he didn't mean it, but it was so terrifying. And on top of everything else I was thinking, I didn't know what to do. So I lost my nerve. I packed a bag and got on my bicycle and went home."

I leaned back on my bench, my shoulders sagging. She hadn't actually seen the ghosts, then. "That was two weeks ago," I said.

"Yes." She sighed. "I've recovered now, and I've had time to think about it. I realize my imagination got away from me, and I'm no further along than when I started. But when you wrote me, I thought . . ."

"You thought Kitty could continue the investigation," Jack said.

Maisey blinked. She seemed surprised he'd spoken, but then I realized she'd noticed the use of my first name. "I don't know. I just know that nothing has been answered, and now I've gone, and perhaps — perhaps if you heard anything, if you found any answers, you could tell me. Perhaps they got sick? All of them?" She looked at me with pathetic hope in her eyes. "It could have happened. But then, who buried them? If Anna is dead, I want to pay my respects to her grave."

"I don't know," I said. "I heard that Mr. Gersbach dismissed all the servants."

"What?" Maisey shook her head. "I didn't

know that. Would he have done that if the family was ill?"

"He told the servants they were moving."

"Then why didn't Anna tell me?" She looked helpless. "When I came home I heard that Mikael died in the war, that he was shot in some horrible way. Sweet, kind Mikael. Then I heard another rumor that he came home after all. I don't know which one is true. Anna never wrote to me about it. If Mikael had died, it would have devastated her."

"I promise, if I find out anything, I'll let you know."

"If *we* find out anything," Jack said. He was still sitting in the grass, listening, looking at me.

"Jack," I said, "it's too risky. You said it yourself."

"And you talked me out of it, remember?" He turned to Maisey, who sat tongue-tied. "Nurse Ravell, if I gave you some letters, would you take them to the village and post them for me?"

I opened my mouth to protest, but Maisey said, "Yes, sir."

"And if the replies were sent to you, could you keep them hidden and bring them here to me somehow?"

"No," I said.

Jack turned to me. "Mikael Gersbach," he said. "If there's a record, no matter how secret, I can find it." His blue eyes sparked. "England's fallen hero is owed a few favors."

"I could bring the replies here," said Maisey. "To this spot. I could come early in the morning and leave them tucked under this bench here, where no one will see them."

Jack stood, brushed the grass from his clothes. "I'll check the spot on my morning run. I'll put my letters out tomorrow morning. If you bring me a reply, wait two days and come again in case I have another."

She sat up straight, her tears drying. "Yes, sir."

"I hope it isn't too much trouble, on that bicycle of yours." He turned to me with half a grin on his face. He knew exactly what I'd been thinking.

"This is a terrible idea," I protested.

"That's too bad, because it's yours." He looked down at me, the sun changing the shade of his dark hair, the wind tousling it against his temples. "Besides, it's no worse than what you're planning."

"I have no idea what you're talking about." How did he *know* everything?

"Yes, you do. And if you're going to do it, you'll need my help. Don't try it without me. And now," he said with perfect solemnity, "exercise is over. Paulus said there'd be fresh pears at tea this afternoon, and I want to know if he was lying. Nurse Ravell —" He nodded good day to her stunned expression, and jogged back off through the trees.

"He seems . . . rather well," Maisey said. "I don't think he was like that when I was here."

"Oh, God," I replied. I'd just given a mental patient access to a bicycle, an accomplice, and private mail. *Just because a man has lost his sanity does not mean he is incapable of subterfuge. In fact, they have no moral qualms at all.* "What have I done?" I said to her. "I've enlisted a madman to help me. Now what should I do?"

"I think you should let him help."

I stood and walked the way Jack had taken, peering through the trees. As he approached the house, Paulus Vries appeared, and another orderly, and another; they'd been looking for him, then. They fanned out in a tense semicircle around him. Jack paused, and then he spoke. One of the orderlies answered. Jack spoke again, and one orderly laughed, and then another. The tension vanished and the four of them walked back to the terrace. Just like that.

I'd enlisted him, but it didn't mean I

could control him. Matron couldn't control him; neither could the doctors. Jack Yates followed only the rules he chose to follow, and only when it suited him.

And now he was working for me.

CHAPTER TWENTY-TWO

"Sleeves," said Matron.

Martha, Nina, Boney, and I stood before her in a line. As one we held out our arms, clothed in the long sleeves we'd fastened on that morning, rows of starchy whiteness hanging parallel in the air.

Matron walked from one end of our short line to the other. Her brow was tensed, her gaze malevolent, a look that meant she was seeking something to criticize. It was another inspection, but this one was not in honor of the doctors.

We'd been hard at work since six that morning — even Nina, who had been given permission to finish night shift at two o'clock and get four hours' rest. We had scrubbed, polished, straightened, hauled linens, dusted, aired every man's room and changed his bed linens — all nineteen of them. My legs were shaking with exhaustion, but it didn't seem quite as bad as when

I'd first started. Perhaps I was getting stronger.

"This is an important day," Matron announced to us, Henry V rallying his battle-worn troops. "This is visitors' day. The day in which members of the outside world come to the inner confines of Portis House. The day in which we make an *impression*."

Behind her, something clanged in the kitchen and someone cursed.

"I cannot express to you," Matron continued, ignoring the sound, "the importance of our conduct today. There will be no breaks. No socializing. Any breach of the rules absolutely will not be tolerated." I thought perhaps her gimlet gaze rested on me as she said this. "Sloppiness is inexcusable. Rudeness is inexcusable. You will speak to our visitors only when spoken to, and only in polite tones. The patients who do not have visitors may be unhappy and may misbehave. It is your duty to see that any such displays are kept from sight and sound of our visitors. If this is not followed, Mr. Deighton will hear of it. Do I make myself clear?"

We stood silent. I swallowed past a lump in my throat.

"You are experienced nurses," Matron said. This time she did not look at me. "Be aware. Be vigilant. These men are our patients, but they are also insane. The insane can be crafty and mischievous, especially on days like these. The orderlies are also on extra guard. You know what to look for. Be sure you recognize it."

"Yes, Matron," said Boney.

"Very well. This is the list." Matron took a piece of paper from her pocket, unfolded it, and read to us the list of men who were to have visitors that day. "Mr. Hodgkins. Mr. Derby. Mr. West. Mr. Creeton." She folded the paper and put it away again.

"Thank goodness it's Creeton this time," Martha said to me in a low voice as we walked down the corridor after dismissal. "He's always the worst to make trouble on visiting days."

"I don't quite understand Creeton," I ventured. Creeton was, without exception, the patient I avoided as much as possible. "He doesn't seem quite insane to me. Just angry."

"You haven't seen how angry he can be," said Nina. "I heard that at the casualty clearing station they had him in, he shot at one of the doctors with a gun he stole from the Germans."

"He what?"

"He missed," Martha put in. "But he had

a gun he'd taken from a dead soldier, and he shot it sure enough. I heard it from another nurse I know. She said he had a breakdown after his squadron was attacked with liquid fire."

I'd heard of liquid fire, petrol sprayed through hoses and lit. It didn't bear thinking about. "And his family hasn't visited him in all this time?"

Nina shrugged. "Most of the families don't. They're too ashamed. Except for Mr. Derby — his fiancée comes every time."

Derby was the patient who slept on the floor of his room, as if he were in a trench. If he had a fiancée, she was in for a bit of a surprise on their wedding night. "I hope they have a competent laundress," I said, and I half meant it, but Martha stifled a giggle, and even Nina looked away quickly, as if to hide a smile.

Breakfast had finished, and the men waited in the common room. The French doors had been thrown open and a warm breeze came in, wafting on kind rays of sunshine and making the air fragrant. "The motorcars are coming," Martha whispered to me, and she and Nina went to the great entry hall at the front of the house to greet the visitors as I stood duty over the men.

"We should be allowed suits," Creeton

complained loudly from his place on one of the sofas. He seemed to be speaking to no one, or to the room at large. "A suit for just one damned day. I have to see my own father while I'm wearing pajamas."

He was keyed up, his face tight, and the other men didn't look much better. I was in charge of a powder keg, and I looked for the familiar form of Paulus, leaning on the wall outside the door in his usual position. He gave me a nod.

A hand touched my arm, and I looked down to see Tom Hodgkins looking up at me from his place in a chair. "Is someone coming today?" he asked me.

"Yes," I said. His name had been on the list. "Your family."

Confusion crossed his face, and then his expression resolved itself. "I'd like to see my mum," he said. "I think I've been away."

I had no idea whether his mother was coming, so I simply said, "Perhaps you will." This pleased him, and I looked around again. There was one face I did not see.

"Good morning," said a voice behind me.

I turned my shoulders just enough to glimpse Jack standing a few feet away, holding a five-week-old newspaper as if it utterly engrossed him. He leaned one shoulder against the wall, hooked one foot behind the other, and did not look at me.

"Good morning," I whispered back, and turned away.

"Creeton had a nightmare last night," he said.

I glanced at Creeton again. He was staring tensely at nothing, waiting to pick a fight. He had thick hands with blond hairs on the backs, with thick fingers that could curl into beefy fists. I realized he reminded me of my father. Elementary, perhaps, and rather pedestrian, but there it was; you don't normally see these things until they are right in front of you. I was glad I had Jack standing vigilant behind my shoulder, and I recalled he'd managed to position himself there the night before as well, as the men sat in the common room after supper. It must be intentional. He was either guarding me or watching me.

"Is it always like this?" I asked him. "Visiting day?"

"I don't know," he replied, "but I know it's complicated. You want to see your family more than anything. It's the thought of it that keeps you going day to day. You'd go to hell for it. But you don't want your family to see you like this."

"And what about you?" I said.

He turned a page in his newspaper. "I

have no family. No one cares if I'm alive or dead, really. Including me."

The voice held no bitterness, only a sort of blankness. This, then, was Jack in a pensive mood. "Perhaps you can get well," I suggested.

"Perhaps I could get my pills back."

"No. I told you, I destroyed them."

"I was hoping you were lying." He sighed. "It's all right. I didn't sleep too badly last night, considering I had to be up early to deliver my letters."

My heart skipped. "So you did it, then."

"Of course. But now I'll be tired when you pull the stunt you're planning."

"I'm not planning anything."

"Let me see." He slowly turned another page. From the front hall I could hear a far-off murmur of voices. The visitors would be offered tea and refreshment before the visits began. "The Gersbachs are gone. We know there were no moving vans. If I were looking into it, as you are, I would conclude that their belongings must still be somewhere in Portis House. All that furniture, all that artwork from the walls — where did it go?"

I said nothing. I kept my gaze on Captain Mabry, who was looking blankly out the window. He had no visitors, either, of course. The thought made me feel hollow.

"If the furniture is still in the house," Jack continued, "where could it be? The only answer must be the west wing, which is kept locked and uninhabited. Am I correct?"

I sighed.

"And the nurses," he said slowly, "have the keys to the west wing."

Damn him. "No, we don't. I'm not sure who has them. Matron, I think. And Boney — Nurse Fellows."

From the corner of my eye, I saw him glance up. "Boney?"

"Don't ask."

"All right, then. So you'll have to lift the keys. I'm curious to see how you do it."

Captain Mabry had looked down at an open book on his lap, but he never turned a page. "I'm not doing anything."

"Tonight, then?"

"I'm not telling you."

"Right. Tonight it is." He paused for a moment, and his voice was deadly serious. "I mean it, Kitty. You're not going into the west wing alone."

"If you want to help so badly," I said, "tell me what the men dream about."

He paused in the act of stuffing the newspaper into his pocket. "Beg pardon?"

"I think the dreams are a clue," I said, "but I don't know how. I don't know what they dream about exactly. None of them will tell me, because they think I'll tell the doctors."

He thought it over for only a second. "All right," he said. "I'll see what I can do."

Mr. Derby's fiancée was a pretty black-haired girl in a well-tailored suit of pastel green with a high lace collar who arrived alongside Derby's mother. Martha put them in the garden, where the women sat on either side of the patient on one of the garden benches, patting him with their gloved hands and discreetly wiping the perspiration of the rapidly sweltering day from their faces. For his part, Derby pulled out a piece of paper and shyly read the girl a poem he'd written, smiling when both women gently praised it.

Nina wheeled Mr. West onto the terrace. There his parents came and sat with him, his father in a suit and formal derby hat, his mother in flowing pink as if dressed for church. Both parents looked not much older than West himself, as if they'd been adolescent when he was born. The three of them sat silent, not catching one another's eyes, presumably pretending West hadn't lost both his legs and his fiancée.

Tom Hodgkins's visitor was not his

mother but his cousin. She was a stout woman of twenty-five, dressed in a suit and high-collared blouse and a hat with a feather on it, carrying a handbag as hefty as a brick. "I didn't even know he was here," she told Boney. "My mother is his aunt, his last living relative except me, and she never said. When I found out, she said she was too ashamed. Ashamed! I don't care what he is — he's blood. I got married last year and we have plenty of room. I've come to see him for myself. Blood shouldn't be in a hospital like a piece of nasty laundry."

I fought the urge to kiss her. "He doesn't remember anything," I said. "And he might think you're his mum."

"Well, bless him — I'm the spitting image of her, so if it makes him happy, it doesn't matter much to me," she said as Boney led her away.

That left me with Creeton.

Creeton's father was visibly mortified, his face red under his heavy whiskers, his eyes flitting uneasily about the room. When he glimpsed the other patients, he looked away, pained, as if every man was disgustingly naked. He cast a single, horrified glance at the bruises on my neck and looked resolutely away again. His wife trailed behind him, hard faced and grim, with the locked posture and determined jaw of a woman attending a funeral. It was not going to be an affectionate reunion.

I put them in the small parlor near the front hall. It had been emptied like the other rooms and now contained a table and three ratty chairs, the window looking out at the dry, mildewed statue of Mary on the front drive. I brought Creeton, who was visibly sweating, into the room and left as quickly as I could, stationing myself outside the door and partway down the corridor. Staff instructions had been clear: We were to give the men privacy for their visits while staying close enough to interfere if there were signs of trouble. I could hear voices from the parlor, but no words.

Boney came down the corridor toward me, tailed by Roger. "Is everything under control here?" she asked, her voice lowered.

"It seems to be."

She nodded, then sighed, crossing her arms. "Visiting day is always the worst. We've never had one go so smoothly."

"Someone always ends up crying," Roger piped in. "Or we have to sedate 'em."

"It's very difficult," said Boney. "A shame."

I looked at her. Something about visiting day had put her in a softer mood. She didn't seem in her usual hurry to get away from me, so I said, "I'd like some advice, if you don't mind."

A thin veil of suspicion came over her gaze. "What is it?"

"Matron told me the men might try to deceive me. In order to escape."

"Of course they will," she answered instantly.

"I'm starting to see that. And it made me think that I need to know better what to guard against. If a patient wanted to escape, he'd need to steal things first, wouldn't he? Are the men's belongings locked up?"

"It depends," she said. "When a man comes here, most of his belongings are kept in a locker downstairs. Money and valuables are kept in a safe in Matron's office. Only Matron and Mr. Deighton have the combination."

"What about keys?" I said. "I worry a patient could steal a set of keys, you know, and escape."

"I'd like to see a single one of them try," Roger snorted.

Boney ignored him. "Kitty, these are madmen, not criminal geniuses. A patient who stole my keys would get into the linens and the store closets. Then what would he do?"

Not Boney, then. "What about the narcotics? Or the west wing?"

"Yes, I suppose he could get into the narcotics, though I don't see how they would help him escape. As for the west wing, I suppose he'd have to get hold of an orderly's keys." She frowned at Roger. "No one wants to get into the mouse droppings and dust sheets, as far as I'm aware. If he's terribly determined, he's welcome to try."

"Nothing there," Roger agreed. He picked idly at his fingernails. "Can't say I've ever used my key, or wanted to."

Boney pressed her lips together, as she always did when about to recite a rule. "We're not to go there at all. The air is bad from disuse, I hear, and there are structural problems with the roof and the walls. It's a hazard."

They moved off. I bit my lip, calculating how to get the orderlies' keys. Because Jack had been right, of course: I planned to go into the west wing, and I planned to do it tonight.

I was alone in the corridor, and I wished I wasn't. I didn't want to be there, staring at the water stains in the ceiling or the cracks in the tiles. Time ticked by. The day was stifling, but it seemed dank and somehow cold in there. My stockings itched, and a bead of cold sweat ran down my back.

"Nurse?"

I jumped. When I turned, my eyes must have been wild, for Creeton's father looked taken aback. He was standing in the doorway of the small parlor, already halfway out the door.

"We wish to leave now," he said.

It wasn't time; the families were given an hour with the men, and barely half that had passed. No one had given me instructions on what to do. "I see," I said evasively, buying time. I approached the doorway and looked into the room.

Creeton sat on the parlor chair, his eyes downcast. I had never liked him, but something about the way he sat there, the look on his face, set off alarms deep in my spine. "Are you certain?" I asked the parents. "Visiting hour is not yet over. Perhaps you would prefer —"

"We would like to leave," Creeton's father said again. "Please show us out."

Creeton had flushed dark red. The tension in the room was horrible, unbearable. There had been some kind of ugly scene. I wished I hadn't witnessed any of it, hadn't seen his embarrassment. He would not look at me. His hands rested on his thighs. I remembered those hands on me, grabbing me.

There was no orderly anywhere, so I would have to leave Creeton alone while I escorted his parents to the door. I leaned a little closer to my patient. "Will you be all right?" I asked him.

He turned a look on me that burned with such utter hatred that I took a step back. Then he looked away.

There was nothing for it. I led Creeton's parents from the room and down the corridor. Not even Creeton's mother looked at him as she left.

"Do you have children, Nurse?" Creeton's father asked me as we walked.

"No, sir," I replied.

"Children can be a great joy," he lectured me, choosing this moment to be talkative. "We had a daughter first. She's married now. The day my son was born was different, though. I believed I'd have a legacy."

"Yes, sir." We'd reached the front hall and I hurried my steps.

"My son," Creeton's father said from behind me, "has been a disappointment. He's never had any strength, any nerve to him. I tried to instill it, but some children can't be taught. And now this." We'd come to the front doors, and he looked around the hall in utter distaste. "He went to war to serve his King and country, and he came back not even half a man. No man at all. I'll never have my legacy now." He put his hand on the door latch, preparing to leave, and suddenly I knew what words he would speak next. I opened my mouth to stop them, not wanting to hear it, not about Creeton or anyone, not from a father. "It would have been better if he'd died," he said to me, and turned away.

The words seemed to echo off the walls. The hairs on the back of my neck stood on end. I watched Creeton's parents leave and walk out into the hot sunshine as cold air crept down the back of my neck, chilled the back of my dress. "Dead is never better," I said to their backs. "Never. The war taught us that." But they didn't hear and they kept walking.

Creeton's face, the hate in his eyes.

I turned and took myself back up the corridor to the front parlor. I heard nothing as I went, saw no one. There was only silence that sucked all the air into it and left a stale deadness behind, and suddenly I started to worry. How long had I left Creeton alone? He was upset, but this was Creeton. Surely he wouldn't —

The parlor where I'd left him was empty.

I stared for a wild moment, and then I shouted, "Paulus!"

He met me in the corridor. "Creeton," I said. "I had to escort his parents out, and he's vanished."

"Bloody hell," Paulus said. "Was he upset?"

"Yes — I think so, yes."

"I'll get Roger," he said. "Go to —"

We were interrupted by a shout and the sound of splintering glass.

"Bloody hell," Paulus said again, and we both ran.

The shouts came from the common room. A pane in one of the French doors was broken, glass littering the terrace. The patients were excited. "He came right through here!" someone shouted. "Broke the glass, opened the door, and went out!"

It was the broken glass that drew my eye. The French doors were unlocked at this time of day; Creeton had not needed to break the window. That meant he had wanted to. Perhaps he'd had a fit of rage. Or perhaps —

I thought of Creeton's parents walking away toward their motorcar. One action that spilled over into another and another, like water running down a slope, inevitable.

"Paulus." This was Jack Yates. One look at his face and I knew he was thinking the same thing I was. "You need to get the visitors out of sight of Creeton. They need to get into the house."

It took Paulus a longer moment, but then he went pale. "Bloody hell — not again," he said, careful to keep his voice too low for the rest of the patients to hear. "Roger!"

"I can help," Jack said.

Paulus aimed a finger at him. "Don't you dare. I've got enough going on." Roger appeared at his shoulder, and the two orderlies quickly conferred.

Matron came in the room, drawn by the commotion. "Nurse Weekes, what is going on here?"

"There's no *time*," I said to her.

"Go," said Jack, almost in a whisper, and in a second I was through the French doors, aiming for the garden gate.

"Kitty!" Nina grabbed my arm. She was on the terrace with Mr. West, whose parents were staring at us, their eyes wide. "Creeton came through here," Nina said.

"I know," I replied.

"He broke the glass and took a piece of it."

My stomach lurched. "Get them out of here," I said. Then I ran into the garden and gave Martha, who was shepherding Mr. Derby, his fiancée, and his mother, the same order. Martha heard the urgency in my voice and jumped to it, asking no questions.

I didn't see Creeton on the grounds outside the garden. I walked quickly through the weeds and called his name, receiving no answer. But I knew where he was going. It was where the others had gone.

His white patient's uniform stood out against the shadows on the grass in front of the isolation room. I called his name again, and broke into a not-quite run; I didn't want to approach him too quickly in case that sent him over the edge. He turned and watched me coming, and when I got close enough to see, he raised one hand and put the jagged point of the large shard of glass he was holding against the soft spot of his throat.

"Go away, Nurse Weekes," he said. His eyes were strangely calm.

I was entering the shadows of the west wing now, choking on the oppressive air. "Creeton, don't!" I shouted.

He dug the glass farther into his neck. "Don't come closer. Do you think I won't do it?"

I stopped where I was. Even though I'd known what he was planning, the sight was still shocking. *This is not a nightmare,* I thought. *This is real.* There may have been shouts or movement far behind us, but I didn't turn to look. It was just the two of us, the day's heat a living thing even here in the shadows, where it pulsed over us and intensified the sour smell of this place. "Please," I managed. "I know that was difficult. But —"

"Where's my Luger?" he said.

"What?" The word meant nothing to me.

"They took it from me when I came here," he said. "I know they have it. I'd rather use a gun than this piece of glass, but if I have to I'll make do." He laughed.

"I can't do that," I said helplessly. "I can't get you a gun."

"You mean you won't." He laughed again, and his gaze darkened when he saw Paulus, Roger, and two other orderlies fan out around us in a circle.

"Put it down," Paulus said.

Creeton's knuckles whitened on the shard of glass. "I can see I'll have to be quick."

He would do it, I knew. It would be messy, imprecise, and it might not even kill him; but here in front of everyone he would do his best to shove that piece of glass into his neck, just like the men who had stood here before him. "Please, for God's sake, stop!" I cried. "It's this *place*, Creeton — can't you feel it? It's this place that's wrong."

He gave no sign that he heard me. His

gaze wandered over the orderlies, who were pressing in closer. "My father fought in the Boer War," he said. "I would have liked to show him my Luger. Maybe then he would be proud of me." He looked directly at me and screamed, *"Give me back my Luger!"*

"Put it down!" Paulus shouted again.

"Do you think you can *help* me?" Creeton said to me, his eyes blazing with a sick, despairing triumph. His knuckles whitened on the shard of glass again. "Nurse Weekes? With your *caring*? With your *concern*? Do you actually think you can help me? Do you actually think you can help *any* of us?"

"What does he say to you?" I asked him, locking my gaze with his. His was so mad I almost felt the madness coming out of him and blooming inside me. "In the nightmares, what does he say? Does he call you a coward?"

His mouth went slack with shock.

"Dead is never better," I said, the same words I'd said to his father's retreating back. "Never."

His pause lasted only a second, but it was long enough for Paulus to come up behind him in three huge, long strides and deliver a powerful kick to the back of Creeton's knees. Creeton overbalanced and fell forward, the glass falling from his hand. The

328

orderlies were on him before he could move.

"You'll want to cooperate with us now," said Paulus calmly as another orderly unfolded a straitjacket. "Off we go."

Creeton struggled only a moment, and then he went slack, facedown in the weedy grass. The orderlies moved his limbs as if he were a heavy rag doll. I looked around and saw Matron some twenty feet away, watching, flanked by Boney. Matron hurried forward, a needle ready in her hand.

The gardens and terrace had emptied. Martha and Nina were presumably inside keeping the other patients quiet, though I could see faces pressed to the glass of the French doors.

The orderlies rolled Creeton over to put the jacket on him. His eyes were open and staring at me. "Go to hell, Nurse Weekes," he said, and he closed his eyes as Matron bent over him and they put his arms in the sleeves.

"It's called a relapse," Roger told me after they'd put Creeton in his room, sedated. "When they top themselves. That's what they put in the letter. 'We regret to inform you your son died after a relapse,' or some such nonsense. They never just say they did themselves in."

I remembered this as I sat in a broom closet, where I'd ducked in looking for a bucket, thinking I was going to throw up. I hung over the dingy bucket, my clean sleeves getting dirty, but nothing happened.

I can't do this, I thought. *I can't, I can't.* I couldn't stop shaking, and my stomach turned again and again. I prayed that no one would come in here, that no one would see me like this.

This house was a vampire, feeding on the pain, the insecurity, the despair of these men. It was feeding on Creeton, it was feeding on Archie, it was feeding on Mabry and Jack. It knew my weaknesses, my fears, and it was only a matter of time before it fed on me. I let go of the bucket, put my head in my hands, and surrendered to my own madness, the madness of this place.

It was killing them, and it was winning. And soon, there would be no time.

Chapter Twenty-Three

In the end, it was easy to get the keys to the west wing. The orderlies had two sets, but at night only one orderly was on duty. After Paulus had gone off shift, I simply walked into the empty orderlies' room next to the kitchen, took the second set of keys from the latched cabinet where Paulus had put them, and walked out again with no one the wiser.

It was late. None of the visiting families had elected to stay the night. Nina had already started night duty, and Martha was asleep. After the afternoon's morbid excitement, Portis House had settled into a dark, quiet night.

I had been debriefed for over an hour by Matron. She had questioned me closely about the exact sequence of events, including the moments I had left Creeton alone. She had written down everything I said for her report. I answered her with numb truth, too tired to consider prevaricating. If I was in trouble, so be it.

But it seemed that I wasn't to be blamed this time. Creeton's parents had left before the appointed time — when an orderly was due to arrive and help — and I had been left with no assistance. Creeton had given no outward signs of suicidal distress, though likely he had been planning it even as I asked him whether he was all right. The mad, as Matron had told me, could be duplicitous.

I was worried that Creeton would be put in the isolation room. Haunted or not, it seemed to be the worst place to put a man who had just tried to kill himself. But when I'd asked Matron, she informed me that "standard procedure" in these cases dictated the patient be placed in his own room, under restraint and sedation, until "his mind has cleared." I remembered that she had dealt with exactly this situation several times already, and I wondered whether she was tired of it. Tired myself, I asked her if she ever thought about why the men kept choosing that particular patch of grass.

"Men who live in close quarters influence each other," she'd replied. "Once one man had tried it there, I knew the others would follow suit. It becomes a sort of group delusion. Madness makes a man's mind more susceptible to such influences. Does that answer your question, Nurse Weekes?"

"Yes, Matron," I'd said.

"Very good. You are dismissed."

Now I wore only my skirt, blouse, and boots, the long sleeves off. I slid quickly down the corridor in the dark, away from the kitchen, where I could hear Nathan talking, probably to Bammy. The lights had gone off and I had no lamp, but I could make my way to the stairs easily enough.

I had a bit of a bad moment before I climbed the first step. It was dark, and I couldn't see exactly where I was going. For a long breath I pictured the shirtless man and my heart turned over in my chest. But there was no breath of cold, only a damp, mildew smell. I had to put exhaustion and fear behind me and push forward. I placed one foot after the other and climbed.

This was the westernmost stairwell of the main wing, and I hadn't had cause to use it before. It was yet another servants' staircase; the stairs for the family were wide and open and far too exposed for what I planned to do. The rough map of Portis House in my head said that one flight up I'd be at the farthest end of the corridors that held the men's bedrooms. That meant that, should I open the stairwell door, Nina would see me if she was doing her rounds in the wrong place at the wrong time. So I climbed to the landing and stopped, holding my breath and listening.

"Kitty."

The breath heaved out of me and my knees buckled, a whistling sound coming from my throat.

"Jesus!" It was a whisper, hoarse and low. "Jesus, I'm sorry."

I clutched my chest like a heroine in a Victorian melodrama. "Jack."

"I'm sorry," he said again, and he moved out of the dark toward me. I could faintly see his white shirt.

"What are you doing here?"

"Waiting for you." He came closer again. "Are you all right?"

"Once I can breathe, yes, I will be."

"I mean after this afternoon." I couldn't see his face, but I could hear concern in his voice. "That wasn't a very good scene with Creeton."

I swallowed. "I'll survive."

He was quiet for a second, and I wondered whether he was thinking of his own suicide attempt. "I wish you hadn't seen that," he said finally. "I wish there had been a way to save you from it."

"That's very gallant, but as Matron made clear, it seems to be part of the job."

"She at least told you that you did well, I hope?"

That surprised me. "Did well?"

"Kept your head. Took action. Kept him talking."

Even in the dark, I stared at his shadow in amazement. "Matron? No. She said nothing like that." The topic was making my cheeks burn, so I changed it. "You haven't told me why you're waiting for me in a stairwell at night."

He shrugged. "I waited last night, but you never came. I'm going with you, Kitty — I told you. You can't get rid of me."

My nerves jangled, but I had to admit that, after everything, I didn't really want to do this alone. And yet . . . "How did you know I would come this way?"

"This is the way, isn't it? The only one left."

It was. There were multiple doors and doorways throughout Portis House, of course, that would take a person into the west wing; every one of them had been discreetly and tidily boarded or bolted shut with hammer and nails. A safety precaution, as the west wing had become a hazard. The only entrance left was this one, past the stairs and across a gallery, through a door that was merely kept locked.

I listened at the door again, but Jack said, "She isn't doing rounds. She's counting linens."

I turned to him. "What's going to happen when she checks and sees you gone?"

"She already knows. I told her I couldn't sleep so I was going for a run."

"Going running? *Now?*"

I almost saw his shrug. "I have authorization. I told her I wanted to go now. What is she going to do?"

What indeed? Nina would not gainsay Patient Sixteen.

"I could have put my pillow under the bedcovers to look like I was sleeping," he said, a grin in his voice. "But she would never have fallen for it."

No, she wouldn't. "We'll have to be silent as we go through the gallery," I said. "I've stashed a lamp in there. I've got the keys."

"Clever *and* beautiful."

I stared at him.

"What?" he said.

"Nothing," I replied. "Let's go."

"One question," said Jack, who was lighting the lamp as I unlocked the door. "Why

336

didn't you do this when you were on night shift?"

"God, no," I replied in a whisper. "The night shift nurse has to do rounds and count linens. She can't get away. And Roger watches like a nanny."

He raised the lamp, and now I saw him in its globe of light. "This hasn't been as easy as you thought it would be, has it?"

"Not even close," I admitted. "What is that smell?"

I had swung open the door to the west wing, and we stepped through, pushing the door shut behind us. Over the smoky odor of the lamp I could smell dampness, mold. It was the smell of the black mold from the men's bathroom.

Jack caught my hesitation. "It's just rot," he said. "Wood and plaster. I don't smell anything dead."

He'd know what death smelled like, of course. I thought of the Gersbachs and all that was at stake and made myself square my shoulders and lift my chin. "Give me the lamp."

"No. I'll lead. If there's a hole in the floor, I'd rather go through it myself than watch you do it."

"Is that supposed to be heroic?"

He grinned. "Follow me."

We crept along the first corridor. Portis House had always seemed decrepit and unwelcoming to me, but as the only door out of the west wing receded, the rest of the house started to seem like a bastion of comfort. There was no other way to put it: The west wing was falling apart. Plaster crunched under our feet on the warped floorboards. The beams were visible in the ceiling above us, stripes of wet black mold rotting through the plaster, which was gone in chunks. The air was still here, but for the faint sound of the wind and the furtive scurrying of something in the walls. The smell of rot was a miasma. I kept my eyes on the back of Jack's white shirt, reading the lettering over and over, and focused on where I was putting my feet.

We reached a room with only a single abandoned dresser in it. Jack set the lamp atop the dresser and opened the drawers as I went to the window, which was cracked just enough to let in a draft. I looked over the unfamiliar vista to the west of Portis House, along the coast and the marshes to the rocky shore. I spent a long moment breathing in the faint scent of clean night air and watching the few trees winking in the moonlight. How long had this day been? A year? Two?

Jack finished with the dresser, which apparently was empty, and I felt him come up behind me.

"What are you doing?" I asked him.

"Watching you." His voice came low, close to my ear. "I can't seem to help it."

"You shouldn't," I said, and I felt a lurch of fear — not of ghosts this time, but of the fact that I was so far beneath him, so unworthy. "You should find someone better."

"Kitty," he said. "You have no idea, do you, what my life was like before you came. If you did, you wouldn't talk like that. In fact," he said gently, "I never want to hear you talk like that again."

I blushed. I felt him breathing. And yet, when he touched me, I jumped.

"Kitty," he said, and sighed. He brushed the backs of his fingers along my bare neck, running them gently up the tender skin beneath my ear. Tension jittered through me and slowly began to seep away.

"You were brave today," Jack said.

My breath caught in my throat and I closed my eyes, feeling the sensation of his skin on mine. "Was I?"

"Creeton owes you a debt."

I couldn't move. I would never move again, not as long as he touched me like that. "He doesn't owe me anything." *Do you think you can help me?* Creeton had shouted at me. *Do you think you can help any of us?*

"You don't even like him," Jack said. He ran the backs of his fingers down and up again, not touching me in any other way, like a man who has found that an animal is willing to sit still for him and he doesn't want to frighten it. "I don't think you're as coldhearted as you pretend."

I sighed again. This place was strange and sinister, but we were alone — truly alone — in a way we'd never been before. I savored it. "You do not get to choose the patients you treat. Matron told me that."

"Exactly my point." His fingers kept rubbing, and I tilted my head, giving him more access. He lowered his head and I felt his breath on my neck, in the spot where his fingers were. "You smell different than you did a few hours ago," he said softly, the words echoing on my skin. "As if you had a bath."

I breathed in, taking in the scent of summer air and rot, and wished I could smell him. He would be spicy and warm. He was right; I had bathed.

He knew it. His fingertip moved softly along the edge of my hairline behind my ear. "Your hair is just a little damp along here." His mouth moved closer. "I think the picture of you in the bath, with your hair down, is the best thought I've ever had."

"You've been locked up for six months." My voice was unsteady.

But he ignored me, and as my breath rasped in my throat, he pressed his lips to the spot on my neck, soft and hot. Just a single kiss. "It doesn't matter," he said. "I'd like to know what makes you laugh. And I'd like to know who has made you so afraid."

My blood was singing and my skin felt raw. That kiss — my first — had erased everything but its own existence, the contact of skin to skin, for a perfect moment. I couldn't speak. Jack put his hands gently on my shoulders and turned me around to face him. His face, half in shadows, was intent on me.

"Is it a husband?" he asked.

"My father." The words slipped out, and I listened to them, stunned.

His gaze seemed to darken, became calculating. "I see. And is he still living?"

"Oh, yes."

He searched my face for another long moment. My heartbeat began the slow process of returning to its normal rhythm. I found I was looking for disgust in his expression,

341

but I found none. He only nodded. "All right."

He turned away and picked up the lamp. I followed him, remembering — barely — to watch my step. "What about you?" I said.

"What do you mean?"

"Do you think — ?" Suddenly I could barely choke out the words. "Do you think you could ever leave here? Do you think you are still sick?"

"I don't know." He sighed. "It was bad, Kitty."

"What happened?"

"I told you what happened. What room is this, do you suppose?"

"A powder room," I said. "And that's a bathroom over there, and if you think I'm going near it after what I've seen in the bathrooms in this house, you'll have to think again. So answer my question. The real one. What happened, Jack?"

He turned in the doorway and looked at me again. It seemed to be his turn to be reluctant, but finally he shrugged, one-shouldered. "My men died."

"Which men?"

"All of them."

He turned away again, and I followed. "So you sat in the tent with the general," I said, "or whoever he was. And they sent you home."

"Yes. And the men I'd led, the ones I'd saved, were reassigned. And while I made speeches, all of them died. Not together, of course. Separately. The last one died in the spring of 1918, of influenza. He was one of forty-eight men who died in a single hospital that day. And then it was over."

Dear God. "That isn't your fault, Jack. You must know that."

"I was *home,* Kitty," he replied. "Staying in hotels and meeting politicians. Sending more men to the Front. They died." His voice had grown as rough as a scrape of gravel. "I never asked to be sent home. But I agreed to it, didn't I? I agreed to all of it. When the Armistice came — and I realized I'd actually *lived* through the damned thing — I suddenly saw that I'd have to go about the rest of my life. And the thought was completely beyond bearing."

I haven't had my chance to die, he'd told the general. "You went over there to die." My voice was almost accusing. "You wanted it."

"No. At least, not exactly. I thought I would die, and I was resigned to it. I expected it. That isn't the same as a wish. But later . . . Later it became a wish. More

343

than that, a desire. I just wanted everything to stop. I was so goddamned tired." His voice was raw with grief. "After I woke up, I came here and I told them to lock me in a room, and in my room I stayed."

I felt sick. "But the pills."

"I wanted a way out. An exit if I needed it. Thornton is practical. I paid him quite a bit of money, after all. And I would take them, sometimes, just to feel nothing for a while. Until you arrived, and you took them from me."

We'd been picking our way along corridors, poking into room after room. Water stains dripped down the walls; plaster had fallen in almost all of them, paint had peeled, and in one broken window a very comfortable bird's nest had been built. It was the ruin of a house that has been abandoned for a decade, not for less than a year. The smell made my head hurt.

And then, ahead of me, Jack stopped. "We've found it," he said.

I looked over his shoulder. He stood before a door that was closed and locked, the first locked door we'd seen. The lock looked much newer than the door did.

"Give me your keys," he said.

I traded him the keys for the lantern and held the light as he tried each key in turn. I wondered whether I would feel a breath of cold at the back of my neck at any moment. "What if he comes?" I whispered.

Jack's hands paused. "There's nothing we can do about that," he finally answered. "If he comes, he comes. There's no stopping him. There never is."

One of the keys hit home, and Jack swung open the door.

It was a long, high room, made perhaps to display portraits or sculptures, the things rich people collected to show to other rich people. It was a room that would have overwhelmed and echoed, but it didn't do so now. It was full to the rafters, items piled and stacked along the walls, covered in sheets and jumbled everywhere. Only a narrow passage had been kept clear down the center of the room, between the monstrous stacks. I jumped as something fluttered against the far window, a bird or a bat.

We moved down the center walkway, Jack holding the lantern aloft. Under one sheet was a grand piano; under another was a thick stack of framed paintings leaning against the wall. Chairs, bookcases, mattresses, bed frames: an entire home, dismantled and stacked. If the Gersbachs had left this house, they'd gone as gypsies, with nothing except what they could carry on their backs.

"My God," Jack said softly.

Boxes were shoved between the legs of the piano, stacked in the corners in toppling piles, placed atop chairs and sheet-covered love seats. Dozens, hundreds of boxes. Jack slid a trunk out from under a table, the scraping sound loud in the silence. In the circle of lamplight, he hesitated, glanced at me. Then he threw open the lid.

The first trunk contained dishes, carelessly stacked and tumbled, the edges of the expensive china plates chipped, the handles of the teacups cracked. We opened a box full of papers — receipts, half-written letters, tradesman's bills, pages ripped from notebooks, old albums. The letters were signed in the bold hand of a man, the writing strong and clear: NILS GERSBACH. Anna and Mikael's father.

Then we opened trunks of clothes. Silk dresses, jackets and skirts, suits and ties. A woman's sun hat. A string of pearls. A dyed, feathered handbag. Men's shirts. And shoes — satiny women's heels, men's shoes polished to a flawless shine, lined up in the bottoms of the boxes as if waiting for their owners to return.

I backed away. The clothes repelled me. We shouldn't be touching them. Here were

346

the shoes of a younger man, not quite fully grown; and the shoes of an older man, conservative and well worn and polished. Something about how those shoes spoke of a living person sent my stomach sinking into a sickening drop.

"They never left," I said. As I spoke it, I knew that a small part of me had held out hope, had wanted the story to be different. "Anna, Mikael. Their mother. Their father. They never left."

Jack's eyes were equally bleak. He ran a hand over his face. "No," he said.

"I'll have to tell Maisey," I said. "No one leaves without their clothes."

"Or their underwear." Jack reached into another box and held up a set of silky women's drawers, made for a teenage girl. He dropped them back on the pile as if he couldn't bear to touch them.

We stood silent for a moment, looking at the belongings of four people who had vanished a year before. "What could it be?" I asked him. "Could they have gone under some kind of compulsion?"

"There's been no demand for ransom," he said. "That we know of, at least. And how can you subdue four grown, healthy people at once, including a grown man? Perhaps they had debts."

"Then why not sell the piano, or the paint-ings? Why abandon thousands of pounds' worth of belongings?" I looked at the shoes, paired up as if their owners had just left them. "I think they're dead, Jack. I can't help it. I do."

"Who would murder an entire family, including the children? And why? It must have been an illness. It's the only way."

"Then someone buried them." I motioned my hand around the room. "And someone did this."

"We have to find their bodies, Kitty." His voice was quiet. "You know that. We don't have a choice anymore."

I thought of the girl who had worn those underthings, a girl who was shy but devoted to her one best friend. A girl who had been excited, perhaps, to wear a string of pearls, made to look like her mother's real ones, not knowing when she put them away that she'd never need them again. The thought of it pressed behind my eyes.

And I thought of Creeton, breaking a window and marching out to the isolation room with a piece of glass. It was all con-nected somehow, the Gersbachs and the madness. Everything that was wrong here, everything that was tainted, was connected to these trunks.

"I know," I said to Jack. "I don't know how we're going to do it, but we have to find their bodies."

CHAPTER TWENTY-FOUR

The next morning the heat was already heavy, promising a stifling day. The wind, smelling of damp and salt, blew hot from the mainland, rolling off into the marshes and tousling the trees. After a morning's work, I slipped into my quiet spot outside the kitchen door and lit a cigarette, thinking about my expedition with Jack the night before. The men were taking their exercise at the other side of the house, out of sight. I had just taken my first puff when a voice came from behind me.

"I'd marry you for one of those."

I whirled. Mr. West was sitting in his chair next to a clump of boxed bushes. He eyed my cigarette hungrily.

I looked around and saw no nurses. "Did they just leave you here?"

"I asked to be alone. You don't think you're the only one who knows about this spot, do you?" He nodded at my cigarette.

"But I don't mind the interruption, as long as you'll give me one. The price of my silence, you know."

I walked over and handed him a smoke. Despite his severe injuries, West was one of the easier patients to deal with; he was quiet and not prone to arguments with the others. He wasn't bad looking by any means, and his arms and shoulders were layered with muscle from maneuvering the chair. As far as I could tell, his mental affliction consisted of quiet periods punctuated by bouts of depression so bad they completely debilitated him.

But he was in a good mood today, and as I held the match to his cigarette, he inhaled with real pleasure. "Ah," he said, his eyes drifting half closed as he exhaled a stream of smoke. "I meant it, you know. I'll marry you for this."

I smiled and took a drag of my own. "Thanks, but no."

"What is it? You don't want a fellow without legs?" His tone was teasing, not touchy, and he gave me an appreciative once-over. "You don't need legs for everything, you know. All of my other parts work just fine."

"I'm happy for you. Go use them on some other girl."

He laughed. "I would, but my fiancée jettisoned me as soon as I came home, and I don't meet many women in this place."

I swallowed. Not a week ago he'd had one of his bouts, pulled from the bed by Paulus like a sack of potatoes, tears streaming heedless down his face. I pushed the memory away. "Are you sure you told her about your parts working?" I said lightly.

"Ah, no." He took another long drag and savored it. "She wasn't the sort of girl you could say that kind of thing to." He didn't even notice my glare, he was so suddenly lost in thought. "Do you know — I don't even think I liked her very much."

"No wonder," I said, thinking of a girl who would disown a man who'd seen his own legs blown off before his eyes. "She sounds like a useless twit."

"You should pity her. She won't get any of my money." He pointed at me with his cigarette. "My family has piles, you know. You could live like a queen. My older brother died at Mons and it all goes to me."

Val, I thought. It was a word he said over and over during his bouts. I'd thought it the name of a woman, but now I knew better. "I'm too lower class for a nob like you, then," I said. "You need a girl who's been to finishing school. A girl who knows her

352

silverware. Carry on the family line, that sort of thing."

"You think I'm shamming? I'm not. How much do you think it costs to be in this place? God, the number would give you nightmares. The monthly fee is more than you make in a year."

"*This* place?"

" 'An exclusive retreat of peace and solace,' " he said, obviously quoting a brochure. " 'A place in which those of distinction can be assured they'll find the proper care.' Our families don't want us mixing with the lower classes, and they prefer to forget that we did it for years in the trenches, so they pay for the privilege. All of us here are officers except for Mac-Innes and Yates. Or didn't you notice?"

I stared at him. With no uniforms on the men, I'd had no idea. There was Captain Mabry, of course, but everyone seemed to call him Captain because he was so obviously gentry. I had no idea of the rank of the others.

"Somersham's family is in railroads," said West, ticking off on his fingers. "Massively rich, they are. Mabry's the only one from old money; his family owns half of Shropshire. Childress's father is a newspaper baron. Even MacInnes has pots of money;

his wife writes tawdry novels that sell like mad, and they live in a mansion in London. Yates is an orphan, but his parents left him their farm, and he doesn't let on but it's profitable as hell. I don't know where Creeton's money comes from, but there's lots of it. My own father is in dairy."

"Dairy?"

"Yes. Not noble, I realize, but you'd be surprised how much money is in milk and butter." He ground out his cigarette and smiled at me. "I'm your best bet, you know. Most of the men have fathers who hate them. My father pities me, but I'm all he's got, and at least I can carry on the family business."

I thought of the parents who had sat with him, awkward and unspeaking. I was reeling. I'd seen blood, piss, vomit, and naked men at Portis House, but none of it had shocked me the way what he'd just said nearly knocked me over. All my life, I'd looked at other people in terms of money. But not here. Never here. This was the only place where I'd forgotten about class.

My own cigarette burned out, forgotten, and I dropped it. Something important tickled in the back of my mind, then receded again. I liked to think of a girl meeting West, falling in love with him, caring for him, making the depression go away. But I'd lived too long in the real world for that. "Then you should go home," I said, "and learn the dairy business."

The look he turned on me was friendly, but had sadness like the keen edge of a razor. "Do you really think it's that simple?"

"No."

"I didn't think you were stupid," he agreed. "Would you wheel me in?"

"Did you know about this?" I asked Martha as we cleared the plates away from supper. "About all the money these men have?"

"I'm sure I never thought about it," she said, not in her usual good humor. "Besides, money isn't much if you haven't got your mind, is it?"

"That isn't the point," I replied. "These men are paying a lot of money to be here. A *lot.* And yet we're completely understaffed, the house is falling down, and we work twenty-four-hour shifts for barely any pay."

Now her eyes widened. "You're not a labor union organizer, are you?"

"Of course not. What I'm saying is that someone is making money from this place. Mr. Deighton, and probably the doctors, too. They're getting rich." And if that had been the plan from the beginning, there was a very good reason to get rid of the Gers-bachs.

"It's nothing to me." She put a plate into the dumbwaiter with something that was almost like force. "I'm just trying to get some work done, unlike some people I know."

I looked at her. "What's the matter?"

She put another plate into the dumb-waiter, her bottom lip pouted out now.

"Martha. Out with it. What is it?"

She looked around, saw the nearest or-derly leave with a tray of dishes, then leaned in and hissed clumsily in my ear. "You left last night."

I went cold. "What?"

"I woke up to get a glass of water and you weren't in your bed. We're not supposed to leave our room at night, Kitty! Where did you go?"

"Martha —"

"And then I talked to Nina this morning and she said Patient Sixteen went for a run last night." She looked at me balefully. "I'm not a fool, you know, Kitty. I'm not."

"I don't think you're a fool." I didn't; I had seen Martha's skills outstrip my own too many times. "It wasn't what you think. We weren't — you know."

"No." Her voice was tight. "I don't know.

356

And you — you shouldn't know. Respectable girls don't. It just — it isn't done between patients and nurses. It isn't!"

"Hush. Lower your voice. I told you there is nothing going on between us." Except he had touched me, and kissed my neck, and I still dreamed about it. "If we don't go to the kitchen for supper, they'll be looking for us. And for God's sake don't say anything."

She followed me only part of the way down the corridor, and then she stopped. "It's easy for the rest of you," she said.

I turned and looked at her. "What?"

"It's easy for Boney, because she's Matron's favorite and Matron would protect her against anything. It's easy for Nina, because she has her fiancé. And it's easy for you — you've worked at Belling Wood and you could get a job anywhere even if you do have incident reports. But this job is all I have." She looked pleadingly at me. "I can't go back to Glenley Crewe. I can't. We've no money, and it's a small place. I'm completely humiliated there. If you mess this up, Kitty — and I don't know what you're up to, but I know it isn't good — you mess it up for all of us. If you're fooling around with patients, we'll all be tarnished with it, no matter what we've done. And it matters to me. It does."

We looked at each other for a long moment after she'd finished. She stood in the dim light of the corridor, her big eyes tired, her pretty cheeks flush with misery. I hadn't thought how what I was doing would affect the other nurses. It was what I did: Look ahead, don't look down, and for God's sake don't start thinking about the people around you.

I blew out a breath. "All right. I won't get you dismissed."

"You'll stop what you're doing?"

"I'll behave," I tempered. "I'll be the soul of a good nurse."

She wanted to believe, but she looked wary. "He isn't just any patient, Kitty."

"Don't you think I know that?" I said to her. "Don't you think I know?"

The words came out heartfelt, and I watched as her face slowly relaxed, the exact moment when she decided to trust me again. I felt no better when she did it, no better at all. No, Martha was not a fool. As she walked with me to supper, I suspected the fool here was me.

CHAPTER TWENTY-FIVE

I awoke from a horrible dream I couldn't remember, something so bad I opened my eyes with my arm already thrown over the side of the bed, feeling under the mattress for my knife. Only when I had my fingers on the handle did sleep start to fall away. I pulled the knife out anyway and rolled over onto my back, exhausted and sweating, the knife resting on my stomach under my hand. I stared into darkness only faintly tinged with dawn, my breath rasping, a primitive part of my mind still living in the dream.

I wouldn't sleep again. Martha slept in the bed next to me, huddled on her side, oblivious. With barely an hour before we were to wake, there was no point in tossing and turning here. I got up and dressed. Perhaps someone was about — Nathan, perhaps, or one of the orderlies. Even a conversation with Roger or Bammy would be better than the silence in my head that left me alone with my own thoughts, my own bad dreams.

I had just picked up my boots, ready to tiptoe out the door in my stockings, when I noticed the knife still on the bed. I'd picked a filleting knife, long and razor sharp, and the kitchen had no doubt missed it. I could bring it down there, say I'd found it, innocently replace it. Instead I put it back under my mattress before I padded off down the corridor.

I descended the servants' stairs to the first landing, halfway between our floor and the men's floor. I sat on the step and took a moment to pull on my boots and lace them. The only illumination came from a high window, through which the dark was beginning to give way to an indigo purple light that made my fingers look blue and frozen as they tied the laces. In the height of the long days of summer, the sun would be up in less than an hour. It was a quiet moment, and as my dreams receded into an ache in my skull, I let myself breathe and begin to wonder whether there would be anything I could snatch from the kitchen for an early breakfast. I had finished lacing my boots when I heard the sound.

Sssh.

I went still, my breath suspended.

Sssh.

I was still bent over my knees, my hands curled motionless in the air above my feet. It was a whisper, yet it was as shrill as nails down a blackboard, and my back teeth clamped together and ground.

Sssh.

My feet were cold now, and the ends of my fingers. The sound was coming from the men's hallway, through the door several feet in front of me. I clasped my hands to my knees and looked back up the stairs I had just come down, thinking about escape. Then the sound came again and I turned back, its pull inexorable. There was no voice in my head, no fist in my stomach. I recognized it now as the dragging shuffle of feet in the corridor, one foot and then the other. Approaching.

Sssh.

It could be a patient, a sleepwalker. I could help. As the thought hit me, I remembered the last time I had had such an idea: the night I had seen the shirtless man go into the stairwell. *This* stairwell. The one I was currently sitting in.

I never see anything walk but the sleepwalkers, Roger had said.

The lamplight, still lit in the corridor at

361

this hour, flickered on the square of floor I could see through the doorway. I had no time to run.

He came into view, slender and white, the naked line of his narrow shoulders clear against the rising light. I saw him through a curious double vision, blurred yet distinct. I did not see his face. He looked down at his feet, which I saw for the first time were bare. He took one step, and then slowly pulled the other foot forward, his heels slipping on the floor. *Sssh.* The movement was defeated, despairing. *Stop,* I wanted to shout. I wanted to get the sound out of my head, wanted the vision to go away and leave me alone. *Please, please, don't look up and see me . . .*

My breath came in short, terrified gasps now, puffing before me in icy steam. My arms tingled and my hands burned hot with panic. *He wasn't this slow before,* I thought wildly, but did I know for certain? I had seen him only as he had disappeared through the doorway, had followed him only after he had gone down the stairs. It had seemed so fast at the time.

His steps now took forever, but never wavered. He walked through the doorway and onto the landing below me, then down one riser, down another. I rose and stood, grasping the railing, just as I had that long-ago night. I moved away from it, from the cold and the despair that came off it in waves, from that inexorable descent down the stairs. My own breath coming high and whistling in my chest, I ran up the stairs again without looking back. *He's doing it over and over,* I thought. *That descent. The same thing, again and again. Why?*

And something new came to me, now that I had seen him in full. I hadn't seen his face, but his body had not been the body of a grown man. His had been the sleek lines of a teenage boy, not yet twenty years old.

I switched staircases and came downstairs another way. I bypassed the kitchen and slipped out the kitchen door, no longer hungry. I saw no one, but as I stepped out into the grounds, trying to put some distance between myself and the house, I saw a solitary figure. It was Jack, heading for the stand of trees that led to the clearing. He was half in a run.

I picked up my skirts and followed. He noticed me almost immediately, turning and waiting for me to catch up. "Did you see her?" he said as I approached.

I shook my head. "Who do you mean?"

"It was Maisey, I think. I saw her come

this way, but I don't see her now. She might have left letters for me."

It was early to be getting replies to the letters he'd sent, but I followed him as he jogged ahead of me through the stand of trees around the clearing. I was glad to see him. My skirts slowed me down, and when I reached the clearing, he'd already checked the hiding spot under the bench. "Nothing," he said.

He stood and turned to me, and I almost found myself smiling. He looked rested and alert, and his gaze took me in inquisitively. I was so used to seeing him in his hospital uniform that I briefly wondered what he looked like in any other clothes. "You're up early," he said.

"I've had the strangest morning," I managed.

His blue gaze traveled over me, up and down again. "Are you all right?"

"I think so."

"What — ?" His gaze moved past my shoulder. "That's not Maisey."

I turned. Through the trees, I briefly saw the figure of a girl; then it disappeared.

I was frozen to the spot, but Jack touched my arm. "Was that the girl you saw the other day?"

"I don't — I don't know."

"I'm going after her." He started to move.

"Jack, what are you doing?"

"She might lead me somewhere," he said. He turned and looked at me. "How much damage can she do if I'm awake?"

I had no choice but to follow him as he took off at a trot. When we emerged, we saw only a flash of fabric through a stand of brush fifty feet away. "Hello?" Jack shouted, but she was gone again before we got there. We fought through the brush until we could see clearly, and then we were only in time to see her figure descend the other side of the rise. She had her back to us and she did not turn. She was slender and she wore the same simple blouse and skirt I'd seen before, her blond hair wound behind her head, her gait stately and unhurried. Her shoulders dipped behind the rise, and then her head, and she was gone.

"Bloody hell," said Jack, and he took a run up the rise, his strides taking him up the slope with no effort at all. I was still halfway up when he reached the top. "Where the hell did she go?" he cried in frustration.

I pointed. "Over there."

She'd made it to Portis House. She was back by the west wing, where I'd seen her before. There were footprints flattening the grass. As we watched, she picked up her skirts and turned the corner out of sight.

"She's not a damned ghost," said Jack.

"No." The realization drained me of fear as I stared at the trail she'd left. "And she's not Maisey, either. Let's catch her."

We ran. He was faster than me, but I'd been working hard and climbing the stairs dozens of times a day; I nearly kept up with him. We followed her trail around the house, giving a wide berth to the patch of weeds in front of the isolation room. We saw nothing, not even when we fanned out and looked from all angles.

"She can't have gone far," Jack said. "We'd see her. She must be hiding somewhere."

The sun had come up now. Martha would be getting up, would find the bed next to her empty, and breakfast would be started in the kitchen. "We can't," I said to him. "We'll get in trouble."

He looked at me. "To hell with trouble, Kitty. We have to find out who she is."

But I shook my head. I'd promised Martha only the day before, and here I was, alone with Jack Yates, outside at the wrong time of day, chasing shadows instead of working. We might have been seen already. "I can't be caught, Jack. Not again. I can't."

He spun around, his gaze looking for the mysterious girl. I backed away.

He swore, colorfully. He was very good at it.

"I'm sorry, Jack," I said, and I turned back toward the house.

No one had noticed that I had broken the rules yet again. I served breakfast in obedient silence. I told a bewildered Martha I'd had a nightmare and had gone for a walk. My explanation seemed to satisfy her.

I fed Archie in the infirmary. He looked as if he hadn't slept in days. I made a note to ask Nina to check on him more frequently, and to see whether a mild sleeping draft would be possible. There must be a way to help a tortured man get a little rest, I thought, without punching him with a drug that would fell cattle. But any draft would likely come from the odious Dr. Thornton, and God only knew what would be in it.

I'd given Archie an aspirin as a weak consolation and was heading back through the downstairs hall when Boney stopped me. "Nurse Weekes," she said.

The words sent an icy bullet of foreboding into my chest, but I kept my chin up. "Yes?"

Two spots of high anger rose on her

cheeks. "I thought you knew the rules," she said accusingly.

I stared at her, fighting dismay.

"You've been here for several weeks now," Boney said. "I thought it would be obvious."

"I —"

"But perhaps," she talked over me, "this particular rule was not *explained.*"

Now I was confused. "What rule?"

She sighed as if she'd lost count of how many times she'd repeated herself. "About visitors. They are not allowed. Especially men."

"What? What are you talking about?"

"Nurse Weekes, I'm telling you there's a man in the front parlor who claims to be your brother. Whoever he is, get rid of him."

Chapter Twenty-Six

My blood rushed in my ears. My skin burned and froze at the same time. This, I thought, was what happened when a girl was about to faint; for a second I was light-headed, and Boney's lips moved in disapproving silence, the way people talked in the films at the cinema. I followed her down the corridor, kept my feet moving when she pointed to the door of the front parlor, her lips still moving. I approached the parlor door alone, its outline jangling in my vision, the sound of my own footsteps echoing up through my body as if my ears were plugged. This could not be happening.

And yet, of course, it was. My brother, Syd, sat in the front parlor, the same room Creeton had seen his family in. Syd sat looking about him in one of the hideous chairs, a high-backed armchair with decrepit maroon upholstering over its sagging seat. The chair was angled slightly away from the window, so the fresh sunlight fell across it in a clean diagonal, and he was tapping his palms nervously on the arms.

My brother. Alive. Hope bloomed in me, sudden and fierce. Syd was home. He could help me.

He'd changed. His face looked older, his hair longer. He carried the set of his shoulders differently, as if something in the last five years had made him stand taller, and he was heavier now than the too thin boy I'd last seen.

Still, when he saw me in the doorway and smiled, rising from the chair, I knew him. This man — his brown hair, his dark eyes, his lean build, the length of his nose and the set of his chin — was unmistakably my brother.

"Kitty," he said, and put his arms around me. He smelled of sweat and the wool of his suit. He didn't smell like Syd anymore.

He pulled back and looked at me. "Thank God I've found you," he said. "Thank God."

"You're dead," I said numbly, thinking of his neatly made bed on the day he'd left for the army. "I mean — you were —"

"Did you think it? Ah, God, Kitty, I'm sorry. I should have written a letter. It was a near thing more than once. But it was madness at the Front, you know, and they censored all the letters. There didn't seem much point."

"Not much *point*?"

"I thought you might rip up like this. Kitty, for God's sake just sit down, will you?"

I lowered myself mechanically into one of the other ugly chairs and stared at him. The one question I most dreaded came out of my throat. "Have you been home?"

He sat down himself. "Yes, for months."

"Months?"

"Of course," he said. "Father's been asking for you, you know. I've been looking for you all this time. It hasn't been easy. You've led me a devil of a time. All over London, and now here. What possessed you, Kitty?"

"You can't be serious," I said.

He sighed. "We have a lot to talk about. So much has changed. It isn't like it was before. Everything is different."

"How did you find me?"

"It wasn't easy. I thought you'd have to get work, you know, so I asked in the shops. And eventually I found a shopgirl who'd worked with you at the glove factory, only she knew you under a different name. When I asked at the factory, they didn't know where you'd gone, but one of the girls told me. She'd been friends with one of your

371

flatmates, I think — I don't remember. And I followed you to your last job, at the wool factory, but someone said they'd heard you left town. That left the train stations." He smiled. "Lucky for me, the man who sold you your ticket remembered you."

I stared at him in horror. Four years of running, of covering my tracks, of false names and anonymous boardinghouses and sleeping in church vestibules — all of it undone by the ticket clerk who'd leered at me when, destitute and starving, I'd bought my ticket for Newcastle on Tyne. It would have been comical if I hadn't felt sick.

"And how did you find me from there?" I managed.

"Oh, I asked around again. These are small towns up here, and lots of people remembered you. Someone remembered you hiring a car, and then —"

"The driver."

"Yes. Surprised, he was. Said he'd thought you were coming to visit a patient."

I leaned forward, put my elbows on my knees. Syd took the opportunity to pull his chair closer. He took my hands in his, looked in my eyes. "I'm just so glad I've found you, Kitty," he said. "I'm just so glad."

I looked into his face. He was my brother,

and he was alive. Perhaps we could both run. Pool our resources, our talents. It didn't matter anymore. We could stand strong together. Perhaps, for the first time, I could be safe.

"Kitty," he said, "I'm living with Father again. He's very worried about you. He's been worried since the day you left. I have some bad news, you see."

I stared at him, uncomprehending.

He squeezed my hands, as if I were weeping. "Father has cancer," he said. "He's terribly sick. He won't last long. He's a changed man, Kitty. Sometimes I think the worry about you has nearly done him in. I've been living with him, nursing him. I've gotten to know him as a man now, as a new man. I have a good job with an insurance agent, and I can afford to support him. His fondest wish is to see you before he dies. Do you understand what I'm saying to you? Do you see?"

"No," I said.

"I'm here to take you home." He smiled at me. "I don't know how you got to this place, but I'm here to take you back with me. You can see Father and —"

I pulled my hands from his. "You can't be serious."

"Of course I'm serious. It's Father's wish

to see his daughter again."

"I'm not going back there," I said. "And you know why, Syd. You know why."

He leaned back in his chair, looking at me. "Well, I have to say it — no, I don't. We had some rough times growing up — I'll admit that. It was a bit hairy after Mother left. But you can't mean that you've held a grudge this long."

My stomach was doing somersaults. I had to remember that he'd been away, that he hadn't seen how bad it had gotten. That, even before he'd left, he hadn't been hit as often as I had and my father had done most of his dirty work to me while Syd was in the other room. I closed my eyes and took a breath.

"All right. I'm going to tell you about it this once, Syd. Just once. I can't repeat it ever again."

"What are you talking about?"

And I told him, in as few words as I could. I told him about the beatings, the chokings, the cracked and bruised ribs. I even told him, so help me, about the knife in my mouth and the night our father had dragged me from under the bed and given me the scar. And that very last night, when he'd climbed over me on the bed, pinned me down, and laughed in my face.

It was a confession, but not just of my own sins. It was a confession of someone else's sins, and for a moment it felt freeing, until I looked at my brother's face.

Syd's expression had fallen. He stared at me with shock, with horror, and it took me a moment to understand. The shock and horror were not directed at the story I told. They were directed at me.

I stopped, and we were silent. There were no voices in the hall. I heard the breeze blow in the eaves.

He turned away, out the window. Then he sighed, a hopeless sound. "Kitty," he said.

"Now you see," I almost pleaded. "You have to see."

He shook his head. "You've made this very difficult."

"It isn't difficult. It's simple."

"It's difficult because I don't believe it."

"What are you talking about?" I said. "Are you saying I'm *lying*?"

"I don't know what you're doing," he said, and he turned back to me. "Kitty, he's your father. Your family. A daughter owes her father a debt."

I pushed my chair back and stood. "I don't owe him a debt, Syd. And I'm not a liar."

"Aren't you?" He looked pointedly at the

375

uniform I wore. "False names, Kitty, false backgrounds — you lied everywhere you went. I don't know what game you're up to now but I'm not believing another of your stories."

"It isn't —" I blinked, hard. "Syd — you were there. He hit you, too. I saw him."

"That was years ago." He pushed back his chair and stood. "You don't understand. He is a changed man, Kitty. He admits he's done wrong in the past, and he regrets it. You can't know how bitterly."

"Now who's a liar?" I said. "He punched me in the stomach and called me a whore, Syd. And that was on a good night."

"You're foulmouthed, too." The corner of his mouth twisted down. "Father wants to make amends. He wants you to come back so it can all be straightened out. He's dying, and I'm his son, and for God's sake I'm bringing you back."

I looked in his eyes, and that was the rub of it: He believed it. He believed every word he said, with passionate devotion. My father probably was dying; that likely wasn't a lie. But my father had convinced Syd of the rest of it, as if he'd found a religion. Syd wanted to believe, and he'd convinced himself I'd made everything up. God knew why — but he did. I felt the hope that had begun to bloom in my chest die sharply, with a quick pain. And then everything I'd taught myself in the past four years came back to me in a rush.

Don't look back, don't look down.

This is how I am going to die.

"Leave," I told him. "Get out. Now."

The corner of his mouth turned down again. "That's not polite, not when we've just found each other again."

"I'm not going back, Syd."

"This is ridiculous. I thought —"

"You thought I'd cringe. *He* thought I'd cringe. You were both wrong." My voice was shaking, but I ignored it. "Now, *leave.*"

He made no move, so I turned and left the room, taking my unsteady steps into the main hall. The circulation in my arms and legs had been cut off but for a painful pin-pricking along the backs of my forearms. My knees had been replaced with half-frozen jelly. I hoped I'd get my body parts back when I watched Syd drive away.

If I found my brother and I lost him again, was it better or worse than never finding him at all?

"What is this?" Syd followed me into the hall. "I don't believe it. You'd rather be in this place — a madhouse — than home, where you belong?"

"Kitty?" It was Martha, approaching tentatively from the corridor. "Is everything all right?" Nina, who had come off night shift that morning, was with her.

I opened my mouth, but Syd said, "Everything is quite all right, sister."

"She's not a sister," I said.

"What is the matter with you? I've come to take you away from here. Father said you'd be difficult."

"Did he?" I said. Martha was looking uncertainly between us, and I hoped to God an orderly would come. "What else did he tell you, Syd? That we'd be reunited as a happy family? That I'd weep at his bedside like a girl in a melodrama? And you believed it?"

"He said . . ." Syd took a breath. "He said he worried about you, that last year after I was gone. He said you might be . . . delusional."

The unfairness of it hit me so hard I could barely speak. "Just get out," I managed. "Just leave."

"I'm not going. For God's sake, Kitty, you're ill. You don't even know what's real anymore. You're as mad as the rest of them."

"I take exception to that," someone said.

I turned. Coming down the corridor behind Martha and Nina were patients,

378

come to see the commotion — West in his wheelchair, and MacInnes, and Mabry. Others trickled in one by one behind them, crowding to see. And Jack, pushing his way forward through them. It was to be an utterly public humiliation, then. My chest burned, and I turned back to Syd.

He'd gone pale, looking at the men. "Are you quite finished?" I said to him now.

"Stay back," he said to the men.

Captain Mabry looked at him coolly. "I believe Nurse Weekes would like you to leave, old chap."

"I agree," said West. His arms flexed massively as hc grasped the wheels of his chair.

"Stay back!" said Syd again. He gazed at the stumps of West's legs sticking out from the seat of his chair in their pinned hospital trousers, and he looked almost sick. He'd fought in the war, and I realized he must have been seeing something in his mind I couldn't see. "Don't come any closer."

I had to defuse the situation somehow. "Syd —"

"What is the meaning of this?"

Matron came stomping down the main staircase, in the middle of all of us, her glasses bouncing on the chain on her chest and her face red with fury. Boney followed behind her, hurrying to keep up. Matron stopped five risers up and leaned over the banister, the better to loom over everyone.

"Nurse Beachcombe," she barked. "Nurse Shouldice. Why are these men not at morning exercise?"

"Matron —"

"Nurse Weekes, what are you doing? This is not part of the schedule. Who are you, sir? *Where* are the orderlies?" As she spoke the last sentence, Boney turned and fled, presumably in search of help.

"Are you in charge here?" said Syd. "Thank God. My name is Sydney Weekes, and this is my sister. Our father is on his deathbed and I've come to take her home."

Matron didn't even pause. "That is well, sir, but I have not given permission for Nurse Weekes to take leave."

If Matron had held out her hand like the Pope, I would have knelt and kissed it, religion be damned.

"That is completely unreasonable," Syd protested. "This is a family matter."

"And this is a medical facility," said Matron, "with professional staff. Applications for leave are taken through the proper channels."

"Matron," shouted one of the men from the corridor. "She don't want to go!"

Syd turned to the room at large. "This

girl is delusional!" he proclaimed. "She is a liar. She's not even a nurse!"

"She is too a nurse!" Martha's cheeks were bright red with outrage. "You just leave her alone!"

"Syd, for God's sake!" I said.

"Look what you've done, Kitty," he said to me. "You've caused a scene. Enough of this foolishness. You're just like Mother, aren't you? Father said so. It's time to leave."

I stepped closer to him, looked him in the eye. "I said I'm not leaving."

It was quick — the space of a second, and yet in my eye it was slow, so slow. It had started minutes before, really, and my mind, which knew the timing so well, had half expected it. And it wasn't much of a hit, not really, just a little slap with the flat of his hand, stinging and very loud. My head rocked back and I took a step, and for a second my ears rang and I didn't see everything that went on behind me. But I heard shouts and voices. And then someone yelled, "Go get him, Jack!" and Jack Yates vaulted out of the corridor and straight at my brother.

He didn't even look angry, just determined, like an athlete doing a sprint. But Paulus Vries had arrived, he had longer legs, and he was surprisingly fast for such a big man. He caught Jack just as he reached Syd, who fell back toward the door.

Paulus grabbed Jack's upper arms from behind, a hard grip that stopped Jack in his tracks. Syd's face was blanched with shock, but he looked past the terrifying madman's uniform at Jack's face, and recognition trickled through. "You're Jack Yates," he said.

Jack didn't struggle against Paulus; he only leaned forward a little, as Paulus's huge hands held him back, and spoke in a calm, taunting voice that barely contained the anger underneath. "How are you feeling, Weekes?" he said. "A little peaked since you got back? You seem prone to violence to me." He watched my brother's expression fall. "It happened to a lot of us. We have a room for patients like you, if you'd like. It's locked. And very, very dark."

"I'm not like you lot," Syd said. "I'm not."

Only someone watching Jack's face as closely as I was would have seen the flinch. It was gone in a second. "Stay a while and find out," he said.

Syd gripped the handle of the door, as if by reflex. His knuckles were white. He looked at Jack and swallowed. Then he looked at me, one last time, and his gaze turned hard. He pushed the door open and left without another word.

Paulus sighed, his hands still on Jack's arms, though I could see his grip had relaxed. "You didn't have to scare him, Yates."

"No," Jack agreed. "I didn't. But it was fun."

"That's enough, everyone," Matron shouted from her place on the stairs. "I want every patient in his room immediately. Morning exercise is canceled."

Jack looked at me. "Are you all right?"

"Yes," I said softly.

"Are you certain?" said Paulus. He'd let Jack go. Their scuffle may have been partly serious, but it had been a little fiction, really, between the two of them, to scare off my brother. I nodded, unable to trust my voice.

"Move it, Yates," Paulus said mildly. He turned back to me. "If you need ice, get it now. I have a feeling Matron is about to call a meeting."

CHAPTER TWENTY-SEVEN

"That," said Boney, "was unacceptable. Unacceptable."

"It isn't Kitty's fault," Martha protested. "She didn't invite him."

We were sitting around the small table in the kitchen, all of the nurses. Matron had called us here, just as Paulus had predicted, but so far she had said almost nothing.

"It was an unseemly scene." Boney looked prim and outraged as usual.

"What were we supposed to do?" said Nina. "Stand there while he carted her off? You heard Matron. She didn't even have leave."

"But the patients!" said Boney. "You left them unsupervised! And look what happened! Complete chaos. And where were the orderlies?"

"I'd like to ask them that myself," said Nina. "We could have used them."

"I think they were trying to keep the

patients from getting into the corridor," said Martha.

"Matron," Boney appealed. "Please tell me there will be an incident report."

Matron looked tired. For the first time since I'd known her, she almost sagged, as if she was carrying a heavy burden. "This day," she said, "has been most trying."

"If there's an incident report," said Nina, "it should be fair. It should say that Kitty's brother wanted to take her without leave and wouldn't go when we requested it. It should say that he struck her in front of everyone."

"That isn't relevant to the situation," said Boney. "Rules were broken."

"It was relevant!" Martha said. "We all saw it!"

"Enough." Matron raised a hand, and they all fell silent. I still couldn't speak. I didn't know what I could say.

Matron sighed. "As it happens, Mr. Deighton is due tomorrow for one of his visits. I will write a report about this situation — and what goes in it will be entirely up to me, as is the rule — and I will give it to him to evaluate. The fact is, this happened on my watch, and there may be consequences even for me. That means I cannot evaluate this incident myself." She looked around at us. "That is all I can do."

I stared at her, my heart accelerating in my chest. She was saying I'd gotten everyone into trouble, even herself. Well, she had no idea. No one was going to be dismissed. Not now, not ever. I'd made a vow to Martha, and I intended to keep it.

"This meeting is adjourned," said Matron. "Nurse Beachcombe, you are excused for rest at supper as you are due to start night shift tonight. For the rest of us, let's salvage this day."

I felt painfully visible all afternoon, as if I had a brand on my chest. The men, however, had apparently found their little rebellion quite satisfying, and when they were released from their rooms for luncheon, they were well behaved. A few of them gave me brief, half-formed smiles or quiet nods, but most of them went back to their own preoccupations. And yet I knew, of course, that in rooms where I wasn't present, among the patients and the staff alike, my scene with Syd was the talk of the day.

The men were sent to afternoon rest after tea, and I was sent on rounds. I took advantage when no one was looking and slipped into Jack's room. He was sitting on his window seat, barefoot again.

"Kitty," he said when he saw me.

"I don't have much time," I told him. "I came to thank you. And to get a moment of privacy. I'd rather not hide in the lav again."

He got up and came toward me, looking at my face. "I can see the mark," he said. "I'd like to go at him again."

I shrugged, my heart skipping. "It will fade." I looked up at him. "You're not being punished in isolation."

"No, I've been banished to my room for the rest of the day. I think it's the best thing Matron could think of. She must be off her game."

I shook my head. "Jack, he recognized you."

"I noticed."

"I haven't seen my brother since before he left for the war. I don't know him, not really. I don't know what he'll do."

"Tell the newspapers, probably." He leaned closer, looking at my cheek. "You told me it was your father you were running from."

"It was."

"You look a little cheerful about it."

"I don't know," I said, the words coming in a rush. "I don't know. I feel so light somehow, Jack. I'm humiliated and afraid, and yet a part of me feels like I'm going to

387

fly away on one of those hot-air balloons. I was so used to running and hiding. But I think now it was an anchor weighing me down. Do you think that's even possible?"

"What happened?" he asked, instead of answering me. "What has changed?"

I ran a hand over one of my cheeks, hot with emotion, wanting to feel myself, wanting to be here inside my own skin for the first time. "He's dying, Jack. My father is dying. That's what Syd came for."

Jack's blue eyes puzzled over this for a moment, and then he understood. "He thought you would go home for a tearful reunion?"

"He was sure of it." I watched his expression cloud over. "I don't care," I confessed. "I'm a bad person for being happy about him dying, and I'll probably go to hell, and I don't care. He'll be dead and he won't be able to hurt me anymore."

Jack listened to this carefully, as he always listened to me. Beneath his shirt I could see the lines of his collarbones, the warm hollow where they met at the base of his throat. If I leaned forward I would feel him breathing, feel his chest rise and fall. He looked down at me for a long moment, watching me look at him. "This seems like a good time to give you your gift," he said.

"Gift?"

He walked to his bedside table — I didn't want to look, but I noticed his bed was mussed, as if he'd been lying on it, and I pushed the picture from my mind — and took up a book. He turned and handed it to me. "It isn't much, but you did ask for it."

It was a battered copy of Homer's *Odyssey,* taken from the library shelf in the common room. I'd never asked him for a book. "What is this for?"

"Open it."

I did, and I saw pieces of letter paper between the pages, perhaps a dozen of them. I examined them.

"It was the best way," Jack said as he watched me. "These uniforms don't have pockets, and I can't leave papers around or they'll be confiscated. So instead I appear to be rereading *The Odyssey* at bedtime."

The papers were all handwritten, each one in a different writing. "What are these?"

"Our dreams," he replied.

I looked up at him, remembering I'd asked him to find out what the men dreamed about. "You got them to write down their dreams?"

"Almost all of them. Tom claims he doesn't dream, or in any case he doesn't remember them. MacInnes is a slow writer, so he's still working on his. And Creeton told me to go fuck myself."

"How did you do this?" I stared in disbelief at the pages. "I didn't see anyone writing."

"We all get paper allotments to write letters every week, but no one uses it. What can we say in a letter, after all? 'Dear Mum, all well, still barking mad. Sorry.' They read them all anyway, so why bother? As for the writing, afternoon rest or the loo are just about the only times. There's no light to write by at night. And the nurses" — he grinned — "usually check on us during afternoon rest."

I riffled through the papers. "What about your dreams?" I asked softly. "Are they in here, too?"

"They have to be, or it wouldn't be fair. Would it?"

"No."

"Then you'll have to guess which one is mine. We didn't sign them."

I folded the pages and put them in the pocket of my apron. I still felt curiously weightless and free, and I smiled up at him. "Thank you."

He blinked. "If it will make you smile like that, I'll hide in the loo and write a novel."

And just like that, the moment changed. I'd wanted to touch him since the moment

I'd walked through the door and seen him, but now he was looking at me, that deep blue gaze on me, and I wouldn't get a chance again. I put my hand on the back of his neck, rose up, and kissed him.

I'd never kissed a man before. Part of me thought it might be a quick thing, a chaste peck, but his mouth was warm and soft, and I lingered. Then he put his hand on my jaw and kissed me back, swift and hungry, as if he meant it. He didn't touch me but for his hand, didn't pull me to him, but he held me close and kissed me a second time, this time softer, but so hungry he bit my lip as we pulled apart, and his eyes when I looked into them had lost all their politeness.

"That was for being Brave Jack," I said, my voice a husky breath.

"I'd brave all the fires of hell," he said, "to see you naked."

I was shocked, but the elated part of my brain flew even higher. I wouldn't have minded the nakedness going the other way, but I didn't know how to say it, not really. Instead I put my palm on his chest, feeling the hard, steady beat of his heart, just as I had imagined it, and said, "I have to go."

He put his hand over mine, that fine, graceful hand, and pulled it from his chest. He turned my arm, bent, and pressed a kiss to the inside of my wrist, hot and lingering, as I ran my tongue along the spot on my lip he'd bitten. "Good night, Kitty," he said.

I took one unsteady step back, and then another. "Good night," I said shakily, and I left the room.

"What did he mean, Kitty," Martha said that evening, "when he said you're not a nurse?"

I was getting ready for bed, putting *The Odyssey* on my bedside table, and I stopped. In her corner, Nina didn't even pause as she undid her apron.

I looked at Martha. She was preparing for night shift after her short sleep, tucking up her hair. "Are you all right?" I said. "You look exhausted."

"It's just a headache, that's all. I've had it all day. A nuisance more than anything. But what about your brother saying you're not a nurse? That was a strange thing for him to say."

I didn't want to lie to her. And perhaps, just perhaps, she could have handled the truth. But I remembered her red-faced exclamation to Syd: *She is too a nurse! You leave her alone!* And I knew that if I spoke now, I'd make a liar out of her. Part of me couldn't countenance it.

"Matron hired me," I hedged. "Do you think she would have hired a girl who wasn't a nurse?"

"Well, I know we've been desperate for girls," Martha said thoughtfully, oblivious to how close she danced to the truth, "but even so, that doesn't sound like something Matron would do."

"Of course," I said. "My brother hasn't seen me in five years. He doesn't know the first thing about me."

She thought it over, looked relieved. "Then you're well rid of him," she said. "Good night."

Nina and I were silent after Martha left. Nina polished her spectacles. Finally I couldn't stand it. "Wonderful," I said to her. "Just wonderful. How long have you known?"

"Since practically the first day," she said without inflection. "You couldn't fold a hospital bedsheet to save your life, Kitty, and it's the first thing we all learn."

I sighed and lay back on my bed. Today was the day, it seemed, when my secrets went up in vapor. And the day I'd kissed Jack Yates. "Don't blame Matron. Mr. Deighton hired me while Matron was away, and by the time she figured it out, I was already here and she was desperate. So she

393

put me to work."

"It does explain why she had you clean that lav," Nina said.

I peered over at her. "You're not angry? I thought you'd be livid."

She sat on the edge of her bed, her night-dress bulky and awkward. "It wasn't my place to say anything," she said. "Matron had sent you, after all. And you worked hard enough. And as for Martha, well, I may as well tell you. You're not the only one lying to her."

This took a moment to sink in, and then I shot upright on the bed. "Your fiancé."

She flushed dull red and looked miserably guilty. "It was true at first — I swear it. Well, sort of. There was a fellow my mother *thought* I should marry. And she planned to have me meet him to see if we would suit. I told Martha I was engaged, because it was practically done. Almost. And I just wanted to be the engaged girl, you know?"

"Yes."

"And Martha took to it — she was as excited as if it was happening to her. And the boy Mother had picked moved away without my ever meeting him, but by then it seemed so real. I found I liked making Martha happy. She's got her faults — we all do — but she's a good girl. She's the best

394

of us, really. So that was it. I'd rather lie to her and make her happy than let her down. I just couldn't bear to let her down."

I lay back on my bed, thinking. "You had me fooled," I said.

"Kitty, I'm a horrible liar."

"No, no, you did all right. You floundered a little when she asked you about the dress, though. A good lie has to be convincing in the details."

"I guess I could take lessons." But she was snickering — *Nina,* actually trying not to laugh — and I couldn't get offended. "I'm turning the lamp out now."

I watched her do it, thinking sorrowfully of the book on my bedside table, and that I wouldn't be able to read it. "What are you going to do?" I asked her. "Eventually she's going to wonder why you don't get married."

"Kitty," she said from the dark space across from me, "I have no idea. And if you say anything, I'll —"

"Find me and skin me, yes." I sat upright in bed again, staring into the dark. "Wait a minute. If you knew about me, then you knew I was lying about having clearance to go into Jack Yates's room."

"Of course I knew it."

"And you let me go in there anyway and

get caught. And get myself an incident report."

"I'm nice," she said, "but I'm not *that* nice. Now for God's sake go to sleep."

I awoke before dawn again and dressed while Nina slept. I'd had no dreams this time, but a strange energy coursed through me. I recognized it as anticipation, though I could not have said of what. My muscles and my nerves seemed fluid, ready. There was no way I would sleep again.

I pulled the handwritten pages out of *The Odyssey,* slid them into my pocket in the still-dark, picked up my boots, and crept from the room. This time I saw nothing when I sat on the staircase to tie my boots. I slipped out the kitchen door and looked around at the horizon, which was slowly turning an eerie pink as the sun began its ascent. I half looked for a figure standing on the rise, and at first I saw nothing; the dark was too impenetrable. Then I made it out, a lone figure stark against the horizon, and I held my breath.

It wasn't Jack. It wasn't Maisey. And it wasn't the strange figure of the woman I'd seen. It was a man, soft and pudgy, his patients' whites flapping against his legs in the rising breeze.

I climbed the rise, huffing. "Tom," I said when I got to the top. "It's early. What are you doing here?"

He was looking out over the marshes, his face, as it so often was, clear of any emotion, any knowledge. He turned and glanced at me. "Oh, hello," he said. "Are you the new nurse?"

I sighed. "Yes."

"I'm trying to remember why I came out here," he said matter-of-factly. Then he pointed at the pinkening horizon. "Over there. That means something's coming."

I gazed at it. "Something?"

"A storm," he said. "A bad one."

That explained the stillness, the readiness in my veins.

"I don't know why I remember that and not anything else," said Tom. "I know I've come out here before, just to this spot. To get away from the house. It's bad in there some nights. The man comes, and he's so terribly angry."

My heart slowed to a hard, measured throb. "The man?"

"Oh, no one likes him, so I've come here before to get away. I always think I'm going to go home. I know exactly where it is. And then I walk out the door, and I stand here, and . . ." He looked around. "I don't know where I would go from here. Do you?"

"No," I said softly.

"It's so confusing. I'd really like to go home. But this . . . this seems to be all there is."

We looked at the sunrise, watching the sky grow light. It was beautiful in its way, but I could believe what Tom had said. Something bad was coming.

"Who is the man, Tom?" I asked. "The angry one."

But he only glanced at me and away again. "He's dead. Horribly, horribly dead. But you won't believe me. No one does."

"I believe you," I said softly.

"Then you'll see him when he comes," Tom replied. His brow creased and trouble crossed his features. "I think it's going to be bad."

His brow smoothed again, and the memory of whatever he had seen, whatever he had heard, left his mind. He went inside to breakfast and left me watching the slow approach of the clouds, wondering exactly what was coming.

■ ■ ■ ■

Part Three:
Nineteen Men

■ ■ ■ ■

So much is written about the war nowa-
days, and in proportion so little of it strikes
a right and wholesome note — and yet it
is so clear. It is nothing but an intimately
personal tragedy to every British (and German) soldier concerned in the fighting part
of it.

— Private A. R. Williams,
in a letter home, October 1916.
Killed in action at Ypres, August 1917

Chapter Twenty-Eight

It is June 1919, and this is the account of my dreams I've been asked to write:

At first I am sleeping and it is quiet. But I awaken and I know someone is there. In the corridor, I think. There's pressure on my chest and I can't breathe. Smell of smoke in the back of my throat that reminds me of the trenches, how it was there. That thick, smoky smell, rotten, wet.

A prickling feeling comes over me then. All over me. It's like fear, but of course I'm not afraid, there's nothing to be afraid of, just the dark and we've all spent time in the dark. But I know he's coming closer. I don't know who he is but I know he's coming, and a voice in my head says, "Coward, you are a coward." I can't move. It's horrible. He grabs me with cold hands and I know I'm going to die and I wake.

This dream is almost always the same, I don't

know why. I'm in bed, and my father comes. He's not really my father (died in Wales when I was four) and yet he is. His footsteps are terrible. He puts a hand on me, it's icy cold, he leans over me and I feel his breath. Get up, get up, you coward, get up. I try to speak. He's not my father, I want to tell him so. The man has a heavy mustache, I can't see him but I know it, and my father was clean shaven. And yet he is my father and I've failed him.

But his cold hands keep grabbing me, telling me to get up you coward, and I open my mouth to scream at him but I've got blood in my mouth, thick and warm, that taste of it in my throat, and I choke on it, and I wake.

This dream is not the truth, my father was a good man.

I am at the hosp. as I am always (that is Portis House) but I am Outside the bldg. Standing by isolation room on west side. You know that part of the house. I do not want to be there. Something v. bad about to happen but cannot move. I am going to die, I feel it. V. strange because I would not mind being dead normally (no more War in my Head) but in the dream I am v. afraid of it. More afraid than we were at the front. Impossible to explain really.

Then I realize I am not going to die but am going to see something v. bad and I close my eyes. Never closed my eyes in all the things I saw There but there you go. Then a voice comes. Kneel you coward, it says, but whether to me or to someone else I do not know. I wake v. confused. There is a bad Taste in my throat. It is like how I heard they executed some of those Poor Fellows but I never saw one (execution) myself so I don't know why I dream of it.

I hope this helps, sorry confusing but the lights are going out

I woke once and saw a man at the foot of my bed. He was young and pale and had no shirt on. He stared and stared at me. I told myself it was a nightmare but I didn't wake. My throat hurt like I'd swallowed smoke. I thought someone was coming but I didn't know who. I don't know when I woke. I told the doctors but they said it was a manifestation of my unbalanced mind and I had to have mind over matter. I never said anything again but I know I can tell this to you, Jack old chap, because you are one of us and a good fellow. I hope you have not had a similar dream as I would not wish it on anyone.

You coward, you goddamned coward. That's all I remember and lately I hear it when I'm awake too. Gunshots at night, it's a rifle, the cracks make me scream and scream like I'm there again.

He was in the mirrors sometimes. When I was awake. His face was there, cloudy, those skinny bare shoulders. I know my privileges will get revoked but I know what I saw. Yes I'm crazy but have you noticed they took out all the mirrors in this place?

. . . I think "he's coming, he's coming" and I am going to die. But the worst thing is that I deserve it, because what am I? Who am I? What am I really, what is left of a man? It's my soul that's gone. I'm sorry about the screaming . . .

"Kitty."
  "Yes?"
  "Are you quite all right?"
  "Yes."
  "You look like you've been weeping."
  "No, of course not. I'm quite myself."
  "Well, all right, if you're certain. Put on your long sleeves. Mr. Deighton is arriving, and it's time for inspection."

Mr. Deighton was somewhere in his thirties, with hair of undistinguished brown and a large pair of reddish eyes with pouches

404

drooping beneath them. He wore a three-piece suit and watch chain, the high collar and tie starched and stiff in the oppressive heat. He did not even remove his hat in deference to us but looked us over distantly, as if he'd been directed to look at a painting he found of no particular interest.

I kept him in my sight right from the first. I studied him closely from the corner of my eye during inspection, trying to appear dull and deferential while looking him over. I watched his expression for quickness, for sparks of cunning and intelligence. I listened to his words and the tone of his voice for bad temper, for erudition and intelligence. I watched the rest of him to see how strong he was, how quick he might be. I watched the leather briefcase he carried in his right hand.

I saw nothing. No sign of deviousness, or unctuousness, or evil that would indicate a man who played a very deep game. No marks of obvious ostentation or pride or money. Just a tired-looking man with a slightly weak chin and a well-made, but not too expensive, three-piece suit.

He did not pay Matron particular attention. He arrived after breakfast and took a brief cup of tea in the front parlor with Matron and Boney. Nurses' inspection came next. Then we were dismissed to our duties. I had arranged it so that my duties took me close to the corridor to Matron's office, where I could see that she was closeted with Mr. Deighton for some thirty minutes, alone, without even Boney in the room. *And that is it,* I thought. *It's done.*

They mustn't have discussed the incident from the day before, because when he emerged his face was as impassive as ever, the pouched eyes still holding their distant expression. Matron, behind him, looked grim and more tired even than she had earlier, as if something had drained her. If she had handed over the incident reports, I thought, then she had possibly just handed him her own doom as Matron. Even so, she didn't look well, and I wondered whether perhaps she had a headache.

I was just figuring what my next move should be, my mind traveling the possibilities, when I passed the head of the corridor and heard him say, "Matron, I would like to have a tour of the building."

"Of course. I would be delighted," she said, sounding not delighted at all.

"No, no. I would not want to take you from your duties. One of the nurses will do."

And there I was, lingering. I had nothing in my hands and was on my way to nowhere in particular, but Matron didn't seem to notice. "Nurse Weekes," she called to me, sounding relieved. "Please give Mr. Deighton a tour, if you would."

"What would you like to see, sir?" I asked him when we were alone. "The patients are at morning exercise. They've been behaving very well today."

For the first time an expression crossed his face, one of such startlement it was almost horror. "The patients? No. No, I do not wish to see the patients."

"Oh, no, sir?" I asked sweetly. I could never resist. "They're your customers, after all. Wouldn't you like to see how they're treated here?"

He looked at me as if I'd started barking like a dog. "That won't be necessary. Not at all. I will start downstairs."

We began in the kitchen, where Nathan and the kitchen boys gave us surprised looks. We did not tour the gardens — the patients were there, of course — but looked at the laundry and the storage rooms before coming back upstairs and going through the empty dining room and common room. "Has anyone reported this crumbling masonry here?" he would say randomly to me, or, "Nurse, this stair seems crooked. Please make a note." And I, quite obviously carrying no means of making notes, would say to his back, "Yes, sir."

It went on and on. I stuck to him as he toured every section of the main floor, dictating notes to me along the way. I stuck to him as we climbed the stairs and started down the corridors of the men's bedrooms. Here he questioned me about supplies, meals, medications, and any sundries the men received, like newspapers — everything, of course, except for the health of the men themselves. He grilled me, spoke down to me, but he never did the one thing I wanted him to do: He never set down his briefcase.

As we approached the lav, he stopped and turned to me. "Nurse, please excuse me for a moment." I nodded, hopeful; any other man would have left his briefcase before using the facilities. But Mr. Deighton walked through the bathroom door, briefcase in hand. Time was running out. I let out a groan of frustration.

"Are you all right, Nurse Weekes?"

I turned. Captain Mabry stood in the corridor at the top of the staircase, regarding me calmly from behind his spectacles.

"Captain," I said. "What are you doing? You're supposed to be at exercise."

"I came to get my book," he replied. "I've

been given permission to read on the veranda. Are you supervising the lav?"

"I'm giving Mr. Deighton a tour." I lowered my voice to a whisper. "He's in there now."

A look of alarm crossed Mabry's face as he whispered back. "Ah. I do hope the pipes behave. The lav can be . . . a little upsetting."

"I know."

He blinked at me. "You don't look very happy."

"I'm fine."

He looked closer. "You are up to something. What might it be?"

I opened my mouth to tell him, and then I remembered his revoked access to his wife and children. "It's nothing, really. You needn't get involved. I'll figure something out."

"Well," he said. "Now I really must know."

I sighed. I could tell him, I supposed, without getting him in trouble. "You don't know how to get a man's briefcase out of his hands, do you?"

"What do you mean?"

"Mr. Deighton. In his briefcase are the incident reports, including Matron's report about yesterday. I'd hoped he'd put it down before going in there, but he didn't."

Mabry's voice grew carefully neutral. "And you wish to get these incident reports out of the briefcase."

"Yes, I do." I looked at his expression and said, "It has nothing to do with me, Captain. My days here are numbered. But I'd rather not be the cause of the other nurses getting dismissed, or the orderlies. Or Matron."

He seemed to consider this critically for a moment, frowning behind his spectacles. "The likelihood is, Nurse Weekes, that he'll find out eventually."

"Possibly."

"And you still wish to do it."

"I have to."

As we heard water running in the lav, Mabry leaned closer and whispered in his crisp voice: "If you want a man to drop something, you have to give him something else to grab onto. Bring him by my room."

And then he was gone, quick and quiet on his long legs, and Mr. Deighton emerged to continue his tour.

Perhaps I should have spared him, but when Captain Mabry gave a command in that patrician voice, you followed it. I led Mr. Deighton down the corridor. He looked a little pale. "Are you quite well, sir?"

"Yes, fine, thank you."

"The air in that lavatory can be rather oppressive, or so I've heard. And there is sometimes a problem with mold. I can make a note."

"There is nothing the matter, Nurse. I appreciate your concern. What is that noise?"

A great racket was coming from Mabry's room. I paused, hoping I wasn't about to heap one catastrophe over another. Then I pressed forward.

We found Mabry in the act of sliding his bed across the room toward the window, sweat breaking out over his pale forehead. He did not look at us as we approached the door.

"Mr. Mabry!" I exclaimed in my best outraged voice. "You're moving your bed again!"

I turned to Mr. Deighton, who had gone even paler at the sight of one of his mental patients apparently in full mania. "I'm so sorry about this, sir," I said. "Mr. Mabry sometimes thinks he's back at the Front, shoring up shell defenses."

"We need more sandbags!" Mabry said gamely as he slid the bed.

"Mr. Mabry!" I snapped. "Stop it right now. You're supposed to be at exercise. Move that bed back right now or I'll have to give you another emetic."

The captain looked at me and slumped.

He really was an admirable actor. "I can't, Nurse," he said in a pitiful voice I could never have imagined coming from him. "I used up all my energy pushing it. I can't put it back."

"Well, this is a pretty problem!" Boney herself could not have been more put out. "Now what are we going to do! If that bed isn't put back in its place, we'll both be in trouble." I turned to Mr. Deighton. "You don't think you could trouble to help him, sir? His fit seems to have passed. I'm quite sure he isn't dangerous at the moment."

Mr. Deighton seemed to have frozen in place. "Beg pardon?"

"I'm so sorry to trouble you," I said. "It won't take a minute. Otherwise I'll be here coaxing him all day. He goes quiet as a kitten when his fits have passed. You'll see. Mr. Mabry! Be nice to the kind gentleman, or you'll get a double dose of castor oil after supper."

"Yes, Nurse."

"Well, I —"

"Please, sir?" I looked up at him, all sweet hopefulness and worship.

He looked down at me, startled, as if he'd just noticed me there. Then he looked about, as if for another candidate. Then his mother's likely lessons about helping ladies

412

and the less fortunate finally awoke, and he sighed. "Very well."

He set down the briefcase and entered the room, poised on the balls of his feet as if hunting a leopard. "Go to the other side," he nearly shouted, as if madness made the captain hard of hearing, his voice nearly cracking with fear. "Grab the end."

They grappled with the thing, and I slid the briefcase neatly out of the doorway with my foot. In the corridor I snapped it open and riffled through it as fast as I could.

"What are you doing!" Mr. Deighton gasped. "The other way. No, the other way!"

There were sheaves of papers in there. I nearly despaired until I found a neat envelope, sealed and uncreased, with the date written on the front in Matron's handwriting. I pulled out the envelope and slid it into the pocket of my apron, next to the handwritten pages from the men.

After Mr. Deighton had emerged, dabbing his forehead with a handkerchief, and we had started off down the corridor with unseemly haste, I turned back to see the captain emerge from his doorway, book in hand. Behind Mr. Deighton's back, I gave him a salute. He looked surprised. At first I thought he wouldn't respond; then, as we turned the corner, he raised his hand to his temple and saluted me back, the gesture strangely dignified in his madman's pajamas.

I didn't know things had gone wrong, not truly, until it came time for Mr. Deighton to take his leave — given the option, it seemed no one ever stayed the night at Portis House — and Matron didn't come to help us see him off.

"I'm sorry, sir," said Boney, contrite. "Matron is feeling unwell and she has gone to lie down for a rest."

Nina and I stared at her in open shock. It was unthinkable for Matron to rest — in bed! — during the workday. Mr. Deighton took it in very bad grace, but he clutched his briefcase and left after giving us a sullen lecture about duty and respect to our superiors. He took his secrets with him, and though I was glad to see him go, I wished I'd had a little more time with the contents of that briefcase.

"You're not serious," I said to Boney when Mr. Deighton had gone.

"You saw her." Boney shook her head. "She didn't look well."

"Well, there's nothing to be done about it now," said Nina. "Supper's to be served in half an hour. We'll just have to do it all without her."

I half expected Matron to reappear during supper or as we cleared the dishes, nagging us about one rule or another, but she didn't. I pulled Paulus aside the first chance I got. "Matron's ill," I said.

He looked amazed. "I wondered where she had got to."

"We're short-staffed," I said. "It worries me."

It wasn't just the shortage, of course; it was the fact that it was Matron who was missing. The threat of Matron's wrath was what kept the men in line during the day-to-day routine. If it got out among the men that she was sick in bed, we might have a discipline problem. I vaguely noticed that the idea didn't terrify me, as it would have on my first day here; it merely seemed like a problem to be solved.

Paulus caught my meaning immediately. "I've got one of my men out back, taking a look at the generator. It's been acting up all day. I'll bring him back into the house and I'll tell the others to be on their guard."

"I think that would be helpful. I hope it's temporary and she's well by tomorrow. There can't be anything worse than Matron getting a serious illness."

But I was wrong. As I passed the common

room, Captain Mabry's voice called to me. "Nurse Weekes, I believe Somersham is unwell."

Somersham was sitting at the end of one of the sofas, sagging over the arm like an unwatered plant. As I watched, he put a hand up and cradled his forehead. "It's just a headache," he said.

"Nonsense, lad," Mr. MacInnes chimed in. "You look like death sitting up."

Somersham's skin was gray under the pale stubble on his cheeks. I touched his forehead. He was feverish, but there was no need to panic the men in the room. "Nurse Shouldice," I said calmly as Nina appeared in the doorway behind me, "I believe Mr. Somersham is not feeling well."

She was equally calm. "Isn't he? Well, let's go, then. Off to bed."

We helped him up the stairs and into bed. He was hot as coals, with alarming red blotches showing high on his cheeks.

Nina, worried, caught my eye as she pulled the cover over him. "Should we take him to the infirmary, do you think?"

"No, no," he protested from the bed between us. "It's just a headache. Had it since yesterday. It'll go away."

Nina and I looked at each other again. "Martha," I said. She'd had a headache the previous night before going on night duty, and she'd been in bed all day.

"I'll take care of him," Nina replied. "You go check on her."

I hurried up the stairs. The hot sun was setting behind a bank of cloud, the air as thick as cotton wool. The storm was coming. *Please,* I thought as my feet hit the steps. *Please, please, don't let Martha get sick.* But when I reached the nursery, the beds were empty, and she didn't answer when I called her name.

She'd gotten almost as far as the bathroom when she collapsed, perhaps in search of a glass of water. She was crumpled on the floor, one arm awkwardly under her head, her cotton nightdress hiked halfway up her thighs. I knelt beside her and pulled the nightdress down. Her legs were thin with sinew, her knees bony.

When I rolled her over, I saw the same feverish spots on her cheeks. Her eyes were glassy. "Kitty," she said. "You have to warn Matron."

"Ssh," I said. "Warn her of what?"

"The men will catch it," she breathed. "You have to warn Matron. It's influenza."

CHAPTER TWENTY-NINE

Everything happened fast after that. Influenza, it seemed, was a quick disease, its onset unstoppable once started, felling people like ninepins. In twenty-four hours half the patients were down with it, and half the orderlies, too.

Nina, Boney, and I worked like dogs. We let Archie out of the infirmary and replaced him with three of the first patients, but as more went down we ran out of room and kept the men in their own beds, making rounds and nursing as best we could. I was apprehensive about going into Creeton's room, where his restraints had just been lifted though he was confined to his room. I shouldn't have worried. He was unaffected by the flu, but he lay in bed and turned his back to us, unmoving and unspeaking.

Boney, whom I'd never seen do much actual nursing, was suddenly everywhere: ordering the able-bodied orderlies to haul supplies, herding the patients to bed, carrying trays, filling pitchers of water. How the fever had come here, we had no way of knowing. Portis House was isolated, but we'd had a string of visitors, including Syd and the patients' families. We also got deliveries of mail and supplies several times per week, and sometimes messages were run over the bridge and into town.

"Rest and fluids," Matron dictated from her bed. She was awake for a few brief minutes and we nurses had crowded into her room, hoping for wisdom. Nina fluffed the pillow behind her head. Matron looked different in her nightdress, her glasses gone and her hair askew, but even with her weakened voice she was still unmistakably Matron.

"They must have rest," she said. "Beef tea if they will take it. As much water as they will drink. Lemon for vitaminic strength. Keep the healthy men segregated as much as possible. Do not leave the sick to lie on sheets they have sweated through. Open the windows for ventilation, especially at night."

"Is that all?" The list seemed alarmingly anemic. "There is nothing else we can do?"

Matron closed her eyes briefly, then opened them again. "Nothing. Make sure you get rest yourselves, and nourishment.

You're no good to them if you come down with it. Alice, you already look exhausted."

It took me a confused moment to understand that Alice was Boney, whose first name I'd never known.

"Nurse Weekes," Matron commanded hoarsely. "There is a telephone in my office. Have you used such an instrument before?"

"Yes."

"You must communicate with the nearest medical hospital. You must speak to the doctor in charge and tell him we need patients evacuated. You must also communicate with the village and warn them of an outbreak."

I had no idea how to do any of this, but I held on to my panic. "Yes, Matron."

"Nurse Shouldice." She turned to Nina. "You are to deal with Paulus. Get an update on the issue with the generator. Make sure the men delivering supplies do not come into the house. The kitchen has permission to reduce meals, as the sick men cannot take solid food, but make sure there is a constant supply of beef tea. Alice, you are to go to bed. You are back on shift to relieve these two for rest in five hours."

That finished her; she could not speak further, and she drifted off into sleep. We went our separate ways. Within a few hours I found Mr. MacInnes at the foot of the stairs, sitting on the bottom step doubled over. We'd sent the men out for exercise, but there was no one to supervise them and a few of them had come back in, wandering the halls. I hoped no one had fallen outside or run off over the marshes. I helped Mac-Innes into bed and tucked him in. That made ten of the patients down.

"Can I help?"

I turned and found Jack in the doorway. He hadn't fallen sick. I was so happy to see him I almost cried.

"Yes," I answered him. "Do you know how to use a telephone?"

Exhaustion turned everything to a blur. There were cloths and pitchers of water, my fingers wrinkling as I endlessly mopped brows, throats, arms, and legs. There were journeys down the long, dark corridors of Portis House, the walls shimmering in my exhaustion, the groans so loud in the walls I wondered whether I imagined them. I sat at the small table in the kitchen, trying to choke down a biscuit and a cup of tea, as Nina told me Boney had gone to bed and not got up again. We had another patient to care for.

At some point I sat in Matron's empty office, uncomfortable in the chair behind her desk, as Jack sat across from me. He had one leg crossed over the other knee and regarded me steadily as I fumbled with the telephone. Gently he gave me suggestions and we sorted out how to get through to the post office in Bascombe, where I told the postmistress what was happening and asked her to spread the word in the village.

Then we spent another twenty minutes reaching the hospital at Newcastle on Tyne. The head doctor there didn't want to talk to me about an influenza outbreak at a madhouse, but I wouldn't let him stop me. I finally got myself patched through to the head administrator and by then I was so frustrated, so angry, and so very tired that I told him Jack Yates, England's hero, was here on his deathbed, along with the sons of many other prominent families, and if help was not sent I would post letters detailing why to the relatives of every single one of my patients, including Archie's father, the newspaper baron. I was told a detachment of ambulances would be sent right away to evacuate us and take in the sick.

I hung up the telephone and looked across the desk at Jack, who was as healthy as ever. He had a half smile on his face.

"Well-done," he said.

"That does it," I told him. "If Syd hasn't

told the newspapers, this will seal it for you."

He raised a brow. "England's hero?"

"It worked, didn't it?"

It took four hours to prepare the patients for evacuation. Any semblance of a routine had vanished now, and the few patients who remained healthy pitched in to work if they were capable. One by one the sick were carried down to the large front hall, using the hospital's single stretcher. Paulus and Roger, the last two orderlies who weren't sick, alternated with Jack and Captain Mabry, while other patients helped if they could. Martha was brought down from the nursery, and Matron and Boney were brought up from their rooms. We put the sick on the floor in neat lines, to ease the process of transferring them to ambulances once the vehicles arrived. As the main hall started to look like the aftermath of a bloodless battle, I looked out the window and saw that it had started to rain.

"Oh, no," I said. "Will the ambulances be able to cross the bridge?"

"I think so." Jack looked out the window over my shoulder. The air was hot and humid, and sweat trickled down his temples from carrying stretchers down the stairs. "It isn't raining very hard. Still, they must get here soon." He paused. "Kitty, look."

But I had already seen. Through the thin curtain of warm rain, a lone girl on a bicycle was approaching from the road.

"It's Maisey," I said, remembering her promise to bring mail. "She can't come in here. You carry on. I'll go talk to her."

From one of the supply closets I grabbed a men's mackintosh, obviously meant for use by the orderlies, and hurried outside. I caught her as the bicycle veered toward the trees at the side of the house, heading for the clearing. I waved my arms and she stopped, uncertain.

"Maisey!" I cried. "It's me!"

"Kitty?"

"Yes — No, don't come closer. Maisey, we have influenza here."

That made her dismount the bicycle. "I'm coming to help."

"No! You'll be exposed."

"Kitty, I'm a nurse! How many patients are down?"

"Ten, along with Matron, Martha, Boney, and four of the six orderlies."

"Oh, my God, Kitty. Has anyone died?"

"No." My brain refused to think about it. The last time Matron had woken, she had given us instructions on what to do if there were bodies. "Not yet."

"You're practically alone, Kitty. Let me help."

"There's no need. Ambulances are coming from Newcastle on Tyne, as long as the bridge holds. We're all to be evacuated in the next hour. You'd be risking yourself for nothing. Do you have an outbreak in Bascombe?"

"No. Not that I know of."

"You'll bring it back there, then. I warned the postmistress about it, but if the infection gets there on its own, you'll be needed."

She hesitated. Even from where I stood, some ten feet away, I could see that something had changed about her. She wore a slender mackintosh topped with a matching rain hat and stylish rubber boots. She looked like a reasonably well-to-do English girl taking a bicycle ride in a summer drizzle, but her face had lost its careless humor. She looked as if she'd taken a blow that had sucked the happiness from her.

"I brought letters," she said. "For Mr. Yates."

"Thank you. Just put them on the steps there."

"Is he sick?"

"No," I said, moving forward as she retreated. "He's fine."

It started to rain harder, the water no

longer soaking into the earth but creating pockets of mud and puddles. I could feel water trickling into the neck of the mackintosh and down my neck. The effect was chilling and uncomfortable.

"Kitty." Maisey had stepped forward. Her pretty face almost sagged with unhappiness as she looked at me.

"What is it?" I put the letters under my coat. "What is the matter, Maisey?"

"I read the letters," she confessed. "I couldn't help it. They had to do with Mikael. I wanted to know." She shook her head, berating herself. "I shouldn't have. Please tell Mr. Yates I'm sorry about it."

I waited. Whatever had made her unhappy, this wasn't it. "All right. I'll tell him."

"What I read there — it made me curious. I did some digging."

"Digging?" What digging could she do from her father's house in Bascombe?

"Nothing is what I thought it was, Kitty," said Maisey. "Nothing. It's worse than you can imagine. I didn't know what to do. I knew I shouldn't have come here over the bridge in the rain, but I just didn't know —" Now I could see she was crying, her tears mixing with the rain on her face. "I didn't know what to do, and now I still don't know."

"Maisey." I tried to be calm. "I have no idea what you're talking about."

"I know, and I'm sorry. I can't tell you now. I didn't think it would be like this here, that this would be happening. But now there's no time. If I don't go back, I won't be able to get my bicycle back over the bridge."

"Maisey, please tell me. What is it? What did you find?"

"Everything," she said miserably. "I made some notes. I'll put them on the step here. They're incomplete because I thought I'd be able to talk to you and Mr. Yates about it. But I think if you read everything, you'll put it together."

As I watched her place a few folded sheets of paper on the step, I felt stricken for reasons I didn't understand. "Maisey. Just tell me. Are they dead?"

"Yes," she said. "And if Portis House is haunted, the ghosts are Mikael and Nils, his father. I'm so grateful you're being evacuated, because if you weren't, I'd ask you to leave with me."

"All right." I took the notepapers in fingers that were numb with cold rain. "I'll be gone in a matter of hours, Maisey. I promise."

"Write me from Newcastle on Tyne," she

said. "When everything is settled. I don't
know what I'm going to do until then, but
I'll find a way through it. And then you can
help me decide what to do."

CHAPTER THIRTY

Nina had made me take a few hours' rest while we waited for the ambulances to come. I'd refused to go upstairs to bed, but spread a blanket in the corner of the floor and curled up to sleep, another blanket that Jack had pulled from the linen closet bundled under my head. "You should sleep, too," I told him, as he crouched next to me.

He shook his head. "I haven't been working your hours. Don't worry, Kitty. I'll be here. I'll wake you if you're needed."

I gave him the letters and the notes that Maisey had brought. As I lay down, my apron rustled, and I pulled out the envelope I'd taken from Mr. Deighton's briefcase a lifetime ago. I turned it over in my hand, looking at Matron's writing, and then I held it out to him. "Take this, too."

"What is it?"

"The incident reports Matron gave Mr. Deighton."

Jack took it, his gaze searching my face. "I see. Are you going to tell me where you got them?"

"Later." I hadn't thought I could rest, but I found myself fading. "It will make a good story for the journey to Newcastle on Tyne."

"Don't you want to read it?"

"I thought I did," I replied, "but now I don't think so. Perhaps you could read it for me."

"All right," he said. "Just rest."

"Jack," I said, the question seeming urgent in my tired mind, "which dream was yours? I read them all twice and I can't tell."

His hand rested lightly on top of the blanket he'd pulled over me. "I'd rather you didn't know," he said after a moment. "We're all dreaming the same thing — I see that now. It doesn't matter which one is mine."

I wanted to argue, but I was asleep before I could try.

I awoke a few hours later as Nina shook me. It was full dark now, and I could hear rain pounding on the windows. The patients on the floor next to me were quiet.

I rolled over. "What time is it?" I asked her.

"Nearly one o'clock," she replied.

"One o'clock!" I gaped at her. The ambu-

lances were over four hours late. "Have the ambulances arrived?"

"Just now," said Nina. "But there's a problem."

I threw off my blanket and stood, straightening my wrinkled skirts. I'd slept fully dressed, including apron, stockings, and shoes. My hair was still wrapped in its braids. It wasn't the best way to sleep, but I'd slept rough before. I followed Nina quietly toward the front door, stepping over the sleeping bodies of the patients.

Paraffin lamps had been brought in to light the hall. The flickering light created an eerie effect: Rows of bodies lined the floor, as still as corpses, while the rain fell relentlessly outside. I could see the men's faces as they slept feverishly, their flushed cheeks and sunken eyes, and I recognized every one of them. Martha, Matron, and Boney had been placed side by side. They all seemed to be sleeping, and Martha tossed uneasily.

We stepped through the front doorway to find Jack Yates standing on the portico, sheltered from the rain by its colonnade. Captain Mabry stood next to him, and they were talking to two men in mackintoshes and watch caps. Four covered ambulances idled on the circular drive, and two other drivers stood in the rain and waited, smoking cigarettes.

"What's going on?" I asked.

Jack turned to me. "Therc are four ambulances," he replied, "and each can only take four patients. They can only take sixteen."

I turned to the drivers. "We've seventeen sick here," I said.

"Twenty-one," Jack corrected me. "Four more fell ill while you were sleeping."

I was appalled. "Are you saying that fourteen of the patients here are now sick?"

"And four orderlies," he said, "and three nurses."

"We can't take them all," said one of the drivers. "We've no room."

"You could put more patients in each ambulance," Jack protested. "That's what I've been trying to tell you."

"I can't do it. Each ambulance only takes four. Otherwise it's overcrowding."

Jack shook his head. "I saw worse than that at the Front."

"So did I," said Captain Mabry.

"It can't be done," said the second driver. "We can't overcrowd ambulances like that. It's against regulations. We'd be sacked."

"What about the rest of the sick?" I asked.

The second driver turned to me. "We'll send back a second detachment, but it won't be until after the rain has stopped and the bridge is passable. As it is, we had a devil of a time getting here, and we have to move now, or we won't get out of here at all."

"These patients could be dead by then."

"That's what I've been saying," Jack said. "Are you going to leave these people to die?"

The ambulance driver turned to him with a look of frightened disgust on his face that I was starting to recognize. The sight of a shirt and trousers with PORTIS HOUSE HOSPITAL stenciled on them seemed to bring it out in everyone. "I know one thing," the man said. "I know I'm not taking orders from a bloody —"

"Stop it," I cut in. "In the absence of Matron, Nurse Shouldice and I are in charge." I glanced at Nina, who was dead on her feet; I wasn't even certain she was listening. "If we don't move soon, the bridge will be impassable. Start loading as many patients as you can. Make sure you take the three nurses — they're just under the windows, over there. Nurse Shouldice will accompany you to help with their care. I'll stay here with the remainder."

He nodded at me and motioned to the other two men, who threw down their smokes and came out of the rain. Soon there were stretchers passing quietly out,

433

some of the feverish patients moaning or crying. I found myself looking at every face, etching it into memory in case I never saw it again. I tried very hard not to care.

I turned back to Jack and Mabry, unable to watch anymore. "You should go with them," I said. "They'd likely let you ride in the front seats with the drivers. It's possible you could be of help."

"And leave you here alone?" Jack looked at Mabry. "What are the odds of our doing that, do you think, Captain?"

"Very long," Mabry replied coolly. "Very long indeed."

"I'm not going, either."

I turned. I'd almost forgotten about Nina, so quiet had she been. "Nina, you should evacuate."

"Those patients are going to a hospital," she said. "These ones aren't. They'll need nursing."

"I can take care of it."

"Kitty." She glanced at Jack and Mabry, then back at me, resigned. "You're not a nurse."

It felt like a slap. In the chaos since I'd found Martha lying on the floor of the corridor over a day earlier, I'd honestly forgotten. "Fluids, beef tea, rest," I said. "I can do all that."

"And what if one of them gets an infection?" Nina shot back. "What if one of them gets fluid in his lungs? Or sleepwalks and hurts himself? What if Mr. West has one of his fits, or Mr. Childress? What will you do then?"

I bit my lip. "All right. But you're half asleep, Nina. It's your turn to go rest. I insist on it."

She pushed up her glasses. "You won't get any argument from me," she said in her old sullen way, and she stomped away to find a blanket.

Captain Mabry was looking through his spectacles and down his patrician nose at me. "What?" I said to him. "You've never seen a girl impersonate a nurse before?"

"It's a bit of a long story," Jack offered.

"Intriguing," said the captain. "It has something to do with that unpleasant chap we ejected the other day, I assume?"

"Something like that," I replied.

"I see." He paused. "Your treatment of nosebleeds was very well-done, Nurse Weekes."

"Thank you. I'm sorry I had to pull rank back there, but he wasn't going to listen to you, and I had to move things along. Now, we need to get Paulus up-to-date on what's going on."

"If we can find him," Jack said.

"What?"

"I've been looking for him for over an hour. Roger's gone, too."

Paulus had never warmed to me, but I was unsettled at the thought of doing without his huge bulk. "He can't have gone far," I said. "Let's help get these ambulances off, and let's keep looking."

Paulus turned up half an hour later with Roger in tow. The two of them came into the hall as the ambulances pulled away, looking sweaty and a little harried. Paulus had drops of rain spattered over his whites. "Where are they going?" he said. "What's going on?"

I turned to him, worry making my voice sharp. "Where the hell have you been?"

"I had work to do," he retorted.

"Well, you have more work to do now. They couldn't fit us all, so they've gone with as many as they can take, and they're coming back after the rain has stopped and the bridge has cleared."

"That's just bloody great." Paulus flushed. "We're all right fucked — that's what we are."

"Speak for yourself," I said. "I want a meeting of everyone left who is able-bodied, except for Nurse Shouldice, who must rest. Round up everyone and go to the dining room. Now."

The meeting was a depressing one. I put a lantern down on one of the long tables and looked around. I was the only nurse; Roger and Paulus were the only orderlies. Jack and Captain Mabry pulled up chairs, and West wheeled in his chair. The disease had passed him over so far.

I exchanged a look with Jack. He appeared tired, but not much the worse for wear. He'd been through harder things than this, of course. I wondered whether he'd read Maisey's papers or the reports from Matron, but I could see no sign of it on his face.

For the first time I missed Matron. Her rules had seemed stupid, but now I knew that she would have kept an itemized ledger noting every staff and patient in the hospital and their current whereabouts. I had to run everything through my tired, jumbled head. "Where are the kitchen staff?" I asked.

"Gone back to the village hours ago," said Paulus. "The gardener, too. The whole building was being evacuated and I thought we wouldn't need them, so I sent them off."

"Nathan doesn't live in the village," I said.

"Bammy does. He said his mum would take Nathan in. Nathan wanted to go, so I let them."

"Paulus, we have a deadly virus here. And you've just sent two people to carry it back to Bascombe."

Both orderlies looked incredulous. "Are you saying we should have sent them on those ambulances to Newcastle on Tyne, even though Bammy lives just across the way?" said Roger.

"Yes." I rubbed my temples. Actually, I didn't know. Would the ambulances have taken people still healthy along with the sick? Matron would have known. "They could at least have stayed long enough to be evaluated by the nursing staff." *Of which I am not one.*

"We didn't have time for that," said Paulus. "Besides, if you want to be the one to get Nathan into one of those ambulances, you can try. I certainly won't."

"Nurse Weekes is right," Jack said. "I didn't know you were scared of Nathan the cook, Vries."

Paulus turned to him. "It isn't my job to wrestle people like him," he said, his accent sounding exotic in our half-dark dining room. "It's my job to wrestle people like *you.*"

"What's done is done," Captain Mabry said in his best aristocratic voice. "We can't get them back now, even if they would come." He looked at me. "We have more pressing problems."

"What do you mean?"

"Do the arithmetic," Jack said. "Count the patients."

I did, shuffling them through my brain. And suddenly I saw it. "Archie Childress," I said. "He wasn't evacuated, and he isn't on the floor in the hall. Where is he?"

"Creeton, too," said Jack. "He didn't need to be carried downstairs, but I told him to come. I didn't want him alone, and I wanted him where we could all keep an eye on him. He said he would come, but he never appeared."

"Oh, my God." I looked around the table. I didn't think that anything could be worse than this. "We're missing two patients."

Paulus raised one of his huge hands. "As to that, we can shed a little light. On one of them, at least."

We all turned to him. His gaze dropped for a second, and I thought I saw uncertainty cross his face. Then he looked back up and spoke. "We found Creeton and Childress in the common room. Creeton was having a go at Childress — you know, teasing him. The stutter and the shaking. He's always liked to take the piss out of Childress, but this time he seemed angry. He hasn't been the same since — well, you know. He was taking it out on Childress rather hard. Said Childress's weakness was what had brought it."

"Him," Roger corrected. "He said Childress's weakness was what had brought *him.*"

Paulus frowned. "I don't think so. What the hell does that mean? Brought who?"

There was silence around the table. Jack and I exchanged a glance. I didn't think Archie had somehow brought the ghost of Mikael Gersbach or his father to Portis House. But if Creeton was not in his right mind . . .

"Anyway, Childress flew at Creeton," Paulus continued. "Started to hit Creeton something fierce. He's thin, that one, but when he's angry he's damned determined."

I put a hand to my mouth. Oh, Archie. *Creeton likes to have a go at me, but I can handle it,* he'd told me. "What happened?"

"We pulled them apart," Paulus said. "It took two of us to take care of Childress, he was struggling so hard. When we came back to the common room, Creeton was gone. We spent over an hour looking for him and had to give up. That's when I came into the

440

main hall and saw the ambulances had gone."

"No trace of him," Roger agreed.

"Wait." West leaned forward in his chair. "What exactly do you mean, you *took care of Childress*?"

Again that flicker of uncertainty crossed Paulus's features. "He's a danger," he said. "He's proven it, hasn't he? With this sickness, I don't have the staff to watch him. I thought it would be just until the evacuation, and then we'd get him out of here."

"What did you do?" I nearly whispered.

"We put him in isolation," Roger replied, his chin up. "The old library. He's there now."

There was a beat of horrified silence.

"Are you saying," I said, "that you took Archie to the isolation room in the west wing and you *left* him there?"

"We had to," said Roger. "That's what it's there for, isn't it?"

"How long?" Jack's voice was almost a croak. "How long has he been locked up in that place?"

"I don't know," Paulus said. "Three hours, perhaps."

I swallowed. I would not have put my worst enemy in that haunted place for three minutes. And Archie . . . fragile Archie, who already had nightmares so horribly bad . . .

And suddenly I knew. It was what Creeton had said that revealed it. No, Archie had not brought the ghosts here, but it was Archie who was making it worse. He was a sort of conduit, his mind the easiest one to reach, his emotions the rawest, his fear the most abject. This place fed on the men, but it fed on Archie first, and as it did, it gained strength. It was why Archie endured a special kind of torture while the men tried to kill themselves and the west wing rotted with eerie speed. It was all tied together. The worse Archie grew, the worse Portis House became.

And now he was locked in the isolation room, the center of the nightmares. Three hours.

"We have to get him out," I said.

"And do what with him?" said Paulus. "Let him strangle someone else?"

I felt him glance at the faded bruises on my neck, and I was angry. "Mr. Childress does not belong in isolation." I tried to sound authoritative, as if terror weren't fighting to take hold of me. "Go get him out."

"I won't."

"You have to," Jack said. His gaze flicked to me, took in the sickened look on my face, and moved back to Paulus. "With Matron sick, her command falls to Nurse Weekes. She has the authority to order it. In fact, without her say-so, you didn't have permission to put him there in the first place."

"You shut it," Paulus said. "Orderlies are given the authority to act when they feel there's danger. It's in the rules. That's why we're given the keys and the nurses aren't."

"You have to get him *out*," I said. "You have to."

"Kitty," Jack said.

I turned to him. "He can't stay there." I looked at Mabry and West, trying to tamp down the panic in my voice. "He's the catalyst," I said to them. "Think about it. He's the center of all of it, the one whose energy they take. And he's getting worse."

West took my meaning right away and turned green. "Jesus," he said. Jack's gaze searched my face as he put the pieces together himself. Mabry had paled but he stayed silent, as if something terrifying were occurring to him.

"For God's sake," came Paulus's incredulous voice. "You're not making any sense. Are you as mad as the rest of them?"

I turned back to him. "It's wrong, and you know it," I said. "Deep down, you know it. Get him *out*."

He didn't give in. But he looked back at me, the knowledge flickering behind his eyes. I didn't know what he thought, what he believed, what he might have pieced together, and I didn't care. I didn't let him go. And so he was still looking at me, and he was caught by surprise when Jack grabbed one arm and Mabry grabbed the other.

They twisted his arms up behind his back, bent at the elbows in a painful posture, as Paulus kicked out with his big legs. In the same moment West twisted in his chair and got his arm around Roger's neck, squeezing with one huge biceps. Roger's reaction lifted West almost completely off his chair, the halves of his legs swinging, but he held on. Roger was strong, but smaller, and he grabbed for purchase at West's muscled arm, held in place.

"Kitty!" said Jack. "Quick!"

There was no time to go around the table, so I stepped up onto my chair and launched myself straight across it, grabbing for Paulus's waist. His ring of keys hung there, clipped to his belt; I grabbed for it and fumbled with the clasp, trying to pry it open. Paulus lifted his hips and torso straight off his chair, heaving, and I nearly lost my grip; I got it again and worked at the clasp as he struggled beneath me. As I lay flat on my stomach on the dining room table, my skirts thrown up and my legs kicking as my own chair went flying, I wondered in a flash what Matron would have thought.

Well, that's just too bad.

I unhooked the key ring and snatched it off Paulus's belt. Then I rolled off the table and ran.

I pounded down the corridor and into the common room. There was no direct way to get to the west wing indoors, as all the doorways were bolted shut; the only way would be to go up a flight of stairs, through the door Jack and I had used before, and back down another staircase. The quickest way to the library was outdoors, straight through the garden and cutting across the grounds to the other end of the building. I took the low steps in the common room two at a time and I flew to the French doors, unlatching them and running out onto the veranda.

The rain was pounding down in a solid sheet. I crossed the veranda and leapt down the steps into the garden, water in my eyes. My cap was gone. I heard shouts behind me, the crash of overturned furniture. My boots clapped on the cobblestone path of the garden as I turned left and then right, and then I was through the garden gate and out into the untended grounds.

I was soaked through already. It was summer rain, chilled but not freezing, driving hard from the sea winds. The ground squelched under my feet and mud flew. I heard the heavy pounding of male steps behind me and harsh male breath. I turned my head for a fraction of a second and saw Roger, head down, arms pumping, chasing me for all he was worth and gaining. But Jack had come out a side door and was heading straight for him, as lithe as an animal. *"Run, Kitty!"* he shouted, and I turned ahead again and pumped faster, my legs churning under my skirts. The main wing of Portis House flew by and I focused on the barred window and barred door of the god-forsaken library, which came into view.

I wouldn't have long. If Jack was tackling Roger, it meant Paulus was free. Paulus was big, he was fast, and he was quiet. His legs were longer than mine. He'd give me no warning, just grab me the way an owl swoops down and grabs a mouse. He was double my size and weight, built for wrestling unruly patients. I had to outrun him, but I wouldn't have much time.

I kept the door to the library in focus and

pushed my whole body, pain blooming in my chest, water and sweat soaking down my back. When I got to the door, I was running so hard I couldn't slow and I more or less crashed into it, hitting it hard. I fumbled with Paulus's key ring in my wet hand and put the right key in the lock just as two huge arms came around my waist from behind.

"Archie!" I screamed. *"Archie!"* I gripped the door as Paulus lifted me off my feet, as easy as if I were a child's doll. I turned the knob and pushed the door open as hard as I could, screaming Archie's name again. Paulus pulled at me as the door swung open with a groan.

And then we stopped.

We froze where we were. Perhaps our position was a bit ridiculous — both my feet off the ground, my torso neatly tucked under one of Paulus's arms like a suitcase — but we didn't notice. There was only that dark doorway, and silence but for the sound of the blowing rain. I was suddenly cold. This was the bad place, the worst place. The place where whatever it was, whatever horror it had been, had happened.

Paulus felt it, too. There was no light in the isolation room; the electric fixture was off, and a paraffin lamp would have been deemed too dangerous to leave with the patient. Paulus put me down and stepped forward into the dark doorway, where the rain blew through the open gap.

There was no sound, no movement from inside.

"Archie," I said. I pushed past Paulus and walked into the room. There was an awful, sour smell. It was so dark I could not see my feet, so quiet I could hear only my own rasping breath. "Archie, answer me."

Silence. I recalled the layout of the room from the time I'd looked in the window, and stepped hesitantly in the direction of the bed. I thought I could hear breathing. *Breathing is good,* I told myself. *Breathing is good.*

I put my arms in front of me and took another step. My foot hit something; I reached down and touched the brass bedstead. I felt along the bed, patting lightly with my hands. Relief rushed over me as I felt a foot, an ankle, a calf that was both bony and warm. "He's alive," I called out.

I glanced back at the doorway, but at that moment Paulus turned away, his attention distracted. Swinging lamplight came up behind him, making his shadow sway on the walls. Jack stepped into the room, soaked with rain, holding a lantern. "Kitty?"

"Here."

"Jesus God," Paulus shouted, his voice hoarse. "I just saw something." He clamped a hand on Jack's shoulder, and Jack turned; the lantern moved, and light played over me and the leg I was holding up, a thin body lying on its side on the bed, knees and arms drawn up. It was Archie, and he didn't move.

"Where?" Jack said to Paulus.

"Stop!" Paulus shouted out into the rain. "Stop!"

I leaned close to Archie. "Archie. Are you all right?"

"It's too late," he whispered. "I'm sorry."

"It isn't," I coaxed him. "I've come to get you out of here. Come with me."

But he stayed curled up, his hands over his head as they had been during that first night shift, when I had witnessed his nightmare. "He's already coming." He moaned. "You're too late, too late. You're too late."

Jack didn't hear it. "Don't go out there!" he shouted to Paulus, who had turned away. "Vries — come back!" There was no response. Archie moaned louder, and Jack turned back into the room. He raised the lamp high and his gaze froze with alarm.

"Oh, my God," he said softly.

I turned and followed the shaft of light, a single square of yellow on the wall above my head. From my angle I saw the beam play over the wall, illuminating the words there. They were high up, near the ceiling, and they were scratched into the plaster, as if with fingernails or the blade of a knife. And part of me knew, knew what the words would spell out in their awful, painful writing.

I AM NOT A COWARD

"He told me," Archie said from the bed. "Someone's going to die."

I looked back down at him. He had taken his hands away from his face, and he lay defeated, his eyes staring at nothing, his thin arms stark against the damp linens. He was still, too still, and it took me a moment to understand what was wrong. I hadn't noticed it at first, but now I stared, transfixed by an eerie dread I could not explain.

My patient's hands had stopped shaking.

CHAPTER THIRTY-ONE

"Oh, good," said Jack. "We're alone."

I looked up from the weak cup of tea I'd been sipping. It was early morning, purplish light filtering through the rain that still poured down the high windows. I was dressed in my uniform and apron, but I'd left off my cap; there hadn't seemed much point to wearing it. I sat at the small table in the kitchen, a picked-over plate before me.

Jack had slept for only a few hours, but he looked much better than I imagined I did. He'd shaved, and his sleeves were rolled up in his usual fashion. In the soft light of morning, his presence seemed larger than life, his brows dark wings over eyes that missed nothing about me as they took me in, the line of his jaw as perfect as if etched in ink.

He pulled up a chair and sat across the corner from me. He leaned back, crossed his arms, and stretched out his legs, which were long enough to reach all the way under my chair. "You cooked," he said.

I nodded. The staff may have gone home, but the kitchen was still well supplied; I'd found bacon, kidneys, eggs, tea, and bread. It hadn't been particularly hard to manage, and I'd prepared large amounts of each. "Are you hungry?"

"Not now, but the others will appreciate it. Have you checked on Archie?"

"Yes, briefly." We'd put him in the main hall with the others; Nina had stayed up with them, and when I finished my breakfast I was to relieve her. "Nina says he may have slept a little, but it's hard to tell. He isn't responsive and he hasn't spoken since last night."

"Mabry and I will go back to the library today. I want to see that lettering in daylight."

"Because you want to see how he wrote it?" I put my teacup down and stirred it unnecessarily. "Archie had no knife on him. And his fingernails were clean."

"No." Jack's voice was soft. "Because I don't think he wrote it."

My throat closed. What had happened, exactly? Would we ever know? "Jack, I don't know how to help him."

"You may not be able to. It may be partly a matter of time."

"We left him there. For three hours."

"Vries left him there."

"It's my fault," I said. "I should have seen he was gone. He was my responsibility. I've mucked it up, Jack. I'm in over my head, and I've mucked this up so badly."

"Ah, now, Kitty." He uncrossed his arms and leaned toward me, taking one of my hands in his. He traced the line of the scar on my hand, his thumb warm on my skin. "No one put you in charge, did they? You weren't trained for command. And yet here you are."

I looked at him, the tight bands around my chest easing a little. "I suppose you know the feeling."

He smiled a little at that. "And how many men have you lost? None."

"I don't even know if that's true," I said bitterly. "They could all have died in the ambulances, and I wouldn't even know. Tom and Somersham and all the rest of them. They could be dead in a rainy ditch somewhere."

"I don't think so." He said it with complete sincerity; it was not meant as a platitude or a patronizing pat on the head, but as a declaration of quiet belief. He cupped

453

his hand over mine and held it. "We'll find Creeton," he said, "wherever he is. He can't have gone very far. We'll keep these men alive for as long as it takes for the ambulances to get back; we've plenty of supplies. And we'll let Archie recover. I saw men like that at the Front sometimes. Sometimes they got well again with rest."

"And Mikael Gersbach?" I said. "What about him?"

He looked up at me, and a shadow crossed his expression.

"It was him, wasn't it?" I said. "The man Paulus saw last night."

"Paulus claims he doesn't know what he saw." Something very dark crossed Jack's features, a memory of something awful. "But he's lying. I saw it myself. He's lying."

"What did he see?"

"It was reflected in the window when I raised the lamp. Just for a second." The darkness crossed his expression again, as if he were fighting it. "There was a tall man holding a rifle. The rifle was held down by his side, and he was staring at us — and then he was gone. I smelled metal and blood."

"That's the man I saw," I said, my voice a rasp. "The one who hit me."

"I know." He looked levelly at me. "It's

Nils Gersbach. Mikael's father."

It made sense. *The man comes, and he's so horribly angry,* Tom had told me. And the men's dreams: *Get up, you coward.* "You've read the letters, and Maisey's notes," I said.

"Yes. I haven't put it all together yet, but I'm close. And I'll tell you everything. I just want to be sure you're ready to hear it."

His hand over mine was warm and strong, and I didn't want him to let go. My gaze dropped to the shirt he wore, with its ever-present stencil, and I shook my head.

"What is it?" said Jack.

"I'm just thinking that we aren't much like nurse and patient anymore," I replied. "If we ever were, really."

The look he gave me was wry. "No, we were never much good at that part."

"It feels stupid to treat you like a patient when I couldn't have done much without you," I said. "Is there . . . anything I can do for you? Anything you want? Except" — I held up a hand as he opened his mouth to speak — "taking my clothes off."

He let my hand go and leaned back in his chair. "Well, now I have to rethink."

"I mean it," I said. "Name something. Except for that. I haven't had a bath in days, and I think you'd regret it."

"I doubt that." His grin had a spark of

mischief in it. "Please tell me that Matron keeps current newspapers somewhere."

"In her office," I affirmed. "And no one's taken black ink to them, either. I'll get them out. Anything else?"

"There is one other thing."

The idea of doing something to please him made me happy. "What is it?"

"Are you certain?"

I bit my lip. "This is going to involve breaking the rules, isn't it?"

"Most certainly."

"All right. Go ahead."

"Well, if you're offering," he said, "I'd like to find my clothes. My own clothes, that is. The ones I was wearing when I arrived at Portis House."

I wasn't sure where the men's belongings were kept, but it didn't prove all that difficult to find out. I knew the key to whatever it was — a room, a storage closet — would be Matron's alone, and that meant it must be in her office.

"My contact at the War Office confirmed that Mikael Gersbach did go to war," Jack told me as I went through Matron's desk drawer by drawer. "He got to Belgium in 1916 and marched to France. But apparently there was trouble."

"What trouble?" I lifted papers on Matron's desk. We'd tried her telephone, a vain attempt to put out another distress call, but the line seemed to be dead — not surprising with the weather outside. Vaguely I became aware that Jack was telling me this while I was half distracted so that the effect would be less upsetting. But I trusted him, and I let him tell it his way.

"He was bullied," Jack said. "Rather mercilessly, in fact. He had a Swiss last name and an accent, for all that he was a British national. His fellow soldiers decided he was an undercover Hun. They saluted him as the Kaiser, held him down and painted Kaiser mustaches on him, that sort of thing."

I stopped what I was doing. "That's horrible."

"It's bad," he admitted. "You have to remember that our soldiers were being trained to kill Germans. They had to be in the mind-set to shoot them, bayonet them, bomb them, mow them down. When you do that to a man, you can't expect him to switch out of it so easily."

"But he wasn't German!"

"He was close enough, with the name and the accent. When Germans have killed your friends and relatives, when they're shooting

457

at you every day . . . Well, some men need a target for their rage and frustration."

He would know more about it than I would, of course. I nodded and went back to my search.

"There are several incidents on record," Jack continued. "In one, Mikael was stripped naked by a bunch of drunken officers and dumped in the center of the nearest town in the middle of the night. They'd painted the words KILL THE BOCHE on him. *Boche* was another word for German, like *Hun.* Two men got reprimands for that. In the second incident, they stole a helmet from a dead German soldier and put it on Gersbach's head. Then they forced him at bayonet point to get out of the trench and stand in the open, right in the German sniper lines."

I paused again. "I get the idea," I said, sickened. "I don't think I need to hear more examples." I turned and saw Matron's thick cardigan hanging from a peg, started going through the pockets.

"There were more reprimands for that one," Jack said. "He was lucky to get out of it alive. Shortly afterward, his section of the line came under heavy attack. It was chaos, but there were several witnesses who agreed on one thing. At the height of the attack,

Mikael ran."

My fingers closed on a slim set of keys in Matron's pocket. I turned and looked at Jack again. He was seated on the chair across from Matron's desk, one leg crossed over the other knee as when I'd sat there using the telephone. "And did he run?" I asked. "Or was that another lie?"

Jack looked grim. "It happened. The witnesses were credible ones, and they all said the same thing. During an artillery attack, Mikael retreated, and they found him hours later, a mile down the road from the front line, sitting on the ground and weeping."

Sweet, kind Mikael, Maisey had called him. Gentleman enough to spend time with his little sister and her friend. How many men like that had been sent off to the front lines, along with the strong ones, the brave ones, the bullies? Shamed by his father, given no choice, he'd been packed off to a hellish place against which he had no defenses.

"What happened?" I asked.

"He was court-martialed," Jack replied. "In the army, desertion is a capital offense. The witnesses proved it, and he didn't deny it. So he was sentenced to execution by firing squad."

Maisey had said that she'd heard he'd been shot in some horrible way. "That's

459

barbaric."

"It's military justice, Kitty," Jack said quietly.

"But if he was shot over there, then how . . . ?"

"He wasn't. A lot of men were convicted of desertion and cowardice during the war, but most had their sentences commuted. Only a few were actually executed. An officer on the tribunal looked at Mikael's case and decided that the bullying was a mitigating factor. He commuted Mikael's sentence and sent him home on a dishonorable discharge."

I walked slowly to the door of Matron's office, thinking. I wandered up and down the corridor, looking for the nearest locked door, barely registering what I was doing. "He came home in disgrace," I said. "He came home a coward."

"Yes," said Jack, following me. "I imagine his father was livid."

I found a locked supply closet I'd never been shown, and touched the handle, running my finger along it. And then I stopped, turning absolutely still.

It is like how I heard they executed some of those Poor Fellows but I never saw one (execution) myself so I don't know why I dream of it.

"His father did it," I said softly. "His father executed him for cowardice. In that spot outside the isolation room."

Jack leaned on the wall next to me and looked down at me. "There's a record of Mikael's body," he said. "Dead of a rifle shot to the middle of the forehead. There's a record of the father's body, too. Nils Gersbach. Also dead of a gunshot, this time to the heart."

"Who shot Nils Gersbach?" I asked no one. "Did Mikael fight back?"

Jack shook his head. "There isn't an account of it. But I wonder, myself, if his wife wasn't involved, or even Anna. There's no record of their bodies. And no one has seen them since."

I turned slowly, my mind churning, and faced him. "What do you mean, record of the bodies? Record kept where?"

"That's where Maisey came in. Remember, she read the letter I received from my contact at the War Office, telling me what had happened to Mikael. I think she read it and suspected what may have occurred. She'd already suspected that Anna was dead. And if there are deaths, if there are bodies, there is one person who tends to know."

My father is the local magistrate, Maisey

461

had said. "Oh, God. Maisey's father. Her father knew."

"According to her notes, she went into his study and looked through his files. And she found records of Nils's and his son's bodies being removed from Portis House and cremated."

"But nothing about Mrs. Gersbach or Anna."

Jack shook his head.

"If Nils killed Mikael," I said slowly, figuring it through, "it's possible he killed the others, too. And the bodies weren't recovered."

"Or they're alive," Jack said. "Who killed Nils?"

Alive. The girl we'd seen in the trees. Was it Anna? Where had she come from? Where was she, that she couldn't contact her best friend?

"And why has no one heard of this?" I asked Jack. "Why was everything covered up?"

"As to that," Jack said slowly, "if Deighton was interested in the property for a hospital, and he was willing to cut in the local authorities . . ."

"Maisey's father," I said. "If there was a cover-up for profit, he must have been part of it. He told his daughter he didn't want her looking into Anna's disappearance, that it was probably nothing. He's been lying to her. No wonder she was so distraught when she came here with the letters."

"Are you certain this is the right closet?" he said.

I looked down at the keys in my hand. "No." I began trying them in the lock, a welcome distraction from thinking about the execution that had taken place on the grass outside the library. *Kneel, he says . . .* "But I think it is."

"How do you know?"

"Because I know Matron," I said. I held up a finger. "First, she would take the keeping of the patients' personal belongings very seriously. Second, she would keep them meticulously organized, labeled, and stored somewhere locked. But not in her office, because she does not need to access them every day. So in a closet nearby. And she would keep the key herself, without giving a copy to Boney, because she would see it as her responsibility alone. Each man's things will have an itemized and dated list included. I'll wager it now."

He was watching my face. He always knew what I was thinking. "She'll be all right," he told me gently. "You'll see."

"Yes, well." I swallowed my worry.

"There was nothing in those papers about you, you know."

I looked up at him. "What?"

"The envelope you gave me. The incident reports you asked me to read for you. I did. And there was nothing in there about you."

"What are you talking about? My brother —"

"Is not mentioned. There is an incident report stating that a visitor arrived on a day not set for visiting and created a commotion. It says the nurses tried to eject him and the patients became disturbed. That was her word, 'disturbed.' It states that the orderlies were late in arriving, and by the time the visitor was shown off the grounds, the patients were very upset. She claims full responsibility for the incident. Kitty, you're never mentioned at all, and neither are the other nurses."

"What about the other incident reports?" I said. "The one in which I went to your room without clearance. And the second time, the night Roger told on me. And the night when Archie attacked me."

"There's one about the attack. I suppose she had to write that one. But it's brief and carefully worded. Matron seems to be an expert in writing a report that doesn't give much away. I have to admire it."

"And the others?"

Jack shook his head. "Nothing. Just those two reports. Nothing else."

My stubborn brain wouldn't take it in. "That can't be right, Jack. She told me she was writing incident reports. She told me Mr. Deighton would read them, and there was nothing she could do. Are you saying she was *lying*?" My face felt hot and tingling. "Oh, my God. She was trying to frighten me all along. She never meant to have me dismissed. When I see her again, I'll kill her myself. I've barely slept, I was so worried."

Jack's voice was thoughtful. "I'm starting to think, perhaps, that Matron puts on quite a good show of being frightening. But a show is what it is."

"She's practical," I replied. "She can't afford to lose a nurse, that's all. It certainly wasn't out of affection for me."

"You may be wrong about that," Jack said.

I shook my head. *I know her,* I was about to say again, but then I remembered that Matron had had a husband, and a son, and I had never guessed. Perhaps I didn't know her as well as I'd thought.

"Fine," I said finally. "We'll leave it. But I know I'm right about this closet."

I was. One of the keys worked, and the door swung open to reveal neatly kept shelves. There were a few small suitcases, and boxes tied with string; there were also a few parcels wrapped simply in brown paper. I realized that these were the belongings each man had come here with, the things of his own life he had surrendered. Some men had come with suitcases, others with a box of beloved items. And some men had come with nothing.

Each item had a paper tag attached to it, with Matron's large, looped handwriting. SOMERSHAM, WILLIAM. D.O.B.: 16 APRIL 1898. ADMITTANCE DATE: 7 JANUARY 1919.

I studied the tags one by one. Jack was silent next to me, looking over my shoulder. It seemed he couldn't find words for those few long moments, as if the sight of that closet had temporarily robbed him. I finally put a hand on the brown paper parcel with his name on it.

I slid it off the shelf, held it in my hands for a moment. It weighed nearly nothing; Jack had come here, it seemed, with the clothes on his back and little else. I turned to him, the small parcel between us, and the ceremonial pose of it, I with an item in both my hands, presenting it to him, struck me with deep truth.

I raised my eyes and looked into his. I could not fathom what I saw there, could

466

not truly understand what this moment would mean to a person who had suffered what he had. He didn't speak; it seemed he couldn't. And yet he put his hand on the parcel and took it from me, and then he ducked down and kissed me swiftly on the lips, his touch telling me more than words ever could.

He stood back and untied the string. The paper fell open to reveal a folded shirt and trousers, a pair of suspenders, a watch, a wallet, a wool jacket. When Jack Yates had checked into Portis House, wishing to kill himself, he had not even worn a tie.

He let out a sigh, a great whoosh of air as if a weight had been lifted from him. He picked a piece of paper from the top of the stack of folded clothes and held it up to me with a half smile. "You should have wagered money," he said.

It was Matron's list of items in the parcel, of course. I smiled back at him.

Jack released the parcel and it dropped to the floor. I blinked in surprise, but before I could recover, he grabbed the bottom hem of his hospital top and wrenched it off over his head in one quick movement. I was left gaping at his bare chest, unexpected and utterly fascinating.

"What are you doing?" I managed.

"These are my clothes," he said simply. He sounded almost happy. He kicked off his shoes. "I'm putting them on."

"Right here?"

"Come, now." He looked up at me and grinned fully, watching my reaction. Too late, I realized he was distracting me as he yanked the drawstring of his hospital trousers and dropped them to the floor. "You're a nurse," he said. "Surely at some point you've seen one of us in the altogether?"

I stood there like a ninny. He wasn't in the altogether — he wore drawers, of course, and at the moment he showed no signs of removing them. But he wore nothing else. *I should turn my back,* I thought stupidly, but I did no such thing. His body was lean, the flat muscles sliding under the skin hypnotic. He had small whorls of hair on his chest, a shade lighter than the hair on his head. His hips were narrow, his legs long and strong, smaller whorls of hair on his thighs and farther down. I stared.

He bent and picked up his trousers, the knobs of his spine moving under the flawless skin of his back. He shook the trousers out and stepped into them, and I felt a short stab of disappointment that I couldn't look at his legs anymore. He fastened the trouser buttons, the movement strangely intimate.

468

He was enjoying the fact that I was looking at him. There was something in my gaze, I realized, something I had not consciously put there, that he was soaking up like a sponge.

He picked up the shirt next and slipped it over his head, and I could see the tufts of hair under his arms as he raised them, the soft, firm undersides of his biceps, the play of skin over his ribs. Then the fabric fell and he tucked the shirt into the trousers as I felt the slow pulse of my heart at the base of my throat.

He attached the suspenders next, slid them over his shoulders. The trousers were a little roomy on him now, but not much; even before he'd come here and gone on a hospital diet, he'd been slim. I saw him now as if through a glass; I could see the patient he'd been, and the man he was, at the same time. They had always been the same person, at least to me.

He put his shoes and socks on and straightened, looked at me.

"How do you feel?" I asked.

He rolled his shoulders, one and then the other, then both at the same time, the movement making the fabric of his shirt play over his skin. Then he stilled and looked at me, his expression dark. "Come here."

I took a step closer, knowing only that I wanted to be nearer, to be as close as I could. He put his arm around my waist and pulled me to him, flush against him. Then he kissed me again.

This kiss was different. He held me tight, and even through layers of fabric I could feel every sinew of him, the beat of his heart and the heat of his hands on my back. I put my arms around his neck and touched his hair with my fingertips. His hips were flush against mine. He teased my mouth open and I let him, the taste of him, mixed with the smell of his skin, overwhelming me. He had kissed me before with need, and the need was still there, but it was tempered with passion that made me ache, made me rise up and open to him as much as he would let me.

He broke the kiss and ran a thumb along my lower lip. He did not let me go. "That's better," he said, breathing hard. "I wanted to kiss you as a man."

"You are a man," I said.

He rubbed my lip again — the sensation of it was raw, as if I had no more defenses — and kissed the corner of my mouth, my jaw, the tender spot on my neck. Then he stopped, holding me, his head dipped to the spot beneath my ear, breathing me in.

I touched his face, ran my fingers along his jaw and his cheekbones. I knew every line of them, every contour, though I'd never touched them before, not like this. The feel of him beneath my hands sent a spark of something through me, dangerous and heady and wonderful.

"Jack," I said after a long moment.

"Hmm?"

"Are you kissing the nurses just to get newspapers?"

When his body shook against mine, I knew he was laughing.

CHAPTER THIRTY-TWO

The rain had not stopped. Though it was morning, the clouds were so thick we needed the electric lights in the patients' hall in order to see through the gloom. The light thrown by the electric bulbs wasn't as strong as the light from the paraffin lamps, and Nina kept a lamp lit as she worked.

"No one's died yet," she told me bluntly when I came to relieve her. "It's well there's only five. It makes it easier."

"Six," I said.

She passed a glance to Archie, who lay still on his blanket. "Yes, well, I meant five infected. I've tried feeding them, but no one will take anything. Did you make the breakfast in the kitchen? Thank God." She stared over my shoulder as Jack came up behind me. She took in his change of clothes and was momentarily speechless.

"Good morning," Jack said.

"Blimey," said Nina.

"I think we ought to regroup," I cut in. "We put the patients on the floor here for evacuation, but the rain hasn't stopped, and we may not get help for another day yet. The floor isn't the best place for them."

"I agree," said Nina. "They should be in their rooms, in bed."

I turned to Jack. "Let's find Paulus and Roger. And Captain Mabry. Let's see if we can move these men back upstairs."

Paulus and Roger were in the kitchen devouring much of the breakfast I'd cooked. We sent them upstairs to prepare the six bedrooms and get a stretcher. Then I put a plate together, poured a cup of hot tea, and brought a tray to West.

He was in the common room, looking out at the rain. He didn't thank me when I gave him the food, but I could tell he was famished. I took a seat in one of the rickety chairs and looked out at the rain as he ate.

"It'll lighten up by tonight," he told me. "And then we can get help."

"How do you know it will stop?"

"I feel it in here." He pointed dismissively to the stumps of his legs. "I felt it coming, and now I can feel it going. Coming is worse. It nearly made my teeth hurt." He took another bite of bacon, didn't look at me. "I'm not useless, you know."

I was surprised. "I never said you were."

"I nearly had that scrawny bastard last night," he went on. I thought vaguely that my patients had long lost any awareness of swearing in my presence, if they had ever had any in the first place. "I learned my choke holds in the army. Another few seconds and I'd have put his lights out, but he fell out of his chair and got away from me." West looked at me. "I'm just saying I don't have to be a drain. I can be of use."

"Very well, Mr. West," I said. "I'll keep it in mind."

"Lieutenant Douglas R. West, First Battalion, Royal Berkshire Regiment, at your service." He gave me a quick salute, then smiled. "Call me Douglas."

"There you are," Jack said, coming into the room. Captain Mabry followed. "Morning, West."

West looked him up and down. "Out of your pajamas at last, Yates?"

"Something like it."

"The look suits you. Though you must be disappointed you're not one of the team." He motioned to the lettering on his shirt.

Jack shook his head. "I've resigned."

"Well, by God." West, cheered up, rubbed his hands. "Brave Jack is here. It's raining, we're stuck here, we're dropping like flies,

474

there's a ghost, and Jack's going to lead us over No Man's Land. I'm game. This ought to be good. What's first?"

Jack pulled up a chair and shrugged. "Mabry's got news. Go ahead, Captain."

Captain Mabry nodded politely at me. He looked pale, and gray shadows hung under his eyes. I hoped to God he wasn't getting sick, but before I could ask him, he began. "The generator's low on fuel. The fuel is kept in the cellar, apparently, so I went to get some, and I found two problems. The first is that the cellar is completely flooded, and getting worse as we speak."

I straightened in my chair. "You're saying we can't fuel the generator?"

"We can't. Sorry. I mucked through as best as I could, but the water's over a foot deep and the fuel container wasn't airtight. The whole supply has watered to nothing by now."

"All right," said Douglas. "Lamps it is."

"The other issue," Mabry continued, "is that I saw evidence that someone had been there. On a shelf was a blanket and two opened tins of meat stolen from the kitchen pantry. The remains in the tins weren't rotten. Someone had been down there recently, camping out. They likely left when the flooding started."

"Creeton," I said.

Jack nodded. "We know where he spent the night, then. But we don't know where he's gone. Or why."

I didn't understand it. Why go into hiding, away from everyone? Creeton hadn't been the same since the awful day of his suicide attempt; he'd been alternately hostile and silent in turn, his comments, when he bothered to speak, almost frighteningly vicious. But he'd been present and aware of his surroundings. His hiding spoke of delusion. Something had pushed Creeton over the edge.

Nina came into the doorway. "Kitty, am I needed to help move the patients? I'm dead on my feet."

I stood. "I can take over. Moving them shouldn't be complicated."

"You may want to rethink that," said a voice from behind Nina.

Paulus and Roger came into the room. Paulus was pale, his expression more grim than I'd ever seen it. I wondered whether he'd recovered from the night before.

"What is it?" said Jack.

"I'm not sure those fellows should go to their rooms after all," Paulus said. "Come take a look."

■ ■ ■ ■

"How did he do this?" Captain Mabry said. "We didn't hear a thing."

We were standing in the bedroom of George Naylor, one of the patients who was currently downstairs lying in the hall. Naylor, a quiet twenty-two-year-old with a gap in his front teeth and a fragile constitution from having been gassed, was a neat and orderly patient. But his meager belongings had been pulled from his dresser drawer, his socks and underthings shredded, his pillow reduced to a pile of fabric and feathers on the floor, his mattress sliced. A single picture frame, the only personal item Naylor had been allowed, lay facedown on the ground.

"This room is just one of them," Roger said. "There are others like this, too."

I glanced at Jack. Creeton had done this while we were downstairs at breakfast, while I had been giving Jack his clothes back. Creeton must have come up past the back servant stairs — it was the fastest way. He'd been passing the stairwell door as Jack and I had stood in the corridor.

Jack's face was stony, impossible to read.

"Excuse me," he said, and walked from the room.

He was going to Jack's own room, of course. We all followed him, clustering in the doorway as he stood looking around the small, dim space where he'd spent six months alone. Creeton hadn't damaged it, not the way he had George Naylor's room. He had littered it with papers, all of them lettered in dark, square writing, the lines close and thick. Pages were strewn across the floor, the window seat, the bed.

Jack picked up one of the pages, scanned it. "His dreams," he said, handing the page to Captain Mabry.

Mabry glanced at the sheet and winced at what he read there, as if it were shocking or painful. "Didn't he give you these when the rest of us did?"

"No." Jack's attention had been drawn to the bed. "He refused." *Go fuck yourself,* the exact words had been.

"Well, it looks like he wrote his dreams after all." Mabry looked around at the dozens of pages littered across the room. "Creeton always denied he had nightmares."

"You all denied it," I said.

"Wait." Jack walked over to the bed, and I could see a single piece of paper placed squarely on the pillow. It was not covered in writing like the others, but had a single message on it that I couldn't read from where I stood. Jack picked up the paper. "Bloody hell."

"What does it say?" said Paulus.

Jack held it up. *"Eliminate the weak."*

We all digested that for a second. Roger spoke first. "I don't like the sound of that."

I thought of Archie telling me, *It's too late. I'm sorry.* The ghost of Nils Gersbach. Creeton going over the edge into delusion at the same time. "The sick men," I said. "Downstairs."

"Archie Childress," said Jack.

"You think he means to harm them?" asked Mabry.

"I think we can't take the risk," Jack replied. "We know he's been in the kitchen, and he sliced Naylor's mattress with a knife. So he's armed himself. He may have found other weapons by now, too. If he's got this idea fixed in his head —"

A sound came from the walls. A low groan, deep and vibrating. By reflex I put my hands to my ears; I knew that sound all too well. It was followed by a hollow *clang,* and then another.

"The lav," I heard Paulus say.

It came again, and from down the corridor, toward the men's lav, we heard a wet gurgling sound. I pressed my hands harder to my ears, but I couldn't block it. I could see the mold in my mind; I could smell it. I could see how it had smeared as I mopped it. And I heard the words in my head, the ones that always presented themselves unbidden. *He's coming.* I opened my mouth to shout it, prepared to run. I had no courage to face it anymore.

And then it stopped.

We looked at one another in the silence.

"By God," said Paulus hoarsely at last. "I hate that bathroom."

"That's the loudest I've ever heard it," Jack said as I reluctantly took my hands from my ears. "Something's happening."

The air was thick — anticipation, fear. I didn't know what it was, but my back ached with tension and my jaw felt stiff. Somewhere, a shutter banged in the rain.

Roger cracked his knuckles. "Let's find this bastard. I don't care about ghosts. Just let me lay my hands on Creeton."

"We need to guard the patients," Jack replied. "If he's planning something, he'll come to them — we won't have to go anywhere."

"They're too exposed in the main hall," Mabry said. His voice was shaky and he looked even paler. "It's dark, and he could come from too many directions."

"I agree," said Jack. "Where should we move them?"

Mabry thought about it. "The common room. There's only the one doorway."

"But it has the French doors to the terrace," I replied. "He could come through there."

"Not without someone seeing him," Mabry replied. "They can be barred. And they let in light. If the generator goes, we want to be in the best-lit room in the house, at least during daylight hours."

I turned to Jack. "Can we move beds in there? I don't like having patients on the floor."

Paulus answered me. "We've no folding beds, but we can move mattresses down. How many would we need?"

"Seven," I replied. "We've five sick men, and Archie. And a mattress for the attending nurse to use."

"Do it," Jack said to the orderlies.

"We'll be quick." Paulus was even paler than before. "I've no desire to be up here longer than I have to. Not after that."

Jack, Mabry, and I descended the stairs to the main floor. "I wish I had a weapon," Mabry said. "I don't like how he's creeping around the house behind our backs. We

481

should be armed."

"I agree," said Jack. "A handgun would be best. Too bad they don't keep them in madhouses."

I halted on the stairs.

The men stopped and turned. "What is it, Kitty?" said Jack.

I looked at them uncertainly. "Is a Luger a handgun?"

Jack and Mabry exchanged a glance. "Yes," Mabry said. "It is."

"Then we have one," I said. "At least, I think we do. It's Creeton's." I bit my lip. "He told me they took it from him when they checked him in here. There's a safe in Matron's office where she locks up the men's valuables, the things she doesn't keep in the main cupboard." I glanced at Jack. "Boney told me about it. If she confiscated Creeton's gun, she wouldn't have discarded it. She would have locked it up."

The men considered this. "And how," Jack said slowly, "would we get into Matron's safe?"

I pulled out the key ring I'd taken from her cardigan pocket. It held the key to the cupboard where I'd found Jack's clothes, but there was a scrap of cloth attached to it as well. I'd noticed it when I'd first grabbed the ring, but I hadn't paid it much attention. Now I did. Because Matron would have kept the two things together — the key to the men's belongings and the key to the valuables, two things that were her responsibility alone.

"I think this is it," I said.

Jack reached for it, but it was Mabry who took it from my hand. He stared at it with what seemed like fascination. Numbers were inked onto the scrap of cloth. Six numbers. A combination.

"The safe," I said, "will have any valuables the men brought in. Money. Watches. Gold. Passports." I bit my lip. "All of it."

Mabry closed his hand around it. He really did look tired, I worried. "Well," he said quietly. "I believe it's official. The inmates are now running the asylum."

"Take it," I said. "But be aware. Creeton's going to want the contents of that safe. And he's going to want his gun."

"We'll get it, and we'll help the orderlies move the sick," Jack said. "Then we'll scout the west wing for signs of Creeton. Roger has a key." He looked at me. "And where are you going?"

"I'm going to find Nina," I said. "She was exhausted. I think she may have gone to bed."

"Upstairs in the nursery?"

"Yes. She doesn't know what Creeton's been up to. I don't want her up there alone."

"Right," said Jack. "Go get her. We'll set up her mattress downstairs with the others." His blue gaze was steady on me. "And for God's sake, Kitty, be careful."

CHAPTER THIRTY-THREE

He'd been there before me. Of course he had. In the pit of my gut, I was starting to know that so far we had always been a step too slow, waiting to see what he'd left behind. This time it was Nina.

She lay on the floor of the nursery, where she'd been undressing to go to bed. There was blood on her temple, as if she'd been struck, but her face was flushed and I could see the rise and fall of her chest. For good measure, Creeton had taken a stocking from her drawer and tied her wrists to the foot of the brass bedstead.

"Nina." I fell to my knees, pressed my hand to her forehead and her temple. She didn't move, didn't groan. She was out cold. I had no idea what to do, of course, if there was anything to be done. But the stocking I could take care of. I lunged for my own bed and felt under the mattress.

My knife wasn't there.

Cold steel touched my throat. "Looking for this?"

I froze.

"Interesting," said Creeton. "One of our own nurses was armed. I guess you were a little bit suspicious of us."

I glanced over my bed. All of my things had been rifled through, my bedding disturbed. Martha's and Nina's things had been searched as well, their undergarments taken from the drawers. *Practical Nursing* lay facedown on the floor as if someone had shaken and dropped it. I'd noticed none of this when I'd come in; I'd seen only Nina.

"What do you want?" I managed.

I was still crouched beside my bed, my hands on the mattress. Creeton shifted behind me, and I could hear his heavy breath. "You know what I want. I wrote a little note and put it on Yates's pillow. You've all found it by now."

" 'Eliminate the weak,' " I quoted.

"Do you hear it?" said Creeton. "He's telling me. I can hear it in my head. Only at night at first, but lately it's been stronger and stronger. There. I can hear him now. Can you?"

I heard nothing but the pounding of my own heart. "He isn't real. It's this place, Creeton. I told you."

"In my mind, he's real. But then, I'm mad, aren't I?" The knife drew tighter against my throat. "I'd like to try killing you. You've never liked me and I've never liked you. But you aren't the *assignment*. You're a means to an end. So was the other nurse."

"What end?" I choked out. "For God's sake, what do you want?"

"The key to the west wing," said Creeton. "I've tried to get in there but all the doors are barred. Just one is locked. I want the key, and I want my Luger. I want the combination to the safe where it's kept."

"I don't know of any safe."

"That's a nice lie," he said. "But I already questioned the other nurse, and she told me that's where it is. But she didn't have the combination. I was finished with her." He leaned closer, exhaling in my ear as he spoke. "I think you have it. I think you have both."

I thought frantically. There was no point in stalling him; everyone was busy with the patients two floors down, and no one was coming this way. If I screamed, how quickly would they come? And would he kill me before they got here?

Creeton pressed the tip of the knife harder into my throat. "Don't scream. I can see you thinking about it. If you try, I'll cut you with this, and then I'll cut her. I swear it."

"Jack Yates has the combination to the safe," I choked. "He has your gun."

"Another lie." His face grew red, and then he sneered. "Oh, perfect Jack, your little lover. Snuck into his room at night, did you? I know all about it. Has he had you yet? Does he know what you are?"

I was blinded by white-hot anger. "You can stick it, you disgusting pig."

He laughed at that. "You're not one of the weak. Not you. I'll get my gun from him; never worry. Now give me the key to the west wing."

Again, I could have put him off. Only the orderlies had the keys to the west wing, but I still had the ring of keys I'd taken off Paulus's belt the night before. At least, if I gave Creeton the key, I'd be able to tell Jack where we could find him. "It's in the pocket of my apron," I said.

"Don't reach," he said. "Keep your hands on the bed where I can see them. I'll get it myself."

He took his time about it, putting his beefy hands into my pockets, making sure his fingers grabbed and pinched me through the layers of fabric. He finally found the right key ring and held it out in front of me. "Is this it?"

"Yes," I said.

"Good girl." He laughed low and put his hand down again, this time grabbing my backside the way he had the first day. "Very nice."

Tears stung my eyes. "You can't hurt me," I said to him. "I've been hurt by worse than you, and he's dead now, or dying."

He dropped his hand. "I would have done it, you know. That day. I could have saved everyone a lot of trouble. I'm one of the weak. My father knows it, and so do I. It would have been best if I'd gone that day, because it's best if the weak are eliminated. But now I have an assignment to carry out. It's the only reason he hasn't had me kill myself already."

"Then go do it," I spat, "and leave me alone."

"Business first. Put your wrists together."

He pulled out another of Nina's stockings. I couldn't do it; it was foolish perhaps, but I'd given in too many times in my life, and all my instincts rose up. I fought him as he grabbed my wrists. I thrashed hard and I screamed. He swore and stuffed the stocking into my mouth, then grabbed another as I choked on it, and he yanked my wrists again.

Still I fought. It was a grim struggle, the

two of us on the ground, I trying to kick him or jab him with my knees, Creeton using his big bulk to pin me down. I was bruised and straining by the end of it, the stocking thick and foul in my mouth, sweat running down my forehead and onto my temples, tears flowing down my face. But he won. He finally wound the stocking around both of my wrists and tied me to the leg of my bedstead, just as he had done to Nina.

He stood, panting, and looked down at me. "You're lucky you're one of the strong ones," he said. "And you're lucky I'm out of time. Otherwise I'd use these, just as I did on your friend." He reached into his pocket and held up the bottle of Jack's pills.

I screamed past the stocking, and it came out a pitiful, muffled sound. If he'd given those pills to Nina, she was as good as dead. I was so bloody helpless. I felt more tears on my face. I kicked my legs, but he stepped easily away.

"I only gave her three," he said. "I made her take them. I didn't want to kill her any more than I want to kill you, but she'll sleep a good while, I think. She won't be much use to anyone even when she wakes up. I was saving the others for you, but I can tell you won't swallow them, even at knifepoint.

And I don't want to take that stocking out of your mouth and hear you scream again."

He put the bottle in his pocket. He looked down at me, and in my haze I wasn't sure whether he spoke again. And then he was gone, and I was tied up on the floor, alone.

Seconds ticked by like hours. Time blurred. The rain pattered on the window. No one else came. Nina was still.

I closed my eyes. Something was happening downstairs; I was sure of it. I hoped Jack and Mabry were ready for it. I hoped the patients had been moved. I thought, incongruously, of Syd, the way he'd looked on the day he came to see me, in his wool suit and new hat. The way he'd smelled. My own brother, who I'd thought dead, coming to get me. Hitting me. I lay back and felt the bitter sting of the stocking in my throat and wept, there on the floor. My anger had faded into black helplessness. It seemed I would always be fighting with men, always wondering when they'd pin me down to get their way. Only Jack touched me with gentleness. And why would Jack ever love someone as worthless as I was?

There was nothing but the sound of the rain on the window, the numbness in my hands, the tight pain in my wrists, and the ache in my arms. My lower back hurt, and my elbow from where I'd cracked it fighting Creeton, and my ribs and legs ached. After I stopped crying I was just this, a body, a collection of varying aches and pains, my heart pushing blood through me as I waited.

Then I heard a creak in the corridor, and a quiet footstep.

I stayed still at first, listening. If it was the shirtless ghost of Mikael Gersbach, I didn't want to see it. I would stay still, and maybe he would go away.

Another footstep, closer this time. Someone had come through the door of the nursery and was crossing the floor toward me.

I didn't feel a flash of cold, and I didn't hear the pipes begin to moan in the walls. I opened my eyes and craned my neck, but the angle was wrong and I couldn't see who was approaching. It was someone tentative, almost tiptoeing. That meant it couldn't be Jack or Mabry. Creeton had finished with me and left. Who was tiptoeing around Portis House?

I heard a rustle of skirts, and gooseflesh broke out on my arms.

She came into my line of vision at last. She was wearing the same dress I'd seen her in before, though it was dusty and bedraggled. Her blond hair was pulled back into a simple braid. She was thin and pale, but she was real, and she was alive. It was the girl from the picture in Maisey's locket. She came forward and knelt next to me.

"Hush," she said. "We must be quiet."

I blinked up at her, amazed.

The girl pulled out a pocketknife and motioned toward my ties. "I'm here to help you," she said. "My name is Anna Gersbach."

"I don't even know where to start," I said when she had pulled the stocking from my mouth.

"I'm sorry," she said. Her accent was flavored with French and something upper class and Continental. "I don't mean to startle you. I'm one of the family who used to live here."

"I know who you are," I said, watching as she sawed the blade of her pocketknife against the stockings around my wrists. Up close, I could see that her hair was coming loose from its braid and her fingernails were caked with dirt. A sour, unwashed smell came off her. "I'm Kitty Weekes. I've seen you before. Outside. You aren't dead."

"No," she said simply, straining as she cut.

"What about your mother?"

"She is dead," Anna replied. "Just three

weeks ago."

"Three weeks? Where have you both been all this time?"

She glanced at me. "It is a long story. I don't know if we have time to hear it now."

"I believe I know most of it," I replied.

She gave me an assessing look, then returned to work on the stocking. There was something removed about her, something a little unnerving, as if she were looking at you through the glass of a lens you could not see.

The stocking gave way and I slumped to the floor. It felt as if someone had shoved wires into my arms. I lay gasping for a long moment, tears of pain rolling down my face, and then I slowly rolled to my side and looked at her again. "Why are you here?" I asked her. "What do you want?"

"I will help your friend," she said as she moved over to Nina and started cutting again. "This man," she said as she worked. "With red hair. He is mad, of course, but it is more than that. Perhaps you'll think I'm mad as well, but my father has him. My father's ghost, that is. He's taken the man's mind." She glanced at me. "I realize this makes no sense."

I lay on my side and felt regular sensation gradually return to my arms and hands.

"You would be surprised at what I think makes sense," I said. "What about your brother? Mikael is here, too."

She stopped her work and looked stricken. "Mikael." For a second she seemed close to tears; then she turned back to Nina's bound hands. "Yes, he's here, too. But he's a prisoner, just like these other men. He wants to be set free." She bit her lip, swallowed her grief. "It was what he wanted in life as well. What we both wanted."

I sat up. *What we both wanted.* I didn't want to think about what those words meant. I knew the possibilities too well. "Did your father kill Mikael?"

"Yes. Out in the grass by the library. He executed Mikael with a rifle."

"And you hid with your mother."

"Not here, no." Nina's ties gave way, and Anna looked down at Nina's sleeping form. "What happened to her?"

"He forced her to swallow drugs, and then he hit her."

The answer didn't seem to affect her. She touched Nina's neck. "Her pulse is strong, but she is asleep. We'll have to leave her here. He'll be downstairs by now, trying to kill the others."

"I don't understand it," I said, struggling to my feet. "Your father was a murderer. He killed Mikael in cold blood. Why did you run? Why are you here, in hiding?"

Anna stood and faced me. "Because if I'm found, I'll be hanged. I'm a murderer, too. After Papa shot Mikael, I took his gun and I shot him myself."

CHAPTER THIRTY-FOUR

Creeton was armed, and he could be anywhere by now; we needed to hurry. Still, I sat on the floor and stared at Anna Gersbach, the shock of her words washing over my body like hot water. "What did he do to you?" I managed. "Your father."

Her face was closed, diffident. "We must go."

"Wait," I said. *That was me,* I wanted to tell her. *That was me, too. Did you tell anyone? Did you cry?* I wanted to know. I needed to know. "What did he do to you?"

Her gaze only glanced over mine, then moved away again. "Enough," she said finally. "He did enough. Now, please get up. We have to move quickly."

We crept down the staircase; we heard no sounds. "Creeton is after the patients," I whispered to Anna. "He'll go for the common room."

She looked at me quizzically, and I realized she didn't know what room I was talking about. What had the room been when the Gersbachs had been here, with all their beautiful furniture? A drawing room? A parlor? I had no time to find out. I pushed past her and led the way.

"How long have you been here?" I asked her as we moved down the stairs.

"A few days," she said. "I think. I don't know. We were in Switzerland, and Mother died. They gave me money . . . They told me I could go to France, or anywhere I wanted. But I have no home in France. My only home is here, and I thought it was empty. So I made my way here."

So she'd been in hiding. How had she thought she could come home and live in Portis House as if nothing had happened? "You must have had a bit of a surprise when you arrived."

"I suppose so."

I frowned and glanced back at her, keeping my voice low. "You said *they* gave you money. Who is 'they'?"

"Men in suits," she replied, shrugging. "Lawyers, perhaps. I don't remember."

I glanced back at her again. For the first time it crossed my mind that Anna Gersbach, who had grown up with a father who had done "enough" to her, watched her father kill her brother, then killed her father herself, might not exactly be in her right mind. This was how she dealt with all of it, I thought: by keeping her distance, as if none of it was happening.

The men had been moved out of the main hall. It stood empty, but for a few crumpled blankets and a left-behind pillow. The light coming through the windows was chalky gray. Was it my imagination, or had the rain eased off a little?

I slipped down the corridor, Anna moving silently behind me. I started to run when I saw what stood in the doorway, pushed off-kilter. It was an empty wheelchair.

The furniture in the common room had been pushed aside, and mattresses had been placed on the floor. The sick men had been placed on them; some were sleeping, one was thrashing, and one groggily asked for water when he saw me. Douglas West sat on the floor twenty feet down the corridor, the halves of his legs flexed upward. He was walking slowly, very slowly, on his hands, pulling himself along the floor toward the door and his chair. He looked up at me. He had blood down one arm and the front of his shirt.

"Don't worry," he said as I rushed to him. "Most of it isn't mine. I don't think so, anyway."

"Are you all right?" I asked stupidly. I squatted next to him. I had no idea how to get him into the chair; that was usually a job for Paulus. "What happened?"

"They put me in charge of sentry duty," he said. "That red-haired bastard came along, as we knew he would. He had a knife in his hand. I wheeled out as he came my way and jumped him, grabbed at the knife. He bloodied my lip, but at least I nicked him before I fell." He stopped his strenuous progress long enough to wipe his forehead. "I got him in the shoulder, I think."

"Do you need help?" Anna came forward. "Perhaps two of us can lift him."

Douglas looked up at her. "Oh, hullo," he said, taking in her unkempt dress and hair. "You're a bit of all right, aren't you?"

"This is Anna Gersbach," I said.

"You don't say? You're pretty, but I have to say your family's a bit of a muck. I don't like to be the bearer of bad news, but your brother's been haunting my nightmares for three months."

Anna had been about to take one of his arms as I took the other, but she blinked at him. "My father is doing it," she said. "He torments Mikael. I'm very sorry."

He grunted as the two of us lifted him.

I'd never known a man could be so heavy with muscle. "It's all right," he said, ever the gentleman. "I was already barking mad." He looked at my face as we settled him into his chair and wheeled him back to the doorway of the common room. "Don't fuss, Nurse Weekes. I'm terribly hard to kill."

"What do we do now?" I said to him. "Where do we go? I thought he would come here to kill the patients."

"I thought so, too, but he didn't. I don't know where he was bloody going. When he shook me off, he headed in the direction of the stairwell."

I thought of what Creeton had said when he attacked me. He had wanted the key to the west wing, and he had wanted to get his Luger. "He may have gone to Matron's office," I said. "He's looking for a way to get into her safe."

"He won't find it," said a voice.

Behind us, inside the common room, one man had sat up on his mattress. It was Archie, hugging his knees, watching us. I hadn't seen him move.

"Archie," I said gently, "are you all right?"

He looked past my shoulder to Anna Gersbach. "He knows you," he said to her. "The man that comes. He knows you."

"Yes," she said.

"Are you here to stop him?" he asked her.

Anna stepped forward, looking down at him, sitting so thin and vulnerable on his mattress. "I was hiding," she told him. "I was afraid. But Mikael — Mikael came to me this morning. He begged me to help. He told me I was the only one who can." She swallowed, but no tears came down her face. "He told me Papa is getting stronger, that he's going to kill someone. He told me to stop it and set him free."

Archie looked up at her from his sunken eyes, all traces of his stutter gone. "I see his face in my dreams," he said. "I heard his thoughts last night. They were in my head. If that was your father, I am truly sorry."

Her mouth opened, but she did not reply. She seemed to have lost her words.

"Do you know how to stop him?" Archie asked her.

Still speechless, Anna shook her head.

"He wants a sacrifice," Archie said. "He's tried, and he's come close." He glanced at me, then looked back at Anna. "But he's never succeeded. If he gets his sacrifice, he will go."

"That means someone has to die," I said.

"Perhaps," said Archie, "and perhaps not." He looked at me again. "Creeton won't get into the safe. The Luger isn't in there anyway. You told him that, didn't you?"

I'd told Creeton that Jack had the combination, but Creeton hadn't believed me. "Yes," I said. "Archie, how — ?"

"It's logic," he replied. "I know what he was after. I know he tried to get it from you. Creeton won't get into the safe himself, so he'll move on. He'll go to the west wing."

"Why?" Douglas asked.

Archie's eyes glittered. "Because the one he wants is there. The one he's going to kill. He's going to eliminate the weak."

My breath came short. Creeton hadn't killed Nina, and he hadn't killed me. *You aren't the assignment,* he'd said to me. I'd thought that meant he was coming to kill the other patients. But it hadn't.

"Jack," I said. "Jack is in the west wing. And so is Mabry."

"We need to hurry," said Anna.

I turned to Douglas. I reached into my pocket and took out a folded rag. Anna and I had made a stop on our way downstairs from the nursery; there was something I'd needed to retrieve from the nurses' night duty desk.

I unfolded the rag and pulled out one of the needles I'd taken from the desk drawer and assembled. "If by any chance Creeton comes back, stick him with this."

Douglas took it from me. His expression was as unsettled as if I'd handed him a live grenade. "I recognize this," he said quietly.

Of course he did. Every man at Portis House could get the needle if he got out of hand. "It'll do the trick," I told him.

He squared away his unease and set the needle gingerly on his thigh, his hand cupped over it. "If he comes back, I'm ready," he said, determined. "Go."

"They've closed off the west wing," I told Anna as we climbed the west servants' stairs. "There's only one door."

"Actually, there's a door through the cellar," Anna said.

"What?"

"It was how I got into the house, through the cellar. There is an outside door and the wood was rotten around the lock. I got in that way and used the connecting tunnel through the cellar to hide in the west wing, where no one would find me."

"I don't understand it," I said, hushed. "I don't understand where you've been, why you came back."

"After I killed Papa, Mama was hysterical," Anna said. "She didn't know what to do. I was in shock. I barely remember. Papa was going to kill us, too — that was why I

504

did it. I still know it, that he would have killed us. But how can I prove that? He'd hurt us for years, but no one outside the family ever knew. He kept it so quiet, so hidden."

"Even from Maisey Ravell," I said.

For the first time she expressed emotion as she flinched in pain. "Maisey never knew. I hope to God she did not. I hid the bruises. Papa said that if I ever told —"

"I know," I said. "I know."

She glanced at me thoughtfully, and then her face returned to its usual impassiveness. "He hurt Mama, too. He hurt all of us. Then Mikael came home disgraced as a coward. It was too much for Papa. He said we would never live down the shame, that we should not live at all. He said he would execute Mikael the way the army should have. He pulled Mikael from his bed one night and did it. He said it was only just. He took Mikael outside. I heard Mikael pleading with him, and I heard the shot, and when I came out I saw Mikael on the ground. So I grabbed the gun from Papa and I shot him."

"Dear God, Anna," I said. "I'm sorry."

"Mama was hysterical," she said, as if I hadn't spoken. She had gone back into her strange trance, distant from the world. "She

505

telephoned the magistrate and he came."

"Maisey's father," I said.

"Yes. I remember he came, and he told us he would take care of it, that there need be no scandal. I had thought I would go to jail, that I would be hanged. But Mr. Ravell said that if we did exactly as he said, it would all go away."

"And what did he tell you to do?"

"Leave," she said. "He helped us book passage back to Switzerland under assumed names, with assumed passports. He told us he would see Mikael and Papa buried, and no one would know." *And make himself a nice profit,* I thought. Anna continued. "Papa had dismissed the servants, because he'd planned very carefully to kill us. There was no one to gossip. Mr. Ravell gave us money and told us to go. I was terrified of being hanged as a murderer, so I took Mama and I went."

We reached the landing and she paused, looking out the small window at the marshes. "We stayed in Switzerland until Mama got sick. When she died, all I wanted was to come home. I thought the house would be empty, that it would still be ours. When I saw that wasn't so, I should have run. But where would I go? I had come into the country on an assumed passport. I wasn't supposed to be in England. Someone had always taken care of us, even in Switzerland, but not now. If I'm found, I'll hang as a murderer. So I broke into the cellar and hid."

I pushed past her and led her out into the deserted corridor, toward the gallery that connected the west wing with this one. I thought of Martha's report to Matron on that first day, of how the orderlies wouldn't go into the cellar because they heard footsteps. "You've been here for days," I said.

"I didn't know what to do. I stole some food from the kitchen. I realized the house was full of madmen. I was going to leave. And then, that first night, I heard Papa."

We'd reached the door. It was unlocked and ajar. I looked at Anna, and another piece fell into place. "That's why his ghost is so angry," I said. "Because you're here."

She swallowed. "I heard his voice. I saw him. It was as if I'd never killed him at all."

We both fell silent for a moment. I tried to imagine what it had been like for her, seeing the ghost of the man she had shot, the man she had thought could never hurt her again. Finally I slipped through into the darkness, Anna behind me.

The smell was the same, that dusty, rotten, wet smell, but it seemed worse. We picked our way down the corridor, stepping over the dust and the fallen debris from the ceiling. I strained my ears, focusing on every sound. At first I thought the rain had grown heavier; then I thought perhaps it was just louder in this part of the house. When we turned the first corner, I realized my mistake. The sound of water was caused by a leak somewhere in the ceiling, and rivulets of dirty rain were trickling down the walls.

I glanced back at Anna. This was her family home, falling apart. But she had seen it already, and her face showed nothing.

Something scurried past us, and I flinched. Where was Jack? Where was Mabry? Had Creeton found them already?

"These men," Anna said to me. "The men that the red-haired man is looking for, that my father is looking for. Are they weak?"

"No," I replied. "Never."

She nodded, and the set of her jaw became grim. "I thought perhaps that was so."

"What do you mean?"

But she grabbed my forearm, her grip hard and cold. "Do you feel that?" she whispered.

I closed my eyes. Inhaled air that was suddenly frigid. "He's here somewhere," I said.

"Mikael," she replied. "I feel him. It's Mikael."

The hair stood up on my arms, but it was easier now. Anna had known him, loved him. *Sweet Mikael.* He had deserved nothing that had happened to him after all. I opened my eyes again. "We have to go forward, Anna. They need our help. Mikael needs our help."

She hesitated, then nodded. But she didn't let me go.

The west wing was now utterly decayed, like a tomb centuries old. "I'm not certain where we are," I confessed. "I came here once before, with Jack. We found all of your old belongings."

"In Papa's gallery," she replied. "It's just to the right. I thought all of our belongings must be there. But it's locked, so I couldn't go in."

We came to the door and I tried the handle. It was locked. I patted my pockets, and then I remembered. The key to this door was on the orderlies' key ring — the one I had given to Creeton. "I don't have the key," I told her. "Only the orderlies have them. We have to keep going."

"Kitty," Anna whispered, "I don't hear anyone."

"Neither do I." It worried me. What if everyone was hiding? Or dead?

The back of my neck prickled with cold,

and then it was gone. My skin felt warm and humid again, clammy with damp from the rain and from my own fear.

Where did ghosts go when they left?

And then, from below us, I heard shouts. Two voices. Three.

I turned back to Anna. "Where is the nearest staircase?"

"This way," she said, and she disappeared around a corridor without me. I followed, taking as much care as I could not to step on a nail or a mouse or a patch of rotten floor. I kept Anna's figure in sight and only looked forward.

We had just reached the stairwell — the door was rotten, warped in its frame, and it took both of us to pry it open — when we heard a single gunshot. "The Luger," I said, pushing past her, running down the rotten stairs that bowed and groaned under my weight. I'd spent enough time on servants' stairs to last me a lifetime. I came out the door at the other end and ran in the direction where I thought I'd heard the sound. Shouts came from before me, and another somewhere to my right, voices echoing off the strange corridors. One of them was Jack's.

I turned toward it, but another sound was closer to me, to my left. It was a groan of pain. I'd lost Anna now, but there was nothing I could do about it. I followed the sound and found Roger lying half inside a closet, his legs out in the corridor, his right arm and torso slicked with blood.

"He shot me," he said without preamble as I knelt beside him. "He's got the Luger. Shot me in the shoulder when I grabbed him. I think it's broken. Good God, it hurts like the goddamned devil —"

So Creeton had found his Luger, then. "I don't know what to do," I said to Roger. "I don't know what to do."

"Give me a strip of something and we'll tie it off. Who the hell is that?"

Anna had appeared over my shoulder. "Do you have something?" I cried at her. "A cloth of some kind. Something!"

She stared at me helplessly. I grabbed the hem of my apron and ripped a strip from it, my arms straining as the thick fabric nearly refused to give way. I handed it to Anna. "Follow his instructions," I told her, "and tie it off. I'm going to find the others."

"In the ballroom," Roger said. "To the left."

And then I was gone, racing down the corridor toward the big, grand double doors that had once led to the ballroom.

Chapter Thirty-Five

I had seen the ballroom from outside that day I'd sat on the lawn with Archie, what felt like years ago. From inside, it dwarfed both the common room and the dining room in size, and probably could have held both of them easily. The floor was marble, the walls accented in gold leaf that carried across the ceiling. Electric lights were installed in the walls, as well as sconces for lamps. It had been a beautiful room once.

Now the gold paint was peeling, the plaster was crumbling with damp, and the floor was slick with leaves and rain. The high windows were crusted with dirt, and the light they let in was murky. I saw a lone figure on the floor, on his knees, his head down.

At first I didn't recognize him. And then I stopped short, just as I approached him, and stared at him in shock.

It was Creeton.

He looked up at me. The anger, the violence were gone from him, and the look he gave me was almost pleading, though he did not speak. He was bloodied on one shoulder, the blood running down his arm. He wasn't holding a gun. We stared at each other for a long moment, in that huge, rotting room, as the rain fell outside and leaked through the ceiling.

"Where is it?" I said to him.

"What?"

"The gun. Your Luger."

He shook his head.

"I mean it," I said. "It's over, Creeton. Give me the gun."

"I was supposed to kill him," Creeton said. "That was the assignment. But I couldn't even do that. I failed. And now . . . now he's gone from my mind. He left me alone at last."

"What are you talking about?" I said. "You didn't fail. You just shot Roger."

But he shook his head again. "I'm sorry, Nurse Weekes. But it isn't over, not yet. I never got my Luger. He always had it. You told me he had it, but I didn't believe you."

My stomach sunk, hard. "If you're saying Jack Yates just shot Roger, then I'm calling you a liar."

"Not Yates," said Creeton. "Mabry. He's

the one who took the gun from the safe. He's the sacrifice. And he never even needed me. Hc's gone to do it himself."

Mabry. Mabry, who had seemed so ill, who had stared at the slip of cloth that held the combination to the safe with such fascination. And then I remembered that Roger had never said a name. *He shot me.* "You're saying —"

"He doesn't have to take just one of us," Creeton said. "That's his power. He can be inside all of us. In our dreams, in our waking nightmares. In this whole house. He can be in more than one mind at the same time."

I looked to the other end of the ballroom, where a large set of double doors opened onto a corridor. The corridor to the library, where men might retreat from a crowded party to smoke or play cards.

"Yes," Creeton said. "He's gone that way."

"You should have stopped him," I said, accusing.

But Creeton shrugged. "I'm finished now," was all he said. "I'm free."

It was hard to run. I felt as if I'd been awake for years, as if I'd never rest again. But I left Creeton behind and I ran to the double doors, and down the corridor to the isolation room.

Nothing in there had changed: not the

narrow bed, the cracked nightstand, the mildewed walls. Mikael's message was still on the wall, staring down at me accusingly. At the other end of the room, the door to the outside had been opened. Jack stood silhouetted there, looking out into the rain.

"Jack," I whispered, not wanting to surprise him.

He did not turn his head. Behind the doorframe, he lifted a hand briefly in acknowledgment. I approached him and looked over his shoulder.

Captain Mabry stood in the grass in front of the isolation room, swaying in the rain.

He had his back to us. He carried a handgun, his arm down at his side. It was a slender, alien-looking thing I had never seen before. The Luger. Mabry's body leaned slightly to one side, and then to the other, as if he was not entirely in control, but otherwise he did not move. Rain sluiced unnoticed down his body, soaked his clothes. He was not looking at anything that I could see.

I looked at Jack. His profile was hard, his gaze unwavering. It was the same as on the day I'd stood in the clearing with Creeton. Too slow an approach, and it would all be over. The gun was lowered, but Mabry's hand was confident on the grip. It would take only a second.

"Andrew," Jack said, gently. I had never heard anyone use Mabry's first name before. "You shot your bullet."

"There were two," Mabry replied, not turning. The rain carried part of his voice away. "There's a second one in the chamber. You know that, Jack."

"Don't do this," said Jack. "This isn't you."

For a second Mabry paused, and then his shoulders sagged. "Don't worry. It will be a relief. It will."

I opened my mouth, took in a breath, but Jack's hand touched my arm. *Wait.* He pointed a finger to the ceiling, turned it in a circle. He meant someone was circling around to the other side of the clearing, probably Paulus. I nodded.

"Andrew," Jack said. "Just listen to me."

"I can't," Mabry said. "I can only hear *him.* Can't you? You can't help me, Jack. No one can. It's over."

Do you think you can help me? Creeton had said to me. *With your caring? With your concern? You can't help any of us.*

Mabry raised his head, as if he heard something. And from the gloom Mikael appeared. He was shirtless, his naked torso impervious to the rain. He was walking slowly, the way he had been when I had last seen him in the stairwell, pulling one foot forward at a time. He was looking at Mabry, coming toward him, the cold coming off him so powerfully I could feel it from where I stood.

Mabry pivoted on his heels and faced Mikael. "What do you want?" he cried. "For God's sake, what do you want?"

Mikael stopped, held out one hand.

A sob came from Mabry's throat. "I can't help you. I can't. I can't even help myself."

I heard an intake of breath, and I turned to see Anna standing beside me. She was looking at Mikael, and her expression was cracked to pieces with grief and love for the brother she had suffered with, the brother she had been unable to save. In one hand, she held a rifle.

"Mikael," she whispered.

Jack turned his head, took her in, his thinking clear in his handsome blue eyes. I wondered whether he recognized her from the time we'd seen her in the clearing.

"Anna Gersbach," I said softly.

He nodded, as if the reappearance of Anna were just another piece of information. His silent gaze went to her rifle.

Anna held the rifle out to him. "Take it." She looked at me. "It was in my father's

517

rifle cabinet. In the gallery with our other things. The orderly had the key." She turned back to Jack. "It's me my father wants. It's me who can end this. It always has been."

He took the rifle from her with sure hands and nodded.

She stepped to the doorway, looked back at him. "If he doesn't shoot me, promise you'll do it," she said. "Promise me."

He didn't hesitate. "I promise."

Anna stepped out into the rain, her arms at her sides, her hands open. "Papa!" she cried.

Mabry turned.

Next to me, Jack cocked the rifle as quietly as he could, but the sound was still loud, even through the muffling of the rain.

Anna had moved out into the clearing, toward Mabry, who was staring at her, dazed. "Anna," he said.

"Don't take him, Papa," she said. "Take me."

"He's one of the weak," said Mabry.

She moved closer to him. Mikael still stood, one hand outstretched, as if he did not see her.

"I don't have a clear shot," Jack whispered to me.

"Don't shoot her," I said through the lump in my throat. "Not yet."

"He isn't weak," Anna said to Mabry, her voice shaking now. Rain had soaked her braid, her bedraggled dress. "I am. I always have been. Shoot me, and then you can go. I'm the last one left, aren't I? The last one to bear the shame?"

Mabry's hand raised the gun slowly, unsteadily, aiming it at her. Blood had begun to trickle sluggishly from his nose. "Anna," he said.

And then it all happened at once. Paulus Vries appeared at the other side of the clearing; he shouted. Mabry jumped. Mikael moved, his eerie form sliding toward his sister. And Jack raised the rifle, sighted it, and fired.

Two shots went off; the noise was deafening. Mabry's leg buckled and he fell. At the same time, his finger squeezed the trigger and he shot at Anna Gersbach with the last bullet in the Luger.

Anna screamed and fell. Jack ran forward into the rain, rifle still at the ready, and Paulus came from the other direction. I followed, my boots squelching in the mud.

Mabry was moaning, his leg drawn up to his chest. "Hold him down!" Paulus shouted, pinning his arms. Mabry had already dropped the gun and lay bleeding into the wet grass, unresisting. I swung a leg over him, straddled him. His spectacles had fallen off, and when he looked up at me, I was reminded of the first day I met him, when he had lain bleeding in my lap. From the look in his eyes, I knew he remembered it, too, and I knew I was looking at the real Andrew Mabry, the kind, gentle captain with the Roman nose and the family he adored and the old-fashioned sense of honor.

I pulled one of the needles from the pocket of my skirt and grabbed his arm. "Sorry," I said, and I stuck him as quickly as I could.

When he fell slack, I turned to Jack, who had dropped the rifle in the grass and had knelt beside Anna. She pulled herself up, wiping water from her face. She had no blood on her at all.

"She wasn't hit," Jack said to me.

"It was Mikael," Anna said to my incredulous expression. She wiped water from her face again, and I realized there were tears mixed in with the rain. "He pushed me. I felt him. Kitty, he's gone." Her breath hitched. "Saving me freed him. He's gone."

CHAPTER THIRTY-SIX

The sun was just breaking over the horizon, and the day was going to be warm. The rain had stopped as night fell, the hem of my skirt sodden as I walked.

Portis House receded behind me. A single, rutted road led from the front door, over the low hills and through the huddle of trees, and eventually to the bridge to the mainland. I could have followed the road, but each pothole and rut was now a puddle deep with rainwater, and the grass actually seemed the drier path. I had never been this way, except for the day I'd arrived here in the hired car. I swung my arms and inhaled the fresh summer air, thinking of that girl I'd been as if she were someone else.

I turned a final curve and stopped, staring. I'd come here in the fog, and nothing had prepared me for how beautiful it was. This was the low part of land, opposite the high, rocky cliffs, the part of land that tilted

521

down into the sea. Long grasses waved on the slope in the early-morning breeze; they finished in a brief, rugged strip of rocks, dark sand, and driftwood before the land vanished into the ocean. The water was choppy, a dark, dangerous blue, with a froth of whitecaps appearing and disappearing, some of the surface slick with fronds of seaweed. Built over this was the bridge, narrow and wooden, launching off over the unsettled water toward the smudged line of the mainland.

Beneath the bridge, the uneasy ocean slapped the wood hard, as if resentful that the storm was over and the bridge had remained standing. The bridge surface was slick with debris and drying water. But it was passable.

I stood watching the water, the bridge, the birds wheeling overhead. I tried to make out details on the mainland, but couldn't. I turned and looked behind me, where the cool stone of Portis House appeared through the trees. The line of windows above the portico, which I knew was the nursery, was just visible. I imagined I could see the abandoned statue of Mary through the waving branches, but the truth was, of course, that she was hidden from here.

I took another breath of salty air, heavy

with oncoming heat, and turned back down the path. There was work to be done.

We now had two injured men, on top of our five sick with influenza. Once we'd moved Roger and Captain Mabry, and Nina had awoken, groggy and rather angry, all of us had set to work. We'd brought three more mattresses to the common room, including one for Douglas West to use when he wasn't in his chair. Roger would need surgery, but we had no means to perform it. We disinfected and bound their wounds as best we could, stanching bleeding and changing dressings. Jack's bullet had taken Mabry through the meat of his calf, a neat flesh wound that hadn't even broken bone. Roger's shoulder wound was more serious, and I worried he would never have full use of his arm again.

Roger had been the first to see that Mabry, with Creeton's gun in his hand, intended not to defend himself but to kill himself. He'd actually tried to stop "the stupid bastard," as he put it. Mabry had shot him; Creeton had witnessed it. Then Mabry had continued on out into the rain. Roger suffered so much pain his first night that, after conferring with the others, I'd finally given him one of Jack's pills to ease him into sleep until help could arrive.

Creeton himself sat subdued. He had come into the common room voluntarily, as we'd been busy with the injured, and now sat quiet and cross-legged on his mattress. Jack had bound his hands as a precaution, though Creeton had not struggled. Creeton would not look at Nina or me.

I came up the circular drive, passed the statue of Mary, and walked up the steps to the portico and through the front door. The main hall was empty now. I passed the little sitting room where I'd met my brother, the dining room where I'd first been so terrified and where I'd sat on the floor with a bleeding Captain Mabry in my lap. I poked my head into the common room and found everything calm; the patients were either asleep or dozing. Nina and Anna weren't there, but Douglas sat comfortably in his chair. "Vries cooked some food," he said to me without preamble. "They've gone down to eat it."

I took a pitcher of water, gave a few sips to the men who asked for it. "All right. I'll go. I just checked and the bridge is clear. We should get help now."

"That's good news," he said.

"D'you want me to bring you some break-fast?"

"Anna said she would. But thank you."

I made myself turn, look down at Creeton, who was now sleeping. He was lying on his back, his mouth open a little as he dozed. His tied hands rested limply on his stomach. "Did he speak?" I asked Douglas.

"Yes. Didn't say much."

"Was he — ?"

"No. I don't think so. He wasn't like before."

I looked around the room. "Someone's missing."

"Archie Childress," Douglas said. "Said he felt well enough to help out. I didn't see a reason to stop him."

I nodded at him and put the pitcher back. Then I went down the corridor to the stairs.

The kitchen smelled like bacon, and suddenly I was ravenous. Everyone was there, filling their plates. Paulus had done a decent job, it seemed; I'd had no idea he could cook. Archie stood at one of the large sinks, his sleeves rolled up, scrubbing pots and pans. He glanced at me and gave me a quick smile.

There was a strange moment when we all sat down at the small table and looked at one another. We were mismatched, for certain: a mental patient, a false nurse, a real nurse, a South African orderly, a murderess, and Brave Jack Yates, sitting down to breakfast. We were like a shipwrecked crew stranded on an island and not sure what to say to one another.

I looked at Jack. He was still wearing his everyday clothes, shirt, suspenders, and trousers. He looked a bit tired, but not much the worse for wear. He was picking thoughtfully at his breakfast, but when he felt my gaze he looked up at me and returned it. He seemed to be looking me over as I'd just done him. My wrists were sore, as were a few spots where I'd gotten the worst of my struggle with Creeton, but otherwise I was fine. I was exhausted, but the walk had given me a second wind, and I felt the blood pumping in my veins again.

I cleared my throat. "I've checked the bridge," I said to everyone. "It's clear."

"Thank God," said Archie. He did not stutter.

"I've just been on the telephone in Matron's office," said Jack. "The phone lines seem to be up again. I spoke to the hospital at Newcastle on Tyne. It seems all the patients arrived safely. I told them we've casualty cases, and they're sending ambulances as fast as they can."

"It will take a few hours," I said.

"That gives us some time," Paulus broke

526

in. When we all looked at him, he said. "Well? What are we going to tell everyone?"

He was right. "The truth doesn't sound . . ." I paused, not certain how to word it.

"It sounds mad," said Archie.

Anna stopped eating and put down her fork.

I pictured it: one of us — any of us — telling the authorities in Newcastle on Tyne that Creeton and Mabry had been possessed by ghosts, and Creeton had tried to kill Mabry in appeasement to the ghost of Nils Gersbach, and Mabry had tried to kill Anna instead, but the ghost of Mikael Gersbach had saved her. "No one would believe me if I said it," I said. "I'm hardly credible."

"Neither am I," offered Archie, gesturing to the prominent lettering on his shirt. "You have the best chance of any of us, Jack."

"I would, if I hadn't just spent six months in a mental hospital," said Jack. "That might tell against me. Paulus or Nurse Shouldice, you're probably the most credible witnesses here."

"God, no," said Paulus. "I need to work, and this place is finished. Who's going to hire an orderly who believes a story like that?"

"I need my job, too," said Nina. She was eating steadily, as always; being struck and drugged seemed to have made her hungry. "Here's the best way. We got hit by the flu. We evacuated as many as we could. The stress got to Creeton and he became aggressive. He attacked Kitty and me, and then Mr. West. Mabry and Yates got the gun out of Matron's safe to defend us. Creeton fought with Mabry, who shot Roger by accident. Yates shot Mabry in the leg when he was aiming at Creeton and his rifle went off by mistake." She put another bite of bacon into her mouth. "I think that works."

Jack had put his fork down and stared at her. "That's missing quite a few pieces of the story. And I'd never let a rifle go off by accident."

She glared back at him from behind her spectacles. "You did this time, Patient Sixteen. You most definitely let your rifle go off by mistake. As for the rest of it, no one's going to know that Mabry shot at Anna if we don't tell them."

"It's not bad," Paulus said. "I come out of it looking rather good. At least I didn't shoot anyone."

"What about me?" said Anna. "Where do I come into the story?"

"Just as you did," Nina replied. "Your

mother died and you came back here. You hid in the west wing. When we found you, we took you in until help arrived."

"Or she was never here at all," said Paulus.

"What does that mean?" said Archie.

"Well, we're the only ones that know she's here, really. She could disappear again and no one would be the wiser." He turned to her. "Is that what you want to do?"

Anna looked down at her plate. "I don't know."

"It's going to come out, Anna," Jack told her softly. "Maisey knows everything, and she can prove it. Whether you're found or not, it will all come out."

She nodded, did not look up.

"The story is rather hard on Creeton," Archie admitted, pouring himself some water with a hand that did not shake. "He did do those things, I know, but he wasn't entirely in charge of his own actions. Neither was Mabry."

"What are you worried about?" Jack asked.

"Well, I assume that we patients will all be reassigned to different hospitals, especially when the scandal breaks. It could go hard on him. He might even face criminal charges."

"I don't think his family will help him," I added.

"Still, they won't want a scandal," said Jack. He sighed. "I don't really know what to do. I'll have to think it over." He looked at Archie. "Where do you think you'll go?"

Archie shrugged. "Wherever they assign me, I suppose." He smiled a little. "Maybe I'll go to a hospital where they have a gramophone."

My mind was turning with an idea. "Has Mabry woken yet?" I asked.

"Only briefly," said Paulus. "He was still groggy."

I nodded, the idea still going round in my mind. I'd talk to Mabry when he was awake.

There was nothing to do, then, but wait. We went our separate ways. Anna took West his breakfast, and they sat talking quietly. Nina flung herself on the spare mattress set up for the on-duty nurse and was asleep in minutes. Paulus disappeared to his own devices, probably to sleep as well, and Jack went to his room. Portis House was silent, the air changed. There were still cracks in the walls and the cellar was still flooded, but it didn't seem like a haunted place. It was a big, somnolent house in the summer heat, a rich man's folly purged of its nightmares, dozing as if already abandoned. I climbed the stairs to the nurses' bathroom and turned on the taps in the bathtub. I unbraided my hair, took off my uniform. I sat in the bath for a long time, thinking about things. About ghosts. About endings. About beginnings.

When I got out, I didn't rebraid my hair. I left it loose and clean; it hung to the middle of my back, swaying with my movements in a way I wasn't used to. It was, I realized, rather a nice chestnut color. I'd never really taken the time to look at my hair in daylight. Perhaps, at almost twenty-one, it was time I did.

I found my cotton nightdress and pulled it over my head, even though the warm sun of midmorning was rising in the sky. Then I padded down the stairs in my bare feet. I made no sound. I saw no ghosts.

Jack's room was darkened. He'd drawn the curtains, and as my eyes adjusted to the gloom, I could see he was lying on his bed, on his back on top of the covers. He'd taken off everything but his undershorts, and he had his fingers linked over his flat stomach as he stared at the ceiling. He went very still when he saw me.

I closed the door behind me, and since it wouldn't lock from the inside, I propped the room's only wooden chair against the knob.

We didn't speak for a moment as my heart careened in my chest. I could hear nothing but the blood rushing in my ears. *Courage, Kitty.* I took a step forward, took my nerves in hand. "You said you'd go through hell to see me naked," I told him. "I think you win."

In one motion, he swung his legs over the edge of the bed and sat up. "Come here," he said softly.

I came closer, fighting shyness, fighting all the fears that had held me back. When I came in range he took my wrists and pulled me in until I stood between his knees. He took my face in his hands and kissed me.

It was everything, that kiss. It was the closeness of him, his skin setting a reaction off mine like sparks, even when we weren't touching. It was the goodness of it, the rightness of it, the fact that I was afraid, and that the fear was right, too. I could be afraid, and I could still do this, still do anything I wanted. It was the fact that he'd come back from that dark, dark place he'd been. It was the fact that both of us had thought ourselves alone in the world, and that we'd both been wrong.

He broke the kiss and bunched his hands in the skirt of my nightgown. "Is there anything under this?" he asked.

"No."

He groaned gently. "Dear God. Give me a moment."

"You don't have a moment. Take it off."

He pulled it up to my waist. "Just your legs are killing me."

I was laughing now. "Jack, stop it."

"Any higher and I may die."

I pulled the fabric from his hands and wrenched the entire nightgown off over my head, dropping it to the floor in one motion. And then I was on the bed with him, on his lap, my legs wrapped around his waist, and we were kissing again, and his hands were traveling everywhere on me. I wanted them everywhere at once. His skin was beautiful in the dimmed, lazy morning light, and I felt the muscles move in his back, the bones of his shoulder blades. His hands cupped my breasts and I laid my cheek on his shoulder, reveling in the sensation of it, the scent of his skin.

He lifted my head a little and kissed his way up the side of my neck, under my ear. He was very, very good at this, I was noticing. "Jack," I whispered, "I'm nervous. You're going to have to be gentle with me."

His teeth scraped my earlobe, and if I hadn't already been sitting, I would have dissolved into a heap of wet lust. Well, perhaps not exactly *gentle.* "I mean it," I said. "I didn't think I would ever do this, so I haven't practiced."

"That makes no sense," he pointed out. Before I could argue, he tenderly nipped the skin behind my ear, and when I shivered and moaned, he slid his hands under me and pulled me even closer, wrapping my legs more tightly around his waist. "I think you'll be very good at it," he said into my ear, and then he pulled away and looked at me. I thought I was about to die. "But you know," he said, "if it makes you feel better, there's a way that we — well, that you can be on top."

I stared at him. "There *is*?"

He watched as the possibilities struck me, and the smile he gave me was slow and nothing if not wicked. "Oh," he said. "This is going to be fun."

CHAPTER THIRTY-SEVEN

The ambulances arrived before supper. We were ready, all of us: the sick prepared for evacuation, the staff and the able-bodied patients standing under the front portico, waiting. Nina and I had even emptied Matron's safe and the cabinet of the men's belongings, putting all of it in a box that now sat between us. A second box contained some of Matron's most important files. When Matron was well, she would want them.

This time, when the ambulances pulled up, we had no argument. Paulus helped the attendants load the sick as the sun stayed high in the clear sky of the long summer day.

An ambulance attendant balked when he saw our boxes. "No one said anything about this," he said. "Are you sure it's important?"

"I'm sure," I said.

"If it's so important," another attendant

broke in, "just come back for it. This place isn't going anywhere."

I glanced at Nina, and then at the others. We were all thinking the same thing. Jack's blue eyes were dark. Even Paulus looked a little pale.

"We won't be back," I assured the attendant. "Load the boxes."

We pulled away in a convoy down the long, muddy drive. I didn't look back as the house receded behind me. And even though I couldn't see them, I knew none of the others looked back either.

In the end, we lost four patients.

It was the likely outcome of influenza. Everyone knew that. *I* knew that. Twenty-one had fallen sick. That seventeen had recovered was a good ratio. *We've seen waves of it over the last year,* the doctor at the hospital in Newcastle on Tyne told me. *It's different strains, I think. This one was not particularly bad.*

Four men buried. Not particularly bad.

George Naylor, with the gap in his teeth, was one of them, his weakened constitution having done him in. The ones who didn't die were sick, or weak, for weeks. Matron had a constitution of iron and was one of the first to recover; Boney, ever her faithful servant, followed shortly after, sitting up in bed with flushed cheeks and trying to give orders before passing out into sleep. I nodded at her and told her I'd do everything she said. She never remembered what she'd told me, anyway.

Martha was one of the sickest. We thought, for a long time, that she wouldn't make it. But Martha had always been stronger than her fragile body appeared.

Matron had Nina and me sit at her bedside. Even in sickness, she knew everything, absolutely everything. "Paperwork," she told us. "Each man must have a transfer form." There was separate paperwork for the men who had died, arrangements to be made to send their bodies back to their families or, if their families refused, to have them buried.

Matron was concerned about Douglas West, Archie Childress, and Captain Mabry, whose flesh wound required only a bandage and a pair of crutches. The hospital had discharged Mabry as quickly as they could, claiming it needed beds. We'd put the three of them in temporary housing under the supposed care of Paulus Vries.

"I do hope he is maintaining their routine," Matron fretted. "Rest and routine are essential to their mental state." Nina and I nodded, not bothering to tell her that Paulus's "care" translated to drinking in the pubs of Newcastle on Tyne and trying — with what success I had no idea, nor did I ask — to pick up girls, while West and Archie smoked cigars and played cards, gambling matchsticks back and forth.

Mabry had been depressed and racked with guilt when he'd awoken. He'd been born to a sense of honor, and even though the blame rested with the ghosts of Portis House, he felt he'd violated his own tenets in the worst possible way. But Archie and West knew Portis House, they knew the truth, and they understood. They had been through a hell just as awful as Mabry's own. They never spoke of what had happened, and they never laid blame. In their way, they looked out for Mabry, one of their fellow soldiers.

In private, in the company of only his comrades, Mabry was able to sit quietly, to think, to read. To write letters. He said he'd finally had the chance to read Boswell's *Life of Johnson,* which Matron had refused to stock in the Portis House library.

And I spoke to him of a way to make amends. He was thoughtful, listening in silence until I finished. "That isn't a bad idea, Nurse Weekes," he said. "I'll see what I can do." If I hadn't known him, I wouldn't have noticed that he almost smiled.

"And what about Mr. Yates?" Matron asked when I visited her. "Why is he not boarded with the others?"

"He's been discharged," I told her.

She thought about this for a moment. "It's just as well. But for God's sake, Nurse Weekes, fill out a discharge form."

She insisted on calling me "Nurse Weekes," even though I didn't wear a uniform. I had changed into my old skirt and blouse before evacuating Portis House, and now I wore my hair in a loose braid down my back or tied with a ribbon. I liked it. I was thinking of cutting it, which was supposed to be the new, scandalous fashion, but in the meantime I liked the feel of my long hair down my back.

Even Nina wore only her civilian dress, though she said it was because she was confused, not working at Portis House yet not exactly working anywhere else. I told Matron I'd left my uniform off because I was resigning. "I wasn't much of a nurse," I said. "You know that."

"You underestimate yourself," she said, and then she flushed, as if the words had slipped out. "You had no training, of course. But a nurse has to have a certain amount of gumption. I hope you don't go off and get

539

married like a ninny and do nothing with your life."

"I want to marry Jack Yates," I told her. We were alone, and I was helping her with her tea. "I think that disqualifies me from ninnyhood."

"It most certainly does," she agreed. She didn't seem surprised, and when I thought of all the times she had threatened to write me up for going to his room, I could see why.

"Besides," I said carefully, taking the cup when she was finished with it and putting it on a tray, "you married."

"Marrying doesn't make you a ninny," she clarified, "and neither does motherhood. But both can certainly contribute to it."

She said nothing about her son, and I didn't ask. There had been too much talk of death already.

It took three surgeries to put Roger's shoulder back together, and he'd never have the full use of it again. At first, he insisted he could still work as an orderly, which was a fiction so obvious no one knew how to reply to it. But when I visited a few days later, he had changed his mind.

"They let Mabry in to see me," Roger told me. "I gave him a piece of my mind. I wasn't happy, I can tell you. He just let me go on and on, and he said he was sorry he shot me. And then he said he'd help, that he owed it to me because I saved his life." Roger motioned me closer from his prone position on the bed. He was pale, but his cheeks were flushed with excitement. "Bloody rich, Mabry's family is. He says he'll tell his father it was an accident, and if I back him up, his father will give me a pension."

"That sounds wonderful," I said.

"Mabry's mad as a hatter," Roger said matter-of-factly, "and his father knows it. But the story is that he was defending the rest of us from Creeton with that gun. His father will soften at that. I was angry before, but now I don't bloody care what the story is. A pension will do just fine for me."

I smiled at him. "I'm glad," I said. I was.

Creeton presented a different problem. As a mental patient who had proven himself a danger, he'd been kept in the hospital under guard. The police had come and gone; so had one doctor, and then another. I never learned what was said in those interviews, but I imagined Creeton claiming innocence, that he had blacked out, that he remembered nothing. I imagined him pointing out how docile he'd been, agreeing to have his hands tied, waiting calmly to be evacuated from Portis House. But no one trusted a madman, not truly, and the fact that he'd assaulted two nurses and a fellow patient — not to mention his very public suicide attempt — must have told against him. Creeton was moved out of Newcastle on Tyne; I heard he was reassigned to a higher-security mental hospital in Dorset.

Somersham recovered, as did MacInnes and Hodgkins. All were slated to be moved to another hospital, but MacInnes went home to his wife, the successful novelist. Somersham's family didn't want him back, but I quietly wrote Hodgkins's cousin and told her what had happened and that he was about to be transferred. She appeared within the week and took him home.

"My God, the paperwork," Matron said as she sat up in her sickbed. "Where are my eyeglasses? It's enough to drive me to drink. What a mess. Why has Mr. Deighton not come?"

Nina and I exchanged a glance and evaded the question.

When I wasn't at the hospital, I was in the temporary flat I'd rented with Jack, two doors down from the room that housed Archie, West, and Mabry. He put Anna Gersbach in a third flat of her own. He'd taken our flat as "Mr. and Mrs. Yates," looking the landlady in the eye and daring her to disagree. She didn't. "We'll fix that part later," he told me when she was gone and we were alone, making my heart flip in my chest. "When we have time." In the meantime, we were busy.

Jack wired his banker, told him he was sane again, and withdrew some funds. Then he wired his man of business, who'd been taking care of the farm Jack had inherited from his parents, and told him he'd be home within the month. "Make sure your books add up," he'd put in the telegram. "I'm quite good at math."

He kissed me, hired a car, and drove to Bascombe. He returned with Maisey Ravell and a stack of files she'd stolen from her father's study.

And then we dealt with Anna Gersbach and what had happened at Portis House.

There was no question about it: Anna had killed her father, which made her a murderer. But she was also a pawn who'd been given no chance to defend herself, whose home had been stolen and sold, who had never been allowed to mourn her brother or tell of how he had been so brutally murdered by the man she'd killed. She was also a girl who had been through too much, and was in mental distress, not quite in her right mind. As we spent more time with her, we could see that she couldn't make many decisions, that she relied on us for even the smallest things, that when we spoke of her case, she stopped listening, as if not hearing our words would make them go away.

Maisey moved into the flat with Anna, made certain she ate and washed, found her more clothes to wear. What they spoke of when they were alone together, whether Anna told Maisey of the pain she'd been hiding all those years, I did not know. But I thought, perhaps, they understood each other.

But there was no way to keep Anna free from what had happened. We had no choice. We went to the magistrate at Newcastle on Tyne and gave him everything — every file, every witness account. Everything but the ghosts.

The resulting scandal was so large even Matron heard of it. The story had already broken that England's Brave Jack had spent six months in a madhouse. *England's Former Hero Shell-Shocked,* read one headline, and most of the others followed suit. Then the second wave of stories washed over the country's newspapers:

SHOCKING SCANDAL AT MENTAL HOME.

Double Murder Led to Scandalous Cover-Up.

Father-Daughter Murder Was Self-Defense.

"I Was a Victim," Anna Gersbach Claims.

Anna was taken into custody by the magistrate to wait for the inquest. Reporters came to our flat in a steady stream, asking for interviews and shooting me very, very interested looks. Jack introduced me to all of them as Mrs. Yates and stared at them as he had the landlady. They were persistent, but he gave them nothing, not a single interview or quote, and they were all disappointed.

It was overwhelming, and our days were full. But at night we never spoke of any of it. At night we got in bed together and the world went away. We talked of nothing, or of everything. Or we did other things. I'd finally found something I was truly good at, if Jack's enthusiasm was anything to judge by. I'd grown achingly used to the feel of him, the smell of his sweat on my skin. And when we slept, it was the dreamless sleep of the exhausted.

In the dark, I told him everything and he told me everything. Those long nights, in the dark, we each understood the other. And then we slept.

Eventually, one by one, the men were removed from the hospital. Mr. Deighton was arrested while trying to flee to France. Maisey's father was arrested for fraud, as were the coroner he had bribed and the sexton who had cremated the Gersbachs for a fee, no questions asked. Dr. Thornton was investigated, though he could not be directly connected to the scandal; he hid, predictably, behind a bank of expensive lawyers. I never discovered what happened to Dr. Oliver.

And at last, the jury at Anna's inquest refused to indict her for reasons of self-defense, and Anna was freed. Portis House itself descended into a legal quagmire; supposedly it was Anna's to inherit, but the wheels of English law turned notoriously slowly. She could not sell it, even if she could find a buyer; she could do nothing with it, it seemed, but live in it, moving back in with her memories and ghosts.

She didn't return to the house. Instead, Anna and Maisey went off on a tour of the Continent together until the scandals died down. They never said where they got the money for the trip, but I knew. Captain Mabry was pleased. "I shot at her," he told me. "It's the least I can do."

Before they left, I had one last interview with Anna, alone. "I don't mean to distress you," I said to her, "but there's something I want to ask."

She looked at me with her curiously disconnected expression, as if she was watching a play.

"At Portis House," I said. "Your father — his ghost — wanted a sacrifice. You said that sacrifice was you. You told Jack to shoot you."

She looked away. "I don't think he would have. I know that now."

She was right; Jack had told me that already. He had always planned to shoot Mabry, not Anna, and he had not shot to kill. "But your father's ghost wanted you dead," I said. "He wanted you dead so that he could go."

"It's true," Anna said.

"But, Anna, you're not dead. Your father never got his sacrifice."

Her lips pressed together.

"He never got what he wanted," I continued. "Mikael is gone — you felt that. But your father . . . If you didn't die, and Mabry didn't die . . ."

Anna's gaze slid to mine, and for a second she was present; for a second she was clear. "Kitty," she said. "Don't go back to Portis House."

Mabry and West got their transfer forms and packed their bags. The story of Mabry defending us from Creeton had stuck; Mabry's wife and her father had heard of it, and though they weren't ready to have him home, Mrs. Mabry wrote that she would apply to visit. She would come alone at first, but perhaps someday she would bring the children.

West had no desire to be discharged. He needed more time — this time, he hoped, in a place that "won't make me madder than I was to begin with."

It was Archie who, at long last, went home. When his father, the newspaper baron, read of the scandal at Portis House, he discharged his son. "He never really wanted me admitted," Archie told me. "Not truly. It was the stuttering and the shaking that made him nervous. I think I've passed some kind of test."

"So you're fully healed, then?" I asked him. "That's what you let your father believe?"

He looked pained. "I had to tell him *some-*

thing, Kitty, or I'd never go home. I told my father I'd glue pages at the paper if he wanted. I still get the nightmares, but not as bad, not now that *he* is gone. I want to try it — normal life, that is. My father doesn't need to know that I'm not right in the head, not really, and that I'll never get well."

Martha recovered enough to go home to Glenley Crewe until she regained her full strength and got another job. Matron was given a prestigious position at a new hospital in Cornwall, including lighter duties and a raise in pay. She took Nina, Martha, and Boney with her. But before she started her new position, Matron herself decided to take six weeks off to walk the Lake District. "I'm not retiring," she told me firmly. "Nursing still needs me, Nurse Weekes."

And then she was gone — everyone was gone.

It was mid-August, and Jack and I were the only two passengers on the platform at the tiny train station at New Thetford, somewhere in Warwick. The sun was massively hot in the middle of the day, and sweat gathered at my temples and on the back of my neck as I adjusted my wide-brimmed hat lower over my face. I shaded my eyes with my gloved hands and stared off down the track.

"It'll come soon enough," said Jack. He'd taken refuge on a wooden bench squeezed into a thin strip of shade and was paging lazily through a newspaper — that day's newspaper, with nary a story blacked out. "We're almost there, you know."

The track seemed to waver in the heat as I watched it, but there was still no sign of a train. "No, I don't know," I said to him. "I'd never been out of London before Portis House. I've no idea where we are."

"We change trains here," he replied easily, "and then we go to Somerset. And then we're home."

"Aren't you nervous?" I asked him. "I'm prickly as a bear. My clothes are all new and I'm not used to them. And I hate wearing gloves."

He put the newspaper down on his lap. He looked impossibly handsome even in a summer suit and tie, and he'd barely broken a sweat, the infernal man. He held out a hand. "Give me your hand."

I walked across the platform and held out my right hand, but he took my left instead and pulled the glove off. He leaned down and gave it a solemn kiss, right on the knuckle near my ring. "You look like a respectable lady, Mrs. Yates."

"Oh, no," I said, and we both laughed.

I put the glove back on and stepped away from him. I had to or the train would come to find me sitting quite comfortably on his lap, heat be damned. "I've never run a farm before," I said.

"You'll do fine," he said, picking up the paper again.

"What if I don't like it?"

"Then I'll sell it and we'll go live like bohemians in the South of France."

"What if I want a job?" I said, remembering Matron's advice. "What if I want to be useful?"

He looked at me. "Do you want to be a nurse? A trained one?"

"I don't know," I said honestly. "I've never done anything but live day to day. I've never really thought about what I want to do."

"I know what you mean," he said. "I was raised on my parents' farm, and I know how to run it. My father taught me since child-hood. But I never really thought about whether I wanted it. And then I went to war."

I looked at him. Oh, how I adored him. That easy competence that he had with everything. The way he treated me as if I mattered. Those gorgeous hands of his. "It's going to be all right," I said. "Isn't it. No matter what happens. No matter what we do."

He thought about it, and his face relaxed almost into a smile. "Yes, it is. The train's coming."

I put a hand on my hat and turned to watch it approach.

And somewhere, miles behind us, Portis House sat solitary, continuing its slow descent into the marshes.

ABOUT THE AUTHOR

Simone St. James is the award-winning author of *The Haunting of Maddy Clare,* which won two RITA® Awards from Romance Writers of America and an Arthur Ellis Award from Crime Writers of Canada. She wrote her first ghost story, about a haunted library, when she was in high school, and spent twenty years behind the scenes in the television business before leaving to write full-time. She lives in Toronto, Canada, with her husband and a spoiled cat.

The employees of Thorndike Press hope you have enjoyed this Large Print book. All our Thorndike, Wheeler, and Kennebec Large Print titles are designed for easy reading, and all our books are made to last. Other Thorndike Press Large Print books are available at your library, through selected bookstores, or directly from us.

For information about titles, please call:
  (800) 223-1244

or visit our Web site at:
  http://gale.cengage.com/thorndike

To share your comments, please write:
  Publisher
  Thorndike Press
  10 Water St., Suite 310
  Waterville, ME 04901